OUR LOVE WAS MEANT TO BE

CJ ANDREWS

ISBN: 978-0-9979087-4-9 (eBook)

ISBN: 978-0-9979087-5-6 (Paperback)

Edited by Joy Editing

Published by Daydreamer Press, PO Box 291, Temple, PA 19560 USA

CONTENTS

AUTHOR'S NOTE

Our Love Was Meant To Be is the conclusion of Danni and Nico's story that began in ***Your Love Is All I Need***.

The books are meant to be read in order. If you haven't already read ***Your Love Is All I Need***, please start there.

Happy reading! ~CJ

INTERVENTION
DANNI

The midwinter days of February and March were dark and dismal, the perfect companion to my mood. Everything positive about my life had been stripped away. I'd lost my husband, my pride, my confidence, and my hope for happiness in the span of one horrid night.

Five weeks had passed since Will's accident. During that time, I'd cut myself off from everything and everyone while I tried to make sense of what had happened, tried to put back together the pieces of my life.

I sat curled up on the couch in the same pajamas I'd been wearing for the past four days. Didn't matter. No one around to impress.

The phone rang. Again. A long beep signaled the lack of space for another message before disconnecting the call. I pulled the blanket tighter around me, gritting my teeth. How much longer would I be able to avoid the rest of the world?

People meant well, offering to help and wanting to make sure I was handling "my loss." What an annoying phrase. They'd all adored Will . . . loved him, worshiped the ground he'd walked on. And they all wanted to talk about him. How many times was I expected to listen to the same damn conversation?

I'd stopped answering the phone weeks ago. Then people had felt the need to check on me in person since they couldn't reach me by phone. That meant I had to stop answering the door, other than when I expected deliveries. I'd even stopped opening any mail that didn't look like a bill in order to avoid the random cards, letters, and packages intended to "make me feel better."

A hint of daylight peeked around the edges of the tightly drawn drapes. Keeping them closed made it easier to hide from the world outside. But I couldn't hide from the memories. Couldn't hide from the lies. Couldn't hide from the goddamn pain and humiliation. And, as screwed up as it was, I couldn't hide from the fact that I agonized over losing Nico as much as I mourned the loss of my husband.

I let out a wistful sigh, sliding my fingers along the silky white petals of a rose on the table beside me. A fresh bouquet had arrived every week since . . . that day. Always without a card, but I knew who'd sent them. I leaned toward the arrangement, bending one of the buds to meet my nose. Its sweet fragrance filled my head as I drew in a slow, deep breath of the scent I'd come to associate with Nico.

Rhythmic pounding on the front door disrupted my dismal reverie. The lock turned, the handle jiggled, and my sister pushed her way inside, mumbling about the stench of week-old takeout containers.

I took another deep breath before releasing my hold on the flower, letting it slip back into the vase. "Smells perfect to me." I grinned and stretched forward to get a better view of where Jen stood in the foyer. "You alone this time?"

"Of course she's not." Kristi, my close friend and coworker, stumbled in backward, struggling to pull an oversized suitcase up the two steps and through the door. She turned to wave, a huge smile covering her face.

"Keep it movin', Tinkerbell." My best friend, Kendra, strolled to the doorway, a small tote slung over her shoulder. She gave Kristi's bag a shove from behind, grunting with exertion. "Christ, Kristi, you smuggling a male stripper in there?"

Kristi giggled. "No, but that would have been a really great idea. I just brought the essentials." She unzipped a pocket and unloaded several bottles, humming a cheery tune.

I didn't get up to greet them. The trio had come every Saturday since Will's funeral, forcing me to do all the things that should have been second nature: shower, dress, take out the garbage, pick up after myself . . . the list went on. But it looked as though they had a different plan this week.

Kristi danced across the room toward the breakfast bar, her arms filled. "I brought José, Bailey, the Captain, and a few of their friends." She lined up the bottles on the counter then stood back, giving a little cheer while admiring her work.

Kendra docked her phone in Will's sound bar, filling the air with rock music. She moved from room to room, opening all the drapes and blinding me with an overabundance of sunlight.

I squinted, looking between Kendra and Jen, who was busy collecting trash and sanitizing every cleared surface. "What's going on?"

"You've mourned long enough." Kendra yanked my blanket away from me and rolled it into a ball as she walked toward the laundry room. "It's time to get off your sagging ass and get on with your life. *We* are here to make sure you do."

Kristi knelt in front of me, taking one of my hands. She gave it a gentle squeeze. "That's right, and we're not leaving until you do."

Jen snuggled in next to me, wrapping me in a tight embrace. "We came prepared to spend the whole weekend. It'll be fun." She looked at me, biting her lip. "You know, like an extended slumber party."

Great. I rolled my eyes and tried to look disinterested enough to discourage them.

Kendra reached the couch in three long strides. "Sweetie, this self-pity shit has got to stop." She motioned for Kristi to slide over and make room for her to perch on the arm. Kendra's eyes glazed over as she stared at the bouquet next to us, her fingers tracing the delicate buds. "Why don't you just call him? You know you want to." She tilted her head toward me, brows raised, as if daring me to deny it.

A devilish smile spread across her face. She tugged one of the roses from the vase, waving it under her nose before handing it to me. "And he clearly can't get you off his mind."

I wanted to hear Nico's voice. See his face. Feel his arms around me. "I—"

The stem snapped in my clenched fist. I drew in a shaky breath and turned away, my gaze landing on the table behind the couch. Will's handsome face smiled at me through the cracked glass covering our wedding picture. The twisted frame leaned to one side. I reached back and gave it a shove, knocking it over.

How many more times could I do that before the frame fell completely apart? How many more times would I need to do it before I felt whole again?

"It's too soon. I can't—I don't want to think about him." My voice tapered off as I struggled to speak.

"Shhh . . . it's okay." Jen rubbed my back, pulling me closer. She stretched toward Kendra, lowering her voice. "Don't push her too hard. Okay?"

"Who's pushing? It's been five weeks, and she hasn't left the damn house. Doesn't even get dressed unless we show up and make her do it."

Jen stared but didn't say a word.

"Fine." Kendra let out an exasperated sigh, her hands raised in surrender. "When you're done moping over that lying, cheating bastard of a husband, maybe you'll wake up and realize who's been waiting right under your nose." She tugged the flower from my hand with a dramatic flair and tossed it on the table then leaned to my ear. "Better hope it's not too late when you finally do."

As much as I wanted to, I couldn't go to Nico so soon after Will's death. What would people think? I closed my eyes, holding back the tears.

Kendra pushed to her feet and moved toward the breakfast bar, glancing over her shoulder at the rest of us. "Let's go, ladies. Time to get this party started."

Monday morning. *At least I think it's Monday.* I groaned and rolled to my back, squinting through the painful daggers of sunlight piercing my bedroom window. It shouldn't hurt to move my eyes, should it? Another agonized groan escaped as I closed them again.

My head throbbed, and it was still a little fuzzy from the weekend. Actually, most of the weekend itself was fuzzy. I'd caved to peer pressure, allowing the girls to obliterate my standard two-drink-maximum rule. Our weekend-long slumber party had seemed more like an out-of-control frat party, minus the guys.

Bits and pieces of the weekend came back to me in flashes. An endless stream of chick flicks, guaranteed to cheer me up or make me cry. Either way, Kendra and Kristi had managed to turn all of them into drinking games and opportunities to bash

Will. Despite my initial reluctance to their plan, it had turned out to be kind of fun . . . a tiny detail I'd kept to myself, thanks to the dismal little voice in the back of my mind that insisted it was wrong to be happy so soon after losing my husband.

My eyes opened again. The sun had shifted, and I felt slightly rested—still hungover, but in less pain. I forced myself out of bed and wandered downstairs, expecting to find a huge mess. Everything had been cleaned up. The vase of white roses had been moved to the breakfast bar. Next to it sat two large bottles of water, a bottle of aspirin, and a note.

Looks like we were right. You weren't dying, drama queen. Call the attorney first thing to get everything straightened out. You'll feel better. ~K. K. & J.

P.S. Don't forget about lunch.

My chest swelled with a warm sense of contentment. I couldn't have asked for a better sister or friends. They'd stuck by me through this whole mess without hovering or crowding . . . or asking a bunch of questions I didn't want to attempt answering.

I called the office of Sherman and Foster, as instructed, returning one of the many messages I'd been ignoring during my dark days of hiding. Luck was on my side for a change. Mr. Foster had a cancellation and could fit me in at eleven forty-five today, which meant I could still meet Kendra for a late lunch.

My stomach roiled at the thought of food, but I'd promised to go and didn't want to disappoint my best friend.

A FEW HOURS LATER, I stepped outside of Sherman and Foster and took a deep breath, soaking in the beauty of an early spring day. My meeting with Mr. Foster had gone much better than I'd expected. He'd reassured me that Will's petition for divorce had died with him since it had never been signed and officially filed. And since my sneaky, lying bastard of a husband hadn't changed his will while filing for divorce, everything passed over to me without a hitch.

With all of the legal stuff out of the way, my future looked brighter already.

Time to get on with my life. I sent a quick text to Kendra, telling her I was on my way, then decided to walk the short distance to Pepper's Deli.

It seemed like ages since the day Nico and Logan had joined us there for lunch—the day Nico had become a complicated part of my life. I'd thought about that "coincidental meeting" a lot over the past few weeks, and about every other moment we'd spent together.

Would I have pushed Nico away if I'd suspected Will was having an affair? Assuming he even *was* having one. I still didn't want to believe it. There had to be another explanation for his sneaky divorce.

Kendra waved as I walked along the glass storefront of Pepper's. She carried her tray to the same table we'd sat at that day. The day she met Logan.

Bits of our conversations from this weekend drifted back to me—animated stories of their weekends together. It could have been the alcohol, but I'd swear she'd even giggled and gushed while talking about him. Guess I'd been so wrapped up in my own life, wallowing in self-pity, that I hadn't noticed how happy and in love my best friend was.

I had no way of knowing if Logan felt the same way. I could only hope he did. It hurt to give someone your heart then realize it didn't mean anything, that he'd stomped on it and thrown it away. Hurt like hell.

But none of that matters anymore. Today is a new day. A fresh start.

I pulled back the heavy glass door and entered the peaceful deli. The familiar atmosphere brought a smile to my face. Soft music drifted from hidden speakers—that awful oldies' station Pepper loved so much.

An elderly couple stood at the counter, pointing at the menu board and bickering about what they'd ordered their last time here. Most of the lunchtime crowd had moved on, but a group of college students still occupied one of the small tables.

Instead of placing my lunch order, I rushed to Kendra and gave her a quick hug.

"Well, look at you." She squeezed me tight. "A little sunshine, some fresh air, and you're glowing. And here I was worrying you'd burn up or something in the daylight."

"Go on, tease all you want. I promise I'll still love you." My stomach growled—the first time in weeks I'd actually felt hungry—but I worried about putting anything in it. I pulled out the chair across from Kendra then sat on the edge.

She squinted at me. "Aren't you eating?"

I waved a dismissive hand. "I had a late breakfast. Enjoy your salad, and I'll just keep you company."

Kendra tilted her head and arched a brow, studying me. "Nope, that's not it. Why aren't you eating?" She stabbed a few green leaves and stuffed them in her mouth.

I gave a short laugh. Why couldn't I ever hide anything from her? "I don't know how you can drink like that all weekend and not feel like crap today."

She held up a finger before swallowing then took a quick sip of water. "First of all, I'm a seasoned pro. And I made sure to drink plenty of water. Is that what's wrong with you though? You're . . . hungover?" She chuckled but quickly pinched her lips together.

"You're joking, right? Jesus, Kendra, with the amount of alcohol you guys poured into me, I'm lucky to be alive—what are you laughing at?"

Kendra slapped her palm on the table, struggling to catch her breath to talk. Her booming laughter attracted the attention of the couple two tables over, and they began chuckling along.

I glanced around the deli. "What am I missing?"

"Oh damn, sweetie, you barely exceeded your two-drink maximum all weekend. Jen monitored every drop Kristi and I poured for you, and she insisted we watered everything down. *Way* down. You just needed to believe you were out of control in order to let go of all the anger and pain you've been holding on to. But . . . but . . ." She gasped, calming another fit of laughter. "I didn't realize you actually thought you were *that* drunk."

I propped my elbows on the table, gripping my head. "What an idiot. I should have known better."

Kendra nudged one of my arms away. "Don't. We were trying to help you. Not trying to make a fool of you." She nodded toward my stomach, which I'd been absentmindedly rubbing. "That pain you're feeling is most likely hunger. Go get some food."

"Fine. I'll be right back." I pushed away from the table, shaking my head as I walked to the counter.

Kendra's staccato bouts of laughter rang through the room and soon had me smiling too. In a matter of minutes, I rejoined her with my Caesar salad and green tea.

"So how are you really doin'?" Kendra covered her mouth, talking around a bite of food. "And spare me the bullshit lies you think everyone wants to hear."

"I'm . . . good." I settled into my seat, biting my lip. "Is it okay to say that?"

I'd been thinking it since leaving the lawyer's office, but actually saying the words out loud made me nervous. I hated to admit I was beginning to feel normal. Not quite happy, but for the first time in months, I felt as though I *would* be.

"As long as you mean it." She lowered her fork mid-bite and leaned forward, her eyes narrowing as she studied me. A satisfied grin spread across her face. "Of course it's okay." She grabbed my hand and gave a reassuring squeeze. "You deserve to be happy. Especially after everything that asshole put you through."

My shoulders sagged. "I'm beginning to realize that."

Kendra lowered her voice. "That bastard never deserved you." She held up a hand. "I know. You think he *saved* you from your *horrible* life. I could never understand why you put up with the way he stared at other women and flirted with them. Right in front of you." She clenched her fists, a frustrated growl escaping her. "Dammit. I should've known better than to believe he wasn't screw—" Kendra's eyes grew wide. She pressed a hand over her mouth.

"Wait . . . what was that? Will really was having an affair? I mean, I spent the last five weeks trying to figure out why he—but I didn't actually believe he'd—he'd—"

"I thought everything was under control." Her fingers flexed around her balled-up napkin.

"You knew? How?" I bit out the words, demanding answers. And this damn well better be information she'd just learned.

"I didn't *know*, Danni. I suspected he was, but—" She looked away, her words squeaking out at a feverish pace. "I saw them *one* time. That's it, and I couldn't be sure."

"You saw them. You actually *saw* them together?" I clutched at my chest. "Oh, my God. You knew. You knew, and you didn't tell me. I can't believe—"

"He told me nothing happened between them. Only dinner. And he swore it was over."

"But you didn't think that was something you should tell your best friend? 'Hey, Danni, just a heads-up, I saw your husband having a romantic dinner with a woman who wasn't you'?" I struggled to keep my voice down. "When?"

She hesitated. "A few months ago. Before Thanksgiving."

"You just let me go on, all those months, trying to spice up my marriage and looking like a fool. The doting wife, too stupid to know her husband's off fucking some two-bit whore."

She reached for my hands, but I pulled them away. "What was I supposed to tell you? I didn't have any proof. He would have denied it. Then you would have accused me of being bitter or said I couldn't stand to see you happy while I was getting divorced."

"Well, I guess we'll never know how I would have reacted, will we?" Tears burned in my eyes, but I fought to hold them back. I shook my head in disbelief, trying to comprehend how my strong, outspoken, brash best friend could have let this happen to me.

I slapped my hands on the table, thrusting myself forward to snarl in her face. "Dammit, Kendra. I can't. Believe. You didn't. Tell me." All the rage I'd buried deep inside since the night of Will's accident exploded with a vengeance.

The couple seated two tables away had turned to watch us again.

I snapped my mouth shut but continued to pin Kendra with the most menacing glare I could muster, my jaw clenched tight. "I need to get out of here."

Kendra caught my arm before I could move away. "Danni, wait. Please don't run off." Her words came out rushed. Tears streaked down her face. "I'm sorry. I never meant to hurt you."

I scoffed, struggling to pull free.

"I just—I needed you. It was selfish, I know. But I'd already pushed Nate away, filed for divorce. Callie hated me. Blamed me for tearing apart our family. I—" She swallowed hard and dragged the back of her hand across her face. "I-I couldn't risk losing you too. You're my best friend."

"Correction—" With another sharp tug, I finally managed to break away from her hold. "I *was* your best friend."

I shoved my lunch tray in her direction then ran toward the

exit. A heavy sob forced its way out, and the tears I'd managed to suppress began to fall. I pushed open the door and rushed blindly onto the busy sidewalk, crashing into a solid male body.

"I-I'm so sorry." I stepped back, rubbing my eyes, and squinted up into Nico's stunned face.

DROWNING SORROWS
DANNI

"Danni?" Nico grabbed my arms, halting my escape. "Hey, beautiful."

His simple touch sent a rush of electricity surging through me. With so many emotions already out of control, I couldn't handle adding my conflicted feelings for Nico to the mix. Not today. I opened my mouth to speak, tell him I had to run, but nothing came out.

Furrows formed in his brow, marring his handsome features. "Danni, what's wrong?"

I tried to step back—struggled to get away—but Nico wouldn't release me.

His grip tightened, and he pulled me closer. His worried expression intensified. "It's okay. I'm here." Concern filled his smooth, deep voice. "Talk to me."

I shook my head and narrowed my eyes to glare at him. "W-what are you doing here? Did Kendra set this up again?" I glanced over my shoulder, relieved she hadn't followed.

"I haven't talked to Kendra in—"

"Whatever. Just . . . just let go of me." Thrashing around

was useless. I groaned through clenched teeth. "I don't. Want. To be. Here."

"Okay. All right. Shh . . ." Nico brushed his thumb across my cheek, swiping away a tear.

His calm tone only irritated me more. I turned away from his touch. Refused to look at him.

Nico leaned to the side, realigning his face with mine. A hint of mischief danced in his eyes. "Give me a minute. Then we'll get away from here, and you can tell me what happened." He turned to the woman next to him, his voice low. "I need to take care of her. Go ahead without me."

She rested her hand on his shoulder. "You sure? I can stay if you want."

He dug in his pocket then handed her a key as he placed a kiss on her cheek. "I'll call for a car to take me home."

Their eyes locked, and an unspoken message seemed to pass between them. I couldn't look away from the familiar scene.

Dark, wavy hair, the way she touched him—the memory hit me like a slap across my face. A month had passed since I stood outside of Giardano's, lusting after Nico while my husband lay dying, but the vivid image of this woman comforting Nico that night had haunted me every day since.

Humiliation fanned the flames already burning in my chest from Kendra's deception. How much lower could I sink before hitting rock bottom? After Will's attempt at a surprise divorce, I'd been sure things couldn't get worse.

Today seemed determined to prove me wrong.

Finally breaking free from Nico's grasp, I wrapped my hands across my stomach and doubled over, silently begging for the pain to stop. "Why are you here?" I choked out the words.

When Nico didn't respond, I tilted my head and glanced up at his face.

"It's Monday." He shrugged and flashed a lopsided smile, acting as though his response made perfect sense. His playful grin only lasted a second before flattening into a straight line, his concerned expression returning.

"What the hell is that—oh." *Monday. The day he comes into the city for a meeting at The Next Level. The day he goes to lunch at Giardano's. The day he borrowed me from my boss to take me with him for an amazing non-date.*

I straightened, clutching my chest. My gaze dashed between him and the other woman. "Oh. Well . . . then don't let me interrupt your little lunch date."

I dodged his attempt to grab me again and bolted down the sidewalk. He'd clearly moved on. More likely, she'd always been there, and I'd been too foolish to realize.

People complained as I pushed past them, barely uttering an apology. The noise inside my head as I raced toward my car drove me mad, my mind spinning in an emotional overload.

Sound bites from my argument with Kendra battled with thoughts about Will. Every despicable nightmare of him screwing around that I'd worked so hard to ignore screamed, *I told you so.*

As if that weren't enough, the feelings for Nico I'd tried to suppress rushed to the surface and demanded my immediate attention. I fought against the sudden urge to run back there and throw myself into his arms.

My heart pounded harder with each faltering step until I couldn't go any further. Doubled over again, hands on my knees, I struggled to catch my breath. *Can't stop. Gotta keep running.*

"You all right, dear?" A slender hand rested on my shoulder then fell away when I jumped.

"Yeah. I just—" I looked back, realizing I'd passed the parking garage about three blocks ago. "Um, I guess I got distracted. But I'm fine." I glanced at the woman, flashing a fake smile, then continued scanning my surroundings.

No sign of Nico, even though I had a strong sense he'd followed me. Bad case of wishful thinking? Or maybe I needed to add paranoia to my growing list of emotional baggage.

The woman cleared her throat, reminding me of her presence. She studied me through narrowed eyes, clearly not buying my lie.

I touched her arm and focused on sounding calm. Sane. "Thank you for your concern, but really, I'm fine. I promise. I have a lot on my mind today, and—" I tipped my head toward the building I'd been fortunate enough to stop in front of, inching closer to the entrance and farther away from this well-intentioned but unappreciated good Samaritan with each word. "I'm just gonna grab some lunch." I lifted one shoulder. "And maybe a drink. Since I'm already here."

Because if I ever truly needed a drink, it's now.

I pulled open the heavy wooden door and slipped inside Farley's Pub. Memories of my last visit to the rustic pub came rushing back—Will and Nico ready to tear into each other in a battle to gain my attention. That was the night I'd decided to forget about Nico and fully devote myself to my husband.

What a foolish choice *that* had been.

After a few deep breaths, I turned and peeked through the etched glass panels. The woman was gone. But still no sign of Nico. The pang of disappointment that followed took me by surprise.

I forced a smile at the man sitting a few feet away, the pub's lone patron. He paused and gave a polite nod before continuing to tap away on his laptop at a furious pace.

A man in a tight black T-shirt stood behind the bar, singing along with the country music playing overhead. The muscles in his forearms flexed as he wiped glasses with a large white rag, drying them before putting them back on the rack. He greeted me as I approached and chatted on about cleaning up from the busy lunchtime rush and . . . something else, before finally asking what he could get for me.

I gave my usual drink order—the same frozen strawberry margarita I ordered everywhere—and placed my credit card on the bar.

He shook his head, pressing his lips together. "Sorry, lass, I don't make none of those girly drinks here." He glanced at my card then grabbed another glass to dry. "Danielle—pretty name for a pretty lady." The bartender winked, flipped the rag over his shoulder, and leaned on the bar top. "Haven't seen ya in here before . . . . least not for lunch, which is the only time I hang out front here. Usually prefer to stick to my office in the back, ya know? 'Less of course they need some help in the kitchen."

He leaned closer to whisper, "Not really good at cooking though, so they need to be pretty desperate."

I held up my hand to stop him. "Listen, um . . ." Great, no name tag on his shirt. Nothing clipped at his waist.

At least he stopped talking. That was really all I wanted anyway. Well, that and a strong drink. *Several* strong drinks. And to be left the hell alone to wallow in self-pity. Was that too much to ask? As my mind drifted back to the current situation, I realized I'd been staring at the chatty bartender this whole time . . . however long it had been.

And he was grinning back, wearing the sappy, hopeful expression of a guy who thought he had a chance. *Great.*

"Rob. Rob Farley." He smiled and lifted his hand, extending it to me.

I gently placed my hand in his. "Nice to meet you."

He was a decent-looking guy and seemed friendly enough, but I wasn't here to search for a date. A weight settled in my chest, and I flashed a glance toward the door. Beyond it was the only man who'd ever made my heart skip. My eyes settled on Nico's troubled expression as he walked back and forth past the entrance, both hands gripping the back of his head.

"So, Rob, how 'bout we get that tab rolling." I tapped my credit card and slid it toward him again. "Maybe line up a few shots for me?"

Nico stopped pacing and reached for the door. My heart pounded faster, but he pulled his hand away and shoved it through his hair again.

"You sure about that?" Rob's question dragged my attention back to him. He studied me, scratching his neck. "Bein' a bartender all these years, I kinda gained a sixth sense for when folks are havin' problems. And I hate to see a pretty g—"

"Rob? Clock's ticking here. Maybe you should just tell me what *you'd* recommend." I crossed my arms and tilted my head, giving him an impatient stare. *When did ordering a drink become such a difficult task?*

"How 'bout a nice club soda and someone to talk to?" He rested his arms on the bar top again, his eyes fixed on mine. A slow smile spread across his face. "I happen to be a great listener."

I arched one brow and continued to stare. *He can't be serious.*

Rob's smile faded. "But I'm guessin' that's not what you have in mind." He cleared his throat. "So . . . I have a nice Killian's on tap. But I'll bet you're probably more of a Guinness Blonde gal. Or I could offer you—"

I placed my hand on his, creating an effective distraction. "Kind of in a hurry here, Rob. Just pour me anything that'll get me drunk and keep it coming. Okay? And while you do that, I'm going to go grab a nice, out-of-the-way seat." I motioned toward the corner by the fireplace. "Can you bring my drink over to me? And—listen up, 'cause this part's really important—if anyone comes in looking for me, *don't* tell him I'm here." I stroked Rob's hand and lowered my voice to a flirtatious whisper. "Promise?"

The pub door flew open, and I took off without waiting for his response. I hid in the shadowy corner with my back to the room and my elbows propped on the table, pressing my forehead into my palms—because secretly loving that Nico had come after me wasn't the same thing as *actually* wanting to see him.

A few tense moments passed. I didn't need to turn around to know he'd found me. The magnetic energy emanating from him made my skin tingle as he approached.

"You seem to have made quite an impression on Farley. He put up a bit of a fight when I told him I'd deliver your drink." Nico moved past me to take the seat on the other side of the table and placed a large mug in front of me. "No pretty pink margaritas today?"

I raised my head enough to see him through my parted fingers. "Turns out, Farley doesn't own a blender. Or so he says." I forced a single, humorless laugh. "Just as well. I'm not here for fun."

Nico folded his arms, leaning forward to rest them on the table. His voice turned serious. "Why *are* you here, Danni?"

"Maybe you forgot, but I recently lost my *sweet, wonderful* husband." The words burned like acid on my tongue. I grabbed my drink to wash it away, swallowing as much of the amber mystery liquid as I could without actually tasting it.

Nico watched, studying me the way he always did. He shook his head. "Nope. That's not it. There's something else." He leaned back and took a slow drink from his glass.

I turned away, staring into the fire to avoid Nico's probing gaze.

Rob came into view in my peripheral vision. He edged

closer as he wiped down nearby tables, his gaze fixed on me. When I tilted my head toward him, he lifted his hands to the side with a shrug. An apology maybe? *At least he feels bad about not following my instructions.* I let out a heavy sigh.

"What happened at Pepper's?" Nico placed his fingers under my chin and gave a gentle tug, forcing me to look at him. "Must've been pretty bad to send you running away in tears." He hesitated before letting his hand slip away, but the arousing effect of his touch lingered.

My grip tightened on the frosted mug. I squeezed my eyes shut, forcing myself to gulp down the bitter brew it held. I shuddered, lowering the empty mug to the table with a heavy thud, and dragged the back of my hand across my mouth then signaled for Rob to bring another.

"He was divorcing me. Had the papers with him the day he died." The words erupted out of me. I waved a dismissive hand, barely looking at Nico. "But I'm sure Kendra already told you everything. Or maybe not. Seems keeping secrets is her style lately."

Nico raised his brows. "I'm—damn, I'm not sure which part of that to dig into first." He shoved a hand through his hair, grabbing the back of his neck. "I'm sorry. I didn't know you were getting divorced."

"Yeah well, neither did I."

Rob approached, delivering my drink with a smile.

"Ah, perfect timing." I wrapped my fingers around the icy handle, grateful for the interruption, and thanked him with a wink.

He cast a slanted look toward Nico then returned his attention to me. "Everything okay here?"

"As long as you keep bringing me drinks, everything is just fine." I raised my mug to him.

"Well, if you need someone—"

"I've got her, Rob. She'll be fine." Nico's dismissive tone

made it clear he was not willing to share the responsibility.

As Rob walked away, I chugged down half the contents of my second vat of poison. A shiver ran through me, making my face scrunch up.

Nico brushed his fingers along my arm. "Why are you drinking beer if you hate it so much?"

"Because Farley doesn't have a blender. Weren't you paying attention earlier?"

Nico didn't even crack a smile. He crossed his arms and took a long, slow breath. Silence hung heavy as his inquisitive gaze pierced through me.

I lowered my head, breaking our connection, and smoothed the edge of my blouse. "Why don't you go back to your new Monday lunch date?"

"What are you—oh." Nico chuckled. "I would have introduced you to Gabs, but you were too eager to run off."

"Why would I want to meet—"

"My sister. Gabriela is my sister. I told you about her. Remember?" A lopsided smile spread across his face, accented with his adorable single dimple. The flickering light of the fire reflected in his sparkling eyes. He leaned back in his chair and took a sip from his glass, continuing to watch me. "You're so damn cute when you're jealous."

"I'm not jealous." I downed another gulp of Farley's disgusting liquid, hoping to pull off my blatant lie, then lowered my empty mug to the table. "I'm a grown woman, Nico. I don't need a babysitter." When he didn't budge, I swept my hand toward him, shooing him away.

He inched forward, eyes locked on mine, and captured my hand in his. "I'm not leaving you alone like this."

There was no stopping the gasp that slipped past my lips, an instinctive reaction to the spark of electricity that surged through me. God, how I'd missed his touch. I'd been sure my memory had blown the sensation out of proportion, but I was wrong.

I grabbed Nico's glass and threw back its contents, sputtering and spitting it out. "What the hell are you drinking?"

He chuckled while mopping up the mess with a cocktail napkin. "It's called water. I figured one of us better stay sober."

Another large mug of . . . whatever that beer was magically landed in front of me, compliments of my new pal Rob, of course. Bits of ice floated to the surface as they broke free from the bottom of the glass. They seemed to vanish as quickly as they appeared. I couldn't tell you how long I stared at the fascinating little show.

"I can't stop wondering if he ever really loved me." My faint, despondent words sounded so distant. "Maybe I've just been a fool all these years, too blind . . ."

I drew my finger through the condensation pooling on the table and used it to trace the rings of the ancient tree trunk. Nico relaxed his posture, caressing my hand, a silent indication for me to go on.

"Thing is, I've had a lot of time to sit and think lately. And that . . . spark? That intense passion? I'm not sure we ever— but he was good to me. I'd never experienced that before." I braved a glance at Nico's face. "It was love. Maybe just not the right kind."

This was all so painful to admit. I pulled in a shaky breath. "But I tried to fix things. Tried to make him love me again. I tried, so hard, to be the perfect wife." I shook my head, unwilling to dwell on the past. "See, without proof of Will cheating, there was always the possibility that the sleazy bastard hadn't replaced me." A bitter laugh slipped out. "I don't know why, but the idea of being traded in sucks a whole lot more than thinking he'd just grown tired of me."

I kept my eyes fixed on the table, my nails gouging the surface as the words continued pouring from my soul. "So imagine my surprise when I learned today that my *alleged* best friend knew Will was having an affair and didn't do a damn thing about it. Couldn't even bother to drop a goddamn hint."

Nico's grip on my hand tightened, but he didn't interrupt.

I downed another dose of liquid courage. "I've never felt more betrayed. Or alone." The screech of my chair on the wooden floor echoed through the vacant room as I shoved away from the table. "Why would he do it? Any of it? I loved him. I gave everything I could to make our marriage work, no matter how I felt about y—"

I pushed to my feet and moved to the fire, away from Nico's stunned expression.

Hugging my empty mug to my chest, I forced myself to press on. The tears I struggled to suppress filled my voice. "I stopped myself. If I could do it, so could he. Which only proves that *he* didn't *want* to."

Anger erupted from me with a brutal force. My mug shattered against the stone fireplace, the thunderous crash blending with my feral scream.

"Christ, Dan—"

"I hate him for lying. For cheating on me. I hate him for fucking humiliating me. Hate him for throwing away everything we had without even giving me a chance to—not even caring enough to try to save our relationship."

My nails cut deeper into my palms with each enraged word. It took several shuddered sobs for me to gain control of my anger. I flexed my fingers, shaking my hands to release the tension as the hypnotic dance of the flames soothed me. I kept my back to Nico, afraid to see judgement or disappointment in his eyes. Maybe even disgust that I could've ranted so wildly about a dead man.

"And I hate him for dying, because now I can't even yell at him, slap him, or throw something at him. All this fury is locked inside me." I turned to face Nico, not bothering to wipe the stream of tears from my face. "He treated me like shit. And I'm the one who looks like an insensitive bitch, because I can't even play the heartbroken, grieving widow."

Rob hovered nearby, shifting uneasily as he monitored the scene.

Nico raised his hand and signaled for another round of drinks. He stood, hesitating before approaching me, his expression guarded. "You are . . . an amazing person, Danni." He reached out and caressed my arms, his eyes locked on mine.

My shoulders eased as his touch melted away my heartache. The intensity of his stare grew, searching my soul. My momentary sense of calm gave way to an inner trembling.

The muscles in Nico's jaw flexed. His chest rose and fell at an increased pace. He stepped forward, erasing the distance between us, and wrapped me in a warm embrace. The world and all its pain seemed to disappear as he held me tight.

"I'm sorry. I wouldn't have stayed away so long if I'd known." His rough cheek brushed along the side of my face, and his warm breath washed over me. "I'm here now though. And I promise to take care of you."

Time seemed to stand still as we held each other, and nothing had ever felt more right. Rob cleared his throat as he approached to deliver our drinks, his intrusion earning a disappointed groan from me this time. The two men exchanged a brief, stony glare. When Rob backed down, Nico took my hand and led me to the table, sliding our chairs close together before sitting. His knee brushed against mine.

Nico asked again what had happened at lunch that had me so upset. His expression made it clear I wouldn't be evading the question this time, so I gave him the short version of how untrustworthy my former best friend had turned out to be. The attentive way he listened to every word made me feel like the most important person in the world.

Gentle touches sent waves of electricity through my body,

destroying the last of my resistance. My self-control. A burning sense of desire quickly took its place. He'd been right under my nose the whole time. Why hadn't I figured it out sooner?

Probably because you were too busy fighting for the wrong man.

Nico continued holding my hand while talking in a soothing voice, but I couldn't stay focused on his words. As his lips moved, my mind wandered, remembering the way they'd felt pressed against mine. The sound he'd made when I'd kissed him that one glorious time.

Mischief played in his eyes as he spoke. He reached out, wrapping his finger in a strand of hair before brushing it behind my shoulder. The feathery touch as his hand skimmed along the side of my neck sent a chill through me. He winked, giving a low chuckle, then leaned on the table, watching me.

The scene reminded me of Logan's party—the night this confident, charming man had introduced himself and taken my breath away.

"Ya know . . . you're really sexy." I walked my fingers along his arm, grinning when he clamped his hand over mine.

"Danni?" Nico drew out my name with a cautious tone and shook his head. "You . . . are trouble, and trying to resist you is gonna kill me."

"Then don't." I lowered my eyes, gathering the courage to go on. "I was just thinking about . . . how much I like being around you. Dancing with you." I bit my lip to stop it from trembling. "Kissing you. Maybe I shoulda even slept with you." I motioned for him to come closer and pressed a finger to my mouth. "Shhh . . . don't tell anybody, but I fantasized about it." A nervous giggle slipped out. "A *lot.*"

He pulled in a slow, deep breath, blowing it out as he scrubbed a hand across his face. "You were married. Neither of us would have allowed that to happen."

"You say that now, but I can be *pretty persuasive.*" I downed the rest of my drink. With one eye closed, I squinted up into the tipped glass, straining to get the last drop. "You know, this stuff's not so bad after a while."

I waited for good ol' Farley to magically appear with my replacement, just like he'd been doing all afternoon. *Doesn't he know a girl can only wait so long for something she really wants?* I giggled and flashed a smile at Nico.

"Where's a waiter when you need one?" I leaned to the side, stretching a little too far toward the bar. Nico grabbed my hand as it slipped from the table, saving me from an embarrassing fall. "Nice ninja reflexes, mister sexy." I waved my empty mug in the air. "Woo-hoo. Hey, Rob? Can I get a refill over here?"

Where did he go?

"Hmmm . . . guess I'll hafta go get it myself." My legs were like rubber when I stood, and my feet didn't want to move right.

Nico caught me by the waist with both hands. "Okay, beautiful, I think you've had enough to drink. Let's get you home."

A warm, tingling sensation spread through my body. No other man had ever made me feel this way. I threw my arms around his neck, sagging against him. His heart pounded against my chest as I pressed a kiss beneath his rough jaw.

"I like the sound of that, but first I want you to dance with me. The way you did that night at Metro Sky." I swayed my hips to the faint country tune drifting through the pub, smiling at the way Nico's body responded to the contact. To me.

The excessive heat in Farley's small pub suddenly hit me. I fumbled with the buttons of my blouse, but they seemed to be stuck. Giving the fabric a good tug, I managed to pop open the first few. Nico released my waist and grabbed my hands, halting my progress. He stared at me, head tipped, letting his raised brows question my actions.

"It's okay. I have on a cami." I wiggled one hand free from

his grip and pulled open my blouse, exposing the pale pink undergarment. "See? It even has pretty lace across the top."

"Christ. Like that's any better." Nico groaned and pulled my blouse closed. "Maybe we should just move away from the fire."

I stretched on my toes to place a kiss by his ear. "I'll go anywhere you wanna go."

About Last Night

DANNI

Oh. My. God.

The throbbing in my head matched the racing beat of my heart. My mouth felt as if someone had taken a blow dryer to it. And the dreadful burning in my eyes warned against even trying to open them. The hangover I'd *thought* I'd had yesterday didn't come close to this morning's misery.

What was I thinking?

A small whimper escaped as I moved. And, of course, the sound pierced through me, making my head hurt even more. I stretched open one eye, then the other, and squinted against the bright sunlight into a bedroom that was definitely not mine.

This had to be Nico's room . . . Nico's bed.

Adrenaline rushed through my veins, palpitations and nervous jitters overshadowing my hangover symptoms. I couldn't decide which felt worse.

Deep breaths. No need to panic. Yet.

I tucked the covers—Nico's covers—firmly under my chin and struggled to remember . . . nothing. No matter how hard I tried to concentrate, tried to figure out how I'd wound up here, my attention kept drifting to the tall posts at the foot of his massive bed.

Each trembling breath filled my head with his familiar scent. My heart beat faster, the previous night still a total blank. *Come on, Danni. Think.* No luck. Only a steady stream of salacious thoughts about Nico played in my mind.

He'd starred in plenty of vivid dreams since the night we'd met, detailed fantasies about how amazing it would feel to lie in his strong arms. I'd imagined the way he'd make love to me. How he'd fill me with a burning passion greater than anything I'd experienced before. Some nights I'd even woken up gasping, on the verge of an orgasm more intense than any Will had ever given me.

I let out a groan, shoving my head deeper into the pillow. A thrumming noise resounded in my brain, mocking me for being so foolish. Laughing at me for forgetting the main event of a real-life night with Nico.

Conjured images of him caressing my body consumed me. Every cell ached with desire, desperate to be touched. I shifted restlessly in Nico's bed, allowing his essence to permeate my senses with each small gasp.

Cool silk sheets skimmed across my skin. My eyes grew wide. My body tensed. Lifting the covers, I ducked under to glance at my legs. My *naked* legs. They extended below a large white dress shirt—also *not* mine—held closed across my midsection by a single fastened button.

Okay, now it's time to panic.

In my fantasies, sex with Nico was always amazing. Better than amazing . . . more like mind-blowing. But now? Well, my fuzzy little mind was clearly *not* blown.

So . . . did I? Did we?

My joints and muscles all felt the same as every other lonely morning. The same tension still lingered inside me like a tightly wound coil waiting to spring free. I slipped one hand under the covers, along the length of my borrowed shirt, to my tiny lace panties—still securely in place.

I should probably be happy Nico had acted as a gentleman and hadn't taken advantage of me. But truth was, I felt cheated.

He'd gotten me undressed. Why stop? Had he decided he just wasn't interested? Maybe he—*well, I'm not one of the twenty-five-year-old perfect little hotties he's used to*—but was I so much of a disappointment he couldn't even go through with it?

The click of an opening door startled me, interrupting my overanalysis of his rejection. But I'd have plenty of time to finish after he threw me out.

I sat up and glanced around the room, the sudden movement making my head spin. Half-naked and trapped in a sexual fantasy-gone-wrong, I hugged my knees to my chest and braced for—well, nothing could be worse than any of the other crap I'd been through lately.

Nico emerged from a steamy bathroom, rubbing a towel over his wet hair. Faded, unsnapped jeans hung low on his hips. I didn't bother pretending to look away. *Might as well enjoy my one and only chance to take in this spectacular view.* My lips parted. A sweet sigh escaped.

He crossed the room at a leisurely pace, muscles rippling with each movement. A mischievous spark danced in his eyes. "See something you like?"

Hell yes. I lifted one shoulder in a nonchalant shrug, biting my lip and trying to play innocent.

Nico dragged the towel across his broad chest, obstructing my view of his perfectly sculpted body. But there was no hiding the heavenly scent that surrounded him. He moved to the side of the bed, staring at me with an assessing gaze.

"Good morning, beautiful." He placed a tender kiss to my forehead, his warm lips sending a chill through me. "You look like shit." He chuckled and grabbed a bottle of water from the bedside table. "Guess I don't have to ask how you feel."

"How did I—why am I here?" My voice sounded so small. I wondered if he'd even heard me. "And w-where did you sleep?"

One brow lifted, and a teasing smile flickered on his gorgeous face. He dropped the bottle next to me then clutched his chest. "You don't remember?" He studied me for a moment, torturing me by drawing out his response. "Next to you, of course."

The heat in his gaze burned through me. A faint gasp slipped out, the prelude to a shriek I somehow managed to contain. I wanted to pull the covers over my head. Disappear.

How could this have happened? I had a headful of things I'd love to forget, but this was the one thing I wouldn't want—

Nico cleared his throat. He tipped his head toward the other side of the bed where a blanket and pillow on the floor marked the place of a makeshift bed.

"Oh. I, um . . ." I hugged my knees tighter and forced a smile. "Guess I should have expected that." *And I guess that means you'll be eager to show me to the door.*

Nico shook his head, grinning, and tossed his towel over a nearby chair. "You were drunk." He stepped closer and placed his palms on the mattress, lowering himself to look into my eyes. "I want to make sure you remember our first time together."

His words ignited a fire that raced through my body, straight to my core. "But . . ." I averted my gaze, afraid to see his reaction. "W-why am I naked?"

"You were pretty trashed when we finally left Farley's. I didn't trust dropping you home and leaving you there alone. And I was worried how it would look to your neighbors if I stayed there with you." He chuckled, rubbing the back of his neck. "You were quite a handful."

"That doesn't explain my missing clothes." I took a sip of the water he'd given me, thankful for the distraction while I tried, again, to remember what had happened. Any small part of it.

Something kept pulling my attention back to those tall posts on his bed. A vague memory lurked in my foggy brain, trying to break free. *Dammit.* Struggling to think only made my head hurt more—which I would have thought impossible a few minutes ago.

A slow mirage of images began to emerge like scattered pieces of a complex puzzle. Singing. Really bad singing, but I wasn't in a bar.

And I was dancing. Swaying provocatively with my arm wrapped around a pole. My eyes flashed to Nico's bedpost—my dance pole. *Oh, God. No.*

A deep laugh rumbled in his chest. "Coming back to you?"

Memories of trying to pole dance on Nico's bedpost played like scenes from a late-night movie that faded into a bad dream. A nightmare. I saw myself slowly unbuttoning my blouse, teasing him, before letting it fall to the floor. Holding onto my *pole* as I shimmied out of my bra and tossed it at him. Standing in front of Nico wearing only my gold heart pendant and a pair of pink lace panties.

I let out a slow, quiet groan and forced myself to face him.

Nico's grin confirmed it all. He hooked his thumbs in his pockets and dipped his head to meet my gaze. "I didn't have to undress you. Did I?"

I shook my head, too humiliated to answer. After the seductive striptease, I'd tried to wrap one leg around his bedpost and stumbled into Nico's arms, where I'd proceeded to grind against him.

I could just die. Now . . . please.

Worst of all, Nico had kept trying to stop me the whole time.

I glanced around the room, looking for my clothes. A place to hide. An exit. Anything that would help me escape the embarrassment.

Nico moved toward the foot of the bed and casually leaned against the post, arms crossed. The tribal band around his bicep strained as his muscles bulged. "I deserve some kind of award, you know—or sainthood—for resisting you. Not saying I didn't enjoy the show. Or cop a feel . . . maybe two. Accidentally, of course." He threw in a wink then sauntered toward me, dragging his fingertips along the mattress.

"As surprised as I was about all of that, you know what I really didn't expect?" He gave a short laugh. "Well, I didn't expect any of it, to be honest. But I never imagined you were hiding such sexy little secrets under all those pretty layers of clothes." Mischief gleamed in his eyes.

I gasped and slapped both hands over my right hip, covering my tiny souvenir from the one-and-only wild weekend of my non-rebellious youth.

One corner of Nico's mouth turned up. His eyes lingered on my hands as though he could see right through them.

"How—" *Dammit*. "Did you, um . . . see? Something?"

Nico tucked his hands in his pockets and rocked forward. "Let's just say you gave a sweet little preview when you tried to wiggle out of your panties."

My chest tightened. My voice shot up an octave. "But they're still on. I didn't—you couldn't have—"

"You sure about that?" He arched a brow and leaned in, lowering his voice. "I can't wait for the day I get to take a closer look at those pretty pink hearts of yours. Among other things."

That couldn't have been a lucky guess. And I never would have told him . . . which left only one explanation. I raised my hands to cover my face.

"Too bad you ran into a little trouble and didn't get to finish."

I spread my fingers enough to peek at him with one eye, unamused by his playful tone. "What kind of trouble?"

His shoulders shook with silent laughter. "Well, you mumbled something about the room spinning right before you passed out cold. Lucky for both of us, I caught you before you hit the floor." He shook his head. "Such a shame though, 'cause I was really looking forward to the finale you'd promised."

My face burst into flames. This time I gave in to the urge to hide and sank beneath the covers, burying myself. Only my clenched fists remained exposed. Which was a lot better than what I'd exposed last night.

This can't be happening. Please, please, please . . . let me wake up.

Nico leaned over me and peeled away my shield. "No point trying to hide. I know where you are. And I've already seen it all." His gaze skimmed the length of my body. "Mmm . . . so incredibly sexy." He gave a satisfied-looking nod as he tapped his temple. "And etched in here forever."

I clutched at my chest, wrapping my fingers around the heart pendant lying there. I'd always treasured the rare occasions when Will had called me sexy. Yet something in Nico's voice sounded more sincere—more hungry—than fifteen years' worth of Will's empty lies.

"You need some rest." Nico tucked my hair behind my ear, letting his hand linger on my neck. He leaned down to kiss my forehead. "I'll be downstairs. You can come find me when you're ready to get up."

"Wait." I reached for him, my fingers catching in the loops of his jeans as he turned to leave. Letting Nico walk out of this room right now felt like I'd be letting him walk out of my life. "Stay with me."

SLEEPING ANGEL
NICO

tay. That one word coming from Danni's luscious lips nearly unraveled me. My feet refused to keep moving toward the door. Toward safety. At least I managed to resist the overwhelming urge to glance back at her, because I'd surely cave and do anything she wanted.

"Please. I-I don't want to be alone." The desperation in her voice tugged at my heart, tearing down another block of the fortress I'd spent months building around it.

My chest rose and fell on several heavy breaths, but I couldn't lock down my emotions. I couldn't walk away. I needed to hold her, comfort her, almost as much as she seemed to need it. Problem was, I wanted so much more than to just hold her, and I'd already pushed my self-control to its limit.

I turned to look at her. "Danni, I don't think—"

"No. Stop thinking." She slid to the center of the bed and tapped the empty spot beside her, never taking her hungry eyes off me.

Long, tense seconds passed in silence, each chipping away at my already weakened willpower.

"Nico?" Her voice shook.

This is such a bad idea. I dragged a hand through my hair, gripping the back of my neck, and looked toward the ceiling, sending up a silent prayer for strength before finally sitting on the edge of the mattress with my back to the angel lying there.

The mattress dipped, and Danni slipped her arms around my waist. "Thank you."

Her soft lips brushed across my shoulder, and I imagined how they'd feel on every other inch of my body. *Christ, this is gonna kill me.* I broke free and pushed myself farther onto the bed, moving to rest my back against the tall mahogany headboard.

"I must be crazy." I shook my head then spread my arms wide. "Come here, beautiful trouble."

Danni bit her lip, which did little to hide her victorious smile. She crawled toward me then curled up on my lap with her arms around my neck, wiggling until she'd snuggled as close as humanly possible. "Mmm . . . now this is nice."

I couldn't disagree, but right now I was too busy fighting a raging hard-on to fully appreciate having her wrapped around me.

She pressed her lips to my neck then let one hand glide down my chest to trace the ridges in my abs. She let out another sexy sigh. "Very nice."

My pulse raced, but I couldn't give in. I'd never forgive myself for taking advantage of her. And she wasn't in a place, emotionally, to make sound relationship decisions.

I stroked her hair, tugging to loosen the tangles before letting my hand skim the length of her back, persuading her to relax a little more with each slow pass.

Danni nuzzled against my neck, purring, and pressed a kiss below my jaw. "You know . . . I'm not drunk anymore."

My hand stopped moving. Every muscle in my body went rigid. "Don't get any ideas."

She sagged against my chest and let out a groan, followed by a faint whimper.

"See? You're still hungover." I kissed the top of her head. "Sleep. It's not negotiable."

Danni didn't argue, and in a matter of minutes, she was sound asleep in my arms. Again.

How many nights had I dreamed of having her in my bed? Under me. Wrapped around me. Our bodies moving as one. It had taken every bit of self-control I'd had to resist her last night . . . and it would again today.

I probably should have admitted I'd spent most of the night holding her, struggling to keep my hands in the neutral zones. I'd only moved to the floor when she'd started grinding against my hard-on in her sleep and moaning my name.

Maybe she wouldn't remember making me promise I'd never lie to her. Or her rambling speech about "honesty" and how everyone she'd ever trusted had lied and hurt her.

I didn't want to be one of those people.

Danni shifted against me. Her lace thong peeked out beneath the hem of my shirt she wore. I brushed my hand over her hip, inches away from her hidden tattoo. I wanted to trace those hearts with my tongue. Follow the trail to her sweet center. Taste her. Drive her wild, then get lost inside her.

But giving in to that temptation would violate her trust in me. I needed her to give herself to me willingly, knowing full well the choice she was making.

I blew out a heavy sigh and took her hand, weaving our fingers together. "Which you're clearly not ready to do yet," I whispered, studying her modest diamond solitaire.

There could only be one logical reason she continued to wear the damn thing.

Commitment.

Loyalty.

Okay, I guess that's two. But the cheating bastard doesn't deserve them.

He didn't deserve her either. Or want her, as it turned out. Regardless, on some level—in her heart and her mind—she was still his. And while she belonged to him, she couldn't be mine.

"But you will be . . . someday, my beautiful angel. I've waited this long. I'm not about to give up." I skimmed my finger along the length of her silky legs with a featherlight touch that left a trail of goosebumps on her skin.

Danni shivered. She squinted up at me through one eye then snuggled deeper into my embrace with a peaceful sigh.

"Welcome back, beautiful. You feeling better?"

"Mmm . . . I am. Much better." A contented smile eased into place, and she gave a dainty stretch. "And this is the perfect way to wake up."

I hummed in agreement, knowing I could easily get used to it.

"However . . ." Danni walked her fingers up my chest then let them slide down to the waistband of my jeans, dipping her fingers beneath the fabric. "I bet I can think of an even better way."

My cock jerked, reaching for her. Eager to be set free. After spending much of the past hour fantasizing about making love to her, I had a hard time remembering why giving in now would be such a bad idea. But then my gaze settled on that fucking ring again, and it all came back to me.

She wasn't ready to move on to a new relationship, and for the first time in a long time, I wanted more than just one night with a woman.

So much more.

IT'S TOO SOON

DANNI

Seconds ticked by as I waited for a response that never came. My hand fell to the mattress, pushed away by the force of his silent rejection.

"Danni . . ." Nico shifted beneath me, retreating, and sat up straighter. "You're still grieving. You need—"

"Don't." I motioned for him to stop, my raised hand successful at holding off his bullshit dismissal. "I'm tired of people thinking I feel anything but disgust for my dead husband. The only thing I *need* is to forget I was ever foolish enough to believe a single word he said."

Dammit. How much longer would I have to suffer for Will's lies? Every time I thought I'd moved past them, the pain resurfaced. And each time the wound cut deeper into my soul, threatening to destroy any hope of finding true love and happiness.

I moved from Nico's lap to kneel beside him on the mattress. "You don't get it. No one seems to get it."

Eyes closed, I searched for the right words—tried to figure out what I could say to make him understand. Baring my soul never came easy for me. I suddenly felt overexposed. Physically and emotionally.

Settling back on my heels, I grabbed a pillow to shield myself and wrapped it across my naked thighs. "He was running around, screwing God knows who. Then he'd come home to me, crawl into *my* bed, and shove his filthy cock into *my* body like nothing ever happened . . . probably on the same damn day."

My body shook with a violent shudder, clenched fists vibrating against the pillow. It took every bit of strength I had not to scream and throw something. My frustration vented out in a strangled groan. "Just the thought of it makes me wanna puke."

Nico tipped his head. His lips pressed together in a straight line. "You sure that's not your body still protesting all the alcohol you downed yesterday?" He covered my hand with his, massaging my tense fingers.

"Not funny." His attempt to make light of the situation—to lighten my mood—wouldn't work. I wanted my moment of anger. Deserved it. After what Will had done, a lifetime of rage could probably be justified . . . and still not be enough. I narrowed my eyes, pinning Nico with a disapproving stare.

His smile faded. He stared past me with a blank expression. "Look, Danni, I get what you're going through. Your husband cheated on you. It sucks. You're angry. You feel humiliated. And you have every right to." Nico's eyes fell closed. "There's nothing more painful than devoting your life to someone, loving them more than you ever imagined you could love someone, only to—"

He lowered his head, brows pinched together as though trying to collect his thoughts. "You dream of the future. A family. You make plans. And then one day . . . one day you realize it was all just a fucking lie." He let out a heavy sigh.

"Nothing hurts more than having your heart ripped out like that."

Wow. No one had come close to understanding the way I felt. Until now. It took a moment for the shock of his accurate description to wear off, but nothing had changed.

And none of this explained why he continued to reject me.

"You talk a good game for a guy who has women throwing themselves at his feet everywhere he goes." I turned away, hugging the pillow to my chest. "I'm sure you've broken more than a few hearts along the way, but that doesn't make you an expert on the subject. And it sure as hell doesn't mean you know how *I* feel."

"Danni, don't—"

I twisted to face him. "Don't what? Don't be stupid enough to think you'd ever be interested in me? Don't get upset because I'm not young enough or sexy enough or—or whatever enough for you? Don't get upset because a guy who has a reputation as a total player won't even lay a goddamned hand on me when I'm half naked in his bed and practically throwing myself at him?"

I straddled his outstretched legs, craning my neck to look him in the eyes. "You've been stalking me for weeks, getting inside my head, making me want you like I've never wanted anyone before. Why?" I jabbed my finger into his chest, driving home my point. "Why bother, if you're not looking to score?"

He didn't move. Didn't respond.

I let out a frustrated groan and collapsed against him. Nothing I said or did seemed to affect this man. At all.

Or did it? Shifting my hips from side to side, I settled deeper into his lap. The hem of my borrowed shirt inched higher with each movement to reveal my pretty lace panties. He could lie and hide his emotions, but he couldn't hide his body's reaction.

I bit my lip, trying to hold back a victorious grin. "Hmmm . . . seems *someone's* trying to hold out on my fun."

Nico scrubbed a hand across his face and blew out a restrained breath. "It's not just about scoring. Not with you."

I pressed my lips to his ear, letting the rough stubble along his jaw graze my cheek, and taunted him with a seductive whisper. "Maybe you just need a little persuasion."

My breasts skimmed along his chest as I moved lower, placing sweet kisses along the length of his neck. Only my borrowed shirt separated us, a barrier I couldn't wait to remove.

Nico's eyes closed. His lips parted with a faint sigh as his head fell back against the headboard. "It's so fucking hard to say no to you."

"Then don't." I guided his hands to my waist.

Heat radiated from his palms, branding me as they slid along my torso. The brush of his thumbs across my breasts sent a shot of electricity through me. My body tingled with excitement, every part of me longing to be claimed. A pleading whimper slipped through my parted lips.

Nico hesitated, his fingers twisting in the designer fabric beneath them. The lone fastened button strained from the tension, exposing the flat stomach I'd earned from weeks of barely eating. Above the button, the curves of my breasts peeked out, begging for his attention.

He remained still, a virtual statue. Except for his wandering eyes. "We need to stop. Let me ex—"

"Shhh . . ." I touched a single finger to his mouth and leaned closer, allowing my lips to skim the edge of his ear. "Nothing you say will explain how you can be this turned on and still refuse to make love to me." I rubbed against him, reveling in the impressive size of his rock-hard erection. "I'm not looking for a commitment. I just want to feel alive. Feel *anything* but empty and broken. Please. Don't make me beg."

His fingers dug deeper into my hips, pulling me tighter to him. He let out a strangled groan, a mixture of ecstasy and agony, before he eased me away from him. His chest rose and fell on several heavy breaths, his forehead resting on mine.

I brushed my lips against his, eager to taste him and feel the passion I remembered so vividly from our last kiss. Our only kiss. Nico stroked the sides of my neck, cradling my face in his hands. Blood rushed through my body at a rapid pace as my anticipation grew, the warmth of his ragged breath caressing my lips.

His arms tensed. He straightened them, holding me at a distance. "I can't."

The subtle shake of his head assured me I hadn't misunderstood. I pressed a fist to my chest, trying to ease the pain, as another piece of my already broken heart chipped away. A single tear slid down my cheek. Nico brushed it away with a soft kiss and pressed his cheek to mine.

"You had your world turned upside down. You need time to adjust. To heal." His lips grazed mine with the faintest touch before leaving a trail of gentle kisses from the tip of my nose to my forehead. He paused, weaving his fingers through my hair. "I'm trying to give you that. I *need* to give you that."

Defeated, I prepared to slink away in humiliation.

Nico released me and blew out a long huff, pinching the bridge of his nose. "I am totally fucking this up." He paused for a moment, rubbing the back of his neck. "Wait here."

He slid me from his lap onto the cool sheets and placed a single kiss to my temple before standing. With slow, labored steps, he crossed the room, stopping in front of a long dresser. He stood there, motionless, time passing in awkward silence. Reaching out with an abrupt movement, he snatched something from atop the dresser then returned to me.

A pained expression crossed his face as our eyes met. Followed by a blank stare, a mask that failed to hide the pain radiating from him. My gut wrenched at his sudden change of mood, a churning sensation in the pit of my stomach far worse than the alcohol-induced nausea I'd endured this morning. Pushing aside my fear, I snuggled next to him as he sat on the bed.

His fingers traced the stitching around the edge of his wallet. The slow minute that passed without a word felt like hours.

My mind raced, trying to imagine why making love to *me* seemed to be such a difficult decision for him.

"I—" He took a deep breath and blew it out slowly while turning the wallet over in his hands. His eyes fell closed. "It's just not the right time."

I could pretend I didn't hear his faint words—they seemed to be directed more to himself anyway—but that didn't stop them from stomping on my heart.

Would there ever be a "right time" for us? I leaned against Nico, brushing tentative kisses along his neck and jaw for what could be the last time. He turned toward me, his lips finding mine. The gentle touch sparked a warm glow in my chest that radiated through me. A glimmer of hope.

I covered his mouth with mine in a slow kiss, savoring the taste of him. No remnants of alcohol this time. No lingering effects to blame for our decisions. No reason for guilt.

It didn't take long for Nico's resistance to fade. He pushed his hand through my hair, taking control, then dropped his other hand to my waist, fingers digging into my flesh to pull me closer. His tongue skimmed across my lips in a sensual assault. The soft moan that followed resonated through me and settled in my core.

I'd dreamed of this moment so many times. Longed for it to come true.

It's too soon. Nico's words replayed, unwelcome, in my mind. My chest constricted. I couldn't stop now. Didn't want to. Reaching between us, I unbuttoned his shirt and let it slip from my shoulders.

Nico broke our kiss, leaving us both breathless. Fire burned in his eyes, a need that mirrored my own. "You're so beautiful." His hands skimmed my torso, leaving a heated trail to my breasts then back to my waist. "And every ounce of my self-control seems to go straight out the window when I'm with you."

He dragged his shirt back up to my shoulders and proceeded to close every single button, grumbling under his breath the whole time, then pressed a chaste kiss to my forehead.

"Come on." Nico took my hands and stood, pulling me with him. "Let's get you home before I do something we'll both regret." He shook his head and stepped back, releasing my hands as he inched toward the door. "There are clean towels in the bathroom, if you'd like to shower before you get dressed. I'll wait downstairs."

This time I didn't try to stop him.

NOT A GOODBYE KISS
DANNI

"You're being ridiculous." I crossed my arms and glared at Nico.

He didn't budge—just stood there holding open the passenger's door of my car.

My car.

"Are you always this stubborn?" A teasing smile eased across his face. "Just get in the car, Danni. I already called Ben, and he's going to meet me at your house." With an exaggerated sweep of his arm, Nico motioned again for me to hop into the seat.

I just wanted to go home. Get away from this humiliating scene. And it seemed this was going to be my only option.

"Fine." I reluctantly climbed in. "But *I'm* not the one being stubborn."

Nico leaned in across me, fastening my seatbelt. The slight brush of his hands along my stomach set off my traitorous hormones. Again.

He gave a low chuckle, clearly knowing the effect he had, then closed the door without a word.

"This isn't funny," I shouted through the glass.

If he heard me, he didn't respond. He took his place in *my* driver's seat, still grinning, and started the engine.

We pulled out of Nico's garage, giving me my first conscious view of his massive house and the beautiful grounds surrounding it. "You live here alone?"

Nico stared straight ahead. "Yep, just me."

"Seems kind of big for one person. Don't you get lost, or feel isolated out here all by yourself?"

He gave a low hum. "That's one of the things that sold me on the place." His tone was flat. Distant.

I twisted in my seat, still absorbing the breathtaking view as we drove down his tree-lined driveway and past the tall stone pillars marking the entrance to his grand estate. Something about the peaceful scene soothed me. Or, more likely, just being around Nico made me happy, even though his mixed signals and constant rejections frustrated me. Either way, despite my best efforts to stay annoyed, my anger faded by the time we reached the highway.

And soon Nico would fade from my life too. I swallowed hard against the sudden lump in my throat and rested my head against the seat, angling enough to watch the silent man of my dreams.

He stayed in his lane, eyes focused on the road, and kept pace with the slow-moving traffic—a total contrast to the other times I'd ridden with him. Those adrenaline-infused adventures in his "toy" had me gripping my seat while Nico shifted gears and zipped across lanes, maneuvering around every potential obstacle.

The memory of how sexy he'd looked—daring but in control—made my heart race. I tugged at my pendant and let out a sigh.

It would have made more sense for me to drive myself home . . . and eliminated the need for all the uncomfortable tension between us during the speechless twenty-minute ride.

At least he held my hand most of that time, his thumb stroking and caressing my skin. All part of what had to be the most caring and gentle brush-off in history.

We turned onto my street. My stomach clenched. Seeing Ben's Maserati parked by the curb meant my time with Nico was coming to an end.

Ben stood lounging against the side of his car, waiting. He pushed away and followed us into the garage, opening my door before Nico shut off the engine.

"Hey, Danni. It's great to see you again." Ben pulled me from the car and into a giant hug, placing a kiss on my cheek.

"All right, Romeo. Hands off." Nico rounded the car and slapped Ben's shoulder. "You've got your own girl."

Ben chuckled and turned to face his brother, keeping one arm draped across my back. "Don't forget about the long line of hopefuls waiting in the wings." He winked before releasing me. "Guess I can let you have this one. Besides, that way I won't have to put up with your constant moping around because you're so desperately miserable without her."

Ben crossed his arms and leaned against my car, his full attention focused on Nico. "So?" He drew out the word in a playful tone. "How was your night?"

Nico shook his head. His gaze flashed to me with an apologetic expression before returning to Ben. "It was . . . none of your damn business." Nico hooked his arm around Ben's neck and led him out of the garage. "Why don't you go wait for me in your car? I'll only be a minute."

"Oh, come on. Where's the fun in tha—ouch." He laughed, breaking free from Nico's chokehold. "Fine. We'll do it your way. *This* time. See you soon, Danni." Ben waved over his head and strolled down the driveway, whistling a cheerful tune.

Nico returned to me, his usual lopsided grin and adorable

dimple back in place. "Sorry. You'll get used to him after a while."

He took my hand and walked me to the door, waiting while I fished my key from my bag. The look in his eyes, the warmth of his touch, and the sincerity in his voice caught me off guard, reigniting that foolish glimmer of hope. But I couldn't allow myself to believe him. Couldn't risk another painful rejection.

"You don't have to hang around." I avoided looking at Nico and unlocked the door. "I mean, I appreciate you taking care of me last night and—well, I'm sure you're anxious to get out of here."

"Hey." He grabbed my arms and turned me to face him, but I couldn't raise my eyes to meet his. I didn't want him to see the heartache they'd reveal.

Nico placed his fingers under my chin, tugging until he forced me to look at him. "This isn't goodbye."

He leaned in and pressed his lips to mine in a slow, sensual kiss that ignited every sinful ounce of desire for him I'd buried deep inside since the night we'd met. His eyes locked on mine, reaching into my soul, stealing the words I didn't dare to tell him. But I couldn't look away. Didn't want to.

Nico brushed his thumb across my lips. "I'll see you soon." He jogged down the driveway and hopped in the passenger's seat of Ben's car, waving as they pulled away from the curb.

My heart pounded. The relentless fire Nico had stoked spread through my body, colliding with the rising fear that I may never see him again. *Wouldn't be the first time a man lied to me.*

I pressed my fingers to my lips, replaying every second of the perfect kiss that still lingered there. Over and over again. Memorizing every detail. Every touch. Every—

"Dammit." The house phone ringing on the other side of the door dragged me back to reality.

I stepped inside and shoved the door closed, berating myself for clinging to foolish dreams about Nico. Wishing I could rewind time and choose him when I'd had the chance, even if it had been for only one night.

I wandered into the family room where the now-quiet phone sat on the table behind the couch . . . right next to a vase filled with wilted white roses. I slid my fingers along one of the limp stems, its head hanging low. The perfect representation of my worries about a future with Nico. A few petals fell to the table like tears scattered among the photos of my former life.

My gaze drifted back to the flashing red light on the phone. It taunted me, reminding me it was filled with pieces of a past I couldn't seem to leave behind. I reached out and pulled in a deep breath, determined to take one giant step toward letting go. With the single push of a button, all the painful messages about Will were gone. A smile eased across my face, followed by short beats of laughter.

The photos were next. I tipped over each one, disgusted by the lies and deceit their cheerful images hid.

The phone rang again, making me jump. I snapped up the handset. "Stop bugging me!"

"Danni? Oh, thank God." Jen's panicked voice blasted through the receiver, stopping me a split second before I slammed it back down. "Where the hell have you been?"

I cringed and eased the phone toward my ear, unsure of how to answer or if I was even ready to discuss the whole mess. "I was . . . out."

"What kind of an answer is that? I've been trying to reach you since yesterday. Yes-ter-day. You haven't answered your cell, and every time I call your house, I get that damn recording telling me I can't leave a message. When are you gonna cl—"

"Well, I wasn't here. And my cell phone died." *Probably.*

"But—oh, my God. Is something wrong? Are Ryan and Caden—"

"They're fine. But now that I know you're okay, I could kill you." She let out a frustrated groan. "Kendra called me after you ran out on her, and I've been worried sick."

"Sorry, I . . . I just stopped at Farley's for a drink." *A lot of drinks.* I pressed my fingers to the side of my head, massaging the dull ache that still lingered. None of this would have happened if my former best friend had just been straight with me from the beginning.

"That was twenty-six hours ago." I pulled the phone away from my ear while Jen went on about not answering my cell phone and the dangers of sitting alone at a bar. Even from a distance, the shrill pitch of her rant screeched like a dentist's drill boring through my skull.

"Hey, you mind if—"

"Do you want to know all the horrible images and scenarios that have been racing through my mind?"

I rolled my eyes at her overactive imagination. "Not really."

Wincing, I pulled away from the phone again, anticipating her strangled scream that followed. When it seemed safe, I continued, determined to stay calm. "Look, I just got home. Give me a few minutes to settle in, then I'll call you back."

Without waiting for her objection, I ended the call and placed the handset on the table.

CHANGING THE SUBJECT
NICO

By some miracle, Ben kept his mouth shut the whole ride to my house. Sure, he'd continued to smirk from the moment I'd kicked him out of Danni's garage, but I could ignore that. Or at least tolerate it for two more minutes. Then I'd be free to sort through everything that had happened in the past twenty-four hours and come up with a plan to make Danni mine.

Ben pulled around the circle at the top of my drive, stopped, and shut off the engine. Before I could say a word, he hopped out of his car.

I leaned across the center console and waved. "Hey, thanks for the ride. I got it from here."

"No problem." Instead of taking the hint that I wanted him to get back in and leave, he reached behind the driver's seat and pulled out his messenger bag. "Since I'm here, figured I'd stick around a while and we can run some numbers for the gala."

Shit. "You mean babysit me to see where my head is now that Danni's back in my life." Not that she'd ever left, at least not in my opinion. "Not necessary." *Or wanted.*

I climbed the steps to my front porch, and of course Ben followed as I expected he would . . . Giardano family rule number something: always watch out for each other.

"I'm thinking about inviting her." The words spilled out of me. Without looking back for his reaction, I crossed the foyer and entered my home office.

The majority of our family believed taking a date to a formal family event—especially one that ran the course of a weekend—implied you were serious about building a future with that person. Ben and I had a different opinion, but we'd decided years ago to avoid confusion—meaning we wanted to avoid the inevitable barrage of unwelcome questions about wedding plans—and made our own rule: no *casual* dates to family events.

"To the gala?" Ben gave a thoughtful hum but didn't sound too surprised. "You tell Dad? And Gabs?"

"Not yet, but I don't see them having a problem with it."

At least not anymore. While I'd never admit it to anyone, I'd been flirting with the idea of inviting Danni long before . . . everything. Not that she would've accepted. That reality had always pissed me off, despite my deep admiration of her values and commitment. I'd just prefer to have them directed at me.

"You taking Kristi?"

"Definitely not." Ben dragged a chair to the front of my desk then plopped down across from me wearing a huge grin. "So. What *really* happened last night?" He raised his wrist with a dramatic flair and overemphasized looking at his watch. "And the better part of today?"

"And now we know why you're *really* here," I grumbled under my breath. "There's nothing to tell. I just helped Danni through a rough day. Period."

Ben laughed. "Oh, come on. You hand Gabs the keys to your precious Ferrari—without even shedding a tear—to run after the girl you've been obsessed with for months. No one hears from you for twenty-some hours."

While he rambled on, ticking off each point on his fingers, I pulled up my files for the gala, intent on putting a rapid end to this conversation.

"Then you call to tell me you're driving Danni home in *her* car and need me to pick you up at her place?" Ben laughed again and rubbed his neck. "And now you want her to spend the gala weekend with our family, but I'm supposed to believe there's *nothing* goin' on between you?"

Works for me. "So Gabs sent me an updated report this morning on confirmed guests, and it looks like—"

"Wow." Ben shifted forward, his brows pinched together. "You *didn't* sleep with her. I thought you were just being all chivalrous and shit earlier since she was there, but—"

"We're not discussing this."

"Wait. Did she—" Ben's shoulders shook with a poor attempt at containing his amusement. He waved a hand between us and gasped a lame apology. "She turned you down. Damn . . . I never thought I'd see the day."

Snippets of Danni trying to seduce me and begging me to make love to her played in my mind. Along with the memory of how damn hard it had been to resist her.

"Then again . . . why are you so happy?" Ben rested his elbows on the desk and leaned closer, staring as though he thought that would make the details magically flow from my mouth.

"I'm not one of your little groupies, rock star." I grabbed my stress ball and bounced it off his forehead. "Doesn't matter how long you give me that fuckin' look, you're not getting what you want."

"Fine. Be all prude-like," Ben grumbled, failing to keep a straight face. He sat back and propped his feet on the corner of my desk, ankles crossed. "But all joking aside, I'm here for you. So talk to me."

"It's complicated."

He lifted one shoulder. "I'm sure I can keep up."

I let out a heavy sigh, appreciating his concern but wishing he'd just cut the inquisition. "She's not available. Can we get to work now?"

Ben dropped his filthy boots to the floor. He rubbed his forehead. "Okay, maybe I can't keep up. I thought her husband died."

Christ, why didn't I shut the door in his face instead of letting him follow me inside? I closed my laptop and turned to face Ben full-on, folded my hands in front of me, and gave him the short version of what had happened . . . leaving out any details that were too personal or might embarrass Danni.

"And after all that, she's still wearing his fucking ring." I pushed to my feet and headed toward the kitchen. "She's not ready to move on, and I'm not interested in being her rebound guy."

"Where you going?"

"I need a drink. Assumed you'd be tagging along?"

"Of course, but please say you didn't tell her that," he groaned.

"That I'm thirsty?" I teased, glancing over my shoulder to smirk at my brother. "I didn't. But I should have. And maybe I—"

"Cut the shit, Nico, 'cause I'm not buyin' it. You seriously think having Danni hook up with some random guy just to check off your arbitrary little 'rebound' box is gonna make you feel better?" Ben leaned against the counter, arms crossed like some hot-shot bouncer, and stared at me as though expecting an answer. "You *want* Danni squirming under another dude while he pounds into her and she screams his name? You want her goin' down on him? You *really* think that'll make her realize—"

"Enough!" I slammed the fridge door shut, waves of jealous anger crashing over me. "You made your point."

"Good." He strolled past me, pulled out a chair, and motioned toward it. "Now sit your stubborn ass down and chill. Let's figure this out."

I opened two bottles of beer and handed him one. "There's nothing to figure out," I said, pacing the length of the kitchen. "She's grieving, confused, and has trust issues—with good reasons. Guess I just need to be patient and hope I can gradually win her over."

"I'm pretty sure she's not the only one with issues," Ben mumbled, rubbing his jaw. "And what about Summer?"

"What about her?" I stopped and took a long pull from my bottle. "She's still calling my office every day, but I have no intentions of responding. I don't want anything to do with her."

"But you've told Danni about her." Ben tipped back his beer but kept his eyes on me.

I slumped into the chair across from him. "I tried. It—it just wasn't the right time. I need to wait."

"She wants honesty, and you're keeping secrets. Doesn't sound like a great plan to me; but hey, it's your life." Ben shook his head. "Let's just hope it doesn't blow up in your face."

Ben's words hung heavy between us. Waiting may not be the best decision, but I wasn't ready to share that piece of my past yet. *Especially since that fucking piece is suddenly refusing to stay in the past.*

"So why aren't you taking Kristi to the gala?" It wasn't a subtle change of subjects, but it would have to do.

Ben let out a single laugh. "Aside from the obvious fact that everyone would get the wrong idea about our relationship?"

"Not the answer I expected. But sure, sounds like a good

place to start." Considering this was probably Ben's longest relationship to date—by a long shot—and the amount of time he spent at Kristi's, I assumed he'd finally found his forever girl.

Ben shrugged. "You've met Kristi. Do you really see her fitting in with the folks who attend the gala? With our family? And I doubt she'd enjoy being there, at least after the initial thrill wore off." He got up and tossed his empty bottle in the recycling bin under the sink then stood with his back to me, staring out the window. "Besides, it might be nice to have a little break, you know? She's a lot of fun, but she's a little scattered, and . . . it gets tiring sometimes."

"So maybe she's not the right girl." I moved to stand next to Ben and nudged him with my elbow. "But that girl's out there. And as busy as you are searching, I'm sure you'll find her."

"Look who's talking, smartass." He shoved me away, laughing, then dragged a hand through his hair and sighed. "Honestly, I'm pretty sure that ship already sailed . . . and I wasn't on it." He strummed his fingers on the counter then turned to look at me. "But we're not talking about my love life, so quit trying to change the subject."

I clapped a hand on his shoulder. "And we're done talking about mine, so let's get to work."

JUMPING TO CONCLUSIONS
DANNI

"About time you got around to calling."

Jen must have been staring at her phone to have answered before the first ring, which would help explain her annoyed tone. Well, that and the fact that I'd intentionally avoided her for three hours . . . okay, more like four. *But who's counting?*

"Sorry." My voice squeaked. "I needed a shower . . . and some aspirin . . . and a nice, long nap." I curled up on the couch, hugged a pillow to my chest, took a sip of tea, and let out a weary sigh. "But I feel better now. I think."

"Well, I'm glad. I think." Jen chuckled, sounding more relaxed. "Does that mean you're finally going to tell me where you were all night?"

I gave a thoughtful hum, pausing to tease her. "I suppose. Just . . . don't go getting any crazy ideas. Okay?" I took a deep breath and forced myself to continue. "I, um . . . I kinda ran into Nico, and—"

"Oh. My. God! You spent the night with Nico?" Jen let out a long, excited squeal.

"Well, I'm glad you didn't jump to any conclusions." I went

on to tell her the whole story about literally running into him yesterday and how he'd taken care of me . . . like a perfect gentleman.

"What? Let me get this straight. You're telling me absolutely nothing happened?" Jen's voice oozed with disappointment. I could picture the pout and slumped shoulders that accompanied the whine in her voice.

For some reason, it made me laugh. "Well . . ." I let her suffer a little longer. "I wouldn't exactly say *nothing*."

"Go on." She drew out the words in a hopeful tone.

I groaned, gathering the courage to thoroughly embarrass myself. "Remember that pole-dancing class Kendra dragged us to last year?"

Saying her name made me cringe. But my overprotective little sister wasn't going to let me escape this call without getting into that whole mess sooner or later, so I'd better get used to it.

Jen hesitated, then her laughter made it clear she remembered that day. "You didn't."

"Mmm . . ." I swallowed the mouthful of tea I'd gulped, expecting a longer answer from her. "Oh, he claims I did. I don't remember much of it, but apparently I did a nice little striptease and tossed my clothes at him. He said he stopped me when I almost fell over trying to shimmy out of my panties."

I scrunched up my nose and suffered through Jen's overzealous amusement.

"Sorry. I'm—" Bursts of laughter bubbled through the phone line. "I'm good." She cleared her throat. "So, he saw? Everything?"

"I'm pretty sure." The memory of Nico propped against the bedpost this morning sprang to life. Along with all the frustration and confusion I'd felt. *Still feel.* "But he didn't touch."

"Wow. The man's a saint."

"Yeah, that's what he said too." I closed my eyes and

replayed our conversation in my mind. "But then he gave me a line of crap about being too drunk and wanting to make sure I remember sleeping with him." I shrugged, even though she couldn't see me. "It was just a polite brush-off."

"I don't know, Danni. It sounds like a valid point to me." She paused, maybe expecting me to agree, then let out a disappointed sigh. "So you just left. Ran off without even talking to him about it?"

My skin tingled, memories of this morning resurfacing. The feel of his body pressed against mine. The hungry look in his eyes. The sounds he'd made when I kissed him.

"Danni?"

I could lie, end the story there. "Well . . . not *quite.*" I bit my lip, warmth filling my cheeks while Jen rambled off a string of excited comments about holding back on the good stuff.

She blew out a long breath. "All right. Spill."

Silence followed. I could imagine her wide-eyed expression as she sat on the edge of her seat, waiting for juicy details. I'd seen it plenty of times—usually aimed at Kendra and her wild escapades.

My chest tightened. Kendra would have been proud of me for throwing myself at Nico, or at least trying to. Maybe someday I'd be able to tell her about it. I shook off the emptiness of missing my best friend and dove into the details of how I'd embarrassed myself by trying to seduce Nico, only to be rejected. Every. Single. Time.

"He insisted on driving me home . . . and kissed me at the door. But I don't expect to hear from him again." The thought had been haunting me since he'd walked out of my garage, but saying the words out loud hurt a lot more than I imagined they could.

"Wow, you need to relax and stop being so hard on yourself. I've seen the two of you together—those sparks could start a fire. Believe me, it'll happen."

Too bad I didn't share her confidence and didn't want to set myself up for more heartache. "Either way, it's time to move on with my life. And on that note, I'm going to head out for—"

"Not. So. Fast. We're not finished here. Because A: I'm not buying your *indifferent act* for one second, 'cause we both know how miserable you'll be if you just give up and move on *without* Nico. And B: I want to know what happened with you and Kendra . . . and you can stop rolling your eyes."

I bit my lip to hold back a guilty laugh and gave my eyes another roll. "Well, I'm done discussing Nico . . . for now. And you already talked to Kendra. I'm sure she told you everything —probably even more than she bothered to tell me—so let's just skip that discussion for today. Please?" I closed my eyes, the pain of yesterday's argument resurfacing.

"Danni, you have every right to be hurt. And angry. And . . . I still can't believe she kept that from you. From all of us." Jen cleared her throat. "But you two have been through a lot together, and you've always been there for each other."

"Until now." My voice cracked, but I took a deep breath and pushed on. "Truth is . . . I don't know if I'll ever be able to forgive her. And right now, I'm not even sure I want to." I groaned, rubbing my forehead. "You know I don't really mean that. I just need some time to process . . . everything."

Jen continued her speech without skipping a beat or acknowledging my response. "Yeah, Kendra screwed up. But—"

"That's an understatement," I grumbled. *More like deceived. Betrayed. Manipulated. Humiliated.*

Okay, so it seems I'm gonna need a lot *of time.*

Jen gave a thoughtful hum. "Possibly. But she loves you like a sister and would do anything for you."

An awkward tension filled Jen's voice. I imagined her

pacing the room, fists flexing, while she played the role of reluctant mediator—no doubt at Kendra's urging.

"Well, she sure has a lousy way of showing it."

"And I won't argue that point either. But *my* point is that I totally get you're hurting—hell, I would be too—but you need to give yourself time to—"

"To what? Laugh it off and say 'hey, no harm done'? Tell her it's no big deal?"

Jen groaned. "I was going to say heal, but if you're good with laughing it off—"

"Not funny." I set my cup on the table and sank deeper into the pillows lining the couch. "It's only been a day, and I was either drunk or passed out for most of that time, so I haven't been able to overanalyze the details yet. But I *trusted* her. Other than you, she was the only person I could always count on to be there for me, and . . . she wasn't."

"I know. Sorry. Just take your time and process this whole mess—what happened, how you're feeling. Nobody's going to rush you."

"Yeah, I—" The doorbell rang, a single chime, followed by a gentle knocking. "Um, I guess. Although—"

After everything that had happened—more like *hadn't* happened—with Nico, I didn't expect to hear from him, but that didn't stop my foolish heart from fluttering to life. I leaned toward the window, pausing with an outstretched arm. *Please let it be him.*

"Danni?" Jen's faint voice called from the distance. "You still there?"

I returned the phone to my ear. "Oh, um . . . yeah. Just got a little distracted. I was saying that Kendra can kind of be, you know . . . persistent."

Jen laughed. "You mean pushy."

I pulled the drapes aside and peeked through the narrow

opening. No sign of Nico, but the familiar purple delivery van from May's Flowers was parked at the bottom of my driveway.

"Someone sent me flowers." I let out a squeal and rushed to the foyer.

"Right now?" Jen echoed my excitement. "They have to be from Nico."

"I hope so. Delivery guy's on my porch. Hang on." I pulled open the door and sucked in a sharp breath. *You've got to be kidding me.*

"Hey, Jen, I gotta go." I ended the call and shoved my phone in my back pocket, cursing under my breath while ice formed in my veins.

Kendra peered around the massive bouquet of white roses she held, a tentative smile on her face. "Special delivery."

I glared at her, arms folded across my chest, while the actual delivery guy drove away.

"I'm impressed he's still sending them," Kendra said, her usual bold voice fading to a timid squeak. "And a little jealous." She paused, maybe expecting a response, then cleared her throat. "But I'm not surprised."

"What are you doing here?"

"I, um . . . I was on my way home from work and—" Kendra looked away and drew in a deep breath. Tears filled her eyes when they returned to mine. "I texted you. And tried to call."

"I know." *And I ignored you.*

Kendra inched closer, moving toward the narrow gap between the doorframe and me. "Are you gonna let me in?"

"Didn't plan to." I rolled my eyes then stepped aside, creating a small opening. "Fine. You have five minutes. Don't waste any of it with your usual smartass arrogant bullshit . . . or do." I lifted one shoulder, trying my best to appear indifferent.

Kendra pushed by, closed the door, and placed the vase on

the foyer table. She swiped the back of her hand across her eyes then stood silent, staring at the floor while smoothing an imaginary wrinkle from her top.

"Clock's tickin'." My foot tapped out a frustrated beat. We'd had some awkward moments over the years, but none had ever been this bad. I just wanted it to end, whatever the outcome.

She shifted her weight from side to side and lifted her gaze to look at me. "You know I suck at this."

"Then feel free to leave." I swept my arm toward the door.

She let out a long puff of air. "I'm sorry you had to find out about Will's affair like that, and I hate that you even had to know about it at all. But keeping it locked inside was eating at me, so I'd be lying if I said I'm sorry it's finally out in the open."

My eyes grew wide. "You're right. You do suck at this." I pressed my fingers to my temples, failing to ease the throbbing headache building there. "So that's what the whole conflict between you and Will was about all that time? You took *his* side, kept *his* secret, and used the knowledge of his affair to blackmail him?"

Kendra's back stiffened. She waved a finger in front of my face. "First of all, I *never* trusted good ol' Will—or even liked him, while we're telling the truth. As for—"

"This was a mistake. You need to leave." I grabbed the handle to pull the door open and escort her out.

"I'm sorry. Okay?" Kendra lurched toward the door, holding it closed. "Sorry your scumbag husband cheated on you. I'm even more sorry I had to witness it. And I'm especially sorry I kept it a secret to protect *your* feelings after he told me they'd broken up."

"This is a really crappy apology." I turned the knob and tugged at the door, unable to move it or my unwelcome guest.

"It is. But I've been a really crappy friend. It kinda fits."

She gave a stiff grin and bumped her shoulder against mine. "Look, I already poured out my heart and soul in all the messages I left. I'm sure you read and listened to them. Nothing's changed."

Finally. Something we agreed on. Nothing *had* changed—from the moment I'd run out of Pepper's—and maybe it never would.

I took a step back, fists clenched, as my frustration grew. "Who was she? You at least owe me that much."

Kendra held up her hands. "I swear I don't know. I was on my way out of the restaurant that night. It was dark. I only caught a glimpse of the back of her head as she leaned across the table to"—she looked away, her voice fading to a whisper—"to kiss him." She swallowed hard and her gaze drifted back to me. "I can tell you she had long, dark hair, but that's it."

"I still can't believe you knew all that time. *Lied* to me all that time." My nails dug into my palms, all the raw anger resurfacing. "You watched me make a fool of myself. Coached me on how to 'spice up my marriage' when you knew—the whole damn time—you knew the bastard was cheating on me."

"Danni, I—"

"Don't. You can't just explain away the damage you did, and it's going to take more than a day—or a few days—for me to move past that and figure out how I can forgive you."

Kendra's shoulders slumped. "Because you love me?" She pulled in a shuddered breath. "We've been like sisters our whole lives. Sometimes we screw up, but—"

I shook my head. "There's a difference between screwing up and . . . this." Tears burned in my eyes, threatening to reveal how deeply she'd hurt me. How much I missed my best friend.

I turned away, needing a moment to pull myself back together, and Nico's flowers provided the perfect distraction. After carefully removing the cellophane wrapping, I took a deep breath. Their fragrant beauty soothed me, reminding me of the amazing man who'd sent them.

"According to Kristi, you and Nico are an item now." Kendra crossed her ankles and leaned against the wall, pinning me with a curious stare. "Did you really spend the night with him?"

Should've figured Ben would tell Kristi. I let out a strangled groan. "Nico took care of me when I got trashed after running out on you. Nothing more."

Kendra bit her lip, but the corner of her mouth continued to twitch upward. She couldn't hide her grin. "I may be a selfish piece-of-shit best friend, but I'd have to be an idiot to believe there's nothing between the two of you." She leaned close to whisper in my ear, "And I'm no idiot."

I fought the urge to give her a playful shove. It would have been easy to slip back into our normal rhythm, but it just didn't feel right. Not yet. I wasn't willing to pretend she hadn't betrayed me. I definitely wasn't ready to trust her. "You should probably get going. I need some time alone to think."

Kendra threw her arms around me, squeezing tight. "Love you too." She gave my cheek a loud kiss before finally releasing me. "Call me tomorrow . . . or I'll call you. We can plan a fun night out. A double date."

I massaged my temples. "It's not that simple, Kendra. Assuming I even decide to forgive you, it'll take—"

"You will." Kendra grinned then reached for the door but paused before opening it. "For what it's worth . . ." She took a deep breath. "Sometimes we only see the things we want to see. Maybe Will *was* trying to make things right. I didn't see it, but that doesn't matter. You're the only one he needed to show."

She shook her head and turned to face me. "Don't let anger cloud your judgment. Prevent you from seeing what's right in front of you." She rested her hands on my shoulders and lowered herself to meet my gaze. "Sweetie, Nico loves you. That's plain as day. And when you're with him, you're happier than I have ever seen you. Ever. You deserve that. Probably more than anyone I know."

Kendra released me, pressed her nose to the bouquet, and took a deep breath. "Give my date night idea some thought." She blew me a kiss then stepped outside.

I closed the door and returned to my flowers, tearing open the envelope that had been tucked among the delicate blooms this time. Nico's voice played in my mind as I read the hand-written note.

Miss you already, beautiful. ~Nico

I pulled the card to my chest, hugging his words as if they were him.

MISSING NICO

DANNI

Walking into Jamison and Walters Thursday morning resurrected all of the insecure feelings I'd spent weeks trying to overcome. My stomach twisted, knots of nervous energy choking out the joy of getting my life back on track.

No doubt the gossip mill would have spread every detail—real and imagined—about my nightmare long before the first shovel of dirt had covered Will's corpse. I didn't expect that to stop people from asking questions though. Verifying facts. Invading my privacy.

I flipped on the lights and approached my desk, surprised to find it as clean and organized as the day I'd rushed out of here. In fact, everything looked the same except for a second desk that had been set up near mine outside of Mr. Jamison's office, which must be Alexia's.

When I'd talked to Mr. Jamison yesterday, he told me she had been filling in for me. He'd also mentioned keeping her in the position a while longer to help me transition back into the "daily grind." An unnecessary step, in my opinion, but I got the impression Peter enjoyed working with his daughter and didn't want it to end.

So maybe I should just be happy I still have a job. I blew out a heavy breath, trying to push that thought aside, and powered up my computer.

"You're back!" Kristi's boisterous greeting grabbed my attention as she raced toward me with open arms. "I mean, I know you said you'd be back today and all that, but you never know." She crashed into me, wrapping me in a tight embrace that lasted too long.

"Um, Kristi." I wiggled to break free. "You can let go now. I'm not going anywhere."

"Hmm? Oh, sorry." She released me and stepped back. "Guess I really missed you . . . or just needed a hug."

This would normally be the point where Kristi exploded with all the details of whatever had triggered such an intense greeting. Instead, she stood there wearing a vacant expression and fumbling with her bracelets, her usual effervescence seeming a bit flat today.

"Hey." I took her hand, halting her trademark nervous habit. "You gonna tell me what's wrong?"

Kristi's eyes drifted toward mine. She blinked a few times then lifted one shoulder. "Sorry 'bout that . . . guess I kinda zoned out a tiny bit. But I'm back now." She gave an awkward laugh and lowered her voice. "I didn't get much sleep last night. I was with Ben, and—well, you know how Ben can be."

A fake version of her usual cheery smile and no babbling about how *amazing* Ben was in bed suggested there could be trouble in paradise. Her gaze flicked between my eyes and her bracelets while I waited in silence.

"We, um . . . we kinda had a fight last night." Kristi let out a heavy sigh. "He said I ramble too much when I talk—if you can imagine that—and it was driving him crazy. Which, of course, meant *I* was driving him crazy." She closed her eyes, pausing on a deep breath. "I didn't sleep much after he left."

Kristi gave a nonchalant shrug and straightened her spine.

"Nothing for you to worry about though. I mean, you've got more than enough of your own problems, right? Especially your *charming* new work buddy." She tipped her head toward Alexia's desk and shuddered. "That alone's gotta be enough to kill the 'good' in anybody's day."

I let out a long hum. "She's not so bad. I'm more concerned about what's gonna happen when Jamison realizes he only needs one assistant. But none of that means I don't have time to listen if you need someone to talk to. We could grab lunch or—"

"Nah. I just stopped up to welcome you back—and to grab some much-needed caffeine—but I'm gonna go hide in my office then . . . you know, try to stay awake and bury myself in work or something like that. Maybe give Ben a call at lunch to see if he's still upset with me. Remind him how much he loves me." Kristi forced a smile. "I'm sure we'll be fine."

She hesitated, biting her lip. "We'll talk later though. Promise." A little spark flashed in her eyes. "Just . . . well, you better make sure to call me if anything exciting happens that you, um, you know . . . wanna share." Kristi pulled me into a quick hug then backed away, a genuine I've-got-a secret smile stretching across her face. "Toodles." She turned and strolled toward the break room.

"Hey, you can't say something like that and just walk away," I called after her.

"Wanna bet?" A tiny laugh followed Kristi's faint response, but she didn't turn around.

Great. Now I'm going to spend my whole day wondering what she knows. And getting my hopes up . . . again.

Mr. Jamison arrived, rushing through the entrance and dodging around Kristi. He bolted past the reception area then crossed the room in long strides with his phone pressed to his ear. His face looked pale as he passed my desk without even acknowledging my return. He headed straight into his office and slammed the door, something he'd never done in all the years I'd worked for him.

Well, this is shaping up to be a very strange day. I sank into my chair and began sifting through an enormous backlog of email, trying to avoid eye contact—and awkward conversations—as my busybody coworkers trickled in.

Mr. Jamison emerged from his office twenty minutes later, still visibly upset. "Alexia won't be in. She's . . . she's not feeling well." He stared at her empty desk and rubbed the back of his neck. "I'm suddenly not feeling too great myself." He gave a slight shake of his head. "I need you to cancel or reschedule everything on my calendar today. And I don't want any inter-ruptions."

My chest tightened at his unusual behavior. Even in the most stressful meetings, Peter always managed to smile. He'd ease everyone's tension with his gentle demeanor and turn things around with a lighthearted story.

And he was always there for *me*, offering sage advice, in times when I would have needed my dad. "Is everything okay? If this is about how long I was off—"

"It's nothing for you to worry about, Danni. Just some personal issues I need to deal with." He turned to walk away, pausing to glance over his shoulder. "Welcome back, by the way. It's good to have you here." His office door clicked shut again.

And that's the second time today I've pretty much been told to mind my own business.

THANKS TO KRISTI's cryptic message, I'd spent the majority of the morning struggling to focus on work while keeping a close watch on the reception doors from the corner of my eye. By eleven o'clock, I'd needed a break—and a reality check—and had decided to head out for an early lunch. A long walk. Some fresh air. Anything to clear my head.

As a result, I'd spent the past forty minutes wandering the streets of downtown Brookdale. Forty minutes being realistic and listing all the reasons Nico would never be interested in a relationship with me. Forty freakin' minutes trying to make sense of my uncontrollable attraction to him.

And after all that time, the only thing I was *sure* of was that I was still really, *really* confused. Because, according to my apparent lack of better judgment no doubt influenced by all those sappy chick flicks I'd binge-watched lately, true love always triumphed over common sense.

But my decision to "move on" with my life meant letting go of unrealistic dreams—especially those about Nico—no matter how painful. And the foolish notion that Tuesday's kiss hadn't been our last definitely fell into that category . . . giant bouquet of roses or not.

I'd reread Nico's note that had come with them a thousand times last night, replayed that perfect kiss on a constant loop, and fallen asleep counting the number of times he'd turned me down in less than twenty-four hours.

But my heart still ached for him—it had since the night we'd first met—and it refused to be sensible enough to acknowledge that Nico could easily crush its fragile remains.

I let out a frustrated groan and turned at the next corner, making my way back to work. My gaze settled on the pink-and-black-striped awning that marked the little deli I'd taken Nico to so many weeks ago—the day I'd decided to give him up in order to save my marriage.

What a huge mistake *that* had been.

My feet stopped moving in front of the large window, the table we'd occupied in plain view. The seats were empty today, but I could still see myself sitting there across from him. Remember how incredibly sexy he'd looked in his business suit and messy hair. His adorable grin. That single dimple. The attentive way he'd looked at me, as if I were the only person in the room.

"He's been waiting right under your nose." Kendra's voice cut through my thoughts. *"Can't get you off his mind."*

I stiffened, glanced around, then drew in a deep breath and continued walking. I had no way of knowing Nico's thoughts, but clearly *he* was all *I* could think about. How natural it always felt talking to him. Being with him. And how every day without him felt incomplete—as though a part of me was missing.

I passed the coffee shop we'd ducked into that day—the one I'd run out of alone. My pace quickened. The buzzing in my head intensified.

"Nico loves you . . . plain as day . . . happier than I've ever seen you." Kendra's words grew louder with each step, replaying in my mind on an infinite loop.

I wasn't ready to forgive her yet, but ignoring the comments she'd made had become impossible. Sure, she'd been right about how happy being around Nico made me. Too bad he didn't seem to feel the same way.

To win the heart of someone like Nico, I'd need a really good plan. And I sucked at making plans. That was always Kendra's—

My feet stopped moving again. Reality hit me like a virtual smack upside my head. "Even when I didn't know one existed."

If Kendra hadn't tricked me into going to the gym that day —set me up to run into Nico—I might not have ever seen him again. Gotten to know him. Fallen in lo— "Whoa, where'd that come from?"

Infatuation? Maybe, but definitely not love.

Anyway, without Kendra's meddling, I'd have gone through the rest of my life with only the memory of our one brief encounter.

"Stop stalling, sweetie. You know what you want. For once in your life, go after it!" Kendra's voice blasted in my mind as though she were standing right next to me.

I rushed along the sidewalk, heart pounding in my ears. "Go after him? She must be crazy."

I mean, that might be a great idea . . . *if* I had a clue how to do it. I'd been with Will for fifteen years. Asking guys out wasn't in my skillset.

I paused outside of Brookdale Tower, laughing at my wide-eyed and slightly panicked reflection in the plate-glass window. Okay. Maybe I was being just a tad overdramatic. After all, how hard could it really be to call Nico and say . . . um, I'd say . . . well, clearly I'd have to work on that part—later—but no big deal. Right?

DREAMS CAN COME TRUE
NICO

Danni charged toward me like a woman on a mission, chewing on her lip and lost in her thoughts with the most adorable bewildered expression on her face. I'd missed her like crazy, even though it had only been two days since I'd seen her. Held her. Kissed her.

And I couldn't wait to do it again.

"Good morning, beautiful." I stepped in front of her and touched her arm.

"Nico," she gasped, pulling a hand to her chest, then mumbled something about being wrong. "I, um . . . I-I didn't expect to see you."

"I could leave if you'd like." I teased, hoping she wouldn't take me up on that foolish offer.

Her eyes grew wide. "No. I was just surprised, but this is—well, this is a *nice* surprise." A timid smile followed, which was a definite improvement from her initial reaction.

"Glad you think so." I leaned close to lower my voice and drew in a deep breath of the same floral sent that lingered on my sheets, surrounding me at night while I dreamed of Danni. "And I'm glad to see you survived your hangover."

Her cheeks turned a deep shade of pink. "That was not one of my proudest moments."

Maybe not, but it was one I wouldn't forget anytime soon. If ever. *Focus, Giardano. Now is not the time to think about Danni stripping for you.*

"I, um—" I shoved my hands in my pockets and watched the lunchtime crowd bustling about. The last time I'd been nervous about asking out a girl was my first middle school dance. Had I lost my touch? Possibly.

Or maybe it's because Danni is the first woman you've ever cared about enough to fear being rejected.

I blew out a long breath. Yeah, that was the reason. "So . . . how's it feel to be back to work?"

"Odd." She stared at me, eyes narrowed. "But you didn't really come all the way into the city to ask how my day was going. Did you?"

"Guess I'm busted, huh?" I let out a single laugh and dragged a hand through my hair to grab the back of my neck. "I wanted to see you. Ask you something." Preferably not on a crowded sidewalk. "Do you have time for a quick walk? Maybe grab some coffee?"

Danni pulled out her phone and looked at the time on its screen. "I'd love to, but I need to get back to work."

I ducked down, meeting her line of vision and trying to recapture her attention. "I promise you'll be back in five minutes. And if you're late, I'll cover for you with Jamison."

She chewed on her bottom lip again. "I, um—"

I held a finger in front of her mouth, barely grazing her soft lips. "Five minutes. Please."

Danni's eyes drifted to meet mine and she blinked a few times. "We could go to the courtyard. Just for a few minutes though." She tipped her head toward the wooden gates to the south of Brookdale Tower. "Kinda like a *mini* walk?"

"That'll work. Lead the way." I swept my arm in front of

Danni then followed her through the entrance to a stunning urban oasis.

We strolled along the brick path, silent aside from a few stilted comments about the beautiful landscaping and the equally beautiful spring day, while I searched for the perfect spot. Someplace private. I tugged at my tie, which seemed determined to choke me today, and loosened it enough to open the top button on my shirt.

"Not sure why this is so much harder than I expected." *Shit. Did I say that out loud?* I groaned and rubbed my neck.

Finding ways to spend time with Danni had, surprisingly, been easier before. Flirting *then* had been just for fun and *more* wasn't an actual option. Getting hurt hadn't been a realistic concern—at least it shouldn't have been—but my heart had still ached every time she'd pushed me away. And a small part of me worried she'd been relieved to use "commitment to her marriage" all those times as an excuse to politely turn me down.

Danni cleared her throat. She sucked in a deep breath. "So, um, I—" Her voice squeaked, and she cringed. "I-I got the flowers you sent—all of them actually—and they're beautiful. Well, the new ones anyway. The previous bouquets . . . they, um—" She snapped her mouth closed and groaned. "Well, they *were* beautiful. Until they died, obviously, and had to be tossed out."

I cast a sideward glance at her. "Obviously," I teased then bumped my arm against hers, oddly comforted by the fact she seemed as nervous as me.

She shrugged. "I never thanked you, so I just—thank you."

"You're welcome. Although I should probably admit I had a slightly selfish ulterior motive in sending them." I tilted my head to catch a glimpse of Danni, trying to gauge her reaction. "I wanted to do the right thing and give you the time you needed to—well, you've been through a lot. But I've thought about you every day."

I took Danni's hand, stopped, and pulled her toward me, surprised by the lines of confusion creasing her face. I wanted to touch her. Comfort her. Smooth away her doubts and make her understand how much I wanted her. "Some days, you were all I could think about. And I wanted to make sure you wouldn't forget about me."

Danni continued staring at me with raised brows. "You really think you're that easy to forget?"

"You know what they say. Out of sight, out of mind." I lifted one shoulder then motioned toward a garden at the far corner of the courtyard. "Let's go over there."

We crossed the lawn hand in hand and stopped beneath a cherry blossom tree that was just beginning to bloom. My eyes locked on Danni's, and so many unspoken words seemed to pass between us in a few short seconds.

My heart raced. I pulled in a slow breath then let it out. *Here goes . . . moment of truth.* "The Executives—Ben's band? They're playing at Metro Sky tomorrow night." I shuffled my feet and took another deep breath. "I'd like to take you there. With me. On a date?" I brushed the hair from her face and let my hand fall to her shoulder. "Our first date."

Long, slow seconds ticked by in total silence, her face shifting in what appeared to be wide range of emotions.

"Danni?" I hooked my fingers under her chin, tipping her face toward mine. "This is the point where you say yes or no." And right now, I felt as if my ability to take my next breath hinged on her response. I searched her eyes, wishing I could read her thoughts. "Hopefully yes."

"I'm—well, I mean . . . I'd like to, but—" Danni pinched her mouth closed, muffling a frustrated scream.

I shook my head, biting back a grin. "Now, before you panic and do something foolish like say no—I talked to Logan last night, and he said Kendra will be spending the weekend with him in New York."

He'd also told me Kendra had visited Danni to apologize and had made a not-so-well-received suggestion for a double date, which I wanted to make clear wasn't part of my plan.

"Oh." Danni hesitated again. Her eyes fell shut.

All hope that her reluctance was based on something other than an aversion to dating me faded away. A giant boulder of disappointment settled in the pit of my stomach, but I needed to hear the words. Needed to know she'd rejected me. "Danni?"

Her eyes floated open and connected with mine. A slow smile stretched across her beautiful face. "Yes!" The word finally exploded from her, and she threw her arms around my neck. "Yes, I would love to go on a date with you."

A huge sense of relief rolled through me. Fear faded, and pure joy took its place. I caught Danni's waist, holding her close as she clung to me. "And here I was worried you were gonna turn me down."

She let out a sweet sigh and snuggled deeper into my embrace.

I kissed her temple, wishing we could stand here like this all day. "I better let you get back to work. And I have a meeting to go to." I took Danni's hand, weaving our fingers together, and led the way toward the lobby. "I'll pick you up at seven, so we can go for dinner before the club."

She beamed up at me, still wearing a huge smile. "I can't wait."

"Me too." We reached the elevators, and I turned to face her. "You still have my number?"

She nodded.

"Call me anytime." I moved closer. "For anything." My gaze settled on Danni's mouth, and her lips parted. Resisting the strong urge to lean in and kiss them, I reached past her to push the call button and whispered, "Especially if it's just to tell me how much you miss me."

The doors opened. I stepped back, releasing her hand, and winked. "See you tomorrow."

I felt like jumping with my fists in the air and letting out a victorious yell but settled for texting Ben.

Me: *I have a date tomorrow!*

Ben responded within seconds.

Ben: *Does Danni know?*

Me: *Dick.*

Ben: *LOL Chill, dude. I was just screwing with you. Told you she'd say yes.*

SMOKE AND MIRRORS
DANNI

I groaned through clenched teeth and tossed my phone on the empty passenger's seat, already dreading my new plans for the evening. The warm bubbly sensation I'd enjoyed all afternoon had gone flat the instant I'd heard Alexia's despondent voice and her request to join me for dinner.

After ignoring my polite attempts to decline, Alexia had resorted to outright begging. She'd even reiterated her silly statement from our first meeting that we were sort of like sisters and claimed she didn't have anyone else to call—the ultimate guilt trip.

Her sudden, if not desperate, desire to hang out raised a proverbial red flag, but I couldn't shake the suspicion that Alexia's mood and Peter's unusual behavior today were somehow connected. Which might also explain the sticky note I'd found on my computer screen when I'd returned from my lunchtime walk. Peter's scribbled message had simply said he'd left for the day to take care of something personal.

Hoping to help, I'd overruled my suspicious gut feeling and reluctantly caved to Alexia's pleas—a decision I already regretted. At least she'd offered to bring the food—a small consolation, but I'd take what I could get these days.

I blew out a long, slow, semi-calming breath and exited the highway. *We'll just have a quick chat while we eat, then she can be on her way. And I can go back to fantasizing about my date with Nico.*

Traffic thinned as I continued the short commute to my quiet, suburban neighborhood. I hugged the bend in the road then followed the sharp turn onto our driveway. My headlights danced across the front lawn, revealing the silhouette of my guest waiting on the front step. Alexia pushed to her feet and followed my car into the garage, a white plastic bag dangling from each hand.

The nearest takeout place was a fifteen-minute drive from my house, provided you didn't have to stop for any red lights and everyone ahead of you was willing to break the speed limit. A quick glance at my phone confirmed she'd only called nine minutes ago.

I painted on a smile and climbed out of my car. "You don't mess around, do you?"

Her step faltered. She stared at me with wide eyes but didn't say a word.

I laughed, nodding at the bags while digging in my purse for my house key. "Relax. I just meant you got here really fast. Were you out driving around with bags of food in your car? You know, searching for someone to share it with?"

Alexia let out a weary sigh, and her shoulders sagged. "Something like that. I was supposed to have dinner with my dad, but I changed my mind partway there." She glanced around the space, a distant look in her eyes. "We had a bit of an argument last night, and I don't think he's settled down yet."

She shrugged then moved past me toward the door. "You know how parents can be." Alexia gasped then turned to face me, pulling a fist to her mouth. "Oh, I'm so sorry. I wasn't thinking—I mean, I forgot you don't really have parents anymore. Well, technically you have your mom, but . . ." She tilted her head and stared at me with a doe-eyed expression. "Well, it's just so sad that she didn't want to stick around."

I blinked, silently counting to ten. Maybe it wasn't too late to change my mind. I could tell her I suddenly felt ill. And since a severe headache seemed inevitable, that probably wouldn't even be considered a lie. Then again, maybe her lack of human compassion and total inability to filter what came out of her mouth had something to do with her argument with Peter. Could I really turn her away after she'd asked for my help?

"Don't worry about it." I pushed open the door and stepped inside. "That might explain your dad's odd mood today though. What did you argue about?"

"Hmmm . . . no big deal really. He doesn't approve of some choices I've made since moving here." She followed me through the kitchen and deposited the bags of food on the counter before moving to the family room. "Thanks for letting me come over. I've really been needing a friend lately."

I pulled the cartons of Chinese takeout from the bag and lined them up on the breakfast bar then grabbed some iced tea from the fridge. "Everything okay? Your dad said you weren't feeling well." Although the feast she'd brought with her contradicted that claim.

"It was just a silly argument. I'd rather not talk about it right now, if that's okay with you." Alexia fumbled with the buttons of her oversized coat as she strolled around the room, pausing to stand up the photos I'd pushed over a few days ago. She studied each one briefly before arranging them on the table.

"Daddy exaggerates. I've just been tired a lot lately. Not

quite myself." She shrugged then dropped her coat on a chair before joining me in the kitchen.

"He, um—" My mind froze, struggling to register what appeared to be a baby bump under Alexia's baggy top. "He seemed pretty worried. Maybe you should see a doctor . . . just to play it safe."

Alexia opened the cabinet above the sink, pulled out two plates, and placed them on the breakfast bar. "Danielle. Stop worrying." She rested her hand on my arm. "I promise I'm fine. Daddy overreacted." She waved a dismissive hand as she crossed the room. "I think he probably felt a little uneasy about how I'd handle stepping aside to give you back your job . . . which is crazy."

After collecting a few napkins from the pantry, Alexia dug in the utensil drawer and found the chopsticks I kept tucked alongside the organizer tray. She climbed onto a bar stool and popped open the containers of food, rambling on without missing a beat. "It was hard growing up—being so far apart. Always feeling like I'd been cast aside. But spending so much time together lately has really helped ease some of that pain. For me, anyway."

She took a bite of a dumpling and washed it down with a gulp of tea. "At least Daddy was lucky he had you to fill that void in his life all those years." A slight hint of jealousy laced her voice.

Alexia would have been around twelve when I began working for Peter fifteen years ago, which was also when I learned he and my dad had been close friends. Peter loved sharing memories about my dad and quickly became a father figure to me, offering sage advice even when I didn't ask for it.

But he also talked a lot about his little girl. "You don't really think Peter saw me as a replacement, do you? Because during 'all those years' of working together, he spent a lot of time—at the office—telling me how much he missed you, and how much he couldn't wait to see you again." I rested my arms on the bar and leaned forward, waiting while she seemed to process that possibility.

Scents of garlic and spicy Szechuan wafted from one of the open containers, making my stomach growl. After running into Nico, I'd never managed to actually eat lunch today. I scooped a huge mound of food onto my plate and dug in while every detail of his surprise visit and invitation replayed in my mind. I popped another piece of shrimp in my mouth and let out a satisfied hum, the smile I'd worn all afternoon finally returning.

"Danielle? Are you listening to me?" Alexia waved her hand in front of my face.

"I—I'm sorry. What were you saying?" I lifted one shoulder. "Guess my mind kinda wandered."

Her expression softened, compassion filling her eyes. "You've been through so much. I understand," she said in a syrupy voice that sounded more condescending than sympathetic. Her gaze drifted across the family room. "I was just saying how much I love your home." A rosy glow filled her cheeks. Her eyes flashed to mine.

"I think about it a lot. How cozy it is." She poked at a piece of broccoli, pushing it around on her plate. "I bet it holds so many wonderful memories of your husband."

Maybe in time some happy memories would surface. Maybe. For now, every place I looked reminded me of the man who'd thrown away the love I gave him. I closed my eyes, trying to hide from the pain.

Alexia's angelic voice broke the awkward silence. "How have you been, by the way? I must seem so insensitive for not asking sooner, but . . . well, I hate to pry." She rubbed her fingers at her temples, giving a faint sigh. "Poor manners. One more thing for Daddy to be disappointed about."

Alexia bowed her head, seeming to study her hands in her lap. "I heard a nasty rumor." She raised only her eyes to peer at me. "That your husband planned to divorce you. That's not true, is it?"

"Yeah, 'fraid so." I stabbed another piece of shrimp and stuffed it into my mouth, hoping to avoid further discussion on the topic.

Alexia winced. "How can that be? You two seemed so happy." She grabbed my hand. Her voice dropped to a scandalous whisper, as though someone might overhear. "You don't think—I mean, was he . . . cheating on you?"

The lights reflected on her ring as she moved her hand. I hadn't noticed it before. A beautiful ruby surrounded by diamonds. My stomach cramped. An icy chill raced down my spine.

"Danielle? What's wrong? You're turning pale."

"I'm—I'm not sure." I pulled my hand free and hugged my midsection, fighting off a wave of nausea. "It must be something in the food."

I couldn't stop staring at that ring. I'd forgotten about the empty jewelry box the police had found in Will's car—presumably my consolation prize to ease the pain of the other Valentine's "gift" he'd planned to give me that day. They'd assumed its contents had been stolen at the scene. *But what if—*

"Where did you get that?" My harsh question shot out as though I were interrogating a suspected felon.

Alexia hummed and pushed the sparkling cluster of gems from side to side, apparently unaffected by my tone.

"Your ring." I forced a smile and a cheery tone, tipping my head toward the shiny bauble. "It's really pretty."

"Oh." She extended her arm to admire the ring from a distance. "It *is* beautiful, isn't it?" She gave a wistful sigh. "This was my engagement ring. I don't think you knew I had plans of getting married."

Alexia rested her hand on her stomach, caressing the tiny bump there, then shifted her focus to me. A cold, dark expression filled her eyes.

"Was?"

"My fiancé . . . *left* me." Her voice took on the acrid tone of a woman scorned. Her eyes narrowed, honing in on the rocks on her hand. "As much as I hated him for it, I couldn't bring myself to get rid of this baby."

She blinked a few times, erasing the fire in her eyes. Her sweet smile eased back into place, and she took a deep breath. "Anyway, I was digging around in my jewelry box last night and found it. Figured just because he's gone, doesn't mean I can't wear it." She held her hand under my nose. "I mean, what girl wouldn't love a ring like this?"

Her gaze fell to my left hand and the ring Will had placed there fifteen years ago. She giggled and brushed her fingers across it. "Looks like we have something in common."

"I—did—" I tilted my head, studying her, confused about *exactly* what we had in common. Afraid to ask the question screaming in my head. *Did she know Will?* It was a crazy idea. Desperate and crazy.

"Did he, um . . . did he leave because—"

"I'm pregnant?" Alexia draped her arms across her belly, giving her unborn child a gentle hug. "No. He was excited about our baby and becoming a dad. But he—well, things changed. And he won't be coming back." She turned away, discreetly wiping the tear that slid down her cheek. "I really don't want to get into the details right now."

My chest tightened, her urgent need for a friend suddenly making sense. No doubt she assumed I'd be able to relate to her anguish over being alone, except I didn't have any experience dealing with the special kind of loser who could abandon his pregnant fiancée after claiming to be so happy.

"I know you're hurting, but you'll get through this." I took her hands and gave them a squeeze. "And you don't have to do it alone. You have your dad, who I'm sure will love having a grandchild to spoil."

Alexia's shoulders shook on a quiet sob. Her head fell forward and swayed side to side, revealing the depth of her argument with Peter.

My heart ached from watching her suffer at what should be such a happy time in her life. "He'll come around. Just give him a little time to adjust."

She bit her lip but didn't respond.

"Alexia?" I waited until her gaze drifted to mine. "You have me too. I don't know much about pregnancy or newborns, but we can figure out all this mommy stuff together. Okay?"

Alexia threw her arms around me in an intense hug, sobbing and trembling. "Thank you. I don't deserve your help or compassion, but I really appreciate it."

"Well, that's what kinda-like-sisters do, right? We take care of each other. Besides, it'll be fun."

She pulled away, dragging her palms across her wet cheeks, and nodded. "I—there's—" She let out a long sigh. Awkward silence followed with Alexia staring blankly across the room. "You, um, mind if we call it an early night? I'm suddenly exhausted." Without waiting for a response, Alexia rushed to the family room.

"Tonight sure didn't go as planned," she whispered, keeping her back to me while pulling on her coat. She collected her bag and scurried toward the foyer, barely pausing long enough to say a quick goodbye.

I closed the door as soon as she had both feet outside then took a moment to replay the last five minutes, searching for clues that might explain her abrupt departure. Nothing stood out.

Alexia was a sweet girl—at least, she could be at times—

but something about her visit had seemed off. Then again, every encounter I'd had with her had been a little strange. Despite that, she needed me. Almost as much as I felt compelled to help her. And her baby.

IT'S BEEN FIFTEEN YEARS
DANNI

My bedroom looked as though it had been ransacked—piles of clothes covered every surface, shoes and handbags laid strewn across the floor.

Jen stared at me from my tablet on the bedside table. "Danni, it's perfect. Just like the last twelve outfits you had on. But you need to settle on one soon, or you're going to be naked when Nico gets there." She gave a devious laugh. "Then again—"

"I can mute you, you know." I wiggled out of the purple dress that made me look like a giant eggplant and tossed it on the bed with the other rejects.

"You could, but then who's going to tell you what dress to wear?" She took a slow sip of wine, watching me over the rim of her glass.

"Yeah well, I don't hear you doing that anyway, so what's the dif—"

"Look, you can never go wrong with a sexy LBD. Go dig that one out of the pile and put it back on. He'll be dying to tear it off you all night." She lifted her phone to the camera, pointing at the time displayed. "And I suggest you get moving."

I let out a scream then dug through the mountain on my bed, finding my little black dress on the very bottom. "Oh. My. God. I am never going to be ready." My voice grew more shrill with each sentence. "I don't even know what I'm doing. Do you know how long it's been since I've been on a date? Do you?"

"Danni, relax. We've been over this—at least twenty times in the past twenty hours—and you're going to be fine." Her patronizing tone sounded like a worn-out recording.

"That's easy for you to say. I don't know what to say or how to act. Hell, I don't even remember how to flirt with a guy." And I'm about to freakin' hyperventilate any second.

"You'll be fine. Nico's crazy about you. Just. Be. Yourself." She stretched to the side then came back into view again. "Oh. And, Danni, most importantly . . . have fun. Okay? Love you, sis." She sent a giant air kiss toward the camera then disappeared.

I stared at the blank screen for a few seconds taking deep, steady breaths. *All right, Danni. This is what you've wanted. What you've been dreaming about. Now get your act together and don't blow what could be your one and only shot at true love.*

By some miracle, I managed to squeeze back into my dress, find the perfect shoes to go with it, and touch up my hair and makeup in fifteen minutes.

Nico arrived at exactly seven. I rushed downstairs, ready to go, and peeked through the window by the door before letting him in. He looked incredibly handsome in his striped button-down shirt, dragging a hand through his ever-messy jet-black hair while he paced on my small porch. His other hand held two roses, clutched to his chest—one white and one pink, just like the ones in the enormous bouquet I'd received only minutes after accepting his invitation yesterday.

Okay, you can do this. I opened the door and greeted him with a genuine smile as it finally sank in—I was going on a *real* date with Nico Giardano.

"Hello, beautiful." His heated gaze skimmed the length of my body, making me melt. "You look absolutely amazing."

He held out the flowers, then slipped his other hand behind my neck and leaned in for a tender kiss. Every cell of my body came alive, quivering with a contradictory blend of fear and anticipation.

Nico pulled away, a warm glow in his eyes as they searched mine. "I've been dreaming of this moment since the night I met you." His thumb traced the line of my jaw before he lowered his hand to take mine.

In the fifteen years I'd spent with Will, he'd never greeted me like this. Never made me feel this desired. I pulled the roses to my nose, breathing in their familiar, sweet fragrance.

"Truth is, so have I. But . . ." I glanced up through my lashes. "I guess you already figured that out."

Nico tilted his head, a crease forming between his eyes.

"I just meant that you must have been pretty confident I'd say yes, considering how quickly the bouquet arrived at my office yesterday." Then again, I couldn't imagine any *single* woman had ever said no to him—pushing him away when I was married had been hard enough.

Nico's head bobbed, and he gave a thoughtful hum. "I'd say more like cautiously hopeful." A shy smile crept into place, and he lifted one shoulder. "I asked my florist to meet me in the lobby just before noon so I could give him the card to deliver with the flowers *after* I talked to you. That way I could make sure my note matched your answer . . . just in case you turned me down."

His response revealed an endearing, vulnerable side I'd never seen from him before.

I bit the inside of my lip, remembering my conversation

with the older gentleman yesterday. "He, um . . . said you told him the roses reminded you of me."

"He did, huh? Seems Carlo's been giving away my secrets." Nico laughed, scratching at the stubble along his jaw. "But he's right. They do." Leaning against the doorframe, he plucked the pink rose from my hand and traced the neckline of my dress with the silky petals, a mischievous sparkle in his eyes. "You wanna know why?"

I wrapped my hand over his thick bicep and nodded.

Nico grinned at me with his adorable lopsided smile. "Because if I were to take a guess, I'd say this pretty shade of pink is your favorite color."

"Hmm . . ." I let my head fall to the side, getting lost in the arousing sensations of his gentle touch. "And just what makes you so sure?"

Nico slipped his arm around my waist. He moved closer, erasing the distance between us, and pressed his lips to my ear. "Because every time I close my eyes, I see your pretty pink cami, the lacy pink bra you wore under it, and that matching sexy-pink-lace thong I foolishly made you keep on."

Nico's warm breath danced across my skin, the deep sultry tone of his voice stirring feelings I'd forgotten even existed.

His lips skimmed the side of my neck, leaving a trail of kisses that made me shiver. He let out a low hum. "Not to mention those hot-as-hell little pink hearts hiding under your panties."

I sucked in a small gasp. A rush of heat flooded my core.

A low chuckle rumbled in Nico's chest. He released me and stepped back. His eyes locked on mine, reaching into my soul with an intense gaze that mirrored my emotions. But there was something else, a hint of uncertainty—that same vulnerability I'd sensed a few minutes ago.

Maybe he worried too that I wouldn't be enough for him.

That it would only be a matter of time before he realized he'd made a huge mistake in asking me out.

Nico closed his eyes, breaking our connection. "We should get going." He stepped back and ran a hand through his hair then led me to his car in silence.

OLD FRIENDS
DANNI

Santarelli's had been named one of the top restaurants in the northeast last year—earning five-plus stars. And I'd heard their menu had price tags to reflect that over-the-top rating, not that Nico seemed to care. He'd spent most of the ride here raving about his many favorite dishes, changing his mind about what he planned to order with each detailed review.

The moment we stepped inside, the hostess shrieked his name and rushed toward us. "I can't believe you're actually here." She greeted Nico with an enthusiastic hug, proving he was more than just a loyal customer, and held on well beyond what anyone would consider acceptable for a casual greeting. "I thought for sure someone was pranking me when I saw your name on the list for tonight."

Nico rested his chin on the top of her head. "You kidding? I wouldn't dare prank you." He wiggled enough to create a small gap between them, raised his hands in surrender, then flashed a grin. "And not just because you'd probably hunt me down to kick my ass."

"Damn right I would." The hostess laughed and dropped

her hands to Nico's arms, continuing to cling to *my* date. "Wow," she said, ogling every square inch of him. "Look at you. Sexy. As. Ever."

I resisted the urge to groan but couldn't refrain from rolling my eyes. Luckily, no one seemed to notice. Guess I'd have to get used to nauseating scenes like this if I planned on being a part of Nico's life. I stood there, invisible, and let my mind wander, taking in the beautiful restaurant's rustic charm while trying to tune out the woman's high-pitched, excited chatter.

Heavenly aromas filled the room—fresh baked breads, savory herbs, and succulent seafood. Will hated seafood and had refused to even step foot in a restaurant that served it unless I'd begged. Even then, he'd rarely concede.

My stomach growled. My mouth watered, eager for a taste, and my attention drifted back to the annoying scene still playing out right in front of me.

The giggling hostess gave Nico a playful jab to his ribs. "So what do I have to do to meet this lucky lady?" She turned to me with an affectionate smile. "Nico doesn't usually bring his dates out here, so you must be pretty special."

Nico wrapped his arm around my waist and pulled me tight against his side. "She is." He motioned toward the other woman. "My good friend Carla Santarelli." He swept his arm back to me, taking hold of my hand. "And this beautiful lady is Danielle DeLaney."

Carla's eyes flashed between the two of us. One corner of her mouth pulled up in a knowing grin. "Well, okay then. It's so nice to finally meet you."

She pulled Nico to her for another hug, stretching up to whisper in his ear. He nodded at whatever she said, and a huge smile lit up his face.

"Wait . . . Santarelli? As in—" I made a sweeping motion with my arm. "Do you own this restaurant?"

Carla beamed with pride. "I do. And Lakeview Cottage, which is about two miles down the road."

Nico brushed my arm. "That's the cute little bed-and-breakfast you pointed out on our drive here. They just opened it last . . . fall, was it?"

"October first. We kicked off with a fall festival that was so popular we're thinking about making it an annual event."

Nico pushed a hand through his hair, a crease forming between his brows. "I should've been there. I'm really sor—"

"Don't. You've already apologized more times than necessary." Carla's gaze flicked toward me then returned to Nico. She shifted from side to side. "You were . . ." She shrugged and lowered her voice. "We understood."

Her cryptic response apparently made perfect sense to Nico. His head bobbed. He sucked in a deep breath and stared past Carla, a stoic expression shielding his emotions.

"Anyway." She touched his arm, drawing him back from . . . wherever his mind had drifted. "You and Danni should come by some weekend." She nudged Nico with her elbow and threw in a wink then leaned toward me with a hand cupped to her mouth. "It's very romantic."

My cheeks warmed. "Oh, we're not—"

"It sounds wonderful." Nico squeezed my hand and placed a gentle kiss to my temple.

Carla's eyes sparkled, her gaze bouncing between Nico and me. "Oh, Danni, the stories I could tell you about this guy." She gave a devious laugh.

This time it was Nico's turn to groan. He bowed his head, squeezing the bridge of his nose. "But you won't. Right?"

"Fine," Carla sighed. "Not tonight." She rested her hand on my arm and leaned closer, lowering her voice. "Call me sometime. We can get together."

"I, um . . . sure." I cast a sideways glance at Nico,

completely "sure" hanging out with one of his exes would *not* be a good idea.

Carla touched her earpiece. "Sounds like your table's ready." She motioned for us to follow then continued to chat over her shoulder while leading us through the spacious dining area to a secluded room overlooking the lake.

Candles burned in each of the large windows lining the wall, and soft, romantic music filled the air. Crisp white linens covered the room's lone table, topped with a vase of Nico's signature roses and a dusting of scattered loose petals. A tall pedestal stood beside the table, holding an opened bottle of wine chilling in a bucket of ice.

"Okay, you two, enjoy your meal. Rachel will be right with you."

I eased away from the table and moved toward the large windows, pretending not to notice Nico holding the chair for me to sit down, and stared out into the sunset while trying to make sense of his decision to bring me *here* for our first date. Hoping it wasn't just an attempt to make Carla jealous . . . although she seemed truly happy to see us together, so probably not.

I'd heard of Nico's reputation as a player, but nothing could have prepared me for seeing it firsthand, up close and way too personal. The weight of his reality closed in on me, threatening to crush my sliver of hope that things could really work out for me. For us.

Nico came up behind me and wrapped his arms across my stomach. He nuzzled my neck, the rough texture of his stubbled beard making me shiver. "Sorry." He dropped a single kiss on the spot, a gentle touch that added another layer to the conflicted emotions swirling inside me.

We stood there, silent for several beats, my doubts about Nico's intentions slowly melting away. I settled into his embrace and let out a contented sigh. This was what I'd been missing—

what I'd craved since the first time he'd held me in his strong arms. Easy. Comfortable. Oh, so right.

Making a conscious decision to enjoy the evening with this amazing man of my dreams, wherever it may lead, I finally relaxed enough to appreciate the picturesque view in front of me. Shades of pink and purple tinted clusters of puffy clouds while the fading rays of light reflected off the calm water, giving it a warm, romantic glow. But all I could focus on was the sensation springing to life low in my belly, compliments of Nico's hard body pressed against mine and the soft caress of his hands along my hips.

"It's beautiful, isn't it? Our first sunset together." His warm breath danced across my skin. He turned me in his arms and lifted my chin until our eyes met. "But not nearly as beautiful as you."

Nico slid his fingers through my hair and held me with a gentle but possessive grasp. His gaze locked on mine, reaching deep into my soul. "God, Danni, the things you do to me."

Eyes wide open, he brushed his lips across mine—a tender touch that ignited every cell of my body. His faint confession echoed in my mind. I had a confession of my own, but it was too soon to tell him. *I think I might be falling in love.*

"Hi, guys. Sorry to interrupt," the bubbly waitress announced as she tiptoed past us and placed a metal basket on our table. "I'm just gonna leave these here for whenever you're ready then let you get back to—" She cleared her throat, failing to mask an obvious giggle.

At least she didn't dump the bucket of ice on us, although her greeting had the same effect. Mood, officially killed.

Nico pulled away but didn't release me. "Thanks, Rachel." His flat response held a teasing undertone.

She turned to face us, inching backward, a mischievous grin stretched across her freckled face. "No problem. Just give a wave when you're ready to order." She hooked a thumb over her shoulder. "In the meantime, I'm gonna go find Carla and pay the five bucks I owe her."

"Why did I think coming here tonight would be a good idea?" Nico mumbled, rubbing the back of his neck.

Rachel laughed then scanned every inch of him with a leisurely sweep of her eyes. She shook her head and gave a low, amused hum. "Yep. Shoulda known better than to bet against her."

When Rachel strolled away, Nico pressed his forehead to mine. His shoulders shook with a quiet laugh. "Now, where were we?"

Well, not sure about you, but I was about to get swept off my feet less than an hour into our first date—right in between visits with two of your exes . . . or currents, or whatever they are to you. So wherever we were, we clearly got there way too fast and without an ounce of common sense.

Not that I would actually ever say any of that out loud to him. Instead, I bit my lip and took a cautious step back. "I, um, believe you were about to decide which of your favorite entrees to order for dinner."

"Right." Nico nodded, masking what may have been a hint of disappointment.

He held my chair again then moved to the other side of the table and placed his phone, screen down, on the far edge before taking his seat. "Sorry, it just gets uncomfortable when I sit for a while with it in my pocket. Promise I won't touch it."

Without a word, I opened my menu, pretending to read the list of house specialties, while my imagination taunted me with images of Nico and Carla together. Questions about their relationship echoed in my mind. Questions I really didn't want answered, but they wouldn't go away.

And then there was Rachel. Not to mention all the other women who'd flirted with Nico in the past, back when my focus was on resisting him rather than staking my claim. But now—

"You have that look in your eyes again." Nico's voice drifted toward me.

My jaw clenched. "And what look would that be?"

"The one that tells me something is upsetting you." Nico's tone remained calm. He tugged at my menu and put it aside then took my hands in his. "Look at me, Danni. Talk to me."

I couldn't hold his gaze and shifted my eyes toward the table and our joined hands. "I'm not upset, I'm just—" I let out a sigh. My marriage had been riddled with lies and hidden truths, and I wouldn't allow another relationship like that. "Well, if I'm being honest, it was just a little . . . awkward. Earlier. Standing there while you two reminisced about—never mind. It's not—"

"You mean Carla?" Nico laughed. He leaned forward and lowered his voice to a concerned whisper laced with a playful tone. "It's a good thing you didn't say that while she was here. She might've thrown us out."

"So you two never—you were never a couple?" This date was beginning to remind me of a secondhand book with the first chapters torn out. "Then what 'stories' does she have to tell?"

Nico lifted one shoulder. "We grew up together. Jake too."

"Jake?"

"Carla's husband. We were talking about him earlier." Nico shook his head, but the humor on his face didn't fade. "Weren't you paying attention?"

"Apparently not," I mumbled, wishing I could rewind the past ten minutes. That must have been the conversation I'd tuned out.

"Anyway, back when we were kids, Carla was the ultimate tomboy. The three of us got into all kinds of trouble together. *Those* are the stories she's way too eager to share."

I gave a thoughtful hum, my concerns only easing a bit. "So what about Rachel?"

My gaze flashed toward the window, my mind reliving the gentle brush of Nico's lips against mine. Imagining the kiss he'd been about to give me when she'd interrupted.

Nico squeezed my hands, drawing my attention back to him. "Rachel is Jake's kid sister. And nope, never dated her either." He tucked a stray curl behind my ear, letting his hand linger on my neck. "But even if I had, it wouldn't matter to me. I'm here with you, and that's exactly where I want to be."

Nico's phone vibrated, indicating a call.

I motioned toward the welcomed interruption. "Wingman checkin' in to see if you need an excuse to bail?"

"Not a chance." He cocked his head and arched a brow, focusing his full attention on me. "And you better not be expecting one of those calls either."

I tapped my chin with a thoughtful hum, giving him a turn to worry . . . even though it seemed my overactive imagination was the only thing to blame for my concerns.

"Really?" Nico pulled a hand to his chest and stared at me with the most adorable wounded puppy dog eyes I'd ever seen.

"Nah, just kidding." I gave his arm a playful nudge. "Here with you is exactly where I want to be too, so you're stuck with me." Despite all of my insecurities, it was the absolute truth. I retrieved my menu and held Nico's out for him. "So, we should probably decide what we're ordering before Rachel comes back."

Nico's phone vibrated again with a single buzz. He cursed under his breath and snapped up the offensive device. Staring at the screen with narrowed eyes, he let out a low growl.

"Do you need to take that?" I tipped my head toward the phone clenched in his fist.

Nico blinked a few times. "Nope. Definitely not." He powered off his phone and returned it to the table with a thud. "Tonight is about us and finally having you all to myself."

SWEET DESSERT
NICO

I scooped up the last bite of Carla's decadent Wild Berry Chocolate Torte—my absolute favorite dessert—and extended my arm. Danni opened wide, wrapped her luscious lips around the fork, and hummed with satisfaction . . . same as she had with every other bite I'd fed her.

The sight of her like that, combined with that sexy little sound, stirred up fantasies I needed to keep under control. *Probably shouldn't even let myself think about them. At all.*

"Oh, wow. Dinner was amazing, but I swear *that* was the most delicious thing I've ever eaten." Danni purred and leaned back in her seat, eyes closed and a dreamy expression on her face—a peaceful look of pure satisfaction.

"Told you you'd love it." I leaned across the table and brushed an invisible crumb from her cheek. "Aren't you glad I convinced you to share?" She'd insisted she was "way too full to even *think* about ordering dessert," but I couldn't let her miss out on this. And I didn't want to either.

Danni's shoulders shook with a silent laugh. She peeked out from under one heavy lid. "Share? Did you even manage to have a bite?"

"I had a few." But I preferred to watch her enjoy it. Loved making her happy any way I could.

Spending time alone with Danni—on an official date—was even more enjoyable than I'd imagined it would . . . once we cleared up those initial jealousy concerns and she relaxed. We fell into a comfortable rhythm, our conversation flowing smoothly through dinner and covering all the typical first-date get-to-know-you topics with ease. Of course, I wasn't surprised to hear her favorite color was pink . . . and I had to admit I'd learned to appreciate the beauty of it myself recently, thanks to her little drunken striptease.

With dessert finished, I was running out of reasons to linger at the restaurant. But I wasn't ready to let go of this perfect moment and move on to Metro Sky, especially with Ben's text message burned in my memory. *Fucking Summer.* I poured the last of our wine, stood, and held out my hand. "Let's take a walk."

Danni hesitated then placed her hand in mine. "Don't we need to wait for Rachel to bring our check before we run out of here?"

"Carla knows I'd never skip out on her." I lifted Danni from her seat and pulled her to me. "Besides, I'm sure she'll know where to find us if she really wants to."

Ignoring Danni's curious stare, I scooped up our wine glasses, led her to the far end of our private dining room, and pressed the small wooden panel on the wall. A hidden door opened to a small vestibule.

"How did you even know about this?" Danni's face lit up. She leaned forward, poking her head into the dimly-lit space. "Are we allowed to go in there?" she whispered.

"Jake, Carla, and I used to hang out here when we were teenagers. And yes." I wrapped my arm around Danni's waist and pressed a kiss to her temple, pausing to draw in a deep breath of her sweet floral perfume, then guided her outside into the . . . chilly . . . evening . . . air. *Shit.*

I rubbed Danni's bare arm. "Are you going to be warm enough? We can go back inside, take a walk another time."

She shivered against me and snuggled closer. "I'm g-good."

I pulled back to look at her. "You sure about that?"

Danni nodded. "Just need a m-minute to adjust." She tugged on my arm and inched away from the building, coaxing me to join her. "So . . . you were s-saying you used to hang out here?"

"I was." I chuckled and draped my arm across her shoulders. We followed the path that wrapped around the restaurant's rear deck and would lead toward the dock. "Back then, this was a rundown old lodge or lake house of some sort—we never could quite agree exactly what it was supposed to be—but we loved the overall feel of the place. We all agreed it could be 'really cool' and imagined all the things we would do with it.

"When Jake and Carla decided to open a restaurant, this was the obvious location. It took some work, but we finally tracked down the owner, and he was more than happy to unload it."

"Well, it's beautiful now."

"Yeah, it really is." I set our wine glasses on the rail along the dock and moved behind Danni, pulling her close to keep her warm . . . and because it felt amazing to hold her like this. Moonlight reflected off the tiny ripples in the lake. The night was quiet—peaceful—with only the sounds of water lapping against the shore and an occasional frog croaking in the distance.

"So I suppose you know every inch—and every hiding spot—out here then?" Danni tilted her head to glance up at me, a tempting spark of mischief dancing in her blue eyes.

"I do." I tapped the tip of her nose. "And I'm pretty confident I can finally steal a kiss right here, without someone sneaking up and interrupting us this time, if that's what you're asking."

I hooked my fingers under her chin and lifted her face toward mine, searching her eyes for permission to do just that. Danni's chest rose on a shuddered breath, and she licked her lips—enough of an invitation for me. I brushed my lips against hers, the gentle contact shooting sparks to every cell in my body.

Danni twisted in my arms and melted against me. Her hands fisted in my shirt, pulling me closer. Holding on as though I'd be foolish enough to let her go. Not this time. I'd waited five long months for this opportunity.

I basked in the moment, letting our kiss evolve slowly. Enjoying every touch, every little sound. Letting my hands roam Danni's back and along the sides of her torso, stopping short of wandering to the places I really wanted to explore.

She responded with a sweet sigh and slid her arms around me, wrapping me in a tight embrace that warmed my soul. Made me feel alive. I swept my tongue past her soft lips and leisurely explored every inch of her mouth, savoring the delectable blend of chocolate, berry, white wine, and Danni.

Danni ducked her head, breaking our kiss, but she didn't pull away from me. She snuggled against my chest, her arms still wrapped tightly around my waist, and let out a slow breath.

"Everything okay?" I pressed my lips against the top of her head, frozen in place, and hoped I hadn't pushed too far. Made her feel uncomfortable.

"Okay?" Her hum vibrated through me. "Much better than just 'okay.' That was probably the most perfect kiss I've ever had. In my whole life, *ever*."

"For me too." I breathed out the words, relief washing over me, and I relaxed into her embrace. "I've been waiting a long time to do that." I bent my knees, lowering myself to her level and caught her lips for another taste. "And thought I'd only ever *imagine* hearing you say something like that."

Danni tilted her head, staring at me with in incredulous expression. "So, um . . ." She glanced up at the restaurant. "What time do we need to leave for Metro Sky?"

"Ben's first set starts at nine." I checked my watch. "So a few minutes ago, but we don't need to be there at any specific time. In fact, if you'd prefer, we could do something else." *Anything else.* "Go wherever you'd like."

A crease formed in her forehead as she appeared to consider my offer. She twisted her lips and shifted her attention back to me. "You promised Ben we'd be there . . . and I do love to dance. But if you'd rather not take me—"

I pressed my fingers to her lips before she could finish that thought. "It was just a suggestion. I'd love to take you dancing."

BRING YOUR A-GAME
DANNI

Thirty seconds flat. I'd swear that was all it took before the first group of ladies in skimpy little dresses sashayed toward us, their hot stares honed in on Nico, devouring him while seeming to barely register me by his side. They whispered amongst themselves then blew kisses as they made their way onto the dance floor, calling out for him to join them.

If Nico noticed them at all, he didn't let on. Then again, he seemed a bit preoccupied scouring the club as though searching for someone, which didn't make sense. He hadn't mentioned meeting anyone here, not even when he'd offered to change our plans. I tried following his line of sight, but nothing —or no one—stood out. Just the typical groups of upscale singles letting off steam and looking to hook up.

The trendy club was more glamorous than I remembered. Mirrored flecks in the pale gray floor shimmered like diamonds, reflecting the blue and purple neon lights above. White crescent-shaped chairs surrounded gray marble tables. And the upbeat alternative rock beat of Ben's band, The Executives, energized the crowd gathered on dance floor.

While Metro Sky's primal, seductive vibe lured me in, the

ominous sense of déjà vu it projected warned me to run out of here as fast as my stilettos would carry me.

Nico wrapped an arm around my waist, anchoring me to his side. "You sure you're up for this? I mean, we could still leave and find something else to do if you'd like."

He'd repeated that offer—the same one he'd made on the dock—on our way here too, but this time it didn't seem like such a bad idea. "Tempting, but I'm not going to be responsible for you breaking your promise to Ben."

Nico gave a thoughtful hum and continued staring off into the distance, scratching the stubble along his jaw.

"But I, um, *I* could go if there's someone else here you'd rather be with." My voice faded as I struggled to force out the words.

Nico's attention drifted back to me, his expression filled with confusion.

"Sorry." I lifted one shoulder. "You just seemed—the way you were looking around. I thought maybe you saw . . . someone." *Better.*

Nico shook his head. "Not even close." He rested his hands on my shoulders, tilting my head until our eyes met. "Did I forget to tell you how much I've been looking forward to our date tonight? How much I want to be with you?"

Without waiting for an answer, he touched his lips to mine in a tender kiss. "If you're leaving, I'm going with you. Understand?" He raised his brows and studied my face as though expecting some sort of response this time.

Thoughts of Will lying and cheating threatened to cloud my judgment, crimes I had no right punishing Nico for. Or myself. The sincerity in his expression as he patiently waited helped diminish my insecurities, but the sense of foreboding that had crept over me the moment we'd entered Metro Sky still lingered.

My eyes fell closed, and I gave a gentle nod. "I've looked

forward to spending time with you too." *Much longer than I should have, but I'll keep that little detail to myself.*

"Good." Nico kissed the tip of my nose then took my hand. "Now that that's settled, let's get something to drink."

Nico led the way, pausing as we reached the bar. He motioned toward the dance floor where Kristi hopped up and down, arms in the air, frantically waving at us from her usual spot by the stage. "Do you want to join Kristi and her friends in the VIP section, or can I be selfish and keep you to myself?"

We waved back with a more normal level of enthusiasm, laughing at her typical high-energy antics.

"Actually, Kristi gave me strict orders to stay away, saying she would be 'perfectly happy if we chose to ignore her for the entire night' . . . as long as I promised to call over the weekend to 'disclose every minute detail of our date without skipping over any of the good stuff.'"

Which I had no intention of doing, of course . . . assuming there would even be any juicy details to share. She'd have to settle for the PG-rated CliffsNotes version.

"So I'm all yours." And I'd be lying if I said I didn't love the sound of that.

Nico squeezed my hand and spun me to face him, grinning his approval. "Every detail, huh?" He caged me between his arms with my back against the bar. Heat radiated from his body, mere inches from mine. "You really gonna tell her *everything?*"

I steadied myself against his chest and bit my lip. "Feeling a little nervous?" I teased, hoping he couldn't hear the tremor in my voice.

Nico's expression turned serious. "Baby, the way I feel about you makes me more nervous than I'm willing to admit." His voice was low and gruff.

He blew out a slow breath and inched closer, erasing the distance between us. The corner of his mouth twitched up, his lopsided grin returning, along with a mischievous sparkle in his eyes. "I just hate the idea of you crushing Kristi's illusion that she's dating the sexiest Giardano. Then again, letting you mess with my baby brother's rock-star ego could be fun."

Nico's impulsive confession about his feelings echoed in my mind, making it difficult for me to think about anything else.

"I, um—" *Focus, Danni.* "Guess you better do your best to sweep me off my feet then." I glanced up at him through my lashes then stretched to whisper in his ear. "You know . . . just in case."

Nico gave a low growl and wrapped his arms around me. "Challenge accepted." He pressed a kiss to the sensitive spot below my ear then lifted me onto the tall seat by the bar—the same one he'd occupied last time I was here.

"Your usual?" His smooth, deep voice rose above Ben's band, concealing any evidence our conversation had affected him, but the passion in his eyes, locked on mine, told a very different story.

Oh my, what did I just get myself into? I nodded, unable to speak, and smoothed the hem of my skirt across my half-exposed thighs while a giant knot twisted in the pit of my stomach. A wave of nausea followed, adding a new element to the emotional turmoil I'd been struggling to keep in check since lunchtime yesterday. Probably longer.

With Nico's reputation and the way women always threw themselves at him, he'd have clear expectations about how tonight would end . . . especially after the way I'd behaved in his bed a few days ago. That was obvious enough by his actions at my front door and that amazing kiss on the dock. Not to mention the ride here with his warm hand resting above my knee, his fingers casually caressing my leg as he spoke.

Until he'd arrived at my house tonight, I'd had the same expectations. Every detail of Nico's seductive greeting replayed in my mind. The way he'd kissed me. Touched me. The sultry tone of his voice. Just thinking about it made my heart race. And that was before my rusty flirting skills had unintentionally challenged him to level up. Bring his A-game. I struggled to pull in a slow, calming breath, but my lungs wouldn't expand.

I'd had plenty of vivid fantasies about making love to Nico. *This* time would be *real*. What if I couldn't measure up to his expectations? I'd overlooked that one major detail, but maybe *he* hadn't, which would explain those occasional flashes of uncertainty he'd failed to hide earlier.

"Hey." Nico's lips brushed my ear. He moved to stand behind me, wrapping his arms across my stomach and pulling me close. "You all right?"

I turned my head, shivering at the feel of his rough cheek against mine. "Of course. Why wouldn't I be?"

He raised one brow then glanced toward my lap and the mangled cocktail napkin in my hands.

When did I even grab that from the bar? I lifted one shoulder. "Guess I'm a little nervous too." *Understandable, and a huge understatement.*

Nico hugged me tighter. "Relax. I want tonight to be fun. About us." He kissed my cheek, letting his lips linger. "I promise I won't hurt you."

A chill ran down my spine. Those were the same words he'd used last time we were here. Right before everything went to hell.

"Nico?" The bartender shrieked and pressed a hand to her chest as she approached, her bright blue eyes sparkling with amusement. "Wow, it really *is* you."

Nico's shoulders shook. "Jazmine, good to see you." He released me and leaned across the bar top, greeting the woman with a casual hug.

She pulled back and squeezed Nico's cheeks, giving a friendly laugh. "Where the hell have you been hiding? And do you have *any* idea how many of your little groupies have been annoying the crap out of me—all begging me to give them your number?" She rolled her eyes and dropped her arms to the bar, lush red curls cascading over her shoulders as she leaned closer. "It's like they think I'm your social secretary or something."

Nico's lips pressed together, forming a tight grin. He rubbed the back of his neck then motioned to me. "This, um . . ." He cleared his throat and spoke louder, still barely audible over the sudden cheer erupting from the dance floor. "This is Danni."

Jazmine's face lit up with a beautiful smile. Her wide eyes locked on Nico's—a thousand unspoken words passing between them in a matter of seconds.

She let out a squeal and reached for me with open arms. "Oh my God, Danni, it's so great to finally meet you."

Finally? I hesitated then stretched forward, as Nico had, intending to give her a loose hug—just enough to be polite—but she latched onto me with a tight squeeze and lifted me from my seat.

Nico laughed and caught my waist, saving me from being dragged across the bar by this crazy woman. He draped one arm across my shoulders and held my hand with the other, lacing our fingers together.

Jazmine watched us, hands on her hips, wearing a satisfied grin. "Well it's about flippin' time."

Nico's face glowed under the neon lights. He winked at me, then looked at Jazmine. "So, what do we need to do to get a drink around here?"

"And I thought you came just to see me." She gave an exaggerated sigh and sank to her forearms again, still grinning at us. "Fine. What can I get ya?"

Nico placed our orders then returned his full attention to me.

"Another friend of yours?" I arched one brow. "Or do you

just spend a ridiculous amount of time here?" I looked away, avoiding his eyes, afraid of what they might reveal.

"Well, I probably *have* spent more time here than I should, but—" Nico brushed the side of my face. "Hey, look at me."

I tilted my head to peek at him—biting his lip and clearly struggling to hold back a smirk.

"You're so adorable. Jaz is a good friend—nothing more. I've known her for a long time." He caught the stray curl that fell across my face, twisting his finger in it before tucking it behind my ear. "You don't need to be jealous. Of her or anyone else."

"I'm not." My cheeks grew warm. "Well, maybe a little . . . at first." Which was odd, because I'd only ever felt this way around Nico.

"Dance with me." His hands slid to my waist. Without waiting for an answer, he lifted me from my seat then guided me the few steps to the dance floor. "I've gone long enough without you in my arms."

Nico pulled me against him and claimed me as his own with a tender kiss. Heat radiated through me as his palms glided along my back, down over my hips, then up to my shoulders before beginning again on the same path. The rhythm of his sensual touch hypnotized me, pulled me deeper under his spell, into a beautiful dream where I imagined spending every night in his arms. I settled my cheek against his chest, listening to the steady beat of his heart.

His hips pressed against mine, swaying to the music. Each movement, a seductive promise of things to come, made me burn with desire. "This is amazing. Holding you like this. Knowing I can."

I hummed my agreement and snuggled closer, reveling in this moment that felt almost too perfect. That tiny seed of doubt—the possibility that this was just another fantasy—grew with each passing second of bliss.

The song ended, but Nico didn't release me. People around us bounced to the upbeat tempo of the new song, casting amused glances our way and chatting with their friends.

"Nico?" I tried to pull away, but he tightened his hold on me. "Nico, people are staring."

He nuzzled my neck. "They're just staring because you're so beautiful."

"No, I'm pretty sure it has more to do with the fact that we're pretending the slow song didn't end." I laughed and tried to wriggle free again.

"Fine," Nico grumbled. He let out a long sigh then raised his hands to frame my face. "But I'm going to have a talk with Ben about playing longer songs." He pressed a quick kiss to my lips then slid his hands to mine, lacing our fingers together. "We should probably go see if our drinks are ready."

Nico helped me back up onto the bar stool, never releasing his hold on me, and rested our joined hands on my lap. His fingers brushed along my thigh as he caressed my palm, the intimate touch sending waves of heat straight to my core.

He had to realize the effect he had on me. Know what he was doing.

Maybe all of this attention was just a part of his standard playbook. His regular game plan to get the girl into his bed—a plan that, according to rumors, he'd had a lot of practice perfecting.

Did that tiny-waisted blonde from Nico's welcoming committee, the one now glaring at us from the dance floor, recognize his moves? Had *she* been with him before?

She swayed her hips and gave a skillful flip of her long hair, reminding me of the woman I'd seen climbing across him—at this very spot—the night I'd been dragged here on that disastrous girls' night. Images of Nico touching her, wrapping his arms around her, and exploring her body flashed in my mind.

An irrational wave of jealousy tore through me. I squeezed

my eyes shut, trying to get my emotions under control. Get a grip on reality. Give myself permission to enjoy this moment. This night. I deserved to be happy. To feel loved. To get lost in the arousing sensation of Nico's touch. Enjoy the tingling in places that had lain dormant for far too long . . . even if it turned out to be for only one night.

And let's be honest, if Nico keeps this up all night, there's no way I'll be able to turn him down. Or want to.

When I opened my eyes, Nico was watching me with a sultry expression. He leaned forward, pausing before brushing his lips across mine. "Care to share the wicked thoughts running through your mind right now?"

I sucked in a sharp breath and pressed my thighs together. "I'm not sure it's safe to tell you." I bit back a grin, hesitating, then gave a seductive sigh. "I think I'll just let you use your imagination."

Nico groaned. "That's a pretty dangerous choice, but let's see where it takes me." He leaned back, stroking his jaw. His eyes locked on mine, growing darker as they bore into my soul.

When his hand slid from my palm to my thigh, my breath hitched with an audible gasp. I caught my bottom lip between my teeth and struggled to maintain control of my body's reaction, but each brush of his fingers beneath the hem of my dress made my pulse race faster.

Nico's grip on my leg tightened, and he leaned toward my ear. "Wanna know what my imagination's telling me?" He let out a low hum. "If it's right, you have a very, *very* sexy mind, and I am one lucky man."

I bit down harder on my lip and gave a light nod. The idea of Nico talking dirty to me was enough to make my insides swirl.

"Aw, you two are just so darn cute together." Jazmine laughed and placed our drinks on the bar, repeating our order as she did. She stepped back, hands on her hips, and grinned.

"Okay. Well, I'm sure you don't want me hangin' around to chat, so just give a yell if you need me."

"Thanks, Jaz." Nico stood and pulled me into his arms. "Let's take our drinks outside. Find a nice quiet spot to finish our conversation."

ROOFTOP OASIS
NICO

The moment Danni answered her door tonight, every drop of blood had rushed from my brain to my dick. And stayed there. It hadn't been easy, but I'd managed to tolerate the discomfort . . . until now. Trying to imagine what sexy thoughts could be filling her mind—wondering if she had the same fantasies I did about us—had pushed my wavering self-control dangerously close to its limit.

Danni chattered on beside me, asking a steady stream of questions about where we were going, clearly oblivious to the moral battle raging inside me. We stepped out into the cool night air, which I'd hoped might act like a cold shower and put me out of my misery.

It didn't.

Then again, none of the cold showers I'd taken over the past three months had done anything to stop the countless hard-ons she'd caused either. But resorting to my soapy fist for relief wasn't an option right now, and neither was bending Danni over a wooden bench and having my way with her.

She deserved better, especially for our first time, and I'd promised to give her that. To give both of us that. And I would. Eventually . . . right after I convinced Danni to let go of her dead, cheating ex, crazy as *that* sounded.

My grip on Danni's hand tightened, and I practically dragged her the last few steps toward my favorite spot on the rooftop lounge—the hidden oasis that I always went to when I wanted to be alone.

"Nico, what are you doing?" Danni whispered, even though no one was near us. She tensed beside me while I punched the code into the panel by the door marked Private. "How did you—are we allowed to go in there?"

"Knowing the owner has its benefits." I grinned and pushed open the door.

Danni's eyes grew wide. "Oh, my. This is . . ."

"Beautiful? Peaceful?" I placed my hand on the small of her back and gently guided her forward. "Romantic?" I whispered as the door clicked closed behind us.

A tranquil waterfall cascaded down the stone facade on the building, splashing into an illuminated pond flanked by potted palm trees wrapped in tiny white lights that gave the small space a warm feel despite the chilly air.

"All of that, and so much more." Danni downed half of her drink before wandering around, exploring and dragging her fingers across every surface.

Muted music from inside the club flowed from hidden speakers. I wanted to pull Danni into my arms and spend the rest of the night dancing with her in our own private paradise . . . preferably while ignoring the large wooden park bench.

I reached into my pocket and repositioned my throbbing erection for what felt like the hundredth time tonight while Danni surveyed her surroundings in nerve-racking silence.

"You're quiet." I took her now-empty drink glass, letting my fingers brush along hers, and placed it with mine on the fire table.

Danni drifted toward the glass wall along the roof's edge and wrapped her arms across her midsection, staring out into the night sky. "Just . . . taking it all in."

Moonlight reflected off the snow-covered mountains beyond the city lights. Most nights I could stare at the tranquil view forever. Tonight, I couldn't take my eyes off the mesmerizing woman in front of me. Or stop myself from overanalyzing her reaction, especially since the last time we were on this rooftop, she'd rejected me and bolted.

Danni shivered and hugged herself tighter. "So. Is this where you bring all your . . . you know, *dates*? To um . . . for . . . I mean, are we going to—"

"Have sex?" Was that the reason her mood had shifted so drastically from fun and flirtatious to stoic and withdrawn? "Someday, I hope. But not here. Not now."

She hadn't brought it up at dinner, but I probably should have assumed she'd heard about my reputation as a player— well earned, but not something I was proud of. And not just because I understood it was only a polite way for people to call me a man-whore. *Whatever. They don't know, or care about, my reasons.*

Deep down I'd hoped Danni would be the one to finally see past all that shit and realize the man hiding there was broken, just like her.

I eased up behind Danni and traced my fingers along her arms, giving in to the overwhelming need to hold her. Comfort her. "This spot is special to me. Like you." I turned her to face me and wove my fingers through her soft hair, tilting her head until our eyes met. "I've never shared it with anyone before. Never wanted to."

Danni nodded but didn't appear convinced.

I knew trust issues all too well, and I'd do whatever it took —for as long as it took—to earn hers. I pulled her close and swayed to the music, humming along to the familiar melody of the Executives' new song. After a few beats, Danni nestled her head against my chest but seemed tense. Distracted.

"You're still quiet. Want to tell me what's bothering you?"

"Nothing. I was just enjoying the music." She angled her head and gave me half a smile. "And my dance partner."

"Hmm . . . partial truth, maybe—and I hope I'm more than just a dance partner to you—but the rest? Nope. Not buyin' it." I twirled Danni around, singing along with the lyrics Ben had agonized over for weeks.

"What are you doing?" She laughed, holding me tight and letting her head fall back.

"Dancing." I picked up with the end of the chorus, dipping Danni low while singing the final line. "Cause it was just one night, one magical night, and I was already fallin' in love. Yeah, I was fallin' in love with you, girl."

She shrieked, clinging to my biceps, and finally rewarded me with a genuine smile that warmed my soul.

"And serenading you." I winked then lifted her into my arms. "You didn't think Ben got all the talent in our family, did you?"

She gave a thoughtful hum. The corner of her mouth twitched up. "So you're saying Gabriela can sing?"

"Ouch!" I teased, slapping a hand over my heart. "I'm so wounded."

"You're so *silly*." Danni brushed her fingers over the side of my face, a gentle touch. She paused, and her mood faded again. "But why are you here? With me?"

"Because I asked you out, and you said yes."

She rolled her eyes. "Seriously."

"Yes, seriously." I took her hands and led her to sit on that bench I'd been hoping to avoid. "Danni, I've been uncontrollably attracted to you since the first moment I saw you. I thought you knew that. I mean, it's not like I've put any effort into avoiding you or hiding my feelings."

Just the opposite—I'd rearranged my whole life on the off chance I might get to see her somewhere, but I preferred to keep that desperate detail to myself.

"If something's upsetting you, it's important to me, so please tell me. Besides, I'm pretty sure you're the one who said you needed honesty in a relationship." Ignoring the irony in that statement, I raised one brow and waited while a series of emotions flashed across her face.

She gave a subtle nod and let out a shaky breath. "I'm trying, but this is unfamiliar territory for me. It's . . . it's only been two months since I lost my husband."

"You mean two months since you found out your lying, cheating husband planned to divorce you." *Shit.* "Danni, I'm sorry. I—"

"Don't. It was kind of a blunt reminder, but you don't need to apologize for the truth." Her gaze fell to the ground. "My point is, it's too soon for me to be doing . . . this." She made a general sweeping motion then pushed to her feet and returned to the railing, staring into the darkness with her back to me.

"Danni?" I eased up behind her and stroked her arms, coaxing her to turn around. "You're going to have to help me out here. What exactly are you doing that's so inappropriate?"

"Dating. Having fun." She kept her head down, staring at my chest and gliding her fingers along the buttons on my shirt. "Feeling . . . things, and . . ."

I caught her chin and tugged, forcing her to look at me. "And what?"

"Anything. Everything. Whatever else all of *that* leads to." She pulled away. "Which I still suspect is the *real* reason you brought me out here, even though you don't want to admit it."

"Danni." I clenched my teeth and scrubbed a hand over my face but couldn't stop the growl tearing through me. "If I was just looking to score with you, I would have fucked you senseless when you were half-naked in my bed and asking for it."

She made a high-pitched gasp and appeared to be frozen in place, which I should probably be grateful for after blurting that out. I reached for her, hesitating before grabbing her shoulders. Afraid she'd bolt, because she sure as hell looked as though she might—staring at me with a wide-eyed, unreadable expression. Her lips parted, but she didn't make a sound.

"Danni." I inched closer. "I'm so sorry. That slipped out before the commonsense portion of my brain had a chance to step in and veto it. I didn't mean to be so crude. But regardless of *how* I said it, it's the God's honest truth." I eased my arms around her and rested my forehead on hers. "That day, with you in my bed, was hands-down my greatest feat in self-control. Ever." *And that's a fucking huge understatement.*

A faint blush danced across her delicate cheeks, her only response to my bold confession.

"I *want* to make love to you, but we're gonna take this slow —as slow as we need—because I want *all* of you. Not just your body, and definitely not just for one night. Got it?"

She gave a slight nod and fisted her hands in the waist of my shirt. "Where have you been all my life?"

"Right here, beautiful. Waiting for you." I pulled her against me, holding her close. Her heart pounded as though she'd just run a marathon, or maybe that was mine.

Everything I'd told Danni was one hundred percent true, even if it wasn't one hundred percent of the truth. Despite her suspicions, my only intention in coming out here was to spend more time alone . . . away from the uncomfortable glares of women who thought they had some sort of claim on me.

But I had to do what was best for Danni. For our relationship. The fact that coming out here also eliminated the risk of running into Summer—even though I hadn't seen her—was just a bonus and not something worth hurting Danni over. "We should probably go back inside."

"Hmm . . . you're probably right." Danni's voice vibrated against my chest.

I slid my hands up her back and framed her face, relieved to see contentment instead of the panic that had been there a few minutes earlier. "Can I kiss you first?"

Her lips curved in an easy smile. "You didn't ask the other times. Why start now?"

"Remember we just talked about taking things slow?" I teased and threw in a wink. "Besides, I realize now that I may have been out of line the other times. I don't want you to feel pressured."

Danni looped her hands behind my neck and stretched on her toes, pressing her lips to mine for a slow, gentle kiss. As much as I wanted to take over and devour her, I let her control the pace, torturing me with sweet nips and teasing licks before finally skimming the length of my lips. She didn't need to ask twice for me to open and welcome the sweep of her tongue across mine.

Her body arched, pressing against the massive hard-on I'd been trying to hide . . . which apparently hadn't been necessary, given the way she sighed and rocked her hips. She slid one hand into my hair and the other down my back, clinging with both as though she couldn't get close enough. The hungry little sounds she made with each stroke of her tongue vibrated through me, making my cock pulse.

My ability to stop this from going any further was fading fast. I cradled Danni's face, forced myself to break our kiss, and pulled her into a tight embrace.

"Nico?" She sounded hurt. Confused.

I hated myself for putting those emotions there, but I'd hate myself even more for taking advantage of her.

"Shhh . . ." I stroked Danni's back and drew in a few slow,

deep breaths, trying to calm my libido before it kicked into overdrive. "That was . . . wow. And quite possibly the best kiss of my life."

"It was for me too." She purred then stared up at me with rosy cheeks and dark eyes. "You sure you want to go back inside?"

I brushed the side of her face, wanting nothing more than to spend the rest of the night kissing her. Trying to convince myself I'd be able to stop there . . . more like *lying* to myself that I'd be able to.

Resisting the temptation of her sexy smile took every bit of strength I had. "No. But I think it's best. I don't want to break my promise to take things slow five minutes after making it." I dropped a single kiss on her swollen lips and extended my hand before I changed my mind. "Let's go tear up that dance floor."

SHOULD'VE KNOWN BETTER
DANNI

Nico led me back toward the entrance, strolling at a leisurely pace that should have given me plenty of time to recover from the twenty-minute emotional rollercoaster ride we'd just taken.

It didn't.

Most of our date so far—okay, all of it—had been complicated by a series of misunderstandings, mixed signals, and unclear expectations. This one was, by far, the most intense. And the most frustrating.

After that raw and unexpected conversation, tonight was also the first time I didn't care what anyone would think about me. What they'd say. I wanted to let go of my inhibitions, give in to my feelings for Nico that I'd fought to hide for so many months . . . and not just because it was convenient since I was already half naked, in his bed, and assuming it would be my one and only chance.

Then again, maybe it was.

"After you." Nico held open the door, waiting for me to pass through. A cacophony of music, blenders, cheers, and shouted conversations beckoned for us to join the fun.

So why did I want to run and hide?

Could be the humiliation of being turned down again. My inability to trust anything he said, thanks to the scars from all of Will's lies. Or maybe because I finally realized this date had been a bad idea, and returning to Metro Sky was too much like tempting fate.

Nico wrapped his arm around my waist before the door closed behind us, pinning me against his side. "Dance?"

I stretched toward his ear. "Could we get a drink first? Find a table?" Because *maybe* putting a table between us again would help reset tonight to the sweet moments we'd shared toasting the sunset and feeding each other bites of wild berry chocolate torte.

"Of course." Threading the fingers of his free hand through my hair, Nico cradled the side of my face. His eyes searched mine. "Everything okay?"

"Yeah. Perfect." I wrapped my hand over his wrist and flashed what I hoped looked like a confident smile. "I just want to freshen up, and I'll join you in a few minutes."

Nico nodded then tipped his head toward the bar. "I'll get another round while I wait." Gaze still locked on mine, he brushed his thumb across my lower lip in a slow, teasing stroke. "Hurry back, beautiful."

He added a wink before walking away, leaving me alone with my swirling thoughts and conflicted emotions.

Nico had only taken a few steps when a female voice called from behind me, "O.M.G. There's Nico . . . and he's alone." She sang the last word, stretching it out to an unnatural three syllables.

I peeked around the large nickel-wrapped pillar separating us and caught a glimpse of Nico's welcoming committee gathered around a high-top table.

"Finally." The perky blonde who'd watched us from the dance floor crossed her arms over her half-exposed chest and pouted. "I just don't get what he's doing here with *her* in the first place."

"I know, right? *Totally* not his type," another chimed in.

The woman with black hair that matched her nails and lipstick picked up her drink, giving the straw a slow, disinterested swirl. "Maybe he was forced to take her out for a bet or some sort of charity deal, because we *all* know he could do *much* better." Her lips twisted in a scandalous sneer. "Isn't that right, Ash?"

I'd heard more than enough and rushed off, skirting along the dance floor—following the same path I'd taken the night I'd left Nico standing alone on the rooftop. My pace quickened with each step, the conversation I'd overheard replaying in my mind making it difficult to remember why I couldn't continue straight to the exit again tonight.

The reason was simple—Nico. I couldn't do that to him. To us. To my chance at love.

But they were right, those women. I wasn't his type. He *could* do so much better . . . and had.

I finally reached the restroom and ducked inside, pulse racing. "What am I doing?" I sighed, sagging against the wall, eyes closed. How could I have been foolish enough to think—

"You okay?"

I gasped, hand on my chest. "Sorry, I thought I was alone." Hoped I was.

The woman at the vanity watched my reflection in the mirror while she blotted at puffy, red-rimmed blue eyes.

"I've been better." I groaned and sank to the floor, crouching with my palms pressed to my face. "How 'bout you? I mean, it kinda looks like we're in here for the same reason."

"Not likely." She ran her fingers through her long, blonde hair, talking with her back to me. "I came here tonight looking for someone I used to know—an ex, actually—hoping to surprise him." Her shoulders shook with a single, bitter laugh.

"Guess the surprise is on me though, because he's here with someone else. Looked pretty into her too, which sucks for me."

She plucked a few items from her small handbag then glanced back at the mirror. "But what could you possibly be upset about? I saw you cozied up at the bar earlier with what has to be the hottest guy in this place."

I bit back the smile I didn't deserve to wear, since this would probably be my one and only date with Nico. "He is amazing, but . . . well, the list of problems is long. I don't want to bore you." Or embarrass myself any further than I already have tonight.

"Ah, so you two have been together for a while?"

"We met a few months ago. New Year's Eve actually." It wasn't a lie . . . technically. And for some reason, it seemed less pathetic than admitting I was hiding in the ladies' room—in tears—on my first date with said totally hot, amazing guy.

"Lucky girl. You know . . . I'm probably *way* out of line for asking, but what are lounges for if not a little bragging about our dates, right?" She twisted the cap on the silver tube she'd been holding and sighed. "Or living vicariously through other women's stories, for those of us unfortunate enough to be alone."

She paused then gave an awkward laugh. "Anyway, rumor around the club is that your guy is quite talented in bed. So spill . . . any truth to that?" She tipped her head but still didn't turn to look at me.

"I—" Aside from not wanting to share my lack-of-sex life with a total stranger, something about this woman felt . . . off.

"Oh, I'm sorry. Guess that *was* too personal." She placed a hand over her chest, but her confident posture and sugary tone suggested a total lack of remorse for invading my privacy.

"No." Whatever. It wasn't like I'd ever see this woman again. "Well . . . yes, actually. It was. But either way, I can't give you an answer." I lifted one shoulder. "Yet."

"Really? That's—" She gave a curious hum and leaned closer to the mirror, focusing on her reflection. Checking her flawless makeup. "Interesting."

She dabbed concealer under her eyes and painted a fresh coat of bright red on her lips, then snapped her bag closed.

"You know, I'm feeling much better . . . thanks to our little chat." She turned toward me, leaning against the edge of the vanity. "But can I give you just a tiny bit of advice? You know, girl to girl?"

The woman sashayed toward me, one corner of her mouth curving up in a catty grin. "I wouldn't leave a guy like Nico unattended for too long. No telling what kind of trouble he could get into with the walking dessert menu out there." She stopped beside me and leaned closer, lowering her voice to an eerie whisper. "And I guarantee those women are *more* than willing to give him what you're not."

Seconds later, the door swooshed open and clicked shut. I was *finally* alone. And feeling more insecure than ever.

"What the hell." I massaged my forehead, wishing I could erase that bizarre conversation from my mind. "Am I the only woman who hasn't had sex with Nico?" Because I'd swear he was the "ex" she'd hoped to hook up with tonight.

"Well, I can't speak for everyone else, but you already know I haven't had sex with him."

Kendra. I clenched my jaw and let out a low groan. *You've got to be kidding me.*

A few weeks ago, I would have been relieved to have my best friend here for support. Encouragement. To talk some sense into me and force me to get back out there instead of having a meltdown on the restroom floor.

Now? After the way she'd betrayed me? Too soon— wounds that deep took more than four days to heal.

Kendra strolled closer, a smug look on her face. No apology for showing up where she wasn't invited. No explanation of why she was here instead of visiting Logan in New York . . . as Nico had promised she would be this weekend.

She stared at me then glanced around the room before letting out a long sigh. "You know . . . I'm not sure this is where I'd be hangin' out if I were on a date with the guy who melts my panties with a single look—real or fantasized. But hey, that's just me."

She held out her hand, but I preferred to stay crouched on the floor and batted it away. "What do you think you're doing?"

"Making sure you don't make a break for the exit. Again. You can thank me later." She gave her usual smart-ass grin and blew me a kiss.

"You really think I'm going to thank you for *anything* right now?" I shook my head. "Wow, how many drinks have you had, 'cause you've completely lost your mind."

Kendra leaned toward me and lowered her voice. "Look, sweetie, you may have been able to fool Nico into believing you're comfortable about coming *here* with him tonight—well, at least until now—but I know you well enough to see through the bullshit act you've been putting on."

"Then you should also know me well enough to recognize my hints to back off, give me some space to work through the pain *you* caused. But ignored calls and texts mean nothing to you. You just do whatever you want—whatever's best for Kendra."

All the anguish from Monday's argument at the diner came bubbling to the surface. I pushed to my feet, pacing in front of her. "You betrayed me, and that's not something that vanishes overnight. You can't drop by the next day to toss out a lame 'sorry' and expect the slate to be wiped clean. That part's up to me, and I'm not ready to trust you or let you back into my life yet."

Kendra closed her eyes and didn't respond. When she opened them again, they were glassy, filled with unshed tears.

A knife twisted in my chest. Maybe she really did just want to be here for moral support. We'd been best friends for as long as I could remember, and she'd helped me through some pretty dark times. But when it counted most? That time she'd let me down—sat back and watched me humiliate myself.

"So why are you really here, Kendra? Guilt? Boredom? Looking to expand your hobby of meddling in my nonexistent love life?"

"Maybe." She narrowed her eyes, giving a sarcastic glare. "Look, I get it. You think you hate me right now, bu—"

"*Know* I—"

"Whatever." She waved a dismissive hand. "Despite what you think of me, I still love you. And I know you better than you know yourself sometimes. I *lied* to Logan so he would bring me here tonight, because I wasn't about to let you chicken out and do something foolish like run away again."

I threw up my arms in frustration. "Well, I'm still here, so it looks like you were wrong. Again."

"Wrong?" She made an exaggerated point of evaluating our less-than-ideal surroundings then rested her hands on my shoulders. "You're scared. That's understandable, but how many times do you think you can run before Nico stops chasing you?"

I rolled my eyes, unwilling to acknowledge her valid points. "Go back to Logan and stay out of my business."

Kendra shook her head. "Can't do that. I lost my best friend by staying out of her business. I learned my lesson and won't make that mistake again."

"Really?" I let out a single laugh. "You call that 'staying out?' Because the way I remember it, you hid a vital piece of information from me. On top of that, you were setting me up with Nico every damn time I turned around."

A Cheshire grin spread across Kendra's face. "Sweetie, I set you up one time—and it was quite entertaining—but the rest of that was *all* Nico." She poked my forehead. "When are you going to get your dense head out of your boney little ass and realize that man is crazy about you?"

We locked eyes in a battle of wills. I refused to concede, even though she could be right. Doubtful, but . . . *dammit.* "I'll say it again. Stay out. Of. My fucking. Business."

Kendra's jaw dropped, and I took advantage of her rare moment of shock to push past her and escape back into the noisy, crowded club. I wove around the groups of people milling around, ignoring Kendra as she followed, calling for me to wait up. The bar came into view, and I stopped in my tracks, paralyzed by the sickening scene playing out in front of me— so similar to the one I'd witnessed my first time here.

The woman on Nico's lap wrapped her arms around his neck, his hands on her hips. She leaned closer, and I closed my eyes, afraid to watch. I wanted to run, but my feet wouldn't move.

"Deep breaths, Danni." Kendra gripped my shoulders, anchoring me in place. "You've got this. Give him a chance to explain."

I eased forward, guided by the calm, steady tone of Kendra's voice by my ear, and opened my eyes to the same horrid scene. My body trembled and my head started to sway, moving of its own accord. "I-I can't."

IT'S NOT WHAT YOU THINK
NICO

"Look, I'm really sorry." *I'm not.* "But I'm here with someone, and she'll be back any minute. So I need you to go. Find someone else." *Before you totally fuck up everything.*

The woman on my lap pouted and wrapped her arms tighter around my neck, making it even more impossible for me to extricate her. Almost as impossible as remembering her damn name. Then again, maybe I'd never even bothered to ask for it when we'd hooked up a few months ago.

"But I missed you, Nico, and—" She looked up and smiled. "Hey, I remember you."

Someone slapped a hand on my back. "Incoming, man."

Logan? No way. I turned to glare at my best friend, who'd sworn he and Kendra would be at his place in New York tonight. "What the fuck? What are you doing here, and—oh, shit. Where's—"

"Chill, dude. I thought you knew." He held up his hands in surrender. "Kendra said she made sure it was okay with Danni, but—"

"And you believed her? Christ, Logan, have you lost your mind?"

"Look, you can yell at me later, but right now I'm tryin' to warn you that you've got bigger problems than Clingy Barbie here." Logan grabbed my head and gave it a sharp twist to the side, where Danni stood watching us. "And that's only part of it."

The panicked expression on Danni's face scared the shit out of me. I'd seen a milder version of it several times before, right before she'd shut down and run away from me. From us. If she took off this time, without even letting me explain, I didn't know if she'd ever open up enough to give me another chance.

Fortunately, Kendra appeared to be preventing that—standing behind Danni, hands on her shoulders. Even though Danni wasn't ready to trust Kendra and needed time apart to heal, I had to appreciate Kendra's persistence and aversion to boundaries. But I could only imagine the thoughts going through Danni's mind right now, the pain she must be feeling. I'd promised her tonight was just about us, no one else.

And I'd promised I wouldn't hurt her.

"Danni!" *I need to get to her before it's too late.*

"No, baby." Miss Blondie giggled, her lips moving toward mine. "It's Ashley." She squeezed my cheeks, trying to pull my attention back to her. "Come on, Nico," she whined, wiggling her hips, "I wanna dance. Come dance with me."

Enough playing Mr. Nice Guy. "For the last time, my answer is no."

I struggled to stand, practically dumping Ashley on the floor, and turned her toward Logan. "Why don't you talk to my friend for a while? Maybe he'll dance with you. But I'm going to go claim my beautiful date before someone else tries to." I rushed to Danni, attempting to appear more confident and in control than I actually felt. "Hey, beautiful. I missed you."

She arched a brow, silently questioning my sincerity.

I leaned down to kiss her cheek. "Dance with me and I'll prove it." Stepping back, I extended my arm and waited.

"Go on. You got this." Kendra nudged Danni forward while pinning me with a menacing glare that warned I'd have her to deal with if this didn't end well.

Normally that kind of attitude would piss me off, but not this time. If I hurt Danni, I'd deserve more than whatever punishment Kendra had in mind.

The music faded. Ben grabbed a stool and dragged it to the front of the stage. "We're gonna slow things down a bit. Give you guys a chance to . . . hold on to that special lady."

His emphasis on the last few words told me he'd witnessed my dilemma. And even though he hadn't finished his remark with "so don't fuck it up," I knew my brother—he thought it.

Illuminated by a single light, Ben adjusted his microphone and nodded in our direction. "This song goes out to a very special couple."

Fear and doubt clouded Danni's expression. After what felt like an eternity, she raised her hand, hesitating before finally placing it in mine. I blew out a breath I hadn't realized I'd been holding then moved to the dance floor and wrapped her in my arms. The way she trembled made my heart ache. I'd done this to her. It wasn't intentional or something I even had control over, but I'd made her doubt my feelings.

And I needed to fix that.

I kissed the top of her head and pulled her closer, eliminating any space between us and hopefully any uncertainty that she was the only lady I wanted to hold. Every soft curve of Danni's body fit so perfectly against mine, like we were made for each other, and we swayed as one to the sultry beat of Ben's band.

I caressed her back, trying to convey my emotions while fighting the urge to kiss her senseless right here. Let her see how desperate she made me. How much I needed her.

Danni's spine stiffened, and a palpable tension rolled off her.

I eased back enough to look in her eyes then followed her line of sight to our spot at the bar, now occupied by fucking Ashley. She sat there, arms crossed, watching every damn move we made as though trying to enforce some sort of delusional claim on me.

"Hey. Look at me." I cupped the side of Danni's face and redirected her attention to me. "It's just you and me. No one else."

"I-I can't do this. I thought I could." She squeezed her eyes shut. "But I'm in way over my head and—I just don't belong here. With you."

Like hell she doesn't. I placed a gentle kiss to her forehead, trying not to panic, and took her hands. "Come with me."

Her head shook. "Nico, please don't make this any harder than it already is." Danni pressed her palms against my chest and pushed me away. "I'd like to go home."

Her eyes fell closed again, shutting me out and closing the door on any chance I had of convincing her to stay.

I sighed. "Wait here. I'll go settle my tab with Jazmine, then we can leave."

Danni gave a slight nod, and I worried she'd be gone by the time I returned.

"Going somewhere?" I'd only taken a few steps when Kendra's sharp tone caught my attention. I turned to find her standing toe to toe with Danni, arms crossed.

"Mind your own damn business and get out of my way," Danni growled, side-stepping in an unsuccessful attempt to slip past Kendra, who seemed to anticipate every move.

While those two squared off, I rushed toward the bar, waving my card at Jazmine like a crazed fool. *Fitting, since that's exactly how the thought of losing Danni makes me feel.*

Jazmine gave me a puzzled look but left the customer she'd

been talking to and moved to meet me. "Hey, what's—oh, no. What happened?"

"Short version, I fucked up again. Can you just run my card quick? I need to get back before she leaves without me."

Jazmine pushed my hand away. "Go. I got you covered."

"You're the best." I gave her a quick kiss on the cheek before running off. "I owe you."

Kendra and Danni were still arguing when I returned. Kristi had also joined on the defensive line, standing shoulder-to-shoulder with Kendra to prevent Danni's escape.

"Why?" Kendra taunted, appearing to enjoy herself a bit to much. "So you can run away again?" She looked at her nails and rubbed them on her shoulder. "Nah, I'll pass."

"I don't owe you either of you any explanations, and I sure as hell don't need your permission." Danni shoved her fists on her hips and glared at her friends. "So if you would just get out of my way, you'll see that I'm trying to—"

"Ladies." I thanked Kendra and Kristi with a wink, draping an arm across Danni's shoulders and easing her to my side. "Let's get you home."

"I'm sorry you didn't have a good time. I wanted tonight to be special," I said, breaking the twenty minutes of silence. Twenty of minutes of Danni clinging to the passenger's door and ignoring my outstretched hand waiting to hold hers.

Twenty minutes of her sweet floral scent swirling around me like a potent drug.

Twenty fucking minutes enduring the raw chemical attraction between us, crackling in this confined space, without so much as a hint of acknowledgement from her. She didn't have me fooled though—she felt it too. But for whatever reason, she'd decided to shut it out. Shut *me* out.

Not. This. Time. No way in *hell* would I let her run away again without a fight. *I just don't belong here. With you.* She couldn't really believe that, could she?

I eased up her driveway, mind racing with all the things I wanted to say to her once we were inside and I could safely demand her full attention. Before my car even came to a stop, Danni threw open the door and bolted toward her house, clutching her shoes and bag to her chest.

"Danni, wait." I chased after her, reaching her on the porch. "We need to talk about this."

She didn't respond, just kept fumbling with her small bag and grumbling under her breath about finding her keys.

When she finally pulled them out, I dove forward, bracing one hand against the storm door to prevent her from opening it. Prevent her from disappearing on the other side of it. "Please. I get that you're upset, and I realize how it must have looked when you came back and saw—but it wasn't what you thought. And if you'll let me explain, you'll realize I didn't do anything wrong." I stroked her hair and tucked it behind her ear, catching a glimpse of her face in the moonlight. "Turn around please. Look at me."

Her head swayed side to side, but she kept her back to me. Several tense minutes passed before she finally relaxed her shoulders and rested her forehead against the door with a weary sigh.

"Somewhere deep inside, I think I already know you didn't." She drew in a slow, deep breath. "Problem is, every-where we go, women are always flirting with you—some practically throwing themselves at you."

Like Ashley.

Danni glanced at me, chewing her lip. "I-I feel like I'm always competing for you. Afraid someone prettier, younger, better is gonna take my place, just like—well, it's just . . . I wouldn't blame you if . . . you know." She shrugged. "I mean, I want you, but I can't make you want me. Make you choose me." Her voice trembled, fading with each word.

I brushed away the tear that slid down her cheek, hating that I'd caused it. Fearing it wouldn't be the last. "You just got out of a really bad relationship with a husband who lied to you and cheated on you. It's only natural to be suspicious of me. And while I'll admit that you *are* adorable when you're jealous, I promise you, I would never intentionally do something to make you feel that way."

I leaned into Danni and wrapped my arm around her waist, ignoring the knot that tightened in my gut. "Why don't we go inside?" I said, stroking her arm.

"Nico, I—" She pulled away from me, shaking her head. "No. That was a really nice speech, but I know what I saw. Intentional or not. That woman was crawling into your lap, and you—"

"And I was trying to get away from her." *Is she kidding me?* "Did you really miss that part, or are you just choosing to ignore it so you have an excuse to push me away again? I can't control what women do, but I sure as hell didn't do anything to encourage her."

How did we get from the amazing evening we'd started out with to . . . this? I couldn't stand still any longer and released Danni, pacing behind her. Trying to regain some sense of calm while my shot at the girl of my dreams slipped away. "Christ, Danni, I know my self-control goes straight out the window when I'm with you. But that woman—"

I grabbed Danni's hands, catching her off guard. Her shoes and bag tumbled to the porch, and she stepped back.

"She's nothing." I closed the gap between us, keeping our joined hands pressed against my chest. I looked into Danni's eyes, willing her to see the truth. "She's. Not. You. None of them are."

"I want to believe you. I-I'm trying to." Danni's eyes fluttered closed. When they reopened, her gaze drifted past me. Her voice faded. "I just don't know if my heart will let me right now. It's too much. Too soon." She pulled her hands away and folded them across her stomach, twisting that damn diamond ring like she did every time she got upset.

"I'm sorry. T-Tonight was a mistake. I—" Her shoulders rose and fell on a shuddered breath. "Please leave."

"So that's it. You're just going to run away again? Refuse to give me a chance, just like before?"

"I was married before, in case you for—"

"And now you're not, but *nothing* else has changed." I reached for her hands again, this time to stop her fidgeting, and repositioned the ring so it sat perfectly on her finger. "Good night, Danni."

I walked away, fighting the urge to look back at her reaction. Maybe she got my point, maybe she didn't. But I wasn't sticking around to find out. By the time I got to my car, she was gone.

BEN AND BLUE
NICO

The doorbell rang—several times—followed by a call from Ben. When I didn't bother to answer either, he resorted to the relentless pounding on my front door—and shouting— that was giving me a fucking headache.

Never should've shot off that "I fucked up again" text to him and Logan from Danni's driveway. Regretted it the second I hit Send. Knew it would only be a matter of time before one of them showed up to make sure I didn't drown my sorrows in whiskey.

"Too late." I downed the last of my drink, shoved aside the empty Chivas 18 bottle, then stormed to the front door—doing a bit of my own shouting along the way—and yanked it open to glare at my pain-in-the-ass brother.

"Hey, you're home," he said with a smirk, acting as though he hadn't spent the past ten minutes being ignored.

I glared harder and growled, "I'm not in the mood for company."

Ben's smug grin stretched wider. He held up a bottle of Johnnie Blue, eyebrows raised. "Still not interested?"

Damn, if I'd known he'd brought reinforcements and

planned to commiserate instead of lecture, I wouldn't have kept him waiting.

"Suppose I can put up with you for a few minutes," I grumbled, stepping aside to let him enter.

Once safely inside, Ben shoved his hands in his pockets and rocked back on his heels while giving me a thorough once-over. He let out a low hum. "Looks like I'm late to the party."

"What's that supposed to mean?"

"It means you look like shit . . . and a little bit shit-faced."

"Perfect." I pushed past him to close the door. "Then I look exactly how I feel."

"Surprised you can still feel anything," he mumbled under his breath, but my hearing wasn't impaired by the comfortable buzz I had going.

"Didn't ask you to come over and offer your judgmental two cents, so feel free to leave if that's why you're here. Shouldn't you be with Kristi anyway?"

"She's entertaining her former roommates from college this weekend. Girls only." He shrugged. "Just as well. Gives me the chance to have a little space without getting into a huge argument about needing it."

"Uh-oh. Trouble in paradise, rock star?" I threw my arm across Ben's shoulders. "Maybe we should talk 'bout it."

"Nice try." He shook off my arm with a laugh. "But I'm here to talk about your pathetic wreck of a love life, not my overactive-to-the-point-of-exhaustion one."

"Right." I blew out a heavy breath and shoved a hand through my hair. "Thanks for rubbing it in."

Ben slapped my back. "Come on, buddy. Let's go find you a place to sit before you fall over." He steered me toward the kitchen then pulled out a chair and pushed me into it. After taking the seat across from me, he poured our drinks and raised his glass. "To the women we can't live with or without."

I glanced from the paltry less-than-one finger of Walker in

my glass to the double in my brother's outstretched hand. "You bring that bottle for you or me?"

"Both of us." He smirked and tipped his head toward the empty on my counter. "But it seems I have some catching up to do. And you definitely need to slow down."

"Fine." He might have a point, even though that bottle hadn't been even close to full when I started. I lifted my glass and tapped it against his. "To our fucked-up love lives."

Ben nodded, took a sip, then slapped his hand on the table. "So, down to business—talk to me."

"Nothing to say. It's over. We're done, not that we ever *were*." And that was the ugly, bitter truth. After months of convincing myself Danni felt the same sparks and instant connection I had, we couldn't even make it through one date before it all went to hell.

"Bullshit. From what I saw, you two were totally into each other when you got there."

"Yeah, I thought so too. Then we got our drinks and went outside to get away from the crowd and the noise."

"And the chance of bumping into Summer."

"Yeah, that too. Least luck was on my side there. Thanks for the heads-up, by the way. I kept trying to convince Danni to skip the club after you texted, but nope. She *insisted* we go be— doesn't matter."

I wasn't trying to blame Ben or make him feel guilty. He didn't need to know the details. Didn't need to know the only reason Danni refused to bail was because I'd promised Ben we'd be there.

Funny how that promise didn't seem to stop her from leaving though.

I finished off my few drops of whiskey and pushed my glass to the center of the table. "Maybe things woulda ended differently if we'd gone somewhere else."

"Maybe. Maybe not. But you can't live your life second-guessing everything. So . . . things were going great, you went outside, and then . . . what changed?"

"Damned if I know."

Ben gave me a questioning look. "Not buying it." He poured another measly finger of whiskey in my glass and slid it in front of me.

I tapped the rim. "You want me to keep talking, you're gonna have to do better than that."

"Just tryin' to make sure you pace yourself."

A laugh burst out of me. "You're a few hours too late for that. Top it off."

We stared each other down for a few beats. Ben let out a sigh. "I'll meet you halfway, then I'm cutting you off." He filled my glass just shy of half full then leaned on the table, arms crossed. "Now continue."

"Fine. I have an idea." I took a slow drink, savoring the burn of alcohol and buying myself a little time, because finally owning up to the reputation I'd earned over the past year sucked—almost as much as having to admit my family was right that one day I'd *"regret my actions and have to face the conse-quences."* "She thought I took her outside looking to score, which I didn't."

Ben nodded, a neutral expression on his face. "I believe you."

I rubbed my forehead, struggling to keep my thoughts together. "We talked about it—agreed we were gonna take things slow. She kissed me, and I *thought* we were back on track. But then we went back into the club, and I could see it in her eyes—we weren't. She looked . . . scared? Confused maybe? I don't know, but she made some 'scuse about freshening up and made a run for it." I dragged a hand over my face. "I shouldn't have let 'er go off on her own."

"What were you gonna do? Follow her into the ladies'

room? Tell her she couldn't go?" He shook his head. "You're not being realistic."

I waved him off. "Anyway, while Danni was gone, that Ash chick snuck up behind me—totally caught me off guard. Thought she was Danni . . . least till I turned around."

Ben coughed, choking on the drink he was taking, and made a bitter face. "Yeah, I'd leave that part out when you talk to Danni."

"Probably right. I'm in deep 'nough shit." I swirled the amber liquid in my glass then took a long sip. "Anyway, I turned, and Ashley literally jumped into my fuckin' lap and latched onto me."

"And of course, Danni had to pick that exact moment to come back," Ben said in a flat tone.

"Exactly." I tapped my nose to let him know he'd hit the mark but wound up with a finger in my eye instead. "She saw us, and . . . yeah."

My head pounded as the scene replayed in my mind for the hundredth time. No matter how hard I squeezed my temples, it wouldn't stop. That painful look of betrayal in her eyes would haunt me forever.

"She accused me of cheatin' on her."

Ben tapped the table. "Hey, I tried to help you."

"I know, and you told me not to fuck it up, but—"

"I thought it, but I'm sure I didn't actually say it." He laughed. "Really screwed up my bandmates switching the song order like that though. We weren't supposed to play 'Sparks' until late in the second set."

"Appreciate the effort, but she'd found her out. A *valid excuse* to end things—least it woulda been if it were true." I sucked in a deep breath and blew it out. "Anyway, she didn't wanna to hear my side of the story. Only wanted to go home, so I took her."

"Did you try talking to her about it?"

"No, I just opened the car door and shoved her out as I rolled past her house." I threw back the contents of my glass, returned it to the table with a thud, and shoved it toward Ben for a refill. "Of course I *tried*. She shut me down—wouldn't even give me a chance to explain."

Ben shoved back my empty glass. "She's just goin' on what she knows, and given how her marriage ended . . ." He lifted one shoulder.

Bastard never deserved her. "Sometimes I wonder if she 'members it ended with him cheating and divorcing her. 'Specially since his fuckin' ring is still securely in place on her finger."

"Seriously?"

"Does it sound like somethin' I'd joke about?" I picked up my empty glass and dropped it back on the table.

Ben gave a low hum. "Guess not. You ask her about it?"

"Nope. Don't need to." Could only be one reason. "She made her choice months ago—him over me. He may be gone, but he's still her choice." *Which makes me second best. Again.*

"I doubt that's it."

"No, it all makes sense now. See, she's so hung up on appearances, worryin' what people are gonna say 'n shit—like her life is any of their fuckin' business. She thinks it's *too soon* to date or, heaven forbid, be *happy*. And even the mere idea of being *attracted* to someone—'specially someone like *me*—is too repulsive for her to handle."

"Someone like you." Ben leaned back in his chair, legs extended and ankles crossed. He stared at me, rubbing his jaw. "I'm not gonna be that sappy guy who sits here and lists all the reasons any woman would be *lucky* to be stuck with you." He smirked and took a slow sip of whiskey. "But that's mostly because your head's already big enough, not because we both know it would be a fucking long list."

"Look who's talking about over'flated egos . . . dick."

Ben flipped me off with a laugh.

"You know damn well what I'm talking about. Hell, the whole female population seems to know my reputation, including Danni. It's like she expected me to nail her the first chance I got and ship her disposable sweet little ass home in an Uber. Not sayin' she's disposable or just a piece of ass—'cause she's definitely not either of those—but it's prob'ly what she thinks I think. I think."

Ben arched a brow but didn't say a word.

I stacked my hands on the table and let my head crash on top of them. "She's the only girl I've been able to think about for months." Since I first laid eyes on her at Logan's party to be exact. "I'm so fucked."

After a long pause, Ben cleared his throat. "So maybe you need to tell her about Summer. Help her understand."

"No. We've been over this already—it's too soon." I sat up and let my head fall against the chair back, staring at the ceiling while the room swayed. "Besides, I already tried. And failed."

Maybe I should just lead with it next time I tried to date someone though—sort of like a "by the way, I'm really emotionally fucked up" disclaimer—so she'd know to run *before* getting close enough to break my heart.

Actually, I should probably write that down, 'cause I may be a little too drunk to 'member it in the morning. It took a few tries, but I finally dug my phone out of my pocket to add a reminder, holding my breath until the screen lit up—like some lovesick teenager with raging hormones, hoping to see a missed call or text from his crush. Nothing there but a string of annoying messages from Logan and Ben.

And my sister.

"What the hell? You called Gabs?"

Ben shrugged. "Just rallying the troops for damage control." He rounded the table, clapped a hand on my shoulder, and leaned down to my ear. "You can thank me for stopping her from calling Dad."

Ben collected our glasses and the bottle of Blue—that I wasn't finished with—chuckling as if any of this was funny.

After putting everything by the sink, he returned and held out a hand. "Let's go, bud."

I pinched the bridge of my nose while his question bounced around in my head. "Where . . . where exactly are we going?" I was in no shape to drop in on Danni, which was the only place I wanted to go.

Ben shook his head with a sigh. "I'm putting you to bed so you can sleep this off. Then tomorrow—or the next day, since I'm guessing you won't be in too great of shape tomorrow—we can figure out where you go from here."

FOCUS ON THE POSITIVE THINGS

DANNI

Jen stood waiting in her doorway on Saturday morning and greeted me with open arms. "I'm so glad you agreed to come."

The deluge of tears I'd been holding back the whole drive here burst free the second I felt safe and loved in my sister's embrace. I dragged my hand across my drenched face. "Me too."

She hugged me tighter. "I was worried you just said you would to shut me up last night."

"I did—originally—but then I realized I really needed you." After hours of tossing, turning, and crying into my pillow.

"Come on, let's go sit." Jen grabbed my hand and led me down the hall to the family room, where an open bottle of wine and two glasses sat waiting on the table by the couch . . . right beside a giant box of tissues. "I should probably offer you coffee or lemonade, considering the time, but I figured you might need something a little stronger."

I nodded. "Good call."

She filled our glasses then settled in next to me, watching

with a concerned expression while I chugged most of my drink before she'd even taken a sip of hers. "Wow . . . that bad, huh?"

I lifted one shoulder. "Let's just say I'll be spending the rest of my life alone."

"I'm sure that's an exaggeration." Jen set her glass on the table and shifted to face me. "But I don't get it. I mean, I'd planned on waiting until this afternoon to call for an update because I didn't want to interrupt . . . you know, just in case your date hadn't quite ended yet?" She shook her head. "What happened?"

I glanced around the room, twisting and tugging at the gold band around my finger. How could something that started out so perfectly end up such a mess?

"Still not ready to take that off?" Jen tipped her head toward my hands, watching me with an arched brow.

"Apparently not." I shrugged. "At least I only wear the diamond." I'd ripped off my wedding band the night of Will's accident—right after discovering our divorce papers—and tossed it in the bottom of my jewelry box. Probably should have hurled it into the lake instead, just like he'd thrown away my love . . . our marriage.

"Ryan took Caden to the park so we could have some time alone." Jen gave my hand a gentle squeeze. "You don't have to talk about any of it if you're not ready. We could watch a movie, bake some cookies, go for a walk, whatever you—"

"I blew it with Nico." I sucked in a ragged breath and pressed on, blurting out the bottom-line summary of last night's disastrous events. "I had my chance with the most amazing man I've ever met, and I totally screwed it up."

Jen grabbed a tissue and blotted the tears from my face. "Maybe it wasn't as bad as you think. Have you talked to Nico?"

I shook my head, struggling to get the words out. "We had

a huge fight before the band even finished their first set. It was all my fault. I panicked. Said things I shouldn't have." I closed my eyes, remembering the wounded expression on Nico's face when I'd basically accused him of cheating as soon as I'd left him alone.

"When I told him I wanted to go home, he didn't even ask me to stay—just insisted on taking me." I pulled a few more tissues from the box and moved to stare out the window. "I tried to sneak out when he went to settle his bill at the bar, but Kendra got—"

"Why was Kendra even—never mind. We can get into that later." Jen wrapped her arms around me, hugging me from behind. "I'm sure you and Nico can work it out. You just need to talk—"

"I doubt he'll ever want to see me again." A heavy sob shook my body. "And I don't blame him." I turned and buried my face in my sister's shoulder.

She held me, rubbing my back while regret and sorrow flowed from my burning eyes. "Shh . . . come on, Danni. It couldn't have been *that* bad."

I lifted my head enough to glare at her. "Trust me. I was there."

Jen tapped her chin, giving a thoughtful hum. A grin stretched across her face. "Nope. Not buyin' it. I've been around you two, remember? And there is some *major* chemistry going on." She arched her brows, daring me to deny it.

I couldn't.

Jen continued to stare at me with a smug, I-told-you-so expression while memories of the way Nico had kissed me last night came rushing back. The soft brush of his lips against mine. The sounds he'd made. The feel of his hard body pressed against mine. A warm glow filled my chest.

"Wait . . . a . . . minute?" She leaned forward, eyes narrowing. "You're holding out on me."

"Hmmm?" I bit my lips, struggling to resist the uncontrollable and inappropriate smile tugging at them, because remembering how amazing it was to kiss Nico didn't change the fact that it wasn't likely to happen again.

But what if it could?

My heart raced, pulse pounding in my ears. There *was* no denying our chemistry, not to mention those sparks—God, I'd never felt anything like that before Nico—but who was I kidding? I'd never be enough for him. Never fit into his life.

"Danni?"

"I, um . . ." *Need to get a grip on reality.* "Did I hear something about cookies earlier?" I asked, escaping toward the kitchen, wishing it were that easy to escape the emotional battle raging inside me . . . and that damn glimmer of hope that just wouldn't go away.

"Hey." Jen rushed past me and blocked the doorway— standing between me and a giant mixing bowl filled with my favorite chocolate chip cookie dough. "Don't you think it's about time you stopped running away and learned to focus on the positive things in your life?"

"Cookie dough is a definite positive, and I'm about to show it a lot of focus . . . just as soon as you move out of my way. Satisfied?" I pasted on my best attempt at a Cheshire grin and squeezed past her.

"Don't give me that look. They're there." She crossed the room and pressed some buttons on the oven before joining me at the island. "And you're going to go over every detail from last night so I can point them out and prove it to you." The corners of her mouth twitched upward. "And because I'm dying to hear them."

I hooked my arm around the mixing bowl and grabbed a spoon, grumbling under my breath, "Knew I should've stayed home alone."

"Not so fast." Jen swiped the bowl, leaving me with an

empty spoon. "I thought we'd try something different this time."

"Like what? Torturing me? 'Cause you're already doing a pretty good job of it."

Jen stuck out her tongue like a typical little sister. "That's just an added bonus." She laughed. "I meant like actually baking the cookies before we eat them." She pulled two cookie sheets from the pantry and set them on the counter.

"You go right ahead and do what you want with your half." I grabbed another bowl from the cabinet and scooped a mound of dough into it. "I'm gonna get a head start and eat mine like this." I took a bite and gave a satisfied hum. "It's much more therapeutic."

Jen shook her head, grinning while she let out an exaggerated sigh. "You're hopeless."

I raised my hands. "See? That's exactly what I've been saying."

"You know that's not what I meant." Jen stared at me, arms folded across her chest. "So . . . last night?"

I slumped into my chair and poked at the chocolate chips in my bowl, shoving them into a line while I organized my thoughts. "Fine." I groaned, adding an exaggerated roll of my eyes. "What do you want to know?"

"Everything." Jen stood across from me, dropping balls of cookie batter onto her baking sheets. "Start at the beginning . . . and don't leave *anything* out."

I closed my eyes, picturing Nico pacing on my front porch when he'd arrived, and the words began to flow . . . along with a few more tears. Jen let me ramble on with only a few interruptions.

When I finally finished, she took my hands and studied my face. "Sounds to me like things were going great most of the time. Right?"

I lifted one shoulder.

"Sure, you hit a few first-date bumps. And having Kendra show up kinda sucked—even though it sounds like it's good she was there—but you can't hold that against Nico. Just like you can't blame him because women are attracted to him. I mean, you have looked at him, right?" She paused to fan her face. "Anyway, it sounds like he was *clearly* into you."

"Yeah, right up until the point where I ruined everything."

"Danni, you've been through hell the past few months. You got scared and reacted the way anyone in your situation would have."

"But what if Kendra's right?" I hopped from my seat and paced the kitchen, rubbing my throbbing temples. The woman from the restroom, who I'd left out of the story for some unexplainable reason, flashed in my mind. "What if Nico decides he's done playing games and moves on to someone else? He certainly has plenty of eager options. For all I know, he might even be waking up next to one of them right now."

I stopped moving, keeping my back to Jen while I rearranged the cookies on the cooling rack to avoid her face. Avoid seeing my worst fears confirmed in her expressions. A few seconds passed in silence.

"I want to spend time with him. See where things go. Know what it's like to be in a relationship with someone who loves me and makes me feel . . . tingly in all the right places, you know?"

Jen let out a dreamy sigh. "Yeah, I know exactly what you mean."

"But after Will—" I turned to face Jen. Face my fears. "Am I ever going to be able trust another man?"

"You will." Jen pulled the last tray of cookies from the oven, glancing over her shoulder at me. "It may take a while, but you'll get there."

My head bobbed while I tried to process the possibility. Visions of Nico and me sharing a normal life drifted through my mind—me standing in the kitchen of his beautiful house, baking cookies, while he played in the yard with our children.

A warm glow radiated through me. "I think I love him." My thoughts spilled out as faint words. I closed my eyes and pulled in a shuddered breath. "No. I'm sure I do."

When I opened my eyes, Jen was standing directly in front of me, beaming, with both hands over her heart.

"What do I do?" A single tear rolled down my cheek. "I can't lose him."

Jen rested her arms on the counter, leaning forward to look me square in the eyes. "Maybe you should start by telling *him* that."

"What?" My eyes flew open wide. "Are you crazy? I can't just walk up to him and say, 'Hey, Nico, how's it going? You look incredibly sexy today. Oh, and by the way, I'm madly in love with you.'"

Jen pushed away from the counter, laughing. "Well, when you put it that way, it sounds a little silly." She grabbed a warm cookie from the tray and took a bite. "Try batting your eyes when you say it. I'm sure that'll make a huge difference." She turned to face me, a mischievous grin on her face. "And don't think I didn't notice you increased the love factor to madly."

I bit my lip while my last words replayed in my mind. The surprising truth sank in, a renewed sense of joy sprang to life, and a wide grin stretched my cheeks. "Thank you." I wrapped my arms around Jen, squeezing her tight. "I'm so happy I have you."

"Me too." Jen pulled back to look at me. "So . . . you hangin' around for the day? Spending the night? Running home to pay a surprise visit to Nico?" She added an exaggerated wink.

As much as the idea of seeing Nico appealed to me, I needed a little more time to gather enough courage to face him again—maybe a lot of time. I tipped my head toward the door and gave Jen a pleading look. "My bag is in the car."

"Well then, go get it," Ryan responded from the doorway. He crossed the room and greeted me with a giant hug. "You're always welcome here."

"How'd you get so lucky, Jen?"

Ryan kissed my cheek and released me. "Nah, I'm the lucky one." He wrapped his arms around Jen's waist, lifting her feet off the floor. "Isn't that right, sweets?"

She squealed, giggling as he nuzzled her neck. "I'm pretty sure you always say you're the one *getting* lucky."

Ryan hummed, tapping a finger against his pursed lips. "Yeah, that sounds about right." A teasing laugh filled his voice. "I always get those two mixed up." He winked then reached past Jen to grab a cookie from the cooling rack.

"Mmm . . . I smell cookies," Caden sang out the words. His little feet echoed in the hall as he ran toward the kitchen. "Can I have—Aunt Danni!" He crashed into me, clinging to my legs. "I didn't know you was comin' to see me."

"That's 'cause I wanted to surprise you." I knelt to give him a giant squeeze and tousle his damp hair. "How's my favorite little man?"

"Good, but I'm really tired. An' hungry." He placed a perfect, sloppy-wet kiss on my cheek. "Daddy and me went to the park an' played soccer for a really long time." Caden stretched to look around the room. "Where's Uncle Will?"

"He—" I squeezed Caden's shoulder to keep my balance. "Uncle Will can't come to see you anymore."

Caden folded his arms. "But I wanna—"

"Hey, buddy." Ryan gently scooped up his son. He kissed his cheek then held him close. "Remember we talked about that?"

Ryan walked out of the room, attempting to re-explain death to a confused five-year-old.

Jen rubbed my back. "Sorry. We've tried, but sometimes it's too hard for him to fully understand."

"He just caught me off guard." I shrugged and fell into my sister's open arms. "Guess my wounds are still healing." *More like being replaced by new ones.*

My eyes fell closed. I pulled in a deep breath and blew it out.

LUNCHTIME LECTURE
NICO

I snapped up my vibrating phone, hoping to see a message from Danni saying she missed me, regretted the way our date had ended . . . wished she hadn't told me to leave.

Logan: *We're going to Pepper's for lunch. Join us.*

Me: *I don't need a fucking babysitter.*

And I didn't need a fuckin' lecture about screwing up either, but guaranteed that was what I'd be getting. More like two, since Kendra was probably gonna make good on her unspoken threat to kick my ass for hurting Danni.

Logan: *Good. We'll pick you up in 15. Don't make me come in and drag your whiney ass out to the car when we get there.*

"Awesome." I tossed my phone on the counter and stepped into the steamy shower, letting the hot water pulse against my numb body. Wising I could wash away the memories of last night's fiasco along with the stench of sweat and stale liquor.

Fourteen minutes later, I ambled down the stairs, fully dressed but still trying to come up with a viable excuse to blow off this lunch charade and go back to bed. No such luck. The second my feet hit the foyer floor, the deep rumble of a car engine on my driveway announced Logan's annoyingly prompt arrival. He laid on the horn at the top of the circle, the unnecessary and offensive noise making my head pound even harder.

I stormed out the front door, squinting behind my sunglasses. "I get what you're doing, and—oh, shit. Lose the fucking 'poor Nico' expressions or I'm going back inside."

Kendra hopped out of the passenger's seat. "Would you rather have me smack you upside your thick skull and call you an idiot for screwing over my best friend?"

"Yes. And look who's talking. Last I heard, you weren't ranked too high on Danni's list of favorite people either."

Kendra squared her shoulders and crossed her arms, pinning me with what I assumed was meant to be a menacing glare. *Two can play that game, and I'll be damned if I'm backing down first.*

Logan leaned across the center console. "Will you two just get in the car so we can eat?"

Kendra's eyes narrowed even further at me for one second, then as if someone flipped a switch, she looked at Logan and turned into some sweet thing. She climbed in the back seat, leaving me to sit up front with my overprotective best friend.

"Sorry, sweetheart." Kendra poked her head between the seats to kiss Logan's cheek. "I didn't realize your friend could be such an ass."

Logan laughed. "Oh, I could've told you that."

"And to think I crawled out of bed and showered for this." I fastened my seatbelt and reclined the seat. With any luck, I could catch a peaceful nap and avoid phase one of this intervention. "Can we at least go to Farley's?"

"Nope." Logan enunciated the word. "Because I don't want you drinking your lunch."

"Whatever. I don't see a point to all this though. Ben already interrogated me last night—so you can check in with him for the details, because I'm done talking about it." I massaged my aching forehead and groaned.

Kendra and Logan exchanged a smug look in the rearview mirror then remained quiet for the rest of the ride.

Of course they dragged my ass to Pepper's and parked it at the same fucking table I'd shared with Danni that first day. "Any particular reason for this emotionally abusive trip down memory lane, or are you just hell-bent on torturing me today?"

"I'm good with torture." Kendra grinned and stabbed her salad with a bit more force than necessary. "Unfortunately, Logan thought a blunt discussion pointing out what a huge mistake you're making by giving up on Danni was a better approach, so here we are."

"Just fucking awesome." I took a huge bite of my lunch to prevent the rest of my complaints from flowing out unchecked.

Logan snapped a picture, chuckled, and tapped away on his phone.

"What the fuck are you doing?"

He had the audacity to laugh louder. "Ben will never believe me if I just tell him you're eating a bacon cheeseburger with whatever that sloppy sauce dripping from your chin is. I'm sending proof."

"Ben knows how drunk I was last night. I'm pretty sure my downing a dose of greasy food won't be a huge surprise," I growled then took another bite.

"Yeah, and he also said he hasn't seen you that fucked up since Summer, so I guess we should just be happy you're out and about today and actually functioning like an almost civilized human being."

My eyes darted to Kendra, who was wearing earbuds and had the decency to at least pretend she was listening to something on her phone instead of paying attention to us. I pulled off my sunglasses and narrowed my eyes at Logan—a silent warning that we were not going to discuss that part of my life right now.

"Don't worry about Kendra." He leaned closer, returning

my stare. "Look, if you care about Danni as much as you keep saying you do, you need to tell her about Summer."

"Christ." I dragged a hand across my face, groaning with frustration. "Doesn't anyone listen to me? I. Tried. I couldn't do it."

"Then you need to try harder. No one is going to understand better than Danni, and it might even help—"

"No." I snapped up my water bottle and took a long, slow drink. "Next topic. This one's closed."

Logan shook his head and leaned back in his seat. "She was there last night."

Okay, so apparently it's open again. I lifted one shoulder, disinterested. That wasn't news to me since Ben had texted to warn me during dinner.

"She came out of the ladies' room right after Kendra followed Danni in there. Was in full runway strut but managed to pause long enough to give me a head tilt and fake smile before storming off."

"Shit." I hadn't seen that part coming. "And you think she said something to Danni." It wasn't a question, because my gut already knew the answer.

"I'd be surprised if she didn't." Logan strummed his fingers on the table. "I'm sure she must've seen the two of you cozied up together. Known who she was talking to."

I blew out a long breath. "She's been calling my office."

"Summer?" Logan's eyes grew wide. He flashed a quick glance at Kendra then leaned toward me, lowering his voice. "This is news. Any clue why?"

To make my life miserable? "I haven't talked to her—Tricia knows not to put her through, and she never leaves a message."

"*Never?* So this has been going on . . . how long?"

"Few weeks." I shrugged, ignoring Logan's incredulous stare. "Figured she'd eventually take the hint to fuck off. Leave it to Summer to show up instead to stir up trouble."

"All the more reason to tell Danni about her yourself. And sooner, rather than later." Logan rubbed his neck, hesitating, then let out a groan. "Much as I hate to say this, you need to deal with Summer too."

"Unfortunately, but I agree. Especially if she screwed with Danni."

"She know everything?" I tipped my head at Kendra, who was laughing and totally engrossed in something on her screen.

"Nah, she's got enough of her own trouble with Danni right now. The less she knows about this, the better."

"That works for me." I snapped my fingers in front of Kendra's face.

Her head snapped up, and she tugged out her earbuds. "You need something?"

"Did you happen to notice if Danni was having a conversation with anyone when you stalked into the ladies' room last night?"

Kendra shook her head. "I didn't hear anything. I'm pretty sure she'd been talking to the woman who strutted past me on her way out though." She let out a heavy sigh. "Danni wasn't exactly happy to see me, but I don't think my presence was the only thing upsetting her. She got angry when she noticed me. But before that, she looked more upset than she had when she'd run in there."

I rubbed at the pulsing vein in my temple. *Yeah, Summer can have that effect on people.*

I couldn't imagine what lies she could have fed Danni to make her overreact like that to the Ashley issue though. No matter, Danni should've talked to me. Trusted me. Given me a chance to explain what had happened instead of shutting me out.

"Figures. I finally meet someone who makes me feel so . . . alive—like she could be *the one*—and she can't even get through one evening with me." I slumped in my seat and stared at the ceiling as if it somehow held the answers to all my problems. "Maybe it's just me. Maybe I'm just not cut out for real relationships."

"Seriously, Logan, how do you put up with him?" Kendra grumbled. She turned to me, rolling her eyes. "Good lord, Nico. Cut the shit. You know you're lovable, blah, blah, blah."

She swept a dismissive hand then leaned on her forearms, pinning me with an intense stare. "*This* is about Danni. And the problem is she's scared of—" Kendra bobbed her head, appearing to weigh her words. "A lot of things actually, but mostly she's scared of getting hurt again. Of having her heart broken."

Okay, that *I can relate to.* I nodded, considering my response before speaking so it wouldn't reveal more than I wanted to share. "Well, she's not the one who has to worry about a broken heart this time, since she's made it quite obvious *she* doesn't want anything to do with *me.*"

Kendra chewed on her lip and strummed her nails on the table, making that annoying clicking sound. She let out a heavy sigh and whispered, "Oh, sweetie, you are *sooo,* so wrong."

I stared at her, certain I must have misunderstood. "Care to elaborate?"

Kendra groaned. "What the hell. I'm already the worst best friend ever. Might as well try to do some good with my evil." She stretched across the table to jab a finger in my chest. "And just so we're clear, Danni would flat-out kill me for betraying her again, so try to keep this to yourself."

She retreated, shaking her head and making a noise that sounded like a cross between a laugh and sigh. "Our dear, sweet Danni is *way* more interested in you than she's willing to show. Has been from the start. And choosing Will over you was probably the most difficult—and foolish—decision of her life. She did what she thought was right, not what her heart told her it wanted."

It took a few minutes for that possible reality to sink in, although it didn't make sense that she'd still choose to wear his ring. Cling to her past. Her memories of their relationship, which honestly seemed to be one-sided from my seat on the fucking bench.

"Anyway, just give her some space and a little time to calm down. Time to think." Kendra held up one finger. "But *don't* wait too long, or she'll get buried so deep in her own head and delusional ideals again about how a widow should—and shouldn't—behave. It took three of us five weeks to drag her out of that damn house last time. Trust me, you *don't* want to go through that."

"Space, but not too much space. Got it." I gave a slight nod.

"And then you need to make her feel comfortable around you. Show her that you're looking for a real relationship—something meaningful that lasts longer than the aftershocks of an amazing double orgasm."

"Okay. Nothing less than a triple orgasm." I teased Kendra with a wink. "Not a problem. Anything else, coach?"

Logan chuckled and jumped in before Kendra could answer. "I'd suggest avoiding Metro Sky with Danni for a while, given your record of striking out there."

I hummed in agreement. "Yeah. Good call."

A CLEAN SLATE
DANNI

Nine full days had passed without a word from Nico. Nine full days that I still hadn't pulled together the courage to call him to apologize. Nine full days, and counting, that I hadn't come to my senses and begged him for another chance. And with each of those long, lonely days, the nagging fear that I'd lost him forever grew stronger and more unbearable.

This morning I'd woken before dawn, drenched in sweat and tangled in my sheets, our latest imaginary romp in the sack still playing in my mind. But I wanted more than dreams. I wanted a dream-come-true *real* relationship with Nico.

I brushed my fingers along his business card and sighed. Sure, it would have made more sense to just program his number into my phone, but then it would have been too easy to accidentally hit the button to call him without knowing what to say.

I'd been carrying his card around for a week. Having to explain to Kristi and Jen—every day—why I hadn't called him yet. Having to ignore daily messages from Kendra telling me to "stop screwing around" and "get my shit together."

Last night I'd written out everything I wanted to tell him,

practiced it a hundred times, and sworn today would *definitely* be the day. Easier said than done, considering I'd chickened out every time I'd picked up my phone so far today, including this time. I slumped in a chair, groaning, and dropped his card on the kitchen table.

Come on, Danni. You can do this.

"Right. Today's not over yet. Still plenty of time to call . . . right after a quick shower. Maybe dinner. And another chapter or two of the book I started reading this morning."

That plan lasted all of ten seconds. My phone lit up, buzzing with Nico's number stretched across the screen. But the call disconnected, leaving me staring at my dark, silent phone. Before I could decide if I was relieved, disappointed, or just imagining things, the buzzing started again.

Afraid this call might disappear too—or I might chicken out—I pounced to press the button and answer. "Hello?"

"Danni. Hey." Nico let out a relieved sigh. "It's so good to hear your voice." Nico's deep voice had a rough edge to it. "I, um . . . I wanted to stop by to see you but realized I should probably call first to make sure that's okay with you?"

My skin tingled with excitement. "Yeah. I'd like that." I sucked in a deep breath and tried to sound calm. "When did you have in mind?"

Nico chuckled. "Answer your door." A gentle knock sounded on my front door.

"Now?" I shrieked and glanced down at my yoga pants, tank top, and bare feet. I'd spent the day lounging around, sipping tea, and devouring the new book by my favorite author . . . in between bouts of missing Nico. "I look a wreck," I mumbled, mostly to myself.

Nico gave a low hum. "I doubt that's possible. But . . . well, I can come back another time if—"

"No! Stay. I'll, um . . . just give me a minute." *Maybe five.*

I ended the call, already racing up the stairs and into my

bathroom, brushed my teeth, twisted my hair into a messy bun, then swiped on a quick coat of mascara and lip gloss. I took a deep breath and blew it out, staring at myself in the mirror. "Okay. That's as good as it's gonna get."

Heart pounding, I ran down the steps and pulled open the front door with a trembling hand. I bit my lip and took in the breathtaking sight in front of me. Nico looked amazing in a pair of faded jeans and a navy T-shirt that hugged his broad chest, revealing just a hint of the chiseled abs I knew were hiding beneath it. "Hi."

His eyes roamed the length of my body before locking on mine. A warm smile stretched across his handsome face, the adorable lopsided one that revealed the dimple in his left cheek. "Hi, beautiful."

He leaned in slightly but pulled back and ran a hand through his perfectly messy dark hair. Maybe I'd imagined it, but I'd thought—hoped—he was going to kiss me.

"Sorry." Nico shook his head, a crease forming between his brows. "I tried to give you time to—but you didn't call." He lifted one shoulder. "I just couldn't wait anymore."

I replayed his words, letting them sink in. Had he missed me as much as I'd been missing him? "Do you want to come in?"

"Yes." His head bobbed, and he stared down at the porch.

I stepped aside, held open the door, and waited. But Nico didn't move. He lifted his eyes to meet mine again. The unmistakable desire they revealed set off a fresh jumble of nerves in my chest.

"But that's probably not the best idea." He shoved his hands in his pockets, letting out a heavy breath, and tipped his head toward the street. "You wanna go for a walk? I noticed a little ice cream shop on my way here."

"Sure. Let me just—" I stooped down, grabbed my

sneakers that were by the door, and held them up before slipping them on.

We strolled side by side in silence along the tree-lined street, his hands still tucked in his pockets. My mind was a total blank. Every bit of the speech I'd prepared last night had vanished the moment he knocked on my door.

Nico cast a quick glance in my direction. He drew in a slow, deep breath and blew it out. "So . . . about the other night."

I raised a hand to stop him. "Before you say anything, I um . . . I just want to—well . . . I'm sorry. For the way I acted and—"

"There's nothing for you to apologize about."

I tipped my head to glance at him from the corner of my eye. "You sure about that? 'Cause I kinda remember things differently, and I'm pretty sure I overreacted a bit."

Nico arched a brow but didn't say anything.

"Okay. A lot." I winced.

The corner of his mouth lifted, and he bumped his arm against mine. "I think we both said some things we didn't really mean."

"I know I sure did," I mumbled to myself, but judging by Nico's growing smirk, he'd heard it too. "Anyway, I've given this a lot of thought, so please—" I stopped, turning to face him, and rested my hand on his forearm. "Let me say what I need to say."

His eyes flashed to where I touched him before meeting mine. He gave a subtle nod. "It's not necessary, but okay."

"It wasn't your fault. I realize that now, but everything—" I blew out a long breath. "I think I just got scared—or at least that's what Jen thinks." A single nervous laugh slipped out. "I'm not very good at this kind of stuff. Talking about what I'm feeling. It's been a really long time since I've been on a date— before that night, I mean—and I guess I wasn't sure what to expect. Things are much different now than they were fifteen years ago. I'm different."

Nico nodded again but didn't interrupt me.

"Anyway, I guess I got a little crazy when I saw that woman with you."

He tilted his head, brows raised. "A little?"

"Sorry," I whispered then turned away, biting my lip.

"Hey, I was teasing. I understand what you're saying, but not everything was your fault that night." Nico nudged me with his elbow. "Danni, look at me."

I shook my head.

"I'm to blame for you feeling overwhelmed that night—or scared, as you put it."

I twisted enough to peek at him.

"I came on too strong. At least that's what Logan told me," Nico said with a wink, imitating my confused tone while borrowing my phrase. "It's just . . . I've made love to you in my mind so many times—" He shoved a hand through his hair, letting out a frustrated groan. "Sorry, I—that sounded better in my head."

Wait . . . what? Did I just imagine that or did he—nope. Judging by Nico's mortified expression, I'm pretty sure I heard him right.

"Seems Logan's lecture didn't help." Nico tucked his hands in his pockets with a nervous laugh. He tipped his head, motioning to continue on our walk. "Maybe we should just keep moving."

"Yeah. Sure." The shaky words squeaked out of me.

His admission played on a constant loop in my mind, filling the awkward silence that hung between us. Stirring up a massive swarm of butterflies in my stomach.

We reached the ice cream shop and stood in line at the window, waiting to place our order. The non-threatening, non-sexual topic of today's featured flavors and our go-to favorites led to a light and easy conversation that melted away some of the tension between us.

Nico paid then passed the cone topped with butter pecan to me. He placed his hand at the small of my back and gently guided me toward the wooden bridge arched across the pond. We stopped on the wide deck at its midpoint, laughing at the single-file parade of geese making their way across the grass then along the trail to the water's edge. One by one, they jumped in and ducked their heads under before splashing around.

"Danni, about earlier." Nico's solemn voice barely rose above a whisper. "I'm really sorry and hope I didn't scare you off with that uncensored glimpse of what goes on inside my head."

"You didn't." I peeked at him from the corner of my eye, catching a flash of his arched brows and skeptical stare. "You just . . . surprised me. I never would have expected you to say that." *At least, not to me.*

Nico let out a low hum. "Well, that makes two of us."

I turned to face him, hating his dejected tone. "Stop beating yourself up. I only meant I'm surprised you'd think about *me* like that."

"I don't understand why you'd—" He paused for a beat then shook his head. "Anyway, the point I was trying to make is that I'd gotten ahead of myself—on our date—forgot that I don't have the right to touch you and kiss you whenever I want. Without your permission." His eyes fell shut. When he opened them again, they locked on mine with an intense stare that reached deep into my soul. "Danni, I probably don't deserve it, but I'd like a second chance."

Nico moved closer, his shoulder pressing against mine. "We can start again with a clean slate. Take things slow. All I ask is that you try to trust me. And that you promise to talk things out when we run into problems—which I'm sure we will—

instead of shutting me out." He rested his hand on the railing in front of us, palm up, offering himself to me. Allowing me to choose. "I promise I'll try to do better. Just please promise you won't run away every time I screw up."

I swallowed hard against the lump in my throat, struggling to speak. "I can't promise." I placed my hand on his. "But I *can* promise I'll try."

Nico smiled and wove our fingers together. "I'll take it." He winked. "And I'll try not to screw up too much."

I glanced at our joined hands, his finger rubbing along the band of my diamond solitaire. My reminder to proceed with caution. "Trust doesn't come easy for me anymore, not since—"

Nico nodded. "Yeah, I get that." He released my hand and blew out a slow breath.

We fell into a comfortable silence and finished our ice cream, enjoying each other's company and the beautiful spring day. Nico rested his arms on the railing, hands folded, and stared out at the water while I studied every detail of his handsome face.

"You look like there's something on your mind."

One corner of his mouth lifted up. "That obvious, huh?" He rubbed his jaw, scratching at the stubble covering it. "I want to ask you something, but I'm not sure how to go about it." He shifted to face me, leaning on one elbow. His eyes locked on mine. "Give me a chance to get all this out before you say anything. Or jump to any conclusions."

"Okay." I drew the word out and nodded, a sense of dread settling in the pit of my stomach. Had he changed his mind already? Regretted asking to start over?

"It's nothing bad. Promise." He stretched his pinkie to the side and tapped it against mine, a hint of a grin on his lips. "My family hosts a fundraising event at Elevations every year. A three-day extravaganza." He made air quotes on the last word then lifted one shoulder. "It attracts a lot of business folks —entrepreneurs with deep pockets, and a few celebrity types."

He reached out to stroke a stray strand of my hair, absently twisting his finger in it as he continued. A shiver from the gentle brush of his hand traveled straight to my core. Focusing on his words while my body made other plans became difficult.

"The money raised goes to help cancer patients and their families." He dropped his hand to mine and paused, his gaze digging deeper into my soul. "I want you to come with me. For the weekend."

My breath hitched, catching in my throat. My body screamed *yes*, but my head needed time to process his invitation. Overanalyze it. I'd only ever been with Will. My gaze fell as panic grew. "I—"

His grip on my hand tightened. "You'll have your own room. No expectations." He placed a finger under my chin, lifting my face toward his. "I promise. I just want us to spend some time together. Get to know each other better." He took my other hand and stepped closer. "I know you worry about being seen with me. About people judging you. What they'll think or say. This is our perfect 'clean slate' for starting over. No one at the gala will know you, aside from my family. And they *fully* support us dating."

"Nico, I—" A whirlwind of contradictory emotions pulsed through me, pulling my thoughts in different directions. "I'm not sure what—"

Nico placed a gentle finger to my lips. "I don't want an answer right now." He leaned closer. His gaze fell to my mouth.

My heart raced as I waited for him to kiss me. Every cell in my body screamed for him to do it. Couldn't he hear them?

Nico let out a shuddered breath. "Take some time and think about it."

He pulled me into his embrace. My body melted against

his, savoring every hard inch of proof that he wanted me as much as I needed him.

"I will." I kissed his neck before resting my cheek over his pounding heart, letting my eyes fall closed.

Nico stroked the length of my back, his fingers flexing against my hips each time but not moving past. He let out a low groan and pulled away. "You ready to head home?"

NEITHER ONE OF us said much on the walk home, but Nico held my hand the whole way. His invitation played over and over in my mind, making my insides swirl. How many nights— and days—had I dreamed of Nico sweeping me off my feet, whisking me away for a romantic weekend? But no expectations? *Hmm . . . maybe he doesn't have any, but I sure do.*

We reached my house and climbed the two steps to my porch.

"I had a really nice time." Nico released my hand and leaned his shoulder against the doorframe, arms crossed. He watched me with a curious expression.

"I did too." I slipped my key in the lock and hesitated. "Are you . . . um . . . coming inside?"

He ran a hand through his hair and gave a thoughtful sigh. "I still don't think that would be a very good idea."

I nodded and stepped across the threshold, trying to hide my disappointment.

Nico caught my wrist. "Don't run. We both know what would happen if I stayed." He tugged my arm, forcing me to face him. "And we'd both regret it."

I swallowed hard, avoiding his gaze. "Would we? Because right now, I don't think I would."

He pushed away from the doorframe and closed the distance between us. The energy flowing from him made every inch of my body tingle with the need to be touched. He placed a finger under my chin, lifting it until our eyes met. "The gala at Elevations is the weekend after next. Take some time to think about my invitation."

"It's all I've been able to think about for the past twenty minutes."

Nico brushed the side of my face, his gaze searching my soul. "Hopefully, they've been good thoughts."

"Mm-hmm . . ." Although I could barely remember my own name when he touched me like that.

"But I don't want you to give me an answer tonight." His hand slipped behind my neck, sending a new wave of desire straight to my core.

"Are you going to kiss me?" My faint question sounded more like a plea.

Nico shifted his weight and inched closer. "I'm trying not to, but—"

His mouth covered mine, devouring it with a hungry kiss. He released my wrist, wrapping his arm around my waist to hold me tighter. My body pulsed, begging for more. I raised my hand to his face and wove my fingers through his hair, clinging to him. To this moment.

Nico broke our kiss, leaving us both breathless. He pressed his forehead to mine. "Christ, Danni. I swear I have no self-control around you."

I brushed my lips against his ear. "You say that like it's a bad thing."

He held me by the waist with both hands and pulled away, shaking his head. "That's because it is." A lopsided grin spread across his face.

I stretched on my toes and pressed my lips to his for a slow, sweet kiss.

Nico hummed against my lips. "Okay, maybe it's not *all* bad."

"So does that mean you're coming in?" I smiled up at him.

He laughed. "Not a chance. Call me when you've made a decision about the gala." He framed my face and pressed his lips to mine for one more quick kiss before turning to leave.

I closed the door, leaning against it for support while my legs regained strength, then let out a scream and danced around the foyer. "Oh. My. God. Did this afternoon really just happen?"

My FINGER HOVERED over Jen's number, my mind a total blank. I'd spent the past hour pacing the full length of my house and practicing what I'd tell her. My heart pounded an erratic rhythm, and my hands shook to the beat. For some strange reason, I felt as though I needed Jen's permission to go away with Nico.

Maybe I just needed her to give me a push.

I'm a forty-year-old woman. Why can't I just say yes?

"Danni? You there?" Jen's voice called through the phone's speaker.

"Nico wants me to go away for a weekend. What should I do?" *So much for my elegant speech.*

Jen's response—a shrill cheer peppered with bursts of creative expletives—surpassed my anxious explosion of words. Panic rose in my chest, the reality of my dilemma sinking in, along with the sudden realization that my sister might not be able to provide objective, unbiased advice when it came to Nico. I moved to the couch, hugging a pillow as I tucked my feet under me and settled in for a long chat . . . eventually.

I waited patiently until Jen finally calmed down. "You done screaming?"

She let out a dreamy sigh. "I'm just so happy for you. I knew it would only be a matter of time before he asked you out again, but a whole weekend? Wow, he doesn't mess around, does he? Oh, wait . . . more like he does. Or at least he plans to."

Jen laughed at her lame attempt at a joke then continued to ramble on, far too giddy and excited. I probably could have put down the phone and wandered to the kitchen for a glass of wine without her noticing I was gone.

"Wait. You did say yes, didn't you?"

I blew out a long breath. "He told me to take some time and think about it. That's what I'm doing." I pressed my palm to my forehead, working to loosen some of the tension there, and groaned. "Who am I kidding? I don't know what to tell him."

I backed up to the beginning and filled Jen in on all the details of Nico's surprise visit, our walk, our decision to start over, and the amazing way he'd kissed me at the end of our impromptu date.

"Thing is, we *barely* know each other. And a whole weekend . . . what do we even talk about for all that time?"

"Well, when you run out of things to talk about, you'll just have to get creative. Find *other* ways to . . . communicate." She chuckled.

"Not. Funny." My eyes fell closed, and images of the ways I *wished* I could "communicate" with Nico flashed in my mind. But the reality was I'd likely panic again, the way I had at Metro Sky when I'd thought Nico wanted to have sex.

"Sorry." The laughter in Jen's voice suggested otherwise. "Please continue."

I shook away the memories of that night and pushed on. "Part of me thinks this is all so sudden—too soon to go away together. Another part wonders why bother taking me away for a weekend if we aren't even going to share a room?" *Despite wondering if I'll ever be ready for more. Ready to explore the way Nico makes me feel with just a gentle touch. A kiss.* I massaged my temples and sighed. "I want to say yes, but . . . I guess I'm just confused."

Especially since an even bigger part of me wants to know why I haven't already called him to accept.

"The grass hasn't even grown over Will's grave yet, and I'm thinking about running off for a weekend of . . . whatever 'no expectations' involves. I mean, how would that even look? Whether we shared a room or not."

"You seem to have forgotten Will was doing that himself. And you were—are—still alive."

I shook my head, not that she could see it, but the mounting frustration needed to escape somewhere. "Not the same thing. No one knew about that."

"And no one there is going to know about Will or care about your past. Danni, it's okay for you to be happy. For once in your life, listen to your heart. What's it telling you to do?" She waited quietly while I thought.

"I—I don't know. It's telling me not to let someone break it again."

"Then I guess you have some more thinking to do. But, Danni? You deserve this. You deserve to have fun. And you deserve a chance at finding true love. Maybe Nico's not the guy you're meant to be with, but maybe he is. If you keep your heart locked up, afraid to take chances, you'll never find out."

AND THE ANSWER IS
DANNI

Thoughts of Nico had occupied every hour of every day—and night—since he'd left my house Sunday afternoon, which was also the last time I'd heard from him. A fact that annoying little voice of insecurity cowering in the back of my mind continued to harp on, insisting his silence all week could only mean he'd changed his mind but was trying to avoid an awkward "never mind" conversation. She made a good point, but I had to hope she was wrong. That he was just giving me time and space to think.

Last night, I'd laid awake for hours thinking about Nico's invitation, my feelings for him, and Jen's advice to follow my heart before eventually drifting off to sleep. The sweetest dreams followed, filling my head with a steady stream of scenes from my future life—joyful moments, created by my own mind, with only one thing in common. They *all* contained Nico.

If that's not my heart telling me what it wants, I don't know what is.

I stepped out onto the deck and stretched one arm toward the sky, breathing in the crisp morning air while birds chirped in a nearby tree. I loved spring—the end of cold, dreary winter and the promise of new life. For the first time in a long time, I was eager to start my day—the first day of *my* new life—because after spending six whole days listing reasons to go away with Nico or turn him down, constantly changing my mind, second-guessing myself and him, and driving myself crazy with all that indecision, I'd finally made my choice—right or wrong—and today I would give Nico my answer.

I sipped the last of my coffee and wandered back into the kitchen, drawn to his business card on the counter. The flyer for birthing classes beside it reminded me I also needed to call Alexia to see if she'd made a decision about attending, but that could wait until later today. Or tomorrow.

Returning my attention to Nico's card, I traced my fingers across the numbers I already knew by heart. He'd told me to call when I was ready to give him my answer, but why just call when giving him my answer in person would be much more fun?

I raced up the stairs and changed into the tiny bits of spandex I'd worn the day I'd gone to The Next Level with Kendra—the day she'd set me up to run into Nico at his gym. The memory of him grinning while unabashedly eavesdropping on our conversation about him popped in my mind.

"Someday I should thank her for that."

Someday. But not today. "So let's just hope I don't run into her when I get there."

Or Trina, Nico's gym-rat groupie. Although it would be fun to see the look on Trina's face when I walked up to Nico and kissed him, then led him into his office so we could talk in private.

An uncontrollable smile stretched across my face. I shoved a few essential items in my bag and grabbed a pair of sneakers from the closet, pausing at the mirror for one last check before rushing off to claim that kiss. I ran down the stairs, rushed to the garage, and tapped the opener. The motor rumbled, and the door rose to reveal a steel-blue Ferrari parked in my driveway.

Nico stood frozen mid-pace in front of his car, dressed in a business suit, both hands gripping the back of his head. His wide eyes locked on mine.

"Nico?" I drew in a sharp breath and pressed a hand over my pounding heart. "I didn't—what are you doing here?"

"You didn't call." Nico shrugged then moved toward the garage, stopping at the entrance. "And I couldn't stay away anymore."

He folded his arms across his broad chest and leaned against the doorframe, crossing one ankle over the other—a casual stance that didn't match the tense set of his jaw. He strummed his fingers, apparently waiting for a response. The sun reflected off the diamond in his signet ring with each movement, reminding me of the night we'd met at Logan's New Year's Eve party—when this confident, sexy man had pulled up a chair and invited himself to join me. I'd immediately realized he was different from any other man I'd know.

My gaze wandered down his tailored suit to his designer shoes, every inch of him pure perfection. But that was only superficial. The man inside was far more complex—a proverbial man of many layers.

And I couldn't wait to explore each and every one of them.

I risked a glance at his face, troubled by his uneasy expression. I couldn't imagine any *single* woman had ever said no to him, yet he seemed so unsure of my response. Anxious.

"I was taking time to think. Like you told me?" My bag slipped from my shoulder as I strolled through the garage and stopped behind my car, directly in front of Nico.

His jaw flexed, but he didn't move. Didn't respond.

"I, um, was just on my way out." I let my bag drop to the floor then leaned against the trunk for support, reaching back with both hands to grip the edge. "On my way to see *you*, actually." I bit my lip and peeked up at him through my lashes. "To surprise you."

"Really." Nico hummed, rubbing the stubble along his jaw. He pushed away from the wall and closed the short distance between us with slow steps.

I pressed my hands to his chest, halting his progress. Trying to maintain a safe distance between us—one that would allow me to focus on what I needed to say instead of how much I wanted to wrap myself around him and never let go. The corner of Nico's mouth twitched up. He reached past me to rest his palms on the car, surrounding me with his presence.

"So . . ." He dipped his head, his cheek brushing against mine. "Does that mean you have an answer for me?"

I drew in a deep breath of his intoxicating scent. "I just want you to know I really *have* given your invitation a lot of thought."

He lifted his head to meet my gaze, a silent acknowledgement encouraging me to continue.

"And this has probably been one of the toughest decisions I've ever made." Of course, the hardest had been pushing him away to save my marriage—which had also turned out to be my worst decision ever.

Nico's jaw tensed, and a crease formed between his brows. "Should I be concerned?"

"I don't think either of us can deny there's some kind of . . . I don't know, uncontrollable force or something that keeps pulling us together.

"Mm-hmm." He inched closer, but I pushed harder against his chest, biting back a smile.

"I want to trust you. But, as much as I hate to admit this, I'm in a pretty vulnerable place right now. Emotionally. The idea of opening myself up enough to let someone in again scares me. A lot."

Nico coasted his finger up my arms. "I get it." His eyes fell closed. He nodded then rested his forehead against mine.

"I keep thinking how easily you could break my heart one day. Walk out my door and never return."

"Danni, I—"

"But I don't want that day to be today." *Or ever, really.*

Nico angled his head. "So . . . what are you saying?"

"I'm saying yes. I'd love to go away with you. Start over. Clean slate and all—"

Nico's lips crushed against mine, claiming me with a powerful kiss that stole my breath. He pulled away, grinning, his eyes searching mine. "You really had me worried, you know? I thought you were turning me down."

"Guess you don't realize just how irresistible you are."

A faint chuckle rumbled in his chest. "I'm glad you think so."

Nico skimmed his fingers along my arms, his touch leaving a trail of goosebumps—a tingling that spread through my entire body. An involuntary sigh slipped past my lips, and I melted against him. His chest rose and fell on shaky breaths, the erratic rhythm matching my own.

Telling him in person had definitely turned out to be a great idea. Although he'd surprised me before I could go to him, so I really couldn't claim credit there. But I could still claim victory. And my prize.

Nico slipped his arms around my waist and pulled me into his strong embrace, making no visible effort to hide his body's impressive reaction to me. Time stood still as we held each other. A perfect moment.

I let my hands fall from his shoulders, exploring his solid torso and the ridges of his abdomen buried beneath their designer packaging—clothing that was probably not his usual weekend attire and warned he was only passing through on his way to someplace more important.

Nico hooked a finger under my chin, tilting my face toward his. The hungry look in his dark eyes erased my irrational judgment of whatever plans he had for today. He covered my mouth with sweet, gentle kisses, each one making me want more—more of this. More of him.

Before I could ask him to come inside, he broke our kiss and brushed his cheek against mine. "We should stop. Take things slow, like I promised."

I stretched on my toes and pressed my lips to his.

"Or not." Nico laughed against my mouth before taking control.

His arm around my waist hugged me closer. His other hand glided to the back of my head, supporting it against the increasing pressure of his lips against mine as his kiss grew more passionate. Nico grabbed my waist and lifted me onto the trunk of my car, continuing his ravenous attack of my mouth. His hands slid over my hips and down my thighs, fingers flexing and digging into my skin through the thin layer of spandex. He eased my knees apart, creating space for him to move between them, and tugged me closer.

I wanted to lose control—take whatever Nico was willing to give me—and shamelessly wrapped my legs around him. He groaned into my mouth and rocked his hips against me, sending an intense wave of pleasure rolling through my entire body. I slipped one hand inside his jacket and tugged on his shirt, but Nico clamped a hand over my wrist and stopped me.

His head fell to my shoulder. "Christ, what am I doing?" He stood there, frozen, for what felt like an eternity then shook his head and stepped back, holding me at arm's length. "This is definitely *not* taking things slow."

Slowing down is not a rejection. At least that was what I kept telling myself—over and over—while Nico drew in several long, slow, steady breaths.

"I'm sorry," he whispered.

I slid off the trunk, still breathing hard and dealing with the throbbing between my legs. "First of all, you weren't *doing* anything I didn't want. Or start. So the only thing you need to apologize about is stopping."

He raised one finger between us and stepped back, shaking his head with a laugh while his hungry gaze swept over me. "Resisting you is going to be real challenge," he mumbled then motioned over his shoulder. "I'm gonna go. Before I break that promise again."

Nico gave a wink, turning to leave, but paused before getting into his car. He glanced at his watch then back at me, leaning on his opened door.

"I wish we could spend more time together—in a public place where I'd be forced to control myself, of course—but I have a meeting I need to get to. Out of town. And then I'll be in New York the rest of the weekend. With Logan. We have some details to go over before his launch." Nico rubbed his neck and groaned. He looked at his watch again. "Guess I'll have to wait until Friday to see you again."

Six more long days apart, then I'd have a whole weekend with Nico . . . and my own *fun* challenge of wearing down his stubborn self-control so we could finish what we'd started today. *Because Jen's right. I do deserve to be happy.*

I blew him a kiss and waved, a huge smile on my face. "I can't wait."

YOU GOT MY BACK?

NICO

One rule—honesty.

Danni had one fucking rule about relationships—not a secret, since she'd mentioned it multiple times—and I'd broken it less than five minutes into our clean slate, fresh start do-over.

It wasn't intentional—at least not all of it. But it wasn't as though I had any other choice. There was no way she'd believe the truth. Hell, I barely believed it.

I pressed a button on my steering wheel. "Call Logan."

"Hey, stranger." His voice sounded from my car's speakers. "I was starting to think you were avoiding me."

I was. "It's been a rough week."

"Sorry, man." The teasing tone disappeared from his voice. "Everything okay?"

I let out a long groan. "I'm not even sure how to answer that. But listen, I need a favor. What are you up to this week-end?" Probably should have known before using him for an alibi, but the damage was already done there.

"Just hanging out. Kendra's at some cheer contest thing

with Callie, so I'm on my own. Care to join me? I'm sure we could find some kind of trouble to get into."

"Can't." I pulled onto the highway, weaving through traffic and cutting across lanes, savoring the rush of adrenaline. "But I told Danni I was gonna spend the weekend with you."

"Okay." Logan drew out the word. "And do I *want* to know why you told her that?"

"Probably not." I let out a single, humorless laugh. "Let's just say the less you know, the better."

"Does that mean you're about to do something stupid?"

"It means I need to take care of something, and I'm counting on my best friend to help me avoid another fight with Danni and a ton of meddling from my family."

Logan gave a short hum. "Yeah, I get it. And lying makes a really strong foundation for a relationship." He paused, maybe expecting me to disagree. "What's your plan B?"

"Don't have one," I snapped.

"Not surprised," he grumbled. "What's so important you're willing to risk fucking things up with Danni? Because you know how she feels about honesty."

"Of course I know." That was how I'd wound up in this whole fucking mess of a situation. "I have . . . a meeting. At noon."

"Meeting someone for lunch. Got it. Business?"

Here we go. "Personal."

"And how does that become a weekend event?" He let out a frustrated sigh. "I'm afraid to even ask who you're . . . *meeting* with."

Christ, he emphasized the word as though it was code for fucking. "Lunch, Logan. In public. No sex."

A long silence followed—typical Logan. This conversation wasn't going any further, which meant he wasn't about to help me, unless I divulged a few details. Gave him at least one pertinent nugget of information. Fuck.

"I'm meeting Summer." I pinched the bridge of my nose, dreading his reaction.

A loud tapping noise came through the speakers. "I'm sorry . . . I could've sworn you said you were sneaking around behind Danni's back to meet your ex?"

He paused, most likely for dramatic effect. He'd clearly heard me. No need to repeat it.

"Are you fucking crazy? Hasn't she screwed up enough of your life? And please . . . *please* don't tell me you're going to throw away everything with Danni to take that cheating bitch back."

"No. Hell yes. And not a fucking chance." The fact that he could even think I wanted anything to do with Summer was ridiculous. "You forgetting you're the one who ordered me to talk to her?"

"Talk. On the phone. As in, have Tricia put her through next time she calls." His weary response oozed with repressed frustration.

Right there with you, buddy. "I tried that, but we're talking about Summer here."

Logan gave an empathetic grunt.

"Anyway, she would only say it's important and something I'd want to know about. Insisted she needed to tell me in person." I took the exit toward Pine Ridge, slowing down enough to navigate the sharp turn. The restaurant we'd agreed on should be right up the road.

"I don't know, man. Feels like a trap."

"Yeah, the thought crossed my mind too. But she's threatening to show up at the gala if I don't meet her today. Danni's going to be there with me, so I'm just trying to avoid another disaster."

"That's big news, and we'll circle back to it later, but it doesn't explain why you'd need to lie about being busy all weekend long."

"Yeah, that part's kinda embarrassing." A pathetic laugh slipped out. "I panicked. Worried Danni would somehow sense I'd been with another woman. Not *been with*, but . . . dammit, you know what I mean. Anyway, I just didn't want to risk making her think I was cheating."

"So you went with lying instead. Only you." Logan laughed. "Do what you gotta do, but you really need to talk to Danni."

I pulled into the parking lot of the Pinnacle and found a suitable, out-of-the-way space. "So you got my back?"

"Against my better judgment, but you know I do. Just don't fuck things up."

I let out a heavy breath. "Thanks, man. I owe you."

"Damn right, and you know I'll collect. Anyway, since we're both free for the weekend, why don't you drag your ass up here after your little meeting? We can hang out, grab a few beers, clear your head—and your conscience, since you technically wouldn't have told Danni a lie then."

"Not sure I agree with that last part. But yeah, it might be good to get away. I'll give you a call when I get in."

DRIVE TO ELEVATIONS

DANNI

'd been pacing the foyer for over an hour, waiting for Nico to pick me up. He'd said he'd be here at seven. I checked my phone for the twentieth time. Six fifty-three. *Any minute now.*

Six and a half days ago, the idea of spending a weekend together sounded exciting. Fun. Now? Well, I'd had all that time to think and realized the implications of this little adventure. And the risks. Not to mention that fuzzy issue of "expectations," or a lack of them, as the case may—or may not—be.

I took a few more steps, twisting and tugging at the gold band around my finger—my constant reminder of what can happen when I open my heart to someone. My reminder that "forever" is a lie.

I'd taken it off and put it back on at least three times while getting dressed after my shower, toying with the idea of leaving it home this weekend and letting my guard down—being free and adventurous—but the risk was too great. If things went the way I hoped they would with Nico, my foolish heart could easily get the wrong idea about our relationship.

Of course, I still planned to explore my feelings for Nico

and hopefully convince him to come to my side of the "expectations" debate. I'd just have to proceed with caution.

Nico's car approached, the engine's distinctive rumble growing louder then stopping in my driveway. A door closed, followed by footsteps on my front porch, then the doorbell.

This is it. My heart pounded an erratic beat while I waited, hand hovering mid-air, poised to open the door . . . right after enough time had passed for me to walk here from the couch.

Nico stepped up to the threshold and captured my face between his hands. He pulled me to him, greeting me with a kiss that made my knees weak. "Hello, beautiful." He brushed his thumb across my lips, a satisfied smile on his face, then stole another quick kiss. "You ready to go?"

"Yeah, I-I was kinda rushing, but . . . I think I have everything." I glanced over my shoulder at my two suitcases along the wall.

Nico laughed, wrapping his arms around me. "You do know we're only going for the weekend, right?"

"I couldn't make up my mind." I lifted one shoulder, averting my gaze as my cheeks grew warm. "Guess I got a little carried away."

Nico moved past me to collect my bags. He loaded the car while I locked up, then we were on our way. Soft rock music drifted from the car's speakers, just loud enough to break the current state of silence but quiet enough to invite conversation.

I folded my arms in my lap and let out a long sigh, staring out the passenger's window. The ride to Elevations would take forty-five minutes, which was a really long time to hold a conversation with someone you barely knew—especially when nervous—so I'd put a lot of thought into creating a mental list of topics we could discuss. But the moment I climbed into Nico's car, my mind went blank, and now all I could think about was the gorgeous man beside me.

Every slow, deep breath I took filled me with the subtle

scent of his cologne—light, airy, sophisticated. It suited him so well. I stifled a satisfied hum and settled back in my seat, gaze fixed on the windshield.

Mostly.

The evening sky ahead of us was beautiful, turning shades of pink and purple as the sun sank into the clouds, but I couldn't keep my eyes off of my handsome date. He zipped through traffic, the muscles of his forearm flexing as he shifted gears. Powerful. So in control.

"Enjoying the ride?" Nico cast a glance in my direction, one corner of his mouth lifting in a slow grin.

"I am." I chewed on my lip and angled to face him. "The scenery is stunning."

A low chuckle rumbled in his chest. "Glad you approve."

His playful tone and the wink that followed made it pretty clear he'd caught me watching him. That tiny gesture, his casual confidence, set off a spark that made my skin tingle.

I loved the effect he had on me. Could easily become addicted to it. Probably already had, if I were to be honest. I'd been craving more of it—more of him—since the day he'd taken me to Giardano's on our non-date . . . which, looking back, may have been more of a date than either of us wanted to admit at the time.

Warm memories of that day flooded my mind. The way Nico had looked at me. Touched me. And how much I'd enjoyed just being there, talking to him.

"What are you smiling at?" Nico's amused tone brought me back to the present.

I twisted toward him and leaned on my elbow, arching one eyebrow. "Shouldn't you be focused on the road, Mario?"

Nico's shoulders shook with a quiet laugh. "Touché." He rubbed his jaw and gave a thoughtful hum. "You know, I can't decide if you're comparing my driving to Mr. Andretti or you think I look like the little guy in those video games. And I'm probably afraid to ask."

"I'll never tell." I relaxed into my seat again and returned my attention to the colorful sunset but continued to sneak peeks at Nico.

His eyes stayed focused straight ahead. "I'm really glad we're doing this." He slid his hand from the gearshift and rested it, palm up, on the console between us.

"Me too." I placed my hand on his. Holding hands—the most basic of romantic gestures, but it felt perfect. Right.

Nico brushed his thumb across the back of my hand. His chest rose and fell on a single heavy breath, and he cleared his throat. "So . . ." He released me and shifted gears, accelerating to change lanes and catch the next exit. "You still didn't tell me what had you smiling."

I bit back a grin. "If you must know, I was thinking about this really hot guy who asked me out."

Nico let out a playful growl. "You better be talking about me, sweetheart." He flashed a grin and offered his hand again.

"Of course I was." With a featherlight touch, I traced circles along his palm, drifting up the exposed portion of his forearm. "You're the only really hot guy I know."

His fingers flexed, curling up to touch mine. "You're making it very hard for me to keep my mind on the road."

"Sorry." I laced my fingers through his and fought the urge to let my thumb continue caressing him.

"Don't be." Nico raised our joined hands to his lips, pressing a kiss to the inside of my wrist, then lowered them to rest on his thigh. "We'll be there soon." He flashed a sexy smile that made my skin tingle. "And then you can distract me as much as you want."

We rode like that for several minutes in silence, but every cell in my body was screaming with excitement. Anticipation.

"So, um, tell me what we'll be doing this weekend." I cringed at the nervous hitch in my voice, hoping he hadn't heard it.

Nico laughed and gave my fingers a gentle squeeze. "We'll settle in and relax tonight. There's an art display set up for silent auction, but we don't need to go to that." He released me to shift, turning onto a steep, winding mountain road. "Tomorrow morning I'll need to work a few hours to make sure everything is set up and in order for the gala, which will be that evening."

"Oh." My shoulders sagged. We hadn't discussed the details before, but I'd assumed we'd be together the whole time.

Nico reached over and brushed my cheek. "Stop pouting. Gabs told me I'm not allowed to invite you for a fun weekend then dump you while I work."

"I think I'm gonna like her."

"You will. And she's gonna love you as much as—the rest of my family already does." Nico shook his head. "Anyway, I thought you might enjoy a relaxing morning at the spa. You can get a massage, facial, manicure . . . anything you want. You won't even care that I'm not around."

I gave a thoughtful hum, considering my response. "I'm sure I'll still miss you, but it does sound nice." And a bit intimi-dating since I'd never gone to a spa without my friends before —and only after they'd guilted me into joining them—but I appreciated Nico's thoughtfulness and kept that part to myself.

"Good. It's already scheduled." Nico dragged a finger across his forehead in mock relief. "After you're finished there, we'll meet up for lunch and spend the day together. Sunday morning we can sleep in, then have brunch with my family before we go back home." Nico pulled up outside the grand entrance to Elevations.

"We're here already? I thought you promised not to speed," I teased, remembering our conversation last night about the adrenalin rush I'd gotten on my first ride with him. Nico had promised, with a playful lack of sincerity, to "take my concerns about his driving habits under consideration since going slow was the new theme for our relationship," even though it would spoil his fun.

"I didn't."

"Didn't speed, or didn't promise?"

He chuckled as he climbed out of the car and moved around to my side, a lighthearted grin still in place. "Little bit of both."

After helping me to my feet, he collected our bags from the efficient bellhop who'd already retrieved them from the trunk, thanking him with a friendly pat on the back. "No worries, Sal. I'll get these."

Nico tossed his travel bag over his shoulder. He rolled my two suitcases with one hand and took my hand in his other, leading me through the large glass doors and down the wide marble walkway toward the elevator at the far end of the elegant lobby.

"Relax," he whispered. "Were gonna take things slow. No expectations, remember?"

Once inside the elevator, Nico dug in his pocket then reached past me to insert the penthouse key in the panel. Every other button went dark, and the elevator moved toward the top floor.

"What are you smiling about?" He grabbed my waist, pulling me close.

"Aside from the fact that I'm going to spend the whole weekend at this beautiful resort with *you*?" I snuggled into his chest, drawing in a deep breath. "I was just thinking about the last time we rode this elevator together. Do you remember it?"

"Of course. What I would have given to be the one holding you that day." His hand slipped lower, caressing my hip.

Maybe Jen was right about Nico's *expectations* after all.

During one of my many melt-down calls to my sister this week, she'd insisted he had them—because *all* guys did—but he was probably just trying to act like a "perfect gentleman" so I'd agree to go away with him.

I pulled away enough to glance up at Nico, biting my lip to hold back a hopeful smile, and tipped my head toward his hand.

"Oops." Nico glanced at me from the corner of his eye wearing a mischievous grin that was anything *but* apologetic. He walked his fingers back up to my waist, rested them in a very PG-rated position, and winked. "Sorry. Reflex." Nico's lips brushed my ear when he spoke, and a soft chuckle followed. "Won't happen again."

"Hmm . . . you sure?" I snuggled into his side and wrapped my arms around his waist, all the excitement I'd felt last weekend returning in a rush. "Because I was kinda hoping it would."

THE ELEVATOR OPENED to a large foyer with the same marble floors and Mediterranean blue hues as the lobby and main areas. Nico pulled open the white double doors, motioning for me to enter. "Here we are."

The penthouse suite looked like a luxury apartment. The great room in the center was warm and welcoming. Large picture windows framed a stone fireplace on the far wall. Cream-colored leather couches piled with blue pillows sat on an ocean-blue area rug.

"Wow, this is so beautiful." To the left of the great room, three steps rose to a small landing with white French doors. "What's through there?"

"That's Nonno's wing, my grandfather's. He lives here." Nico shook his head and laughed. "He's probably downstairs getting into trouble. We'll find him later." He placed his hand in the small of my back. "Let's get you settled into your room first."

He led me past a gourmet kitchen with granite counters and a large island in the center. The room flowed into a cozy alcove with a crystal chandelier centered above a family-sized dining table. We moved into a wide hallway with four white doors.

"Ben, Gabriela, and I all have rooms here. With our long hours, sometimes it's just easier than driving home every night." He walked past the first two doors and continued to the end of the hall. He opened the door on the right and flipped on a light, stepping back to allow me to enter first. "This is the guest room."

I pulled a hand to my chest as I wandered the spacious room, taking in the elegant decor and amazing view. Plush pillows lined a cozy window seat overlooking a large, lighted hill that appeared to be one of the ski runs, although there wouldn't be any snow covering the grassy slope for the next six months.

A bouquet of white roses sat in the center of a small round table by the bed. "They're beautiful." I stroked the silky petals before bending over to breathe in the familiar sweet scent.

"Almost as beautiful as you." Nico hadn't moved from the doorway.

I dragged my hand along the raised king-sized bed, flashing a glance at him. "This is an awfully big bed for just one person."

He hesitated, following me with his eyes. "My room is across the hall." He dragged a hand through his hair and cleared his throat. "There's a closet around the corner, and you have your own bath through there." He motioned to the door at the far side of the room.

"Why don't you take a few minutes to unpack and settle

in?" He hoisted my bags onto the bed. "And I can make us something to eat. What would you like?"

Um, you. "I'm not hungry, but if you want—"

"Nope. Just trying to be a good host." Nico moved to stand in front of me and took my hands. "How 'bout a walk instead?"

"A walk sounds perfect." *Or at least safe.* I forced a smile to hide my disappointment.

"Take your time." He brushed a strand of hair from my face, letting his hand glide along the side of my neck to rest on my shoulder. Wearing a tight grin, he tipped his head toward the great room. "I'll be out on the couch."

I MANAGED to find a home for the excessive amount of clothing I'd brought with me for the weekend then wandered toward the great room, slowing at the sound of two men's voices. Nico stood talking to a silver-haired man who turned around when I approached, a bright smile spreading across his face.

"Ms. Danni. *Buona sera.* It is so nice to see you again." He placed his hands on my shoulders, leaning in to kiss my cheeks.

"Ernesto?" I looked at Nico, confused about finding his limo driver in the suite. "Are we going somewhere?"

Nico's gaze shifted from me to Ernesto then back again, a crease forming between his brows. He shook his head and laughed. "Ah . . . that's right. I forgot you met when you had your girls' night at Metro Sky." Nico placed his hand at the small of my back. "Allow me to *officially* introduce my grandfather. Remember I told you he likes to fill in?"

Ernesto wagged a finger at Nico. "And it's a good thing I was there that night. 'Tis a shame for a beautiful young lady to run away in tears."

"*Si, Nonno.* I've apologized to Danni." He slid his hand to my waist, pulling me tight to his side.

"He has," I said.

Ernesto laid his hand on Nico's cheek. "That's because my Nico, he's a good boy." He leaned toward me and lowered his voice. "But he has been known to break a lot of hearts."

"I can imagine he does." *And hope mine doesn't become one of them.* "But I was as much to blame for our . . . misunderstanding that night."

Nico cleared his throat. "All right, you two. Don't forget I'm standing right here." He flexed his fingers against my waist and pulled me closer. "Danni and I were going to take a walk, but we can stay here and watch a movie if you'd like some company."

Ernesto chuckled. "You two don't want an old man—even one as charming as me—hanging around." He turned to wink at me. "Enjoy your evening. Danni and I, we get to know each other tomorrow. *Si?* I make breakfast." Without waiting for an answer, he kissed both our cheeks then moved toward his room. "*Buono notte.*"

CHANGE OF PLANS
DANNI

"Where are we going?"

"For a walk." Nico laughed and nudged my side. "There's a path that circles the lake. We can walk for a while if you want, but there are also spots where we can just sit and relax." Nico closed the door then took my hand, lacing our fingers together. He pulled me to him and kissed my cheek. "Thank you." His words were a whisper.

"For what?" I hadn't done anything.

"Being here. Agreeing to come this weekend." He smoothed his thumb across the spot his lips had touched. "I imagine it wasn't an easy decision for you."

I leaned into his touch, loving the feel of his skin on mine. "Nothing in my life is easy anymore, but choosing whether to spend time with you is definitely the best problem I have."

The dim moonlight illuminating Nico's face revealed a lopsided grin and his adorable single dimple. He gave my hand a gentle squeeze then started down a cobblestone path away from the building. We strolled for a few minutes in comfortable silence, enjoying each other's company and the sounds of nature.

"Was there rain in the forecast?" I held up my palm. "Because I'm pretty sure I felt a few rather large drops."

"There wasn't. I checked while you were unpacking." Nico looked up, swiped the back of his hand across his face, then laughed and made an exaggerated show of shaking it dry. "But I think you may be right. We should probably—"

A bright flash of lightning lit the sky, followed by booming thunder and a torrential downpour.

"Head back?" I shouted, finishing Nico's sentence.

"Exactly! This way." He tugged my arm, dragging me in a different direction than the one we'd taken to get here. "I know a shortcut."

We sprinted, hunched over, each with one arm thrown over our heads as though it would somehow help keep us dry. I struggled to keep up, my wet fingers slipping through Nico's as he led the way across the courtyard toward an unmarked door. We ducked inside, shrieking with laughter, and shook off the cool spring rain.

"Well *that* didn't go as planned." Nico cradled my face, pushing away the wet hair clinging to it. "Guess we'll need to come up with a new one."

I tapped my jaw and hummed, pretending to think. "We should probably get out of these wet clothes."

"You think so, huh?" Nico moved closer, a teasing sparkle in his eyes. He traced the backs of his fingers along my arm.

The featherlight touch made me shiver. "See? I'm already getting chills."

Nico shook his head, failing to suppress a grin. "What am I gonna do with you?" He pressed his fingers over my mouth before I could offer my suggestions. "Rhetorical question . . . don't answer. How 'bout we go someplace public to dry out instead?"

I smiled against his fingers and motioned for him to lean

closer. "I've never really been into *that* sort of thing, but I guess we could give it a try."

Nico groaned, lowering his forehead to my shoulder. "*You* are trouble. Beautiful, sexy, maddening trouble." He pulled me to him, pressing his rock-hard body against mine. His rough cheek skimmed along my neck, followed by a trail of tender kisses. "Come with me. I know the perfect place."

We wandered through a maze of busy corridors, past several posh shops, and into the grand ballroom. Nico kept moving with determined steps like a man on a mission, his fingers laced in mine. We entered a cozy alcove with a few people gathered by the bar.

"I remember this place." I skimmed my hand along the table where Nico had introduced himself to me the night of Logan's party.

Nico's hold on my other hand tightened. He looked over his shoulder to give me a wink. "Me too."

We finally reached an exit that led to an outdoor seating area. Mellow jazz music filled the air, rivaled by the occasional roll of distant thunder. Clusters of tables surrounded a roaring fire pit that glowed in the center of the covered patio. Only a few open tables remained.

"Looks like everyone else got turned down—I mean, had the same idea too." I sat in the chair Nico held out for me and continued looking around, wanting to absorb every detail— every memory—of our time together.

Marble Tuscan pillars accented the wide stone archways, similar to the decor of the grand ballroom. Tiny lights danced above like stars in the night sky.

"This is really pretty." I reached across the table, taking his hand. "And very romantic."

"It's one of my favorite places to relax after a long day." He motioned for the waiter and requested a bottle of the house red.

"So, you said this weekend is an annual event at Elevations?" I gave myself an internal high-five, impressed I'd finally remembered one of the topics from my elusive mental list of conversation starters.

Nico's head bobbed. "It is." His attention drifted back to me. "This the tenth anniversary—ten years since my mother lost her brief battle with cancer." He leaned forward and captured my hands, caressing them while he talked. "The gala is our way of honoring her. She always took care of everyone, so an event like this to raise money in her name is the perfect way to keep that spirit alive."

I pulled one hand free and pressed it over my heart. "That's beautiful. And I see why this event means so much to you. Thank you for asking me to be a part of it."

The waiter returned with our wine, pouring us each a glass before leaving us alone again.

Nico raised his and tapped the rim to mine. "Here's to our first official weekend getaway. Hopefully the first of many." He took a sip then stared at the wine swirling in his glass, appearing lost in thought.

"Hey. You in there?" I waved my hand in front of his face.

"Hmm?" His eyes snapped up to meet mine. "Oh, sorry." His mouth curved in a half smile. "I was just thinking about how happy I am to be able to sit here with you, holding your hand. Have you here with me for the weekend." He stared at our joined hands resting on the table, stroking my wrist with his thumb.

"But?"

Nico's chest rose on a deep inhale. "But nothing. Sometimes I . . ." He squeezed my hand and finally raised his eyes to meet mine. "My mind just wandered off, that's all."

I pulled back and crossed my arms on the table, searching his face. "I'll buy that your mind wandered off, but I get the feeling there's a reason you don't want to share where it went." And it wasn't a good vibe.

"It wasn't anything bad." He brushed my cheek. "Promise. I was just feeling a little guilty about—"

"There you are." A woman's cheerful voice sang out her discovery as she approached our table. "And it looks like you were out playing in the rain."

Nico's sister, the woman I'd seen comforting him the night of Will's accident, stood smiling as she looked from Nico to me, then back again.

"I heard a rumor you were here. More specifically, that you brought a beautiful woman with you." She leaned down to hug Nico. "Disappointed guests"—she glanced at me—"female of course, have been coming up to me all evening asking if it's true." She laughed, rolling her eyes.

Nico's rugged stubble couldn't hide the hint of pink that shaded his cheeks. "She exaggerates." He squeezed his eyes shut, muttering something about strength and regretting an introduction. He swept his hand between his sister and me. "Danni, this is Gabriela. Gabs . . . Danni."

"Hi. It's nice to—"

Gabriela pushed past my extended hand and threw her arms around me. "I am so happy to finally meet you." She continued hugging me beyond what anyone would consider an acceptable length for an introduction—even if my blouse had been dry—then let out a frustrated sigh and finally released me. "I really wish I could stay and chat with you, but it's getting late. I need to get home to my family, and you two need to get changed out of your wet clothes." She gave my hands a squeeze. "Tomorrow. I promise we'll have time at the gala."

Nico asked her for a quick update on the event, and they shifted into professional mode long enough to discuss business.

Gabriela gave Nico another hug then pulled back to look at him, squishing his face between her hands. "You be good."

"Haven't had any complaints yet." He laughed and ducked a second before she tried to swat him.

"See you tomorrow." Gabriela waved, already on her way.

"Yep, I think I'm gonna like her." I slid my chair next to Nico's and leaned into him, draping my hand across his chest. "By the way, I'm happy to be here with you too."

He pulled me closer and pressed a kiss to the top of my head. "You ready to go back upstairs?" His fingers drifted up and down my arm, a lazy rhythm that stoked a fire of need inside me. "We can get changed and watch a movie. Finish our wine."

I wiggled, settling deeper into his embrace. Getting lost in the seductive sensations he created. "Sounds nice. But only if you promise to let me snuggle."

Nico hummed, a contented sound vibrating through his chest. "That was already part of my plan."

"Then yes." I smiled and pressed a kiss over his heart. *Let's hope the rest of your "plan" for the evening matches mine.*

A Little Slice of Heaven
NICO

Danni had fallen asleep less than ten minutes into the movie we'd picked after returning to the suite last night, and I'd spent the next two hours holding her—watching her sleep instead of paying attention to the story on the screen. She'd made the cutest little sounds and adorable faces that made me hope she was dreaming about me. About us.

At some point, long after the movie had ended, I'd scooped her up and carried her to bed . . . *her* bed. Leaving her there alone had been fucking hard. But I'd kept my promise and dragged my ass across the hall, like the gentleman my parents had raised me to be. Climbed into my own cold, lonely bed. And stared at the damn ceiling, imagining all the things I wanted to do to Danni.

I'd eventually resorted to a cold shower and taking matters into my own hand—twice—before finally relaxing enough to doze off . . . dreaming about her.

Leaving the suite this morning without seeing Danni had been just as difficult. I'd stood outside her closed door for a full five minutes, tempted to knock and wake her just to say good-bye. Steal a kiss.

I checked my watch again, then jogged up the three steps to Aurora Spa's entrance and strolled inside. "Good morning, Anabelle."

"Mr. Giardano." She greeted me with an amused smile. "Perfect timing—I was just messaging to let you know Danni's getting dressed and will be out in a few minutes."

"Thank you." I nodded and tucked my hands in my pockets, trying to appear calm, then turned toward the waiting area. My gaze locked on the large window that overlooked the front lawn—the exact spot I'd spent the past twenty-five minutes pacing, eager to see Danni.

I dropped my chin to my chest, chuckling to myself, then twisted to glance back at Anabelle. Her shoulders shook with a suppressed laugh, that same smile still on her face.

"Guess I'm busted, huh?"

"Afraid so. But I promise not to tell." She drew a little X over her heart.

"Hey, handsome." I turned toward Danni's voice, and her warm smile melted away all my anxiety. She drifted toward me, eyes sparkling. "I didn't realize you were meeting me here."

"That's because I wanted to surprise you." I pulled her into a tight embrace, breathing in the soothing scent of massage oils mixed with her floral perfume. "I swear you get more beautiful every time I see you."

Anabelle sighed. "Every girl should be so lucky."

I chuckled in Danni's ear and whispered, "See? No one's judging us here." Not even if I were to give in to my constant desire to kiss her right now. Forcing myself to step back, I dropped my hands to hers. "I thought we could try taking that walk again. There's a quiet little spot by the lake I think you'll like. It's one of my favorite places."

"I'll go anywhere if it means I get to spend time alone with you."

Once outside, I led her toward the path we'd retreated

from last night. "You look very relaxed. Did you enjoy your morning?"

"I did." She hesitated, scrunching up her nose.

"But?"

"It's nothing really. I was just a little . . . uncomfortable at first. Everyone kept referring to me as 'Mr. Giardano's special guest' and treating me like . . . royalty?" She shrugged, and a rosy glow covered her cheeks. "I feel silly even mentioning it."

"Hmm . . . I have a feeling that may be my fault."

Danni tipped her face toward me, a cute little wrinkle in her forehead. "What'dya mean?"

"You're very special to me." I lifted one shoulder. "Guess the staff picked up on that when I asked them to take extra-good care of you." I slipped my arm around her waist and pulled her close, pressing a kiss to her temple. "Sorry. I didn't mean to ruin your experience."

"Are you kidding? I just spent four glorious hours having every inch of my body kneaded, buffed, and polished by a very talented team of . . . technicians? Therapists? Not sure what to call them, but my point is, it was perfect." She bit her lip and glanced up at me. "Can I tell you a secret, though?"

"Of course."

"When you told me yesterday you'd arranged all that, I was worried I wouldn't enjoy it. At. All. But I gotta admit, I loved it —a lot—and could really get used to that kind of pampering."

"Good." Because I planned to spoil her as often as I could. "So I guess that means I'm forgiven for deserting you all morning?" I winked.

"I suppose." Danni drew out the word in a teasing tone then glanced to the side. "I mean, I missed you like crazy, but wow . . . I don't think I've ever felt this amazing." She rested her head on my shoulder and let out a contented hum. "Thank you."

"You're welcome." *And someday soon, I hope to show you all the ways I can make you feel even more amazing.*

We strolled arm-in-arm beneath a canopy of pink blossoms created by the dogwood trees lining the bank of the crystal-clear lake. A few ice dams from the cold, harsh winter still bobbed on the current, glistening under the mid-day sun, but the spring thaw was well under way.

I traced my fingers along Danni's hip, picturing the tiny hearts hiding beneath her skin-tight jeans. "So . . . are you hungry?"

Her stomach growled as if to answer for her, just in case she tried to lie. "Oops." She giggled and pressed her hand over it.

"I'll take that as a firm yes." I hugged her closer. "Almost there."

We crossed the arched wooden bridge over Little Pine Creek and veered off onto a narrow path dotted with stepping stones that led to a wooded area. Danni clung to my hand through the short, twenty-yard stretch of dense forest, climbing over fallen tree trunks that she could have easily walked around.

"And here we are." I swept my hand in front of Danni and ushered her into a private cove on Pine Lake, surrounded on three sides by large weigela bushes in full bloom and tall shade trees.

"Oh, Nico, this is beautiful." She released my hand and covered her heart, turning to take in every inch of my little slice of heaven.

"Is that for us?" She asked over her shoulder, already wandering toward the picnic I'd set up on the wooden deck overlooking the lake before meeting her at Aurora.

"It is. I had the chef put together a lunch for us."

Danni stopped at the edge of the red-and-white checkered blanket and stooped to examine the old milk can I'd filled with fresh-cut flowers from the greenhouse. I eased up beside her and brushed her shoulders.

"Nico, this is so sweet." Danni stood and wrapped me in a tight hug. "And romantic." She pressed her lips to my chest. "I can't believe you worked all morning and still found time to do this."

I could have stood there all day with her in my arms, but she was hungry. I kneeled on the blanket and patted the spot next to me, motioning for Danni to join me, then began unpacking the contents of the wicker basket.

"So, what are we having?" She slipped off her shoes and sat beside me, peeking into one of the containers. "Mmm . . . this smells delicious."

"That is crostini with a citrus pesto spread. We also have paninis with chicken, roasted peppers, basil, and Chef's amazing balsamic dressing. Cannoli for dessert. And, of course, wine." I pulled out the bottle of Riesling I'd grabbed from our private reserve and popped the cork. After filling two glasses, I passed one to Danni and raised mine. "To making memories."

She beamed, her sparkling eyes locked on mine. "I like the sound of that." She tapped the rim of her glass to mine then took a slow sip, hugging her knees to her chest and staring off in the distance.

I draped my arm across her back and leaned closer. "See that over there?" I used my wine glass to point toward the mountain on the other side of the lake. "The small chalet in the spot where the pine trees are thinned out?"

Danni nodded.

"That was the original building here at Elevations. My grandparents lived there before moving into the penthouse. Then it became my parents' house, the one I grew up in."

"It looks like something out of a fairytale. I can't imagine growing up in a place like this." She turned to face me, a dreamy look in her eyes. "Who lives there now?"

"No one, really. Ben, Gabs, and I have all stayed there short-term at some point, but we usually rent it out or open it up for friends who want a quiet getaway." I brushed the hair from her face. "We can stay there the next time we come up if you'd like."

She stared at me, narrowing her eyes. "You're serious?"

"Of course. It'll be fun." I could already picture us snuggled up by the stone fireplace on a cold winter night, watching the snow fall outside.

Danni leaned against me, resting her head on my shoulder, and stared across the lake. She drew in a deep breath and let out a contented sigh. "Your grandfather made me breakfast this morning, along with the best hazelnut cappuccino I've ever tasted, and we had a really nice chat."

"Should I be concerned?"

"No." Danni drew out the word and gave my arm a playful shove. "I mean, he may have mentioned you a *tiny* bit." She held up her thumb and forefinger, showing the tiniest gap between them. "He mostly talked about how much he loved raising his family here at Elevations—I assume in that beautiful house.

"And he told me a little bit about the history, how he and your grandmother started with nothing and worked hard to build the resort they'd always dreamed of. I love the way his eyes sparkled when he talked about his 'beautiful Lorena.' He even showed me the picture from his bedside table." Danni smiled. "It was so sweet . . . so easy to see she had truly been the love of his life."

Thank you, Nonno.

I knew the picture well, the two of them wrapped in each other's arms and lost in each other's eyes. That image, taken only a few months before the stroke that ended her life, had captured the genuine love they'd shared for fifty-six years.

"Yeah, they were amazing together. Same with my parents . . . Gabs and Troy too." Someday I hoped to be lucky enough to experience that kind of love as well.

I wrapped my arms around Danni, hugging her closer, and every cell of my body came alive. We sat in silence for a few minutes, sipping our wine. Each lost in our own thoughts.

Danni's stomach grumbled again. "Oops, sorry."

"No need to apologize. I've kept you waiting too long." I kissed her temple. "Let's get you something to eat."

I plated our food then continued pointing out special places on the massive grounds of Elevations while we ate. Sharing lighthearted stories about growing up here, like learning to ski around the same time I'd mastered walking, summer weekends spent tent-camping in the woods with my family, and my obsession with playing in the lake—leaving out the part about getting caught skinny dipping more than a few times in my late teens and college years.

I finished the last bite of my panini then leaned back on my elbows, savoring the moment. "This spot has always been my favorite though. The one I go to when I want to be alone." And spending time alone here with Danni had turned out to be even more enjoyable than I'd imagined it would be.

Danni snuggled up next to me and leaned back, imitating my posture. "I can see why. It's so peaceful." She tipped her head back, raising her face to the warm rays of sunshine peeking through the budding trees. "What is that? Up there." She pointed toward the small wooden structure tucked in the sturdy branches of one of the old oak trees.

"That . . . is *Casa di Nico*," I said with an air of dignity.

"I'm sorry. *Casa di* what?" Danni's warm laughter wrapped around my heart.

"You heard me." I tickled her side, making her laugh

harder. "That fine architectural specimen is my childhood tree-house and hideout, so no making fun of it."

Danni pinched her lips shut then closed an imaginary zipper across them.

She looked adorable as hell, but now I couldn't focus on anything but wanting to kiss those sweet lips. I cleared my throat and tried to push that thought aside for now. "Anyway, Dad and I built the treehouse when I was seven or eight—this deck too—although I suspect Mom had the carpentry crew come out every night and re-do all of our work to make sure everything was safe and looked perfect."

"Sounds like a mom thing to do." Danni glanced around, silent for a moment.

I always imagined I'd have a family of my own someday—children I could share the cove and treehouse with, build new memories together.

Danni got up and walked toward the tree, continuing to study the treehouse. "This is adorable. Even has a cute little built-in ladder." She traced her fingers along the wooden slats we'd nailed to the trunk.

"Glad you approve," I teased, moving behind her and sliding my arms around her waist. "As I got older, it also became a great place to hide from Mom when I'd misbehave and she'd threaten to get out her wooden spoon. Mom was afraid of heights and would *never* climb up there."

Danni laughed and relaxed against my chest, tipping her head to look up at me. "Why do I get the feeling you got into a lot of trouble when you were younger?"

I nuzzled Danni's neck, humming against her soft skin. "Who said I ever stopped?"

She turned in my arms, looped her hands around my neck, and stretched on tiptoes to brush her lips against my ear. "You know . . . I can be bad too."

Oh, damn. I bet she could. I'd sure as hell fantasized about it enough times—as recently as last night. My grip on her waist tightened while I struggled to shut down the sudden urge to push her up against that old tree trunk and find out how accurate my imagination had been. She dropped her hands to my chest and eased open my shirt buttons, her fingers brushing against my skin as she moved from one button to the next, each deliberate movement sending sparks of desire shooting through me.

"Danni?" I drew out each syllable. "What do you think you're doing?"

"You said you wanted to get to know each other better this weekend, right?" She finished with the remaining buttons, biting her bottom lip, then looked up at me. "What better way is there?"

She tugged my shirt open and slid her hands under the fabric, caressing and exploring every inch of my torso. My eyes fell closed. I let out a soft groan and lowered my forehead to hers, surrendering to the exhilarating sensation rolling through me. Making it difficult to remember why I needed to stop when all I wanted to do was claim every inch of Danni as mine.

I dipped my head lower, brushing my cheek against hers. Then my lips. When Danni tipped her head to the side, sliding my lips to hers just felt like the right thing to do—the most natural thing in the world. And when she parted her lips on a gentle sigh, my tongue glided past without a conscious thought —teasing with slow, gentle strokes. Tasting the lingering wine from our lunch. Our toast.

Danni melted against me, and I wrapped my arms around her to keep her close. Hold on to this perfect moment. This perfect kiss.

Each minute that followed became an exercise in focus and self-control, a concentrated effort to keep my promise to her and to myself—a battle I believed I was winning until her fingers dipped beneath the waistband of my jeans. I grabbed her wrists, stopping her while I still could, and laced our fingers together.

"Seems I should have been a little more specific," I said, my voice sounding gravelly and unfamiliar. I cleared my throat, pressed our joined hands along the outsides of Danni's thighs, and stared down into her eyes. "And *you* seem to have forgotten we're taking things slow."

Danni let out a thoughtful hum, the corner of her mouth twitching up in a tiny grin. "I'm pretty sure *I'm* not the one who was kissing me." She pulled one hand free and walked her fingers up my chest. "Now . . . you didn't really mean all that silly 'no expectations' stuff, did you? 'Cause I'm perfectly fine with forgetting you ever mentioned it."

"Tempting." I dropped a kiss on the tip of her nose. "But no. And I'm pretty sure *I'm* not the one who unbuttoned my shirt *before* that kiss."

Danni shrugged, gaze locked on mine with a playful-but-seductive sparkle in those baby blues. She skimmed her fingers down my exposed chest to the top of my waistband. "Oops?"

I let out a low groan. "And despite how much I love where this is heading right now, I really *did* mean 'all that silly no expectations stuff.' Still do."

Her eyes fell closed. She turned away, shoulders sagging on a heavy sigh.

"Hey, this isn't a rejection . . . not even close." I tugged at her chin, pulling her attention back to me. "In case you haven't noticed, I'm a very patient man. We're just slowing down. Taking our time."

"Sure feels a lot like stopping." Danni grumbled, rolling her eyes.

I inched closer and raised our joined hands between us. "My point is, two months ago, I couldn't even hold your hand." The reminder of *why* glistened in the sun, as if on cue, mocking me.

Danni arched a brow. "So that's enough for you? We're just gonna hold hands all weekend long?"

"Of course not." I winked. "I planned to steal another kiss or two before it's over." I pressed my lips below her ear. "Maybe even cop a feel, if things are going really good."

Danni pressed her palm against my chest, forcing me to take a step back. "Maybe this was a one-time offer, and you just missed your chance." She lifted her chin and turned away, peeking at me over her shoulder with a mischievous grin. "If you're not interested, guess I'll just have to find someone else who is."

I caught her by the waist before she could take a single step, spun her around, and pulled her flush against my body, making no attempt to hide the effect she had on me. Solid proof that I was definitely interested—*too* fucking interested.

Danni gasped, clinging to my shoulders. She caught her bottom lip between her teeth and took a deep breath.

"Pretty sure you can figure out how much I want you right now," I whispered against her ear. "But I'm not willing to rush things and risk losing you."

A few seconds passed, the sounds of nature barely audible above our ragged breaths. Danni gave a slight nod, finally conceding.

"Thank you." I tugged her lip free and kissed her, making sure to keep it sweet and brief even though we both wanted much more. "What d'ya say we finish our picnic? We still have dessert and a half bottle of wine to finish before we head back."

CHALLENGE ACCEPTED

DANNI

If anyone were to ask me to describe the perfect day, I would have to tell them about today. Especially if tonight ended the way I hoped it would.

If. That one tiny word had my insides swirling. Or maybe that was the lingering effect from my afternoon with Nico. If he hadn't stopped me—stopped us—I could only imagine how far things would have gone. Right there. Out in the open.

"Danni?" Nico's warm voice preceded a gentle knock on the bedroom door. "Hey, beautiful, we need to leave in a few minutes."

I stood in front of the full-length mirror, twisting to inspect my naked back—feeling even better about my brazen wardrobe choice than when I'd bought my dress a few days ago.

"I'll be right out." I brushed a layer of gloss on my lips as his footsteps faded down the hall.

If. The word still echoed in my mind, taunting me. Asking *what if* "no expectations" was simply Nico's polite way of saying he didn't *want* more from me? Warning *that* was the real reason he'd stopped earlier.

I pulled in a deep breath, forcing that toxic thought out of my mind, and smoothed my hands across the shimmering blue fabric that clung to my body like a second skin. *By the time we return to the privacy of Nico's room tonight, he won't be able to keep his hands—and every other body part—off of me. I hope.*

With the help of a few more deep breaths, I managed to calm the whirlwind in my stomach and made my way down the long hallway toward my handsome date. One look at Nico lounging in the overstuffed chair—waiting for *me*—and those butterflies took off again. I paused at the entrance to the living room, my feet frozen in place. I'd forgotten how intimidating he looked in his formal attire. Every fine detail showcased the wealthy and powerful man inside—details he somehow managed to disguise when he blended into my simple, middle-class world.

He stood to face me, exuding the casual confidence that lured women to him in droves. "You look . . . wow . . . even more beautiful than I could have imagined."

Memories of New Year's Eve came rushing back—the way he'd swooped in and stolen my heart before I'd even realized it'd happened. Not to mention the way his mere presence that night had turned me into a babbling imbecile, unable to form a coherent sentence.

I lifted my chin, determined to avoid a repeat performance, and imitated his confidence. I strolled forward, giving an appreciative hum. "I have to say . . . you clean up quite well yourself, Mr. Giardano."

A lopsided grin spread across his face, complete with the adorable dimple in his left cheek. He stood motionless, following me with only his eyes as I scanned every magnificent inch of him.

I placed my hand on his shoulder, letting it skim along his back to the other side as I circled behind him. "Mmm . . . absolute perfection."

My breasts brushed his arm as I rounded to face him, letting my fingers trace the lapel of his jacket. His playful smile disappeared, replaced by a smoldering gaze that sent sparks of desire blazing straight to my core.

Nico grabbed my wrist, trapping it against his chest. "You're playing with fire, Ms. DeLaney." A deep, seductive tone laced his voice. His gaze dropped to my lips, lingering there.

Seconds ticked by, my heart pounding harder with each beat. I stretched toward his mouth, anticipation building. "Are you going to kiss me?" The words floated out as a whispered plea.

Nico slipped his arm around my waist, moving in slow motion, and pulled me to him.

"I haven't decided yet." His lips brushed against mine with the faintest of contact. Mischief danced in his eyes.

"You're being a tease, you know." I rolled my hips forward, grinding against his erection. "But two can play at that game."

I pushed away from him and sashayed across the room, glancing over my shoulder. "You'll have *all* night to think about what you missed out on." After pressing the call button for the elevator, I turned to face the stunned man watching me. "You better get your sexy self over here, or we're going to be late to the party."

Nico laughed, shaking his head and mumbling as he approached. "What am I going to do with you?"

The elevator door opened. "Hmm . . . well, I guess you'll have all evening to think about *that* too." I blew a kiss at him then stepped inside.

Nico entered and stood beside me, hands tucked in his pockets and his head hung low. An amused grin still stretched across his face, accompanied by the low rumble of restrained laughter.

As the elevator descended, I tipped my head to the side to

peek at our reflections in the polished steel wall. Every inch of Nico *was* pure perfection, as always, but realizing how perfect we looked together tonight stunned me. I hooked my arm around Nico's bent elbow and leaned into him, moving my leg to reveal the slit that ran halfway up my thigh and exposed a whole lot more than my sparkling gold stilettos. I'd never worn anything so daring before, but I wanted to impress—more like tempt—my handsome date. And from the expression on Nico's face, I'd say it was working.

I bit the inside of my lip, trying to hold back a smile. "You're staring."

His eyes met mine in the mirror then swept the length of my body with a heated gaze. He let out a low hum. "You're beautiful. I'd be a fool not to." He bent to nuzzle my neck, pressing his lips by my ear. "But don't pretend you weren't checking me out again too."

Nico wrapped his arms around me, pulling me close. "You better get used to the attention. With the way you look tonight, there'll be plenty more people who won't be able to take their eyes off of you." A crease formed between his brows. "Guess I should prepare myself for that too. I don't think I like the idea of other men ogling you that way."

After all the times he'd teased me about acting jealous, it felt strange to be on the receiving end of that emotion. I nudged him with my hip, laughing at his troubled expression. "You're so adorable when you're jealous."

The elevator doors opened. Mellow tunes from a string quartet drifted inside. My grip on Nico's arm tightened. We stepped out onto the plush lavender carpet that had been rolled across Elevations' ornate marble floor, marking the path to the Foundation's event in the grand ballroom. Large bouquets of flowers greeted us, their sweet fragrance filling the air.

Nico leaned down, whispering in my ear as we walked.

"Relax. It's just like any other party you've ever gone to—cocktails, dinner, dancing . . . a charming speaker." He squeezed my hand. "This one just has a fancy name."

"And a giant price tag." One thousand dollars a plate, to be exact. No wonder the gala only drew people with deep pockets. I bit my lip and peeked up at his grinning face. "But if you can arrange a dance for me with that charming speaker?"

He winked. "Already done. I was hoping for more than just one dance though."

"Me too." I brushed his cheek. "A *whole* lot more."

MINGLING AND DRINKS
DANNI

We passed through the wide double doors into the grand ballroom, pausing for the photographer to snap our picture.

Crystal chandeliers sparkled above large round tables covered in lavender and white linens, each adorned with a smaller version of the floral arrangements used to decorate the lobby. The tables surrounded a spacious dance floor with a raised platform at the far end where the band would play after dinner. The scene looked as if it had been pulled straight from a fairytale, complete with my very own prince charming.

Heads turned as Nico escorted me across the room. The attention he drew reminded me of his entrance to Logan's New Year's Eve party—strangers smiling, their gazes lingering on him. Nico stopped occasionally, introducing me as he greeted guests and made polite conversation, skillfully dodging their frequent attempts to flirt.

"Do you know all of these people?" I clung to his arm, feeling more self-conscious and insecure by the minute.

"I've met most of them, but there are only a few I actually

know well." Nico placed his hand on mine. "Would you like to take a little break? Get a drink from the bar?"

The idea of a giant margarita to calm my nerves *sounded* perfect, but—"Maybe a club soda?" I lifted one shoulder. "I don't wanna risk doing something to embarrass myself in front of your entire family." Or all these important people.

Nico touched my cheek. "You won't. And they already love you, so stop worrying."

I nodded and glanced around the room, hoping he was right. "Where are they, by the way?"

"Dad and Nonno are probably in the kitchen, driving the chefs crazy." He gave a single laugh. "They're the only ones who can get away with that without getting thrown out. The rest? I'm not sure, but they're around here. Somewhere."

We strolled under one of the wide stone archways lining the edge of the ballroom and entered a cozy alcove. Nico placed his hand at the small of my back, guiding me toward the bar.

"Mr. Giardano, good to see you, sir."

Nico extended his hand to the tall, young bartender waiting for us to approach. "Good evening, Lucas. How are your classes going?"

While the two men chatted, I glanced around the room. My gaze settled on the table where I'd sat four months ago, anxiously waiting for my husband to return, not realizing I was about to meet this amazing man of my dreams. I snuggled closer to Nico, wrapping my arms around his waist, and breathed in the light scent of his cologne.

Lucas pulled a bottle from the top shelf. "What can I get for you and your lovely date?" He grabbed a rocks glass and added ice.

"Looks like you've got my order down." Nico laughed and rubbed his jaw. "Can we have a Berry Hopeful Cosmo for Danni?"

"Absolutely." Lucas moved to the other end of the bar, gathering ingredients.

"But I—"

Nico pressed a finger to my lips. "You don't have to drink it if you don't like it. It's this year's special signature drink that we'll be serving through the summer—all proceeds go to the Valentina Giardano Foundation's Hope for a Better Tomorrow, which is the program that funds cancer research. Anyway, it's fruity and sweet." He winked. "Like you. And I thought you might like it."

"All set. You two have a wonderful evening." Lucas returned with my drink and placed it on the bar next to Nico's then moved on to another couple.

A stack of plump, fresh blackberries clung to the wide rim of my glass, dipping into a tempting lavender drink. I slid the glass closer, watching the sugar coating on the berries sparkle under the lights. "It's so pretty."

Nico moved to stand behind me, his tux grazing the exposed skin on my back. He wrapped one arm across my stomach and pulled me against his solid chest. "It is. But not near as pretty as you are." He reached past me to take his glass, swirling the contents before taking a long drink. Nico chuckled and rested his chin on my shoulder. "I don't think I've ever seen someone so entertained by watching a cocktail before."

I twisted in his arms, the brush of our bodies making me shiver, and glanced up at him through my lashes. "Do you have a better suggestion of how I could entertain myself?"

Nico took another sip of his drink, failing to hide his smile. "I might." He leaned against me and stretched to put his glass on the bar. "Too bad we have a gala we need to attend instead."

Images of all the ways Nico could "entertain" me flooded my mind. My knees felt weak. "Can I, um . . . try my drink first?"

"Of course." He grinned and eased back just enough to allow me to turn toward the bar again, but he didn't move his arm and continued to trace his fingers along my stomach, my side, my bare back.

I wrapped my hand around the stem of my glass, gripping so tight I worried it might snap, and slid it toward my lips.

"Are you enjoying our game?" Nico whispered against my ear. "Because I sure am."

The tiny sip I'd intended to take turned into a giant gulp. "You're gonna pay for that, you know?"

Nico's eyes locked on mine. "Counting on it." He winked and brushed his fingers along the side of my face then let out a sigh. "As much as I'd like to keep you all to myself for the rest of the evening, we're supposed to be mingling with the guests right now." Nico finished his drink and placed the empty glass on the bar then extended his hand. "Shall we?"

We only made it halfway across the room before a tall man with a runner's build and light brown hair rushed toward us.

"Nico Giardano, as I live and breathe. It is so good to see you, man." He grabbed Nico, pulling him into a robust hug. "I heard you were out our way the other night and meant to give you a call, but . . . well, you know how hectic things can get when you're juggling two businesses and a family."

The man released him but kept one hand clasped on Nico's shoulder and drilled him with a curious stare. "So. What's new?"

Nico shook his head, chuckling under his breath. He caught me by the waist. "I'll assume you already know this is Danni." He pressed a kiss to my temple. "This is Jake Santarelli, one of my best friends since we were kids."

"Oh, you must be Carla's husband." I held out my hand to him.

Jake pulled me into a hug that rivaled the one he'd given Nico. "Sure am, and I've heard *all* about you."

"That's enough," Nico teased and tugged at Jake's arms. "You still trying to steal my dates?"

"Only the pretty ones." Jake laughed, finally releasing me —sort of. His hands slid to mine then stopped, a deep crease forming between his brows.

"*Don't* get any ideas." Nico's voice was low and flat. He shoved a hand through his hair. "We'll talk later."

Jake's gaze drifted to Nico then back to me. He gave a subtle nod. "All right. We can get into the details later. Whatever they are though, let me just say *now* that it's good to see you happy again, and that I hope this means you're—"

"Where's Carla hiding?" Nico's change of subject was about as smooth as a speed bump.

"See you still haven't mastered the fine art of subtle transitions." Jake chuckled. "She ran back up to our room for her phone so she can check on Mia."

Nico's face lit up. "How is sweet little Mia?" He turned to me before Jake could answer. "I think I told you Jake and Carla have a daughter, didn't I?"

"You did. She's three, right?"

"Almost four now." Jake slid his phone from inside his jacket, tapping on the screen while he talked. "I may be a bit biased, but she's the absolute best." His face glowed with love and pride.

Nico took Jake's phone, the screen displaying a picture of a little girl with light brown curls and big green eyes.

"She's beautiful." I pressed a hand over my heart and leaned into Nico's side.

"She is, and I can't believe how much she's grown." He returned Jake's phone then rubbed his jaw, giving a thoughtful hum. "Guess it *has* been a while since I've seen her—too long —I'll need to fix that."

I closed my eyes, trying to imagine Nico with a little girl.

Thinking about the way he treated his sister. His playful banter with friends.

Jake chuckled. "I can see your wheels spinning, Danni. He's actually amazing with her." He flashed a mischievous grin at Nico. "He'll make a great dad someday."

"Jake Santarelli, don't you go making trouble." A woman's voice teased from behind us. Carla smacked Jake's arm then gave me a hug. "Danni, you look absolutely beautiful. This is a nice surprise—seeing you again. Here." She gave Nico an inquisitive glance. "Anything you'd like to share, my friend?"

"Nope. But Jake was about to tell us about Mia." Nico pulled me closer, resting his head against mine. "She's the most adorable thing ever."

"Are we talking about Mia or Danni?" Carla laughed, shaking her head at Nico. "Other than a slight fever, Mia's great. It's probably nothing, but I still worry a little."

"More like a lot," Jake chimed in.

Carla arched a brow at Jake and gave him a playful nudge. "Anyway, Mom has Mia and is supposed to check in with me before she puts her to bed, which she can't do if I can't even remember to take my phone off the charger and bring it down here with me." She let out a weary sigh and swept a hand at Jake's phone, which he'd been waving next to her head. "Sorry, guess I'm a little stressed."

Jake wrapped his arms around Carla. "She'll be fine, sweetheart. Try to relax and enjoy yourself." He pressed a kiss to her cheek then looked at Nico, the corner of his mouth curling up. "You know, you're long overdue for a play date with Mia . . . and with us. Next time you come over, you should bring Danni."

Carla's face lit up. "That's a great idea. Plus it would give Danni and me a chance to chat—you know, get in that girl time we talked about."

"I, um—" I glanced at Nico, unsure how to answer.

Getting together with his friends—socializing like a real couple —sounded like a lot of fun, but maybe he didn't feel the same.

Nico smiled, his warm eyes searching my face. "We'd love to."

Their conversation shifted to business, and while the three of them discussed their various properties, I took in my beautiful surroundings then settled my attention on the growing crowd on the patio. Ben leaned against the stone railing, surrounded by three beautiful women, which made it pretty clear why he hadn't invited Kristi to the gala. He turned my way, a huge smile spreading across his face, and raised his cocktail glass, greeting me with a nod before returning his attention to his companions.

My gaze drifted to the other guests, all chatting and laughing as though they were close friends. But, as Nico had promised, none of them knew me. A reality that both soothed and unsettled me, because—wait a second. "Oh. My. God."

"Danni? What's wrong?" Nico's grip on my waist tightened, his voice laced with concern.

"That looks like—" I leaned forward, squinted, and blinked several times, but he was still there. "Is that . . ." It couldn't be. Could it? "Is that Tanner Grayson?"

Every girl had a celebrity crush. At least that was what I'd always told myself. And mine stood a mere fifty feet away, looking as perfect and sexy as he did on the big screen.

"Uh-oh." Carla laughed, turning to follow my line of sight. "Yep, sure is." The sparkle in her eyes didn't match her nonchalant reaction. She draped her arm across my shoulders and leaned close to whisper, "He's pretty dreamy up close too."

Jake groaned. "You're playin' with fire."

Carla just winked at him then continued, her volume increased enough that the men would easily overhear her. "Bet you could convince Nico to introduce you."

I turned to him, heart racing. "Could you? I mean, I guess you must know him at least a little bit, right? But I'd love to—"

"I'd rather not." Nico's fingers flexed, digging into my waist. He flashed a narrow-eyed glare at Carla.

"Please? Just a quick introduction?" I pleaded, smiling at Nico and batting my lashes. "It's not like I'm going to run off with him."

An awkward silence followed.

Jake slapped Nico's arm. "She's joking, dude. Relax."

"Right." Nico took a deep breath. He ran a hand through his hair. "Yeah. Sure. Um, I'm sure we can grab a minute of his time after dinner."

I threw my arms around Nico's neck. "Thank you."

Carla's phone buzzed. She looked at her screen, pressed a button, and asked the person on the other end to hang on. "Hey, I gotta take this. But let's all get together soon. Okay, Nico?" She gave him a quick hug then grabbed his cheeks and pulled him toward her, talking in hushed tones.

Nico nodded. He grinned then seemed to relax before pushing her away, laughing. "Jake, do something to control your wife."

Jake scratched the side of his jaw. "I'm not sure that's even possible." He said a quick goodbye then followed Carla toward the lobby.

ROMANCE AND RIVALS
NICO

"Well, I've mingled enough." I raised our joined hands and pressed a kiss to Danni's wrist then slipped her arm through mine. "What do you say we get a little fresh air before dinner?"

Danni let out a faint sigh and smiled, her shoulders relaxing. "That sounds like a really nice idea."

We moved out to the patio, wandering beyond the groups of guests gathered there until we reached a spot overlooking the gardens where we could be alone. I stepped behind Danni and pulled her against me, wrapping my arms across her middle. Having her here this weekend felt so right. As though I'd finally found the missing piece of my heart. My life.

"I'm sorry about the way I acted earlier. Pressuring you about Tanner." Danni twisted to face me, chewing on her bottom lip. "Guess I just got a little starstruck."

"A little?" I teased, tugging her chin so she'd meet my gaze.

A faint blush covered her cheeks. "If you'd rather not introduce me to him, that's fine."

"Don't be silly. We'll find him later." The thought of that fucking asshole anywhere near my girl made my blood boil, but it seemed I'd do anything she wanted when she batted those gorgeous baby blues at me.

Danni slipped her arms under my jacket and wrapped them around my waist, snuggling against my chest and sending a warm wave of contentment rolling through me.

"I saw Ben earlier," she said without moving. "Surrounded by a group of women."

I gave a cautious hum, unsure where she was going with this. "Sounds like Ben." And me, most years.

Her head bobbed with a little nod. "Suppose that's why he didn't want to bring Kristi." Danni drew in a deep breath. "She's crazy about him."

She didn't need to finish her thought. I got it. Kendra hadn't told her Will was cheating, and now Danni felt she was in the same situation—even though the circumstances weren't quite the same. Ben had told me he only ever agreed to open relationships, not that I actually believed he'd ever taken advantage of that stipulation.

I skimmed my fingers along the exposed skin of Danni's back, tracing the outline of the fabric. "I wouldn't read too much into it. We don't usually bring dates to the gala."

Which was true, but given Ben's comments a few weeks ago, our "rule" wasn't his only reason. Just a good excuse.

"We?" Danni tipped her head, brows arched, and gave an inquisitive hum. "Well, I guess that helps explain all the commotion you caused yesterday, showing up with me."

I tapped her nose. "Gabriela exaggerates."

Although I was sure there were a few disappointed ladies, based on my own observations while we were making our rounds. Some had decided to openly flirt anyway, right in front of Danni, as though they somehow thought they could take her place.

Not a fucking chance.

In the past, I would've been mingling alone. Making a

mental list of which ladies I wanted to dance with later, maybe even get a little personal with. But that would be it. I'd always go back to my own room. Alone.

The gala had been created to honor my mother, and she never would have approved of me sleeping with a girl I didn't intend to make a part of our family . . . not that I bothered letting that guilt stop me any other time. Far from it. But a meaningless fling or one-night stand just felt wrong on *this* night.

Danni smoothed her hands over my jacket and adjusted my tie. "You're sweet." Her eyes flicked to mine. "But I think your sister was right." Danni stretched toward my ear. "I was there too while we were mingling, and just because you pretended those beautiful women weren't hitting on you doesn't mean I didn't notice it." She pressed a kiss to my cheek. "Thank you."

I slid my hands to Danni's and stepped back, letting my gaze roam over every glorious inch of her before settling on her eyes, reaching into her soul. "The only beautiful woman I see is right here in my arms. And she can flirt with me all she wants."

Danni stood motionless for several seconds. She blinked a few times and drew in a deep breath. "Oh, yeah?" The corner of her mouth twitched up. She drifted closer, her body grazing mine. "I like the sound of that."

"Danni? What are you doing?"

She rested one hand by my shoulder and skimmed the fingertips of her other down the front of my jacket. "Flirting." She raised her eyes to meet mine and nibbled on her bottom lip. "Am I doing it wrong?"

I let out a low groan. This was my own damn fault— should've thought it through before giving her free rein to torture me. "Wrong? No." I tugged her lip free and rubbed my thumb over the spot. "But I think you skipped over flirting and jumped straight into seduction."

Danni eased closer, her hips swaying against mine. "I see. So which one of those gives me a better chance of having you kiss me?" She traced her fingers along the side of my face and batted her lashes. "Because I really . . . really want you to kiss me."

Ah, fuck. I caught the back of Danni's neck and pulled her toward me, stopping myself right before our lips touched. It would be so easy to lower my face that fraction of an inch to kiss her, put an end to the torture of being so close and not giving in to what we both wanted.

Danni's wide eyes locked on mine, pleading for more. Begging me to kiss her.

Just one little taste. That's it, except . . . "I'm pretty sure you told me I'd have the rest of the night to think about not kissing you back in the suite." I brushed my lips across her cheek to her ear. "Time's not up yet."

Danni smacked my chest. "You are *such* a giant tease." She laughed and shook her head.

The dinner chimes sounded behind us.

I released Danni's neck and eased away, licking my own damn lips instead of hers, and winked. "Looks like everyone is taking their seats for dinner." I pressed my lips to the top of her head, which didn't come close to satisfying my need to kiss her. Prove to her that she's the only woman I want.

I swear all of this "taking it slow," delayed gratification shit is gonna kill me.

I stepped back and bent my arm, inviting Danni to take it, and put on my best attempt at a relaxed smile. "We should probably go join my family."

"THERE YOU ARE. I thought I was going to have to send out a search party for you two lovebirds." Gabriela stood to greet us and pulled Danni into a hug. "You look absolutely beautiful. My brother's a lucky man."

I'd been telling myself that every day for weeks . . . except for the days I'd fucked up and nearly lost her. But even those days had turned out to be lucky, since she'd agreed to give me another chance.

Danni cast a shy look over her shoulder at me then sat in the chair I held for her. She smiled and waved at my niece, who was wearing a pink evening gown, sparkly shoes, and a tiara.

I scooped up Bella, lifting her for a giant hug, and tickled her tummy. "How's my favorite little munchkin tonight?"

"Uncle Nico!" She squirmed until I put her back down. "You hav'ta be careful or you'll wrinkle me." She shook her head and smoothed every inch of her dress, explaining the whole time that we needed to bow and curtsy when we were dressed for a ball.

Gabriela and Danni exchanged a look and shielded their faces, trying to hide their laughter.

"It's your own fault, Nico." Gabriela reached for Danni. "She's been convinced she's a princess ever since Nico watched her for a weekend and decided to spoil her with a giant dress-up trunk and every Disney princess movie ever made."

"We had a very fun weekend, didn't we, Bel?"

"So much fun!" She hopped and clapped her hands. "We had tea parties an' watched movies. And Uncle Nico pretended ta' be a frog. Then he turned into a han'some prince when I kissed his cheek." Bella looked up at me with that gigantic grin that melted my heart then hooked a finger, motioning for me to bend down. She cupped her hands around my ear and whispered, "Your friend is very pretty. Is she a princess too?"

"I think she is," I whispered back. "Would you like to meet her?"

She nodded and turned to face Danni.

I grinned at Danni, hoping she was okay with this. "Princess Danielle, allow me to introduce Princess Isabella."

Danni stood and curtsied then took Bella's hand. "It's a pleasure to meet you." She stooped down to Bella's level. "And you can call me Danni."

Gabriela picked up her phone then glanced toward the ballroom entrance and nodded. "Bella, Daddy's looking for you. Can you *walk* to the big doors by the music people to meet him?"

"Okay, Mommy." Bella took a few steps then ran back and threw her arms around Danni's hips. "I hav'ta go sit at the special table for big kids, but I'll be back."

"Oh, my God. She's adorable," Danni laughed, returning to her seat.

"Yeah, but I think I've been replaced as her favorite adult." I sat next to Danni and draped my arm across her shoulders. "Thank you for indulging her."

Gabs ended her call with Troy. "He's going to get Bella and the boys settled in the kids' room, then he'll finally be ready to join us." She tucked her phone inside her small bag. "Hey, Ben mentioned earlier that Logan's dad was rushed to the hospital this morning. Everything okay?"

"Yeah, Logan called this afternoon to tell me they were there. Fortunately, his dad's chest pain appears to be a strained muscle and not a heart attack. They want to keep him overnight for observation though, just to be safe, so Logan's gonna stay there with him."

He'd apologized multiple times for missing the gala, especially tonight, even though it wasn't necessary. After all these years, he had to know I'd have kicked his ass back to New York if he'd shown up here.

"It's too bad Logan won't be here, but I'm glad his dad is okay." Gabriela folded her arms on the table and stretched toward me, one corner of her mouth twitching upward.

"So . . . I also heard you convinced Chef to put together a special picnic lunch today. Do I need to ask where you went?"

I rubbed my jaw, trying to hide my grin. My family had practically made a career out of harassing me about my spot by the lake, and they had a whole catalogue of "stories" that may or may not have actually happened there. Hopefully, she'd keep them all to herself tonight.

"You know we went to the cove," I said.

Danni jumped in, recapping our afternoon together in great detail, right up to the part where things almost spiraled out of control. She gave a contented sigh.

"It was . . . just about perfect." Danni smiled at me, a mischievous sparkle in her eyes. "The meal was delicious and a really sweet surprise. But spending time talking—getting to know each other better—that was the *best* part." She bit her lip. "I can't wait to do it again."

I brushed my fingers along Danni's arms, remembering her version of "getting to know each other better." The way she'd touched me by the lake. Tempted me. How close I'd come to throwing out my whole damn plan to wait for her to let go of her past before moving forward with our future.

"Well, that was a fun little display you two put on by the gardens." Ben popped his head between ours, draping one arm over mine across Danni's shoulders and hooking the other around my neck.

"Just giving the gossips something real to buzz about for a change." Not the real reason I couldn't keep a respectable distance from Danni, but it was a definite added bonus.

"Oh, they're buzzing all right. And there are some pretty imaginative scenarios flying around. Wanna hear them?"

"Not really." I groaned and pushed Ben away.

"Fine. But you're spoiling my fun." Ben plopped into the seat next to Danni and asked if she was enjoying herself.

"What d'ya know, seems there may be some truth in rumors."

Tanner Grayson. *Fuck.* I'd hoped to avoid him until long after dinner. Avoid the risk that Danni would ditch me and cave to her fan-girl crush on that piece of shit.

"Sounds like Hollywood discovered you," I grumbled to Danni, taking her hand and helping her stand. Owning up to my promise to introduce them, even though it appeared I would be an unnecessary—and likely unwanted—participant in this conversation.

Grayson scanned every inch of Danni's body, practically stripping her with his eyes. Bastard. He winked, gaze still fixed on her, but leaned toward me. "Sure didn't waste any time picking out a sweet little piece of arm candy this year." He slapped my arm and laughed.

Danni tapped our joined hands against my leg. She flashed me a glance, and I could only imagine the thoughts going through her mind. Hoped she realized what a vile piece of trash her idol was in real life.

Ice pumped through my veins. I stood tall and glared down at Tanner, taking advantage of the three inches I had on him, and slipped my arm around Danni's waist. *Just get it over with, Giardano.*

"This is Danielle DeLaney—my girlfriend." I gritted out the words, unsure if my jaw even moved, and pulled Danni closer to my side. We hadn't discussed labels, so introducing her as mine was a gamble. Judging by her easy smile and the way she settled into my hold on her, I'd made a good call.

"It's very nice to meet you." Tanner scooped up Danni's hand and dragged it to his lips for an awkward kiss that he probably thought was romantic.

Danni tugged her hand away, reclaiming it from the over-confident slimeball, and reached for me.

I linked our fingers and grinned at Tanner. "So what are you working on these days?"

Tanner leaned against a chair back, appearing bored by the question. "Same shit as always—another sappy chick flick. You know, nothing too exciting . . . just don't let my agent know I said that." He shook his head and laughed.

"I'd like to do an action-packed thriller. Something manly, but that's not what my female fanbase wants." He shrugged. "I'm sure they could still work in some half-naked scenes to keep the ladies happy and flocking to the theaters. Right, sugar?" Tanner brushed Danni's arm and glanced around the room.

"Looks like they're beginning to serve the first course." Tanner slapped my shoulder. "We'll have to find time to talk later." He focused his attention on Danni, his gaze wandering down the front of her dress. "Maybe I can even steal you away from Nico for a dance or two."

My grip on Danni's hand tightened while I waited for her response.

She chewed on her lip then put on a tight smile, unfamiliar to me. "Thank you for the offer, but I've already convinced Nico to let me spend every dance in his arms."

The corner of my mouth twitched, a satisfied grin trying to break free, but I held it back. Waited.

It seemed to take a few moments for Danni's rejection to sink in, but Tanner's face eventually dropped. He rubbed his jaw. "I can't remember the last time I was turned down." He shook his head and looked at me. "Not sure how you managed that, but man, that's some damn good luck."

Grayson wandered off toward the bar without bothering to say goodbye—typical.

I held Danni's chair while she settled back in, ignoring the probing gazes from my siblings, then took a seat next to her. "So now you met Tanner." I fidgeted with my place setting, adjusting and rearranging everything that had been perfectly placed, anything to avoid looking at Danni. "Satisfied?"

She let out a low hum. "Not really. He's kind of a jerk."

Gabs and Ben chuckled then turned away and resumed their conversation about the soccer game Gabriela's sons played in this morning, giving Danni and me space to talk privately.

"That's a polite way of putting it, I guess." And a gross understatement. I glanced at Danni then returned my attention to the table. "You could've accepted his offer, you know." I pulled in a heavy breath and struggled to continue. "I get that he's famous. Women gush over him. And—"

Danni pressed her fingers to my lips. "None of that matters." She touched my cheek, coaxing me to look at her. "I know I could have accepted, but I meant what I said. You're the *only* man I want holding me."

"Thank you." I leaned into Danni's hand, turning to press a kiss to her palm. "I'm not sure I could've handled seeing you in his arms."

DELICIOUS
DANNI

Nico watched as I finished the last bites of my dessert, meringata with a chocolate-espresso sauce, and placed my fork on the table.

He leaned in, pressing his lips to my ear. "I don't have to ask if you enjoyed your meal." The warm rush of breath from his whispered words tickled my neck. "I think you were doing it on purpose. Teasing me with those sweet sounds."

"It wasn't intentional, just delicious. Almost as delicious as your hand on my skin all through dinner."

Nico had managed to eat most of his meal one-handed, opting to keep the other one tucked in the long slit on my dress and resting on my thigh.

I blotted my mouth with my napkin and looked at Gabriela. "I'm going to go freshen up. Care to join me?"

"Sure, I could—" She looked past me and pressed her lips together in an amused tight line. "On second thought, I'm good. Besides, I think you already have an escort."

I turned around to find Nico standing beside me with his hand extended. I bit back a grin and placed my hand in his. "I'm not taking you into the ladies' room with me."

He pulled me to his chest, catching me around the waist with his other arm. "I'd go willingly if it meant getting you alone right now." He stepped aside, still holding my hand, and motioned for me to lead the way. "Excuse us please. We'll be back in a few minutes."

"Don't get lost, you two," Ben teased. "You have a speech to make."

Nico checked his watch. "Plenty of time. Don't worry."

His hand drifted to the exposed skin of my lower back, and he guided me through the ballroom. When we reached the lobby, he steered me toward a dimly lit corridor—away from the ladies' room, at least the only one I knew about.

"Where are we going? Isn't—"

"I'm kidnapping you." He angled his face to glance at me wearing a suggestive grin. "I need five minutes alone with you before you paint that shiny red stop sign on your lips again."

Finally. I let out a long, thoughtful hum. "So what happened to that whole take-it-slow, you're-not-gonna-kiss-me plan?"

Nico tugged my waist and stopped walking, pulling me flush against his broad chest in one swift movement. "Fuck the plan." He inched forward until my back bumped against the cool marble wall. "I'd much rather kiss—"

"Hot damn. Look at you." A woman's voice, laced with a hint of laughter, filled the corridor.

Nico groaned and shifted toward the slow click of approaching heels. "Jazmine, you have the *worst* timing."

"Aww . . . you always did know how to make a girl feel loved." She laughed and pulled Nico into an overdramatic hug, humming as though *she'd* taken a bite of the world's most delicious dessert. "Just having the chance to see you all hot and sexy in your tux is well worth the huge price tag for tonight's shindig."

Nico chuckled. "I'll keep that in mind when I negotiate my

contract renewal. Maybe I can get that corner office I've been dreaming of."

She slapped his chest. "You already have a big fancy corner office, sweet cheeks."

Nico took my hand. "You remember Jazmine? We met her at Metro Sky the other week."

She looked stunning in a shimmering black dress with her red curls pulled to one side and cascading over her shoulder.

"I do. It's nice to see you again," I said.

"Considering what I interrupted, I doubt you mean that." Jazmine pulled me into a hug. "Relax. I'm not the competition." She released me and stepped back, hooking a thumb over her shoulder. "But believe me, there are plenty of gals in there who think they are."

I nodded, the insecurity I'd felt earlier tonight returning.

Jazmine touched my arm. "You don't need to worry about them. Or me." She waved a dismissive hand and shifted back to her usual easygoing demeanor. "Nah, this lovable hunk broke my heart years ago." Her eyes fell closed with an exaggerated sigh. A dreamy smile spread across her face.

"Jazmine." Nico's playful tone weakened his attempt to reprimand her.

She winked at Nico. "It was short-lived but a lot of fun." She cupped the side of her mouth and leaned toward me. "Keep in mind we were barely teenagers, so that was long before he mastered that killer charm of his . . . not to mention the killer body." Her eyes scanned Nico from head to toe, and she gave another exaggerated hum.

"Okay, Jaz, that's enough. Don't you have a date you need to get back to before you scare Danni away?"

Jazmine stretched to prop her elbow on Nico's shoulder. "That depends. Where's Logan tonight?"

Nico shook his head and removed her arm. "He had to cancel—unexpected family matter."

"Hopefully nothing serious, but . . . damn, that's . . . disappointing, if I'm being selfishly honest." She folded her arms over her chest, watching Nico with an assessing gaze. "So you're flying without your wingman? Interesting."

One corner of Nico's mouth twitched up. "Guess you could say that, but I gotta admit I kind of miss him right now."

"Eh, his loss." Jaz flipped her hair and gave a single laugh, acting as though it didn't matter. "Anyway, I'm really happy you decided to bring Danni instead."

"Glad you approve." Nico's tone was dry as he teased her.

"No, you're not." She smacked his shoulder then rested her hand on my arm. "I gotta tell you, Danni, I've known Nico my whole life, and—"

"Excuse me. Mr. Giardano?" A woman in a navy pencil skirt and white blouse approached, clutching a tablet to her chest. She tapped the Bluetooth set above her ear. "I found him."

Nico's posture shifted from the casual man I knew to a powerful business executive. "Tricia?"

"Sorry to interrupt, sir, but they're ready to get started." She glanced at Jazmine and me. "Would you like me to have them delay to give you a few more minutes?"

Nico let out a heavy breath. "No, that's not necessary. But can you escort Danni back to my family for me?"

I raised a finger between them. "*After* I visit the ladies' room."

"Absolutely." Tricia gave me a kind smile. "It would be my pleasure."

"No need. I was heading there myself. I'll keep Danni company . . . point out all the exits for her." Jazmine grinned at me and winked, unfazed by Nico's scowl. "Sheesh, so serious. I was just trying to have a little bit of fun." She laughed and rolled her eyes. "Fine. You know I'll take good care of her for you."

Nico's assistant swung her gaze back to him, waiting until he nodded his approval. "Okay. Then I'm off to meet with Simon in security regarding . . . the issue we discussed this morning. If there's anything urgent, I'll find you later for an update." Tricia tapped her Bluetooth again as she hustled down the hall. "Mr. Giardano is on his way."

Nico chuckled. "That's her way of telling me to get moving." He pressed a kiss to my temple. "Fifteen minutes, and then you're all mine for the rest of the night."

All his. Hopefully, that meant he planned to finish that kiss . . . and more. "Talk fast . . . but don't start until I get back. I don't want to miss a word."

Nico gave Jazmine a quick hug and thanked her before turning to leave.

My heart ached already, missing him, and he wasn't even out of sight yet. How could that be possible?

"You're a very lucky lady. I hope you realize that." Jazmine's casual comment pulled me back to the present. "Nico's one in a million and worth several. And he's a dear friend." She looked at me with a sweet smile. "You really hurt him. Twice."

"I know. I didn't mean to, but I—well, it's complicated. And not something I feel comfortable talking about."

"No need. Nico's already told me, and I'm really sorry for everything you've been through." She hooked her arm around mine and tugged me toward the ladies' room. "But you're not the only one trying to get over a crappy, complicated past. Keep that in mind the next time you're tempted to run off."

STEAMY STROLL
DANNI

Jazmine escorted me back to the grand ballroom, as instructed. She released my arm and strolled up to Nico, shaking her head, then patted his cheek. "You're so darn predictable it's cute."

"Is something wrong?" I asked, unsure why Nico was lounging against the wall *outside* of the ballroom's double doors instead of standing on the stage *inside*, giving his speech.

"Not at all." He took my hand, lacing our fingers together, and pulled it to his lips. "You said you didn't want to miss a word."

"So you waited for me?"

"Always." He brushed a curl from my face, his eyes locked on mine. The tender expression in them made my heart flutter.

"Okay then." Jazmine cleared her throat. "Looks like my services are no longer needed." She leaned toward my ear and lowered her voice to whisper. "Don't break his heart."

I nodded, acknowledging her, even though my heart was more likely the one to be shattered.

Nico pulled me into his arms the second she was gone,

holding me in silence for a full minute. He let out a slow breath. "You ready?"

"I think the real question is, are you?"

His head bobbed. "Yeah. This is just gonna be a little rough. I'm glad you're here with me."

Nico escorted me to my seat, seeming oblivious to the hundred pairs of eyes on us, held my hand while I sat down, then winked and made his way to the stage.

He said a few words to welcome the guests, thanking them for their more-than-generous donations and continued support of the Valentina Giardano Foundation. "My family selected me to do all of the talking tonight, claiming I was the only one of us who could get through this presentation without breaking down. So if you're placing bets on whether or not they're right, now's your last chance."

A light rumble of laughter spread through the crowd.

Gabriela leaned across the table, grinning, and tapped my arm. "That's actually the truth."

When the crowd settled, Nico continued. "As you know, tonight is our tenth annual gala. But for my family, it marks the ten-year anniversary of the loss of my mother. And since we created this foundation to honor her memory—rooted in the unconditional love and unyielding support that represented her way of living—we would like to take time to remember her."

The lights dimmed, and the wall behind Nico lit up with a photo of a young woman with dark hair and sparkling eyes that matched his. He began telling stories of his mother's youth and how she'd met his father.

As he spoke, the images changed, showing the history of his family with her as the center of it. The heart and soul, as he'd once told me. Seeing pictures of Nico as a child melted my heart. He was absolutely adorable with his trademark messy hair, lopsided grin, and single dimple already established.

"You look bored." A gentle touch on my arm accompanied Tanner's whispered interruption. He'd pushed his chair away from his table. Too close to mine.

"Not at all." I shifted away from his hand. "I love listening to Nico, and I'm enjoying his speech."

Tanner gave a low hum. "I'd much rather hear your sweet voice."

I scooted my chair away from his and returned my full attention to Nico. His heated gaze was fixed on me, staring as though I were the only person in the room.

The screen went dark, so did Nico's mood. His voice cracked, raw with emotion, as he talked about his mother's diagnosis and her grim prognosis. My heart broke for him, and I wished I could rush up there. Hold him.

He took a deep breath and blew it out slowly. "Mom would've threatened to pull out her wooden spoon if she could see us wallowing in self-pity right now."

A few people chuckled, and Ben glanced over his shoulder. "Also a true story, although she never actually used it on any of us."

Gabriela nudged Ben's arm. "Which is a true testament to her patience, considering all the trouble you and Nico got into."

The lights grew brighter, and Nico talked about families who were able to spend precious time with their loved ones thanks to the Foundation's new program, Home for Hope. He introduced a few who had joined us tonight.

"So how long you and Nico know each other?" Tanner brushed the hair from my shoulder then rested his hand on the back of my chair.

This conversation didn't warrant my attention, so I didn't turn to face him. "Not long. We met New Year's Eve." Which felt like a lifetime ago considering everything that had happened since then.

"At Logan's party? Damn, I'm really sorry I missed it now."

I gave Tanner a curious glance.

He grinned and leaned closer. "If I'd been there, I'd be the lucky one to have you on his arm tonight."

The brush of his fingers along the exposed skin of my back startled me. I slid forward in my seat and flashed him an annoyed look. A few months ago, the mere thought of Tanner Grayson asking me out would have sent my heart racing, married or not. I'd seen every one of his movies—many times—and had imagined myself as each of his lucky leading ladies. That was before I'd met Nico . . . and Tanner.

"I doubt you would have even noticed me." I turned away, hoping he would take the hint to do the same, and returned my full attention to Nico.

"So are the rumors about you two true?"

I groaned and glared at Tanner from the corner of my eye. "Excuse me?"

He gave a sarcastic laugh. "I mean, the idea of Nico in another committed relationship is a bit far-fetched, but—"

Applause sounded as Nico finished his speech, drowning out the rest of Tanner's comment. I stood with the rest of the guests, welcoming the opportunity to slip beyond his reach.

Nico lingered on the stage, talking to one of the band members, but his gaze remained locked on me the whole time —the same possessive stare I'd noticed during his speech. He clapped a hand on the man's back, ending their conversation, then stalked toward me, exuding power and confidence. Determination.

"Have I told you how incredibly beautiful you look tonight?" Nico brushed his fingertips down my arms, awakening every cell in my body with one tender touch.

I swallowed hard, my pulse racing. "Only about a dozen times, but I won't stop you from saying it a dozen more."

"Dance with me." He took my hand and guided me to the center of the dance floor. He raised one arm and twirled me beneath it, then pulled me into his embrace. "I need an excuse to hold you right now."

The band started playing—a slow, romantic song about holding someone through the night and needing her. Nico settled our joined hands against his chest then pressed his other hand to the small of my back and pulled me close. He danced with graceful ease, moving our bodies as if we were one.

"I enjoyed your speech."

"Did you?" His tone was flat but seemed to suggest a hint of doubt.

I lifted my eyes and stared up into his. "Of course. It was beautiful. Moving."

He gave a slight nod and looked past me. "I wasn't sure you were listening."

"Why would you think that?" My stomach knotted. He'd waited for me then thought I hadn't even paid attention, and the reason was obvious—my former favorite actor.

"Did Tanner enjoy it too?" Nico's grip on my hand tightened. "You two looked pretty cozy."

Wait, he's . . . he's jealous? Wow. Did not see that coming.

"Really?" I looked at Nico with wide eyes, struggling to bite back a grin. "I mean, Tanner's a mega-hot, sexy superstar and *every* woman with a pulse has had fantasies about him."

Nico leaned back, looking at me with an arched brow. "*Every* woman?"

"Well, yeah." I lowered my gaze to his lapel, tracing my fingers along the edge of the fabric. "Of course, that was before I knew he was an egotistical jerk who's too in love with himself to ever be capable of a meaningful relationship with someone else."

Nico's chest shook with a concealed laugh. He nodded. "And now?"

I lifted one shoulder. "He's not my type." I rested my cheek on Nico's chest, snuggling into his warmth.

Nico's shoulders relaxed. He slid his hand from the small of my back to my waist, pulling me closer, and rested his head against mine. After a few beats, the arm around my waist drifted lower, his fingers flexing on my hip.

"People are watching us." *But please don't let go.*

He gave a low hum, seeming unconcerned. "They're watching you." He spun us around. "Wishing they were me."

Nico extended one arm, spinning me away. With a gentle tug, he twirled me under his arm again and pulled my back to his chest. His hand slid across my stomach, holding me from behind.

"And who could blame them?" he said, his mouth pressed to my ear. Before I could respond, Nico twisted me to face him again.

I clung to his shoulder for balance. "Are you trying to show off or make me dizzy?"

Nico laughed. "Maybe a little bit of both. Is it working?"

"Yes. To both." I tightened my hold on him, wondering if I'd ever had more fun. Felt so light.

He gave a thoughtful hum. "Then maybe I better slow down." He skimmed his nose along the side of my face. "Can't have you falling."

Too late. I've already fallen . . . for you. I chewed on my lip, pushing that thought aside. "So um, where did you learn to dance like that?"

"Mom made Ben and me take lessons when we were teenagers. She wanted her sons to be perfect gentlemen, and according to Mom, that included knowing how to sweep a lady off her feet on the dance floor."

"She sounds amazing. I wish I could've met her."

"Yeah, me too."

"But does that mean Ben can dance like this too? Because I bet Kristi doesn't know."

"Well, he's nowhere near as good as I am." Nico flashed a dazzling smile. "But he does well enough to impress the ladies . . . when he wants to. And only when it doesn't interfere with his badass rocker image."

Nico pulled our joined hands to his chest. Our bodies swayed to the music while he traced circles on my back, each loop stirring up more butterflies inside me.

"So . . ." The drawn-out word echoed in Nico's chest. "If Tanner's not your type, what kind of guy are you looking for?" He tipped his head to the left, then to the right, making a subtle show of searching the room. "Maybe I can help you find him."

I tapped my chin. "Well, he'd be tall. And sexy." I brushed my fingers along his stubbled cheek then pressed my palm over his heart. "Rugged looking on the outside but tender on the inside. Caring. Honest. And fun to be with. Oh . . . and he'd have to be a really great dancer."

Nico's mouth curved up in that adorable lopsided grin. "He sounds amazing."

"Doesn't he?" I casually swept an imaginary piece of lint from his tux jacket. "I don't really need help finding him though."

"No? Why's that?"

I looped my arm around his neck. "Maybe I already found him on my own . . . well, more like he found me. But either way, he's mine." I raised my eyes to meet his. "At least I hope he is."

Nico slid his fingers into my hair, angling my face toward his, holding me as he gazed into my eyes. "Yeah, baby. I'm all yours."

He lowered his head, pressing his lips to mine in a slow,

sweet kiss that made my knees go weak. His arm tightened around my hip, supporting my weight, and he pulled me to him. When he ended the kiss, he brushed his thumb along my bottom lip but didn't release me, his eyes searching mine.

I stared at him, wide-eyed and speechless. Caught totally off guard. So many thoughts swirled in my mind, but the loudest one was how fast and hard I was falling for this man.

"Danni, say something." A crease formed between Nico's brows. "Please tell me I didn't screw things up again."

"You—of course not." I caught my lip between my teeth, tasting him there. "But you . . . kissed me."

"Glad you noticed." A sexy smirk spread across his face. Fire danced in his eyes.

"In the middle of the dance floor. In front of all these people. In front of your entire family." A quick glance around confirmed they'd all seen it. And were all still watching.

"Relax. My family isn't stupid. They've already figured out how I feel about you. As for the rest of the people, their opinions don't matter to me." He tapped the tip of my nose. "And no, I'm not drunk."

I threw my arms around his neck and pushed up on my toes to kiss him.

Nico's shoulders shook with laughter. He leaned down and whispered in my ear, "I could've sworn you said you weren't into public displays."

"Good point. Maybe we should go somewhere private." I bit my lip, straightening his tie and smoothing the front of his jacket.

Nico framed my face, his eyes locked on mine. "I know the perfect place. Come with me." He placed his hand at the small of my back and guided me toward the wall of folding glass doors that opened onto the patio.

"Have fun, you two," a woman called from behind us.

Nico slowed but didn't turn around. "Good night,

Jazmine." He chuckled and mumbled something under his breath. "Let's get out of here before she decides she wants to chat again."

We made it outside, where several other couples milled around under the stars. "So where are we going?"

"I thought we could take a short walk." Nico turned to the right and continued to the end of the patio. "There's a gazebo that overlooks the lake, and the gardens around it are beautiful this time year."

"Hmm . . . I think you're just trying to get me alone." I nudged him with my hip and glanced back at the ballroom, all the unfamiliar faces—everyone in their formal attire—and Jazmine, who seemed to blend in with ease.

"That too." Nico took my hands to help me down a set of wide stone steps, hesitating at the bottom. He drew in a slow breath. "If you changed your mind, we can go back."

"What? No, I just—"

"Keep turning around?"

"No. Well, yes . . . I guess I was. But I definitely want to keep going." I stretched up to kiss his cheek then looped my arm through his. "Especially if it means you're going to kiss me again."

Nico gave a single nod, and his grin returned. "That's the plan."

After walking in silence for a minute or two, Nico cleared his throat. "So are you going to tell me what had you distracted back there?"

"It's nothing really. I was just . . . surprised, I guess. To see Jazmine here."

"Really? Why?"

I shrugged. "It's just, well, a thousand dollars seems like a lot for a bartender to shell out for one dinner. Not to mention the cost of her dress and everything else."

Nico nodded. "Jaz comes from money, and she earns a

decent living on her own with her paintings. She only tends bar because it's fun." He made air quotes on the last two words with his free hand. "Her father owns Metro Sky . . . and the building it's in. Along with a few others."

"Well, she's very protective of you." I glanced at him from the corner of my eye, wanting to gauge his reaction. Hoping it didn't reveal a spark of romantic interest.

"She's a good friend." Nico grinned and shook his head. "Jazmine's an only child. So when dating didn't work out for us, she decided I'd be her brother instead—said that fit better for the way we felt about each other anyway. We've been close ever since."

We continued along a cobblestone path lined with luminaries, their flickering flames casting a romantic glow. I clung to Nico's arm, thrilled to be sneaking off with him. Confident we both had the same plan for our stroll this time.

So why couldn't I just enjoy that and stop focusing on how wealthy and powerful everyone in Nico's life seemed to be? *Everyone except me, that is.*

My perpetual fear resurfaced, warning that it would only be a matter of time until he realized I didn't fit into this world. Into his life. There was no denying we had an intense chemical attraction, but how could we have anything in common?

He brushed my arm, drawing my attention back to the present. "What's on your mind? You seem miles away."

How could he know me so well already? "You. This place. The people. Everything about tonight. There's a lot for a simple girl like me to absorb."

He glanced my way. "Simple is perfect for me. As for the rest? I'm not sure—are those things good or bad?"

"They're good. Mostly. Just different than what I'm used to. For example, big fancy parties like this—they're normal for you?"

Nico nodded. "Believe it or not, they lose their appeal after the first few and become pretty routine. Monotonous even. But I'll admit, getting dressed up tonight to spend the evening with you has a whole new feel." He slipped his arm around my waist, pulling me to his side. "This is the first party I've enjoyed in a long time."

I rested my head against his shoulder, my fear subsiding. "It all feels like a fairytale to me. I keep thinking I'm going to wake up and realize this whole weekend has been a dream."

Nico pressed a kiss to the top of my head. "More like a dream come true."

He took my hand and pulled me up a step into a cozy white gazebo. Tiny lights twinkled around the perimeter of the ceiling like distant stars in the night sky. A gentle breeze blew through, rustling the needles of nearby pine trees, and the moon glistened off the tiny ripples on the lake's surface.

"This is so beautiful." I drifted toward the railing to get a better view, a sense of calm and anticipation stirring inside me.

Nico moved to stand behind me and wrapped me in his warm embrace. "Funny, I was just thinking the same thing about you."

The sounds of nature surrounded us, peaceful and sooth-ing, but they couldn't calm the racing beat of my heart. Nico's hips swayed as though dancing to an imaginary tune. His gentle hands brushed my sides in long, slow strokes, sending chills through me. He took my hand and twirled me away from him, then pulled me into his strong arms and rested his hand on the curve above my backside.

"Where's the music?" I teased, touching the side of his face. The tension I'd noticed earlier had faded.

"Right here." He grinned and tapped his fingers to his chest. "Being with you makes my heart sing."

I laughed. "I swear you must be drunk."

"Nope. Unless you count being drunk on you." He spun us around then dipped me with one arm, making me shriek. He paused there, holding me, his face hovering mere inches above mine. His eyes searched mine with an intensity that made me weak. "This is just what being with you does to me."

"Aah, but have you decided what you're going to do with me yet?" I clung tighter to his triceps, waiting for him to kiss me.

A crease formed in Nico's brow. He straightened, pulling me with him. After a moment, his grin stretched wider, obviously remembering our conversation before we'd left the penthouse this evening.

"About that . . ." He stepped away, lifted the top off of one of the lanterns, and blew out the candle inside. "I've had a few ideas cross my mind"—he moved to a lantern on the other side of the path and glanced over his shoulder at me—"but they've all been pretty inappropriate."

"Then they sound perfect to me." I hooked my finger, motioning for him to come closer.

"I was hoping you'd say that." Nico grinned then extinguished the second flame, cloaking the back half of the gazebo in a veil of darkness. He returned to me and brushed the sides of my face with gentle strokes, letting his hands slide to my neck. "You realize you're to blame for those thoughts with the way you've been teasing me all night."

I bit my lip then smoothed my tongue over the spot, aching to kiss him again. "It's only teasing if I don't plan to follow through." I glanced up at him through my lashes, slipped my hands to his shoulders, and stretched toward his ear. "I wasn't teasing."

Nico's warm breath caressed my face. He inched forward, his chest brushing against my breasts. Each subtle touch sent a new wave of desire racing through me. Every cell of my body tingled, longing for his touch. His kiss. Our eyes met, the intensity of his stare revealing more than words could express. His soul mirrored every emotion swirling around my heart.

"God, you're so beautiful." Nico lowered his face, pressing his lips to mine in a tender kiss that shot sparks straight to my core.

His lips began to move, gentle at first then becoming more firm. Hungry. Greedy. He swept his tongue into my mouth, brushing it across mine, and deepened our kiss. The sounds he made—faint moans—vibrated through me, making me feel more desired than I ever had before.

Nico grabbed my waist, his lips never leaving mine, and guided me backward until I bumped against a wide lattice support post at the back of the gazebo. He took another step, pinning me there with the full length of his rock-hard body. His mouth slipped from mine and moved to my neck, kissing and nipping a slow trail to my shoulder.

My head fell to the side on a sigh, opening myself up to him. Welcoming the sensual whirlwind he created inside me with such ease.

"So sexy." Nico kissed his way back up my neck, stopping below my ear. "I love the way your body responds to me."

"Mmm . . . I love what you do to my body."

He slid one hand lower, gliding over the curve of my hip. "This dress has been driving me wild all night. Flashing little glimpses of your sexy body every damn time you moved." He ran his fingers under the slit in my dress and gave a satisfied hum, stoking the embers of the fire he'd ignited.

Nico tensed. His fist clenched in the fabric, frozen, and he dropped his forehead to my shoulder. "Danni—"

"No. Don't you dare stop." Panic clawed at my chest, fear of another rejection ringing in my ears. I nuzzled the side of his face, struggling to calm down. Catch my breath. "Please, Nico. I want this as much as you do." I reached up between us and pulled his mouth back to mine.

Nico resisted my kiss for a moment then swept his tongue past my lips, picking up where he'd left off. He pushed aside the gaping fabric along my thigh and stroked my exposed skin, growling into my mouth and rolling his hips against mine.

Each touch, each sound, made me want more. I scraped my nails along the rugged stubble on his face and slid my fingers into his thick, lush hair.

Nico eased his hand down my thigh and lifted my leg, pinning it against his hip. His hand drifted higher, fingertips dancing along the edge of my panties. He wedged his leg between mine and adjusted the angle, creating an exquisite pressure in just the right spot.

Waves of pleasure rolled through me, and an involuntary whimper slipped past my lips. I slid my hands inside his jacket and clung to his back, tugging his shirt free so I could touch his skin.

Nico trailed kisses along my jaw to the spot below my ear, sucking and nipping at the sensitive spot. Driving me wild. "We should probably head upstairs." His chest rose and fell on heavy breaths.

In that moment, I belonged to him. Mind, body, and soul. My eyes fell closed as I surrendered to the uncontrollable desire consuming every part of me. I wanted everything from him— needed all of him. "Won't your family wonder what happened to us if we don't go back?" *Please say no.*

He kissed me again then smiled against my lips. "They don't expect to see us anymore tonight."

SATURDAY NIGHT FUN ENDS
NICO

I'd been dying to kiss Danni—and more—all night. All weekend. But especially tonight. And since I'd already lost our little game of delayed gratification by kissing her on the dance floor, thanks to a wild case of jealousy, my plan to hold out for a sweet-but-memorable good-night kiss had been shot to hell. No point in continuing to torture myself. Or her.

My grip on her delicate fingers tightened as we rushed along the trail, racing back to the penthouse like a couple of kids, where I planned to rip that dress off Danni and explore every inch of her body. We should slow down to a respectable pace—an inconspicuous stroll—but every time I tried, my girl would plead with me to get moving.

We ducked through a service entrance near the kitchen, avoiding the risk of random mood-killing conversations with family or guests in the grand ballroom. I pulled Danni into my arms for another deep kiss before strolling down the long corridor, both of us laughing and trying to act as though we weren't about to—

"Mr. Giardano. Nico," my assistant called out, her heels

clicking on the marble floor as she rushed toward us from the main lobby.

I groaned and stopped, giving Danni's hand a squeeze, and bowed my head. "Sorry. I should see what she needs." Damn sense of responsibility.

Tricia reached us, slightly out of breath. "So glad I caught you. I just need a few minutes." She tipped her head to the side, indicating we should step away to talk in private. "It's important."

Great. Tricia had been with me since I'd moved into the COO position thirteen years ago, long enough for me to pick up on her subtle hint that this had something to do with our earlier conversation about Summer.

"I'll only be a minute." I gave Danni a quick kiss on her cheek then added a playful wink, not wanting her to sense my tension. "Try not to miss me too much."

Tricia stood waiting, clutching her tablet to her chest, and grinning ear-to-ear as I approached. I shook my head.

"What's with the look?" I teased.

Tricia had also been one of my mom's closest friends for as long as I could remember, and she'd taken it upon herself to watch out for Gabs, Ben, and me after we lost Mom.

"It's just so nice to see you happy." She leaned in and whispered, "I like her."

I laughed. "Glad you approve . . . *mom.* Hopefully, you didn't drag me away from my beautiful date just to tell me that."

"That does sound like something your mother would have done."

Very true, especially if she'd seen the way I'd been looking at Danni at that moment. Mom would have known exactly what we'd been up to.

Tricia sighed. "Unfortunately, that's not why I interrupted you two. You asked me to update you if security had anything to report."

After last weekend's meeting didn't go the way Summer had wanted, I'd put my staff on alert, anticipating she'd follow through with her original threat.

Tricia glanced in Danni's direction. "Simon said she arrived, alone, right when everyone was being seated for dinner. She gave security a difficult time when they turned her away, demanding to speak to you, but she eventually left."

"Let me guess—only after they threatened to call the police."

Tricia gave me a sympathetic look and nodded. "Afraid so." She touched my arm, holding it until I met her eyes. "I'm sorry for ruining your mood, and possibly your plans for the evening, but I wanted to make you aware of the situation before you *turned in* for the night."

Shit. My plans *were* shot to hell now. But this mess reminded me I never should have let things with Danni go as far—and as quickly—as they had. If Tricia hadn't stopped us, I'd probably have Danni naked in my bed and be buried deep inside her right now. I needed to cool things down before we both wound up getting hurt. Again.

"Thank you." I patted Tricia's hand. "I needed to know."

She disappeared toward the elevators leading to the executive suite, leaving me along with my thoughts.

Summer hadn't been happy when I'd rejected her ridiculous proposition last weekend, especially after she'd blindsided me with—damn, I still couldn't even think the words. I shoved a hand through my hair and let my head fall back.

She wasn't going to make this whole ordeal easy, but I wasn't about to give in—or back off. I just needed to be patient. Gather all the facts before I planned my next move.

"Hey. Everything okay?" Danni slipped her arms around me and rested her head against my chest.

Not even close. "Yeah." I pulled her to me and pressed my lips to her forehead. The ache in my chest threatened to consume me. I needed Danni like I needed my next breath, an unobtainable breath I'd be craving for the unforeseeable future. "Tricia just wanted to update me on an issue I need to deal with."

In the meantime, I had to protect Danni's heart—and my own—and try not to lose her in the fucking process.

I wove my fingers through Danni's hair and lifted her face toward mine. "Thank you for tonight. For this whole weekend." Like a bee to honey—despite knowing better—I pressed my lips to Danni's, moving slow, savoring their sweetness.

With a heavy sigh, I pulled away and extended my hand. "You ready to call it a night?"

Danni led me through the penthouse, her fingers laced with mine. She glanced over her shoulder every few steps. "Your room or mine?"

The sultry smile on her luscious lips, still swollen from kissing me, made it hard to remember why I couldn't drag her into my room. I stopped in the hallway and pulled her into my arms, reveling in the feel of her soft body pressed against mine. Breathing in her sweet floral scent.

I lifted her chin, tipping her face toward mine. Her eyes burned with passion. Need. The same emotions I felt but couldn't give in to. I brushed my lips against hers, a tender kiss good night. "Yours. And mine."

Danni bit her lip, a soft blush creeping over her cheeks. "Okay, both. I like the sound of that."

I shook my head, telling her no. Telling myself no? I couldn't be sure anymore. My gaze fell to her mouth, and her tongue peeked out, licking her lips. I groaned and pressed my lips to hers again, one last taste to get me through the night.

She purred and melted against me, clinging to my shirt and pulling me closer. Testing my faltering restraint with each rock of her hips against mine. Every stroke of her tongue across the seam of my mouth, begging for me to open to her. Then she nipped at my lower lip, and that was all it took to break my shaky resolve. I swept my tongue into her mouth, taking control. Taking whatever she'd give me.

Danni let out a small gasp when her back bumped against the wall, but her arms tightened around me, preventing a retreat. Encouraging me to keep going.

I pinned her with my hips and continued devouring her mouth while exploring her body with a slow caress. A faint voice in the back of my head kept telling me I needed to stop, but I couldn't. Something about this woman just made it impossible for me to walk away.

Danni shifted beneath me. She reached for her bedroom door, pushed it open, and tugged me toward the opening.

That damn voice of reason shouted, demanding I find some fucking self-control before it was too late. I released Danni and braced my hands on the doorframe, forcing myself to break our kiss.

"What are you doing?" Danni stared at me, dazed and breathing as hard as me.

"I'm saying good night." *Like a fucking idiot.* "Like I meant to ten minutes ago."

She grinned and snaked her arms around my waist. "We need to work on your joke timing, 'cause that's not funny."

I caught her wrists and pulled her hands to her sides before things—meaning me—got out of control again. "Danni—"

"No." She raised her hands between us, two dainty stop signs, then steepled her fingers between her eyes as they fell closed. "Dammit, Nico. No. Don't do this."

My chest tightened—guilt, fear, and the weight of her pain crushing me. I brushed her arms and forced out the only explanation I could give. "Sweetheart, I promised you nothing would happen."

"Yeah, well . . . I'm a little slow, but I get that now." She turned away, wrapping her arms across her stomach. "You've made it abundantly clear—several times—that you didn't bring me here so you'd have someone to screw all weekend long. So why *am* I here?"

"Because I want you here." I eased up behind her, gripping her shoulders, and rested my head against hers.

"Why, Nico? I seriously don't get what we're doing." She turned in my arms but pressed her palm over my racing heart, pushing me away. "Is this all just some game to you? Entertainment? Putting on a show to give people something to talk about? Because—"

"I don't give a fuck about other people. This is about you and me, Danni. No one else matters." I reached for Danni's face, slipping my fingers through her hair, and looked into her eyes. "It's just us—two people exploring some pretty intense feelings and getting to know each other better. For now."

"For now?" Danni's voice shot up, her eyes wide. Wounded. She pulled away and moved toward the hallway.

I caught her arm and tugged her to my chest. "Where do you think you're gonna to run to, Danni? You're sixty miles from home, and your only choice this time is to stick around and talk about what's *really* upsetting you."

Danni squared her shoulders and lifted her chin, glaring at me with utter contempt. "You mean other than the fact that you were dry-humping me against a wall one minute then acting like someone dumped a bucket of ice over you the next?" She swept her arm toward the hall, not that I really needed clarification.

"You're so damn hot and cold, Nico. All. The. Time." She jabbed a finger in my chest, driving home her point. "Constantly flipping between treating me like I'm the most important person in the world to you—"

I opened my mouth to tell Danni she was, but she raised her palm, silencing me before I could get out a word.

She continued without missing a beat. "And acting like I'm a deadly toxin you're determined to avoid at all costs."

Her blunt but accurate description hit like a punch to my gut.

"You'll thank me for that later," I grumbled, shoving my hand through my hair. Tugging on the strands while taking a slow, deep breath. "But yes, beyond . . . that. *You're* always looking for an excuse to run off. Run away from me. Away from us." I raised my face toward the ceiling and blew out a weary breath. "It's getting really exhausting."

"*You're* exhausted? Your constant back and forth is giving me freakin' whiplash, Nico. I'm so confused." Danni turned away. "I . . . I don't know what I'm doing here. I keep fooling myself into thinking you care about me, and then—" She wandered over to the window, staring out into the darkness. "I don't want to get hurt again."

But she had. And I was to blame. My heart ached for her, because I knew that feeling—that pain—all too well.

I eased deeper into her room, desperate to fix this. "Do you really think I would have brought you here, invited you to spend a weekend with my entire family at an event honoring my mother, if I didn't care about you?" I joined Danni by the window, sitting to face her.

"What I meant by 'for now' is that I want *more*. When the time is right." I took her hand, brushing my thumb across the top of it. Across my proof that I was making the right decision. "It's too soon, Danni, and I'm not willing to rush things. For both our sakes."

Sometimes doing the right thing really sucks.

A single tear slid down Danni's face. I stood and swiped it away, letting my hand rest on her shoulder. My gaze locked on hers, and I let out a sigh.

"This was supposed to be a fun trip, and I'm so happy to have you here. With me. It's what I want." I hooked a finger under her chin, tipping her face toward mine. "But I'll take you home if you don't want to be here."

That was also part of the promise I'd made for this weekend. I just never imagined I'd need to own up to it.

Seconds ticked by, stretching into a full minute. Danni didn't respond. Didn't move.

"I'm really upset right now." Her faint words drifted toward the window. She twisted her lips, her brows scrunched together. "Angry might be closer to accurate."

She took a deep breath and placed her palm on my cheek. Her eyes met mine with a tender expression that touched my soul. "But despite everything, wherever you are is where I want to be."

UNCHARTED TERRITORY
DANNI

I tossed and turned, unable to drift off to sleep. Unable to let go of the frustration and disappointment at how my *almost* perfect day had ended.

I'd assumed—quite foolishly—that "call it a night" was guy code for "let me take you to bed before I lose control and fuck you in public." How was I to know he actually meant "let's say good night and go to our respective beds?" Alone.

Especially after we'd continued to make out like honeymooners in the elevator to the penthouse, then raced down the dimly lit hall to our rooms, where Nico had pressed me up against my door, kissing me breathless.

Kissing me good night.

Maybe I shouldn't have opened that door, tried to pull him inside with me, and just let things progress right there. In the hallway. Where any one of his family members could have walked in on us.

Maybe staying in his family's penthouse was his way of *preventing* anything more from happening between us. *Damn "No expectations."* I dragged a pillow over my head, muffling my agonized groan.

He'd brushed the hair from my face, twisting his finger in one of the long curls. "It's too soon. I'm not willing to rush things," he'd said. His dark eyes had betrayed him though, revealing the same passion and desire that had burned inside me.

And still did.

I pulled the pillow away and touched my fingers to my mouth, remembering the feel of his lips against mine. Hearing the passionate sounds he'd made. Longing for the thrill of his hands on my skin again.

With each second that ticked by, I became more tortured by Nico's presence—so close, but too far away. I imagined him standing outside my door, hands in his hair, struggling to decide if he should come in.

I wished he would. My body ached, needing to be with him. Every touch, every kiss, every moment spent in his arms tonight had only left me wanting more.

Enough of this. I threw off the covers, swung my legs over the side of the bed, stretched to grab my robe, then headed for the door—girl on a mission to get her man.

Ignoring the twinge of disappointment at finding an empty hall, I took a deep breath and reached for Nico's door with a trembling hand, hesitating before gently pressing down on the lever.

Locked. *Dammit.*

Without pausing to think, I tapped lightly, whispering his name. The lock clicked, and the door opened. He must have been standing right there to have answered so quickly.

Holy shit. The sight of Nico, bare chested, took my breath away. Navy silk lounge pants sitting low on his hips. Chiseled six-pack and deep-cut V-lines on full display. And a sexy little happy trail just begging to be followed.

Perfect. The way he looked. The way I felt. The perfect opportunity.

"Were you waiting for me?" I bit my lip, glancing up at him through my lashes.

"I—" He dragged a hand through his already messy hair and leaned into the doorframe. "I couldn't sleep."

"Me either." I stepped closer and pressed a hand to his chest, coaxing him to take a step back. Allow me to enter. "And since we're both awake . . ." I pulled the sash around my waist, letting my robe slide off my shoulders and fall to the floor. "And barely dressed . . ." I traced one finger down the center of his smooth chest. "We might as well have a little fun."

Nico let out a slow hiss, the muscles of his torso flexing. His lounge pants strained across his growing erection.

I skimmed the top of the silky fabric, imagining how he looked beneath it—anxious to finally find out—and dipped my fingers below the waistband.

Nico wrapped his hand around my wrist, fingers flexing on my racing pulse. His grip tightened, putting an end to my exploration. "Danni—"

"What's stopping you, Nico?" I let the fingertips of my free hand lightly dance across his shoulder and down his arm, tracing the lines of the tribal band around his bicep.

He blew out a heavy breath. "Right now? A hell of a lot of self-control." He raised my hand from his waist and held it over his pounding heart. His eyes locked on mine, reaching into my soul.

I stretched toward his ear and whispered, "Lose it."

His eyes grew dark. He slipped his other hand behind my head and pulled me to him. Our breath mingled, lips brushing. He let out a strangled groan, and his mouth covered mine.

Nico's hand slid down my back then drifted lower and cupped my bottom. He pulled me closer, his erection pressing against my abdomen while his fingertips skimmed the edge of my satin shorts, each gentle brush sending sparks of pleasure pulsing through me. A small whimper escaped me as I rolled my hips against his.

Nico groaned and pulled away, licking his lips. His chest heaved on heavy breaths. "Danni, please. Saying no to you is killing me, but—"

"Then don't."

He closed his eyes, a pained expression on his face. His jaw flexed as seconds ticked by in silence. "I want you more than I've ever wanted anyone, but we need to wait. *I* need to wait."

Nico grabbed my left hand, stroking my palm with his fingers before raising it between us. The dim light from his bedside table lamp reflected off my diamond solitaire—the ring that had branded me as Will's for so many years.

"Why do you still wear this?"

My mouth opened and closed several times. "I-I don't know." I turned away, searching for something to look at. Anything. As long as it would help me avoid staring at the pain in his eyes. "Habit, I guess." How could I explain to Nico why I wore the damn ring when I didn't fully understand it myself?

I hated Will for what he did to me—did to us—so I should hate wearing his ring too. And I did.

But some days taking it off just felt wrong. Other days, wearing it was a conscious effort—a reminder of everything I'd been through. A reminder to never let someone else lie and hurt me the way Will had.

A reminder to protect my heart.

I met Nico's gaze, staring deep into his wounded soul. "It's just a piece of jewelry. It doesn't mean anything to me. Not anymore." At least not anything I wanted to share.

Nico shrugged. "Maybe. But I think there's a part of you that still loves Will and needs to grieve."

"Doubtful." I moved closer, snaking my arms around him and letting my hands glide over his lounge pants. "Maybe I just need someone to make me forget about him."

Nico reached behind his waist, grabbed my wrists, and pulled my hands to my sides. "I'm looking to build a future with you, not be a solution to your past."

"That's not what I meant. I want you *for* you, not because of . . . him. Or what he did to me." I lowered my head, hiding the rejection that burned in my eyes.

"I get it. More than you realize." Nico placed a finger under my chin, coaxing my gaze back to his. "When I make love to you, I need to be sure it's *me* you see when you close your eyes."

He scrubbed a hand across his face, pulled in a deep breath, then released it with a slow, muffled groan.

"Stay here." Nico placed a single kiss to my temple then crossed the room with slow, labored steps, stopping in front of a long dresser. He stood there, motionless, time passing in awkward silence. Reaching out with an abrupt movement, he snatched something from atop the dresser then sat on the edge of his bed and tapped the empty spot next to him.

A pained expression crossed his face as our eyes met, followed by a blank stare—a mask that failed to hide the pain radiating from him.

My gut wrenched at his sudden change of mood, a churning sensation in the pit of my stomach. But I pushed aside my fear, climbed onto his pillow-topped mattress, and snuggled against him.

His fingers traced the stitching around the edge of his wallet, then he opened it without looking up and flipped to the lone photo it contained. "This is Summer. My wife." He bobbed his head. "Ex-wife."

"She's, um." I wrapped my arms across my midsection and swallowed hard against the bile rising in my throat. "She's beautiful . . . and still in your wallet." My trembling voice echoed the panicked rhythm of my heart.

Long blonde hair glistened in the sunlight, framing the petite tanned face staring at me. Her blue eyes sparkled with the seductive energy of a woman in love as she blew a kiss at the man of my dreams. She was . . . perfect. I couldn't compete. Couldn't even come close. *No wonder he can't bring himself to settle for me.*

I closed my eyes, wanting her to vanish, and focused on the subtle hum of Nico's voice.

"We met in college, dated for a while." His thumb brushed across her lips as he spoke, the distant tone of his voice matching his vacant stare. He seemed lost, reliving a time in his past. "She moved to Europe at the start of my junior year. Wanted to be a model." His chest heaved on a heavy sigh. "Broke my heart when she left."

"We've all been dumped. And it hurts." I brushed my fingers along the side of his rugged face. "You're sweet for trying to help me see that, but . . . well, that's not quite the same as what I've been through."

Nico leaned into my touch, turning to place a kiss to my palm. "She moved back a few years later. Got a job in New York City. Logan and I ran into her at a club one night." His eyes fell closed. "God, she was just so beautiful."

The crushing words hung heavy in my chest, making it hard to breathe.

He flashed a glance at me, an apologetic expression. "We started seeing each other again and were married the following year."

So many questions swirled in my mind, making me dizzy. Trying to choose the right one to ask first seemed impossible. I opened my mouth, but nothing came out.

"She made me feel alive. Something I haven't felt for a while. Too long." He turned to face me, a warm smile in place. "Until I met you."

Nico returned his gaze to the floor and continued his story in the same somber tone as before. "We bought a place in

Mountainside, close to Elevations. She quit her job. Said she wanted to stay home and be the *perfect wife*."

His shoulders shook as a bitter laugh escaped him. "I decided to surprise her for our first anniversary. Booked a romantic trip to the islands and came home early from work to whisk her away. I made my way through the house, past the messy bed she never made, and moved toward the splashing water of the shower.

"I paused outside the bathroom. Aroused by the mere images of her in my mind, I decided to join her and slipped past the door, already beginning to undress. There she was. On her knees, moaning with pleasure as she sucked another man's cock."

Nico's fists clenched around his wallet, crushing the photo inside its protective sleeve.

"I—damn. Nico, I—" Nothing I could say would be enough. I climbed on his lap, overwhelmed by the need to comfort him.

He wrapped his arms around my waist, clinging to me. "Needless to say, I didn't stick around for an introduction. Didn't want to hear her lies or shake the hand of the fucking bastard who'd taken my wife. I didn't even want to expend enough energy to smash his pretty-boy face against the tiled wall, although I probably should have."

Nico's wounded eyes stared past me. "The woman who'd vowed to love me for the rest of my life had betrayed me in the worst possible way. Nothing else mattered."

He stroked my back, pulling me closer. "I walked out. Filed for divorce the next day, and swore I'd never give another woman the chance to destroy me the way she had."

He shook his head, an amused grin on his face. "That *was* working out for me."

"I . . . I didn't know. You must have—I couldn't—" How

could I tell him I understood his heartache, make him believe me, when I couldn't seem to figure out my own?

"Make love to me." I pressed a tender kiss to the side of his neck. "Take away the pain. For both of us."

Nico cradled my face, staring deep into my eyes with a passion that rivaled my own. His eyes fell closed, shielding his emotions. "It's not enough." He rested his forehead against mine. "I can't be a stand-in—just some random warm body filling a void until you get over losing your husband."

"You won't be." I brushed my lips across his, a silent plea for him to trust me. Let me in.

His body tensed, but he didn't move. Didn't tell me to stop.

I covered his mouth with mine in a slow kiss, savoring the taste of him. It didn't take long for his resistance to fade. His lips vibrated against mine, a soft moan that resonated through me and settled in my core. Nico's hands fisted in my hair as he took control, kissing me with an animalistic hunger. His tongue skimmed across my lips in a sensual assault that left me breathless.

I'd dreamed of this moment so many times. Longed for it to come true. An anxious gasp slipped past my parted lips. My body began to rock against his, an instinctive response to his seductive power over me. Each slow stroke across the silk that barely concealed his bulging erection created an erotic sensation that increased the throbbing between my legs.

His hands fell to my waist, fingers digging into my flesh. He pulled me closer and let out a slow hiss as his body moved in time with mine.

Nico stood, lifting me with him, our bodies pressed together. His mouth caught mine in another urgent kiss that made me sway, despite my firm grip on his broad shoulders. His hands skimmed my torso, leaving a heated trail to my breasts then back to my waist. He eased away to look at me and licked his lips. Fire burned in his eyes, a need that mirrored my own.

"You're so fucking beautiful." Nico pressed his lips to my forehead, drew in a slow breath, then released me and crossed the room. He stood by the door with his back to me and shoved his hands through his hair, grasping the back of his head. Waves of tension rolled off him as he stared at the ceiling.

Seconds ticked by in silence. Nico shook his head and pushed out a single laugh. "I must be fucking crazy."

He scooped my robe from the floor and turned to face me. My chest tightened, waiting for him to tell me to leave. Bracing for another painful blow of rejection.

"Actually . . . I'm sure I am." He moved toward me with hesitant steps. "Problem is, I'm too selfish. I won't give you what you want, but I don't want you to leave."

He reached behind me, draping my robe across my shoulders, then guided each of my arms into the sleeves.

Nico framed my face. "Stay with me. I want to hold you all night long. But when we get into this bed, it's to sleep." Dark eyes searched mine. "No sex. No foreplay. No fooling around."

"Well, that's *no* fun. What if I want to fool around and don't agree to your boring rules?"

Nico winked then brushed his lips against mine. "My bed. My rules."

A firm, passionate kiss replaced the light, gentle touch. His hands slid from my face and glided along my arms to my waist. He pushed aside the robe and slipped his hands under the hem of my camisole. Strong, gentle hands caressed my stomach, inching their way higher with each stroke. Nico brushed the underside of my breasts, letting out a low hum that blended with my desperate sigh.

"Christ, if I survive tonight, it will be an absolute miracle." He took my hands and led me to his massive bed. After one more tender kiss, he released me. "That was good night, beautiful."

Nico tugged my top back into place. He overlapped the front edges of my robe as far as they would reach and tied the sash in a double knot behind my back.

He scooped me up in his strong arms and placed me in the center of his soft bed. "Turn on your side, facing away from me."

I propped myself on one elbow, tapping the mattress in front of me.

Nico rolled his eyes and shook his head. "I need your hands where they're less likely to get into trouble." He motioned for me to turn around.

I pressed my head into one of Nico's plush pillows, surrounded by his intoxicating scent. The mattress dipped as he climbed in behind me. He snuggled close, as promised, draping one arm across my stomach and pulling me against him. Every inch of his perfect body molded to mine.

"This is totally uncharted territory for me. But who knows, spending the whole night aroused and resisting you—taking that 'delayed gratification' thing to a whole new level—may turn out to be intensely erotic."

I reached behind me, stroking the silky fabric that covered his thigh.

Nico groaned. He caught my wrist and trapped it against my stomach. "You're not going to make this easy, are you?"

"Afraid you can't handle the challenge?"

I wanted him to cave. Toss aside his ridiculous plan to wait and make love to me all night long. I pushed back, settling into his embrace, and rocked my butt against his massive erection.

"Danni—" His hand slid lower, gripping my hip and pinning me tighter against him.

I lifted my head, grinning over my shoulder at him. "Hmmm?"

He shook his head then kissed my cheek. "Sleep, my beautiful angel."

I let out a heavy sigh, deflating as my head crashed back into the pillow. Every cell in my body hummed with desire, desperate for Nico to push me over the edge. But it seemed I'd have to settle for *almost*. Again.

THE TENSE RIDE HOME
DANNI

I 'd hoped to wake up Nico's arms. Dreamed that he'd come to his senses by morning—change his mind about making love to me.

Should've known better.

I stretched and gave a faint yawn, alone again in his king-sized bed and still filled with unreleased sexual tension. Nico's room was quiet. Bright sunshine peeked around the curtain edges, and a soft light glowed inside his walk-in closet.

I scooted to kneel at the foot of his bed, holding onto the tall wooden post. "Good morning."

Nico appeared in the closet doorway, fully dressed and rolling up the sleeves on a casual plaid shirt. A lazy smile spread across his contented face. "Good morning, beautiful. You sleep well?"

I avoided his gaze, pulling on the sash of my robe and twisting my hand in it. "Did you sleep on the floor again?"

He laughed and moved toward me. "I should have. But no, I didn't." Nico hooked one arm around the bed post and caught my chin with his other hand, tilting my face upward. He pressed his lips to mine for a gentle kiss then pulled back to study me, a crease forming between his brows. "Everything okay?"

"Sure. Why wouldn't it be?" *Other than the fact that we ended what was probably the most amazing day of my life with a PG-rated snuggle fest. And you apparently couldn't wait for even that to end.* "I'm still waking up." I pulled free from his hold and looked away. "Guess I didn't expect to do it alone."

Nico stepped to the side, back into my line of vision. He brushed my cheek and let his fingers float down my neck. "You looked so beautiful sprawled out on my bed. Peaceful. I didn't want to disturb you." The corner of his mouth curved up in a lopsided grin. "Or do something I'd promised I wouldn't."

I bit the inside of my lip, struggling to prevent my body's usual reaction to his touch. To him. "Maybe I was hoping you would."

He released me and shoved his hand through his hair, still damp from the shower. His smile faded. "I'm sorry. I know last night didn't end the way you wanted it to, but we talked about that. I explained wh—"

I held up my hand to silence him before he chimed in with another word on the subject. "I get it. Well . . . not really, but I at least remember what you said. So let's just drop it."

I'm done with rejections. Done embarrassing myself.

I slid off the edge of his bed and backed away, adjusting my robe. "If it's okay with you, I'd like to go home now."

"Danni, I—" Nico dragged his hands through his hair. His eyes squeezed shut, failing to shield the pain he felt.

"Don't." I turned away, afraid I'd cave again and run to Nico. Tell him I'd changed my mind. "You just got done telling me you didn't want to break your promises. Well, you also promised I could leave whenever I wanted to."

He blew out a heavy breath but didn't try to stop me as I ran out of his room.

NICO SHIFTED GEARS, zipping his Ferrari along the open road. "Don't be mad at me." He reached across the console to take my hand.

"I'm not." It wasn't a total lie. I was mostly frustrated . . . and disappointed, but with myself as much as with him. Not to mention humiliated. I turned away, staring out the passenger's window. "It's my own fault. Guess I just misunderstood."

Nico took a deep breath and blew it out. He let the subject drop without pushing me to talk about it but never let go of my hand. The rest of the ride home was quiet, aside from his rock music and the noise in my head—my damn inner voice recapping every failed attempt at romance and reminding me how foolish I'd been to think Nico might actually want more from me than companionship.

We turned onto my driveway. Nico cut the engine. He shifted in his seat and brushed the hair from my face. "Hey, beautiful. We're home."

I flinched, pulling away from his touch, then got out of his car without saying a word.

Nico carried my bags inside and dropped them in the foyer. "Danni, you're gonna have to help me out here." He stood facing the family room, both hands in his hair. "I get that you're angry with me. I'm just not sure why. We said 'no expectations' this weekend."

"*You* said—"

"It's. Too. Soon." He bit out the words in a low, determined voice then turned to face me. "We're not ready for that kind of a relationship."

"Sorry. I should have realized 'no expectations' was just guy code for 'I don't want to have sex with you, Danni.' My mistake."

Silly me for assuming the way he'd kissed me in the gazebo

then raced toward the penthouse had something to do with wanting comfort and privacy to finish what we'd started. *Clearly not.*

Nico stood there silent, his jaw flexing. Pupils growing dark.

"I hear the whispers, you know?" I said, meeting his stare. "Everywhere we go. Other women saying how 'lucky' I am, among other crude comments about your 'insatiable sexual appetite.' You have quite a reputation as a player—charming the panties off ladies with that sexy smile of yours and the sweet way you treat them.

"Yet here I am, practically untouched and panties fully intact. Why *wouldn't* that make me mad, Nico? I literally threw myself at you all weekend—not something I normally do, by the way—and you shot me down. Every. Single. Time." I poked his shoulder to emphasize each word.

Nico grabbed my finger. His eyes narrowed as his gaze bore into me. "Is that the only reason you agreed to go with me this weekend? You were looking for some sort of wild rebound fling?" He broke his hold on me and paced, one hand gripping the back of his neck. "Looks like *I'm* the fool who misunderstood."

He paused, heaved a heavy sigh, then resumed pacing. "Yes, I've gone out with a *lot* of women the past eighteen months. Most of them meant absolutely nothing to me. They were just warm, soft bodies. Eager to please and willing to be used just so they could say they'd had a piece of me.

"I'm not proud of it. I don't run around bragging or keep a tally somewhere. After Summer . . . I never expected I'd want more from a relationship again." Nico stopped in front of me and dragged a hand through his hair. "Never imagined I'd—"

"Why? I want to know why, Nico. You'll sleep with all those women, but you won't venture past second base with me." I pounded my fists against his chest. "Is it my age? My body? Is it because I have something inside my head besides vacant space? Why is it I'm not good enough?"

He grabbed my hands, trapping them between us. "You're beyond 'good enough.' You're—" Nico's eyes fell closed. His chest rose and fell on several breaths, each slower than the last. "Danni, you're perfect. I wouldn't change a thing about you."

"Oh, well, that makes perfect sense. Thanks for clearing it up." I struggled to pull my hands free from his strong grip.

"Stop. Do you really need me to admit how selfish I can be? Because that's all it was with those other women. They were just easy scores who took care of my physical needs. I didn't waste time trying to strike up a meaningful conversation. Didn't care about their lives or thoughts, beyond whether or not they wanted to fuck. Hell, most times I didn't even bother asking their names." He paused, taking several ragged breaths.

"And none of them ever meant a goddamn thing to me beyond that. You—" He brushed a tear from my face. "*You* are the only one who has the power to destroy me. The only one I *feel* anything for in here." He laid our joined hands on his chest. "The only one I dream of making love to."

None of this made sense. I raised my stinging eyes to meet his.

He placed a soft kiss to my forehead then rested his head against mine. "I need to protect myself. Protect my heart. I *can't* cross that last boundary with you unless I'm sure you feel the same way about me. And it takes more than words or a roll in the sack to prove it."

He released me and turned away, fists clenched. "I know what it's like to give my heart to someone only to have it ripped to shreds . . . and so should you."

I did. First with Will . . . and now by Nico.

"I haven't slept with anyone since Will's accident." Nico kept his back to me, his voice faint and despondent. "I'm embarrassed to admit it's because, deep down, I'm relieved to have him out of the picture—which I realize makes me some sort of depraved monster."

Nico drifted into the family room, shoving his hands in his pockets as he wandered around. "But all I could think was, 'She's single now.' I finally had an opening that didn't cross moral boundaries and hope that I could win you over. Make you mine."

I went to Nico and reached for him, desperate to ease the pain his voice revealed. "Nico, I—"

"But you can't let go." He pulled away, tension rolling off him. "The fucking bastard lied to you, cheated on you, and planned a surprise divorce, and your house still looks the same as it did two months ago. Like he'll be coming home any minute to his devoted little wife, who's still walking around wearing his ring."

Nico grabbed my left hand, raising it between us as he had the night before, and shook his head. "You're worried about women I don't give a damn about? I'm competing with a fucking ghost."

He blew out a bitter laugh and let my hand fall. "Talk about having a disadvantage. Sure, I don't have to worry about him coming back and claiming you, but how am I to know you're making love to *me* and not some distorted memory of the man you chose over me?" Nico inched closer, crowding me. Pinning me with an intense stare. "I won't be a stand-in, Danni. That's not enough for me. Not with you."

Fire burned in his eyes. He grabbed my head, twisting his fingers into my hair, and kissed me. There was nothing tender about this kiss. It was raw, delivered with a possessive passion that left me trembling. Gasping for air. I clung to his arms, afraid my legs wouldn't support me.

Desperate whimpers slipped past my lips as he continued to devour them. I wanted to feel his body against mine, but he stood back, maintaining enough distance to deny me even the slightest brush.

Nico grabbed my waist. He lowered me to the couch, breaking our connection. "You take some time. Figure things out. When you decide—*if* you decide—to let go of your past, you can let me know if you want a future with me."

He walked away, leaving me breathless and speechless. His car door closed. The engine roared to life then faded into the distance.

CAN YOU BELIEVE IT?

DANNI

A short nap did little to clear my head. I wandered through my empty house, each step echoing against the wood floor. My stomach growled, the only other sound to break the silence.

I skipped dinner, opting instead for a therapeutic pint of Ben & Jerry's. *The perfect remedy for a wounded heart.* I curled up on the couch, flipped through the channels until I found some sappy chick flick to watch, then wrapped my lips around a giant glob of sweet dark chocolate.

The doorbell rang, followed by impatient pounding and a brash voice I hadn't heard in weeks. "Come on, Danni. Open the damn door and let me in."

I slid to the edge of my seat and took another bite of ice cream. Deep down, I needed my best friend right now. But she was one of the last people I felt like seeing today . . . not that I really wanted to see anyone else.

My phone buzzed. I rejected Kendra's call and settled back into my seat. Seconds later, the voicemail alert sounded. I tapped to listen, not because I cared—I was just curious. At least that's what I told myself.

"Look, sweetie, nobody in their right mind would believe you don't hear me out here, so you can stop ignoring me. Get off your ass and answer the damn door 'cause I'm not leaving."

I jabbed my spoon into my ice cream with a groan and plopped it on the table before moving toward the foyer and my persistent friend. *Might as well get this over with.* I grabbed the knob and eased the door back enough to create a small gap to glare through. "What?"

Kendra pressed her face against the crack. "You look like hell." She arched a brow at me, hands on her hips.

"I'm sure I already figured that out without your help. But thanks for interrupting me to confirm it."

Kendra winked. "Just making sure I don't keep any more secrets from you." She pushed the door open and threw her arms around me. "I'm so sorry, Danni. I've been a shitty best friend, but—"

"Shouldn't you be with Logan?"

"Nah." She released me and waved a dismissive hand. "His dad's fine. They don't need me hanging around pestering them."

"So you decided to come here." I stared, torn between asking her to leave and wanting her to stay.

Kendra rolled her eyes. "Nico called Logan this morning." She closed the door and took my hands, towing me back to the couch. "I overheard part of their conversation and dragged the rest of the details from Logan after they hung up." She grabbed my ice cream from the table, pausing to take a closer look at the label, then passed it to me with a teasing laugh. "New York Super Fudge? Uh-oh, pulling out the heavy guns."

Kendra knew me better than anyone, probably even better than Jen. I'd missed that closeness.

"It's kinda been a rough weekend—couple of weeks actually—but mostly the weekend." I shrugged and poked at my absolute favorite super sweet, super rich indulgence before scooping up a glob.

"Anyway, there is some deep shit going on that you need to know about." Kendra shifted to sit sideways and hugged one of the throw pillows to her chest. "Turns out Nico was married —can you believe it—to some super-hot model—"

"Is this supposed to make me feel better?" I held up my hand. "Don't worry. I already know about Summer. Not sure why Nico hid that part of his life from me for so long, but he finally told me about her last night—right after rejecting me for the hundredth time." I sighed. "And right before rejecting me a couple more."

Kendra pushed out her lower lip, silent for possibly the first time ever. Except for when she didn't tell me about Will's affair. But having her stare at me with pity in her eyes turned out to be more annoying than putting up with all the pathetic looks other people had been giving me the past two months.

She took my hand and gave it a gentle squeeze. "Anyway, Logan said Nico's family all have these perfect, forever, true-love kind of relationships." Kendra drew air quotes on each description. "His grandparents. His parents. His sister. So when he married that Summer chick, he went all in. Opened his heart completely and expected the same type of amazing happily-ever-after life he'd seen all of them have." She rolled her eyes.

"Which didn't happen."

"Right. And Logan said he'd never seen someone so 'fucked up over a failed relationship' in his life." She lifted one shoulder. "His exact words."

I let my mind wander back to last night. Every word. Every raw emotion wrapping around my heart. "Nico told me what he feels for me is stronger than what he felt for Summer."

"Which is why he's terrified to surrender to those feelings. He thinks about how much *more* it will hurt if *you* walk away or decide you don't want him."

"That's just crazy." But something from Nico's speech this morning came back to me—*protect my heart*—and the words finally made sense. So did the pain and disgust his voice had revealed when he'd asked if I'd only gone with him in hopes of having a rebound fling.

"Nico's pure alpha male and hot as hell—always appearing to be so confident and in control. Not that I need to tell you that." Kendra gave an exaggerated wink then wiped the imaginary sweat from her brow.

A sweet sigh slipped out as I imagined him in nothing but his lounge pants last night. He'd definitely taken charge when he'd pushed me up against the door, kissing me into a frenzy of need. For one brief but glorious moment he'd tossed aside that infuriating self-control he always claimed didn't exist.

"Mm-hmm." Kendra laughed and nudged my shoulder. She grabbed my spoon and helped herself to a bite of my ice cream. "But . . . he's an emotional wreck too."

"He certainly hides it well."

Kendra hummed in agreement. "I still believe you two are perfect for each other though." She narrowed her eyes at me. "And I dare you to try to deny it. To me or to yourself."

I couldn't. I crumbled under the weight of her gaze and looked away. She didn't need to know I was pretty sure I'd already fallen in love with Nico.

"He's right though. You need to get your act together if you expect him to trust you with his heart." Kendra touched my arm then let out a sigh. "I better get going. Don't want to overstay my welcome, but I had to make sure you were okay." She stood and pulled me to her for a hug. "I love you, you know."

"Yeah, I do. Not sure I'm over being hurt by you yet, but I'm trying . . . and I love you too."

Kendra squeezed me tighter then pulled back, swiping at the corner of her eye. "Damn allergies." She shrugged and hooked a thumb over her shoulder. "I'll, um . . . I'll let myself out."

BIG, IMPORTANT NEWS
NICO

A five-mile run on the trail along the lake usually left me feeling cleansed and renewed—physically and mentally. Today, it hadn't even come close. No matter how high I'd cranked the volume on my earbuds, the pulsing beat of Linkin Park echoing in my head couldn't drown out the noise of this morning's argument with Danni.

This weekend *should* have been the perfect opportunity for us to set a solid foundation for a meaningful relationship. The perfect setting—my home turf—to show her the values I was raised with and what I really wanted out of life.

Family. Love. Commitment.

I needed Danni to realize I wasn't just "some rich, shallow player out to have a good time and sleep his way through the Brookdale Heights' female population." Yeah, I heard the gossip too—*fucking clueless people*—but that shit couldn't be further from the truth, and this weekend I'd *intended* to prove it.

I'd failed.

Ben let out a long groan from the driver's seat of his Maserati and flashed a quick glance in my direction. "If you want to talk—"

"I don't."

I continued staring out the passenger's side window, catching a glimpse of my brother's reflection in the glass. He nodded, but didn't push the subject. For now.

I hadn't been surprised to find him lounging on my deck when I'd returned from my run, or to learn that Logan had joined him via FaceTime by the time I'd dragged my tired ass up the steps.

The two of them had launched into a well-prepared speech about taking a step back and needing to get out of my own way. Then they'd informed me we'd be spending some time in New York to make sure I followed their advice . . . and they wouldn't be taking "no" for an answer.

"So how long you planning to hold me hostage?"

"As long as it takes—couple days, all week. I told Gabs we'd be remote for the week, just to be safe." Ben shook his head and laughed. "You make it sound like I plan to lock you up in a basement with nothing to eat or drink."

"Nah. I just like giving you a hard time." Honestly, I'd have gone along willingly if they'd only even hinted at their plan. I loved my apartment in the city and welcomed the idea of hiding out there for a few days.

Logan and I had the only two units on the 23rd floor of CP Tower—his occupying the south half, mine the north—and he'd been leaning against his door, waiting for Ben and me when we stepped off the elevator. The three of us settled into my apartment, relaxing and chatting over a couple of beers . . . all of us acting as though there wasn't a proverbial elephant in the room—the *actual* conversation they'd brought me here for.

"By the way . . ." Ben grinned, handing me his empty bottle as I walked toward the kitchen. "Gabs and I noticed you introduced Danni to Tanner as your 'girlfriend' last night. You just staking your claim against that douchebag, or is that title finally official?"

"Well, she didn't correct me, so I guess she's good with it. At least she was before this morning." After the things we'd said and the way I'd stormed out of her house, I didn't expect to hear from her again.

"Since you brought it up . . ." Logan drew out the words. "Let's recap what you told me this morning when you called—make sure I got it straight." He tapped one finger, preparing to tick off the list of events. "You drove Danni home."

"Because she wanted to leave!" I'd planned to spend the whole day together—a romantic walk after brunch, maybe take her to the chalet I grew up in, spend some time alone at my cove on the lake.

Logan tipped his head, his brows raised. "And was there a reason?"

I dragged a hand across my face. "Just continue."

"Okay, I'll take that as a 'yes.' So you drove her home, picked a fight, kissed her senseless, then just . . . walked out?"

"Yup. That pretty much sums it up." I handed out the next round of Sam Adams then moved to the window, preferring the view of Central Park over the judgmental stares of my brother and best friend. I appreciated their support—needed it—and knew that "hang out together" had been code for "subject myself to their prying questions and uncensored opinions."

That didn't mean I was ready for them. And this was only the beginning—the easy-to-explain part of the mess I'd created for myself.

I closed my eyes and massaged the tense knot between my brows. "It's fucking killing me to hold back."

"So why are you?" Logan said.

Shit. Didn't realize I said that out loud.

"Because I'm a fool?" I kept my back to them and took a long pull from my bottle, buying myself a little time. "You know, I actually believed Danni wanted to spend the weekend together because she was interested in building a relationship and getting to know each other better." A single humorless laugh slipped out. "Should'a known better. Turns out she was only looking for a wild rebound fling to help her get over her husband."

Not sure how I hadn't seen through her charade, but I'd convinced myself we wanted the same things and were headed in the right direction. *Guess love really* is *blind.*

"I don't know. Danni seemed genuine to me—like she was totally into you." Ben hesitated, humming as though searching for the right words. "Not everyone . . . *reacts* . . . the way you did after what happened with Summer."

Logan chuckled. "You mean, like he wants to make every woman pay for what she did to him?"

"More like prevent any woman from getting close enough to hurt me the way she did," I grumbled.

"And you're afraid Danni's gonna hurt you too." Logan's blunt statement made it clear he wouldn't be pulling any punches today.

"Hell yeah!" I flashed an annoyed glance over my shoulder then returned my focus to the soothing world outside while chaos raged inside me, wondering what it said about my current emotional state that I could find peace in the bustling madness of New York City. "I never want to go through that again, and the way I feel about Danni . . . it would destroy me."

"I can't guarantee she never will, but I don't see Danni as someone who's gonna cheat on you . . . or just use you until someone better comes along." Logan paused, maybe expecting me to respond, then sighed. "I get the feeling there's more to this story than what you're telling us? Something else is holding you back."

"You could say that." I let out a low groan and dragged a hand through my hair. "It has to do with Summer. More or less." I sat on the edge of the chair, facing them, but kept my gaze locked on the floor. "That day I met her for lunch—"

"Wait . . . what?" Ben coughed and sputtered, choking on a sip of beer. "You went out with Summer? When? And why is this the first I'm hearing about it?"

"No! Well, last weekend. But it's not like—it wasn't a date!"

Logan chuckled. "Yeah, right after he locked down his plans to spend *this* weekend with Danni."

"It was a lunch meeting. Nothing. More. So don't even think about giving me shit for this. Besides, you're the one— both of you, actually—who kept pushing me to talk to Summer after the stunt she pulled with Danni at Metro Sky."

Ben shook his head. He picked up his phone and waved it in front of me. "They make these things called phones, which are great for talking to people you don't want to be around, so—"

"No shit." I swatted his hand away. "But they're not very helpful when the person you're trying to avoid *insists* what she needs to tell you is 'way too important for a phone call.' Summer threatened to show up at the gala if I didn't agree to meet with her before then, so I didn't really have much of a choice." Details of that disastrous lunch replayed in my mind. The shock —the anger—still as raw in my memory as it had been that day.

Ben dropped his phone to his lap. "Okay. So what was her big, important news?"

"That's not something I wanna get into." I swirled the beer in my bottle then took a long drink, wishing they'd drop the subject, but I knew avoiding this discussion wouldn't be an option.

Ben and Logan exchanged a confused look. They both shook their heads and let out exasperated groans. "Maybe you didn't notice, but we didn't ask if you *wanted* to talk about it," Logan said.

I shoved a hand through my hair and returned to the window. Seconds ticked by, so many emotions weighing heavy on my chest while I searched for the right words. I drew in a deep breath. "She wanted to tell me I have a daughter."

Silence. A really long stretch of absolute silence. And I could only imagine the expressions on their faces.

Ben cleared his throat. "I'm sorry. I don't think we . . . could you repeat that, because I'd swear you said—"

"That I have a daughter?" I turned to face them. "No, you heard correctly."

"Wow!" Logan gripped the back of his neck, his eyes wide with shock. "When you came here to hide out that day, you refused to talk about what she wanted—shut me down every time I got anywhere near the damn topic." He leaned forward, elbows on his knees, and shook his head. "I had a feeling something major went down, but . . ."

"Damn." Ben picked up where Logan left off. "Sure as hell didn't see *that* coming. And I can't believe you've been keeping this to yourself . . . you have, right?" He looked at me for confirmation, then rubbed his jaw. "I'm confused, though. It's been what, eighteen months?"

I nodded. "Sophia—the little girl—just turned one. Summer claims she found out she was pregnant the week after I left her. The math works out, but—"

"You're not the only guy she was sleeping with." Logan's tone was flat. Sympathetic.

"Yup. And that's really fuckin' with my head." And my heart.

Silence returned. Their heads bobbed while they appeared to process.

Ben blew out a long, slow breath. "I hate to even ask this, but you're not considering going back, are you?"

"To Summer? Hell no! I told her she was fucking crazy to even *think* I'd want anything to do with her."

The corner of Ben's mouth twitched upward. "I can't imagine she handled that well."

"That's an understatement. I think she had some grand delusion that I'd be thrilled and eager to take her up on her suggestion to reunite our 'happy little family.'"

I couldn't sit still anymore and stood, pacing the length of my living room. "But if Sophia *is* mine . . . it hurts like hell to know I missed the whole first year of her life." So many moments I didn't get to share. Memories I didn't get to make. "I don't want to miss another minute."

"Assuming she's really yours . . ." Logan's flat tone made it clear he didn't trust my ex. "Did Summer offer any proof? Agree to a paternity test?"

"She showed me a picture of Sophia, and my name on her birth certificate. The paternity test is still a point of contention." My shoulders shook with a single laugh. "She actually had the nerve to tell me I should just be able to trust her."

"When I demanded the test, she went back to her original threat about showing up at the gala—even gave me a preview of the performance she had planned—some bullshit story that I'd abandoned her when I found out she was pregnant. Left her penniless. Oh, and then there's the whole deadbeat dad bit she'd concocted."

"Sounds like typical Summer drama." Ben grabbed my arm when I passed in front of the couch, forcing me to stop and look at him. "You know none of us—family, friends, or anyone else at the gala—would've believed a single word of her story."

Deep down, I knew that. But hearing the words, and the depth of conviction in his voice, meant more than I could say. I nodded and choked out an insufficient, "Thank you."

"Well, at least she didn't follow through with that threat," Logan said.

"Oh, she tried." I collected our empty bottles and tossed them in the recycling bin, then grabbed another round from the fridge. "I'd tipped off security and instructed them to escort her from the property if she showed up, and to call the police if she refused to leave peacefully.

"But learning she was there and realizing how desperate she is to stir up trouble was the reminder I needed to take things slow with Danni. At least until I can figure this mess out. Unfortunately, that seems to be making an even bigger mess, because Danni assumed my holding back meant I didn't want her." And that couldn't be further from the truth.

Ben hummed, as though assessing the situation. "So I take it that means you haven't told Danni about this either?"

"Danni's had enough stress in her life, thanks to her own cheating ex. How can I drag her into this shit show? Subject her to God only knows what stunt Summer decides to pull next?" I sank down on the edge of the chair and leaned forward, elbows on my knees. "Besides, I don't even know if Danni likes kids. She might not want anything to do with me when she finds out."

I loved Danni. But if Sophia was my daughter, and I couldn't have them both, the choice was obvious—family first. Always. "None of that may matter anyway after the argument we had at her house this morning."

Ben and Logan spent the next hour dragging every detail from last night and this morning out of me, overanalyzing it all until my head was spinning. 'Course the amount of alcohol I'd consumed during that conversation could have been to blame for some of that too.

"Anyway . . ." Logan moved to stand beside me at the window. "Remember what Kendra told you at Pepper's a few weeks ago? Just give Danni some space and a little time to calm down and think."

"But not too long." I added, remembering Kendra's speech well.

"Right, and then show her that you're serious and want a *real* relationship with her . . . which means you gotta stop shutting her down in the bedroom, dude."

Something meaningful that lasts longer than the aftershocks of an amazing double orgasm. The rest of Kendra's advice that day played in my mind, and I couldn't hold back the grin that followed. Judging by the look on Logan's face, he knew exactly what I was thinking.

Logan shook his head and laughed. "According to Kendra, Danni's spent her whole life looking for love. For someone to make her feel special. Wanted. Complete." He shrugged. "Her words, not mine." He slung one arm across my shoulders and slapped my chest with the other. "Kendra never believed Will was that guy. Her money's on you, my friend, so don't fuck it up."

"Probably too late for that, but good advice . . . I'll keep it in mind *if* she ever talks to me again."

"She will." Logan smirked. "I'll never understand why, but women just can't seem to resist you."

"Ha! One of life's great mysteries." Ben kicked off his shoes, propped his feet on the coffee table, and grabbed the TV remote. "Basketball or hockey?"

Just like that, the inquisition was over and I could relax a little. But I had a lot to think about—like how to fix things with my girl—because I may have *fucked* up, but I wasn't ready to *give* up.

OH, THAT KISS!

DANNI

I'd spent the past ten days in a daze, definitely not dwelling on the most remarkable kiss of my life . . . or the fact that Nico had stormed out of my life right after it.

Okay, so it *was* all I could think about, but it didn't *mean* anything. Didn't mean Nico would ever decide to sleep with me . . . and not just to snuggle. Didn't mean he'd ever believe I'd let go of my past. And it definitely didn't mean he'd ever be interested in spending forever with me. It was just a kiss. A totally amazing, earth-sha—

"Good morning, Danni."

"Logan!" I'd been so immersed in my reality check that I'd lost track of time, hadn't seen him arrive for his meeting, and barely registered his greeting.

"Sorry, didn't mean to startle you. Kind of even hated to interrupt you." He winked, and a teasing smile stretched across his rugged face. "You looked pretty deep in some happy thoughts."

"No. I just—" My gaze drifted to my computer screen, registering 10:08 displayed in the corner. "I'm the one who should apologize."

"I'm a little early." Logan shoved his hands in his pockets and rocked back on his heels.

"That's fine. It's, um . . . it's good to see you again." *And even better that you're alone.* "How's your dad?"

Logan folded his arms on the reception ledge above my desk and slouched forward, as though settling in for a long chat. "He gave us quite a scare, but he's good. Back to driving Mom crazy with all the things he wants to do now that he's retired."

"Glad to hear it. Well, not the 'crazy' part, but . . . you know what I mean." I grabbed my phone, casually folding in half the flyer on birthing classes I'd tucked next to it this morning, and pressed the button for Peter's office.

"Yes?"

"Logan VanBergen is here for his 10:30 meeting."

"Thank you, Danni. Go ahead and send him in."

"Sure thing." I fumbled the phone, snagging it before it hit my desk, and pressed it back in the cradle . . . using both hands. "Mr. Jamison is ready for you."

Logan chuckled. "Looks like Nico's not the only one who's been a wreck lately."

"I wouldn't know about Nico, since I haven't heard from him in ten days. But *I'm* perfectly fine." I tidied a stack of folders on my desk, trying to look busy.

"Glad to hear that." Logan strummed his fingers. "You know, Nico told me everything that happened, so I'd completely understand if you weren't." He gave a short laugh and leaned closer, lowering his voice. "Well, he *said* it was everything. But don't worry, I'm pretty sure he left out more than a few details."

Heat flooded my cheeks. "I, um—" I angled my face away from Logan, hoping to hide my obvious embarrassment. "Sorry to disappoint, but I'm sure you got the full story. Nothing really happened between us. Nico made sure of that."

Logan rubbed his jaw. He let out a strangled groan. "Nico would kick my ass if he heard me say any of this shit, but I can't sit back and watch you two continue to torture yourselves. Or each other."

"Look, it's really sweet of you to play matchmaker, but——"

Logan raised his hand between us. "I know he told you about Summer." His firm voice made it clear he intended to make me listen to his explanation of Nico's bizarre behavior. "But I doubt he told you that what happened with her nearly destroyed him." Logan glanced around the quiet office. He moved to the side of my desk and leaned against the edge, angling to face me. "He'd set high expectations for himself about their relationship—too high, if you ask me."

I rolled my eyes. "I know all about Nico's *expectations*." All. Too. Freakin'. Well.

"Good. Then it shouldn't be hard for you to understand that, in Nico's mind, he'd failed at being a man—at least the type of man he needed to be—when things didn't go the way he'd envisioned." Logan checked his watch then glanced across the still-empty reception area. "You've met the whole Giardano clan. Spent enough time with them to know the tight bonds they have. Family is everything to them. Their deepest core value.

"That's what Nico expected *his* family to be like. Christ, it was all he talked about after he'd put that giant rock on Summer's finger."

The idea of Nico so in love with someone else twisted like a knife in my heart. "You can spare me the details. Kendra already gave me the whole 'poor heartbroken Nico' story, but none of it really makes much sense. Seems to me like he over-reacted. He's not the only person ever to be cheated on. And it sucks, believe me, but he's been hanging on to this for eighteen months. That's an awful long time."

Logan chuckled. "I don't disagree. But believe it or not, his current behavior is a major improvement compared to how he spent the first year."

"Screwing anyone who'd get into bed with him?"

"Yeah, that too." Logan pinched the bridge of his nose. "He . . . let's just say he hit rock bottom for a few weeks. After . . . that, he threw himself into his businesses—worked hard and crazy-long hours then partied even harder. It was tough watching him self-destruct."

"So what changed? Because the man you're describing isn't the one I know."

Logan shrugged. "Guess his family finally started to get through to him. But the real change came when he met you."

The office door opened, and Nico strolled in looking more gorgeous than in my wildest fantasies. My skin tingled from the magnetic energy flowing from him. I wanted to jump up to greet him, throw my arms around his neck. Tell him how sorry I was and how much I'd missed him, but I couldn't make myself move. *He'd* walked out on *me*.

He tugged at the knot in his tie and smoothed the front of his jacket as he crossed the room at a leisurely pace.

Logan laughed. "I'm not sure which of your expressions is more entertaining." He stepped away to greet his best friend and business partner. The two men spoke in hushed tones for a few minutes.

"Take your time. I've got the meeting." Logan adjusted Nico's tie then clapped his hands on Nico's shoulders. "You just worry about gettin' the girl."

Logan laughed and walked toward Mr. Jamison's office, stopping as he passed me. He looked down and winked. "Trust me, you two don't need a matchmaker. Just a good, hard kick in your stubborn asses."

I bit my lip and lowered my head but continued to peek at Nico from the corner of my eye, trying to pretend I didn't notice him or the jumble of nervous energy bouncing around inside my chest.

Nico stood watching me, his hands tucked in his pockets. He cleared his throat and approached with slow, measured steps. "Good morning, beautiful." His subdued greeting lacked its usual effervescence.

"Good morning, Mr. Giardano. You can go ahead and join Logan in Mr. Jamison's office. He's ready for you."

Nico arched a brow, his only reaction to my cold greeting. "I've been waiting to hear from you."

"Well, I've been busy trying to figure out what you want from me." I swept my arm toward Peter's office then turned my attention toward my computer.

"Danni, please don't do this. I've missed you." Nico slipped in beside me and leaned on the edge of my desk, hesitating before brushing his fingers along my arm. He kept his voice low, even though there wasn't anyone in the front office to overhear us. "Go to lunch with me after my meeting. Someplace quiet, where we can be alone."

"Can't today."

"Then dinner tomorrow night, and we can go dancing after if you'd like. Spend a few hours holding each other close?"

I averted my gaze, afraid of drowning in his warm chocolate eyes. But I couldn't hide from the heavenly scent surrounding him, the seductive tone of his deep voice, or the longing in his words. My heart ached, begging me to give him another chance. Give *us* another chance.

But that chance would probably end the same as the last one . . . and the one before that. I clung to my fear of another painful rejection and glanced up at his hopeful expression. "Why bother, Nico?"

He flinched as though my words had slapped him. "Did I—"

"You hit on me one minute, then push me away the next. You say I need more time to get over my ex—which I totally disagree with, by the way—but you constantly show up everywhere expecting us to spend time together." I twisted to face him, arms folded over my chest.

Nico pushed his fingers through his hair. A crease formed between his brows. "I didn't realize wanting to spend time together was such a terrible thing."

"It's not . . . for normal people. But nothing about our relationship has been normal." I emphasized the last word, complete with air quotes.

Nico took my left hand. He rubbed his thumb across the tops of my fingers then lifted my hand between us, glancing at Will's ring. "Then again, I shouldn't be asking out a married woman."

The pain in his voice sent an icy chill through me. I tried to pull my hand free, but he wouldn't release it. "It's just a piece of jewelry. Nothing. More."

He nodded, seeming to consider my answer. "Then you shouldn't have any trouble taking it off."

I'd tried—several times—but after fifteen years of wearing Will's ring, it had become a part of me . . . for better or worse. Not that I'd ever be able to explain that to Nico.

"You know, Nico, I may be guilty of wearing an old piece of jewelry, but—"

"It's more than that."

"But I'm not the one carrying around a picture of my cheating ex-wife. Maybe you need to think things through yourself and decide what *you* really want."

Nico's grip on my hand tightened. He pulled me to my feet and stepped closer, our bodies nearly touching. "I know exactly what I want. *Who* I want. And she's standing right in front of me."

"Words, Nico. Beautiful words. But still *just* words. And like you told me, it takes more than that." I lifted my face to meet his gaze. "Your heart isn't the only one at risk here. The only one that could get destroyed."

I tugged my hand free and turned away. "You hid a very important part of your past from me." The faint words slipped out.

Nico slid closer, positioning himself in front of me again. "I never lied to you, Danni."

"Maybe not, but you didn't exactly tell me the truth either." I lifted one shoulder. "All those conversations we had about my failed marriage, my 'cheating bastard' husband . . . and you never saw an opening to say, 'Hey, Danni, I've been there myself'?"

His eyes fell closed. "I was trying to protect you."

"From what? Realizing that you're still pining over your ex-wife a year and a half after you walked out?" I shook my head. "We both need to learn how to trust again. Until we do, you're not going to believe I'm making love to *you* and not some twisted memory of my ex any more than I can be sure you're holding *me* and not imaging I'm Summer."

"It sounds like you've already decided to give up on us," Nico grumbled, rubbing his neck. "Go out with me tomorrow night and let me change your mind."

"I have other plans." Which were likely going to be cancelled, but he didn't need to know that.

A stunned expression flashed on Nico's face. "You have plans? Like a date?"

"I believe you have a meeting to get to. We've already kept Logan and Mr. Jamison waiting too long."

"Logan's fine on his own. I wasn't even supposed to be here today, which I'm sure you already knew." Nico's eyes narrowed, and he drilled me with an intense, heated stare. "I came so I could see you, and I'm not going anywhere until we straighten this out. Where's your break room?"

I gestured toward my boss's office again, hoping Nico would take the hint and head on in. "Mr. Jamison has coffee in—"

"I'm not interested in goddamned coffee." Nico's voice was deep and low. He stepped closer, invading my personal space. "I prefer to settle this in private, but we can do it right here if you'd like, where anyone could walk in. So last chance, are we moving this to the break room?"

I nodded, unable to argue, and took a tentative step in that direction. Nico fell in place beside me and pressed his hand to the small of my back. The heat of his touch scorched me through my silk blouse.

"Well, this is it," I said when we entered the small space. "What would you like?"

The door closed behind me. Nico caught me by the waist and pressed my back to the wall in one swift move. He hovered above me, our faces mere inches apart.

My heart raced. My breaths came faster. Shorter. While I waited for what felt like an eternity, aching for him to kiss me. Wanting him to leave me alone.

Nico brushed the side of my face. "You have two seconds to tell me no."

His lips crushed against mine in a passionate kiss that rivaled the one he'd given me Sunday morning. A hungry groan rumbled against my mouth. Nico inched closer, his hips pressing against mine. He made no effort to hide the massive erection between us. I reached for him, but he caught my wrists and raised them above my head, pinning me in place as he continued to devour my mouth.

Nico pulled away. His chest rose and fell on heavy breaths as he pressed slow kisses along the side of my face and down my neck. "Now tell me, does that feel like a man who doesn't want you?"

My knees grew weak. Nico rested his forehead on my shoulder. He took another deep breath.

"I better get going. I have a meeting to go to." He released my wrists, letting his hands slide to my waist, then stepped back. "And you have a date to cancel."

Cool air surrounded me, replacing the warmth of his strong body.

Nico grinned at me with that damn lopsided smile. "Don't want to keep Logan and Peter waiting."

"You don't play fair."

"Never planned to." He winked then lowered his lips to my ear. "First rule of any game, Danni. 'Always play to win.' I'll pick you up tomorrow at seven."

He opened the door and stepped through the opening, leaving me hot, bothered, and alone. *Damn him.*

I paced the room, pressing my fingers to my mouth. *You wanted it, Danni. Been dreaming about it for days.* My lips still throbbed from Nico's luscious assault. But that was only half of my problem. I yanked open the freezer door and shoved my head inside, trying to ignore the pulsing in my core.

Thirty seconds—sixty, tops—and he owned me. "God, I'm so weak."

"Did I just see Nic—oh, my. Never mind." Kristi laughed and moved to stand beside me. "I'm pretty sure this answers my question." She craned her neck to catch my eye. "Whatcha doin?"

"Smug bastard dragged me in here then kissed me like—like —" I waved toward the door. "And then he just strolled out of here looking all hot, sexy, and completely in control. And I—ugh —I can't even think straight." My voice climbed higher with each sentence. "It's like he thinks this is some kind of a freakin' game. Even said as much. Well, I'm not—what are you laughing at?"

Kristi folded her hands and pulled them to her chest, spinning in a circle. "Danni's in love." She sang the words, a huge sappy grin on her face.

I slammed the freezer door shut and sagged against it. "Lotta good it does me. Nico refuses to believe me. How the hell am I supposed to convince him?"

"Oh, come on, Danni. I'm sure it's not that bad. I mean, Nico *has* to know how you feel about him. After all, you two slept together."

"*Slept*, Kristi. That's the key word in that sentence. Having a PG-rated slumber party doesn't count." Just like wanting to run my lips over every inch of Nico's perfectly sculpted body didn't mean he'd let me. And desperately needing an orgasm—or ten—hadn't made one happen.

Kristi shoved her hands on her hips. "Well, not for lack of effort on your part, right? I mean, that man's got more self-control than all the guys I've ever dated. Combined. Probably times five." She giggled. "Maybe he's got all of Ben's too, which would explain why he's such an insatiable beast."

I let out a frustrated groan and pressed my fingers to my temples. "Is this supposed to make me feel better? 'Cause it's not working."

Kristi twisted her lips. After a few seconds, her eyes lit up. "Ooo, I know exactly what you need." She grabbed my hands and pulled them from my face. Her bright blue eyes sparkled. "You're gonna love it . . . ." She drew out each word in an excited squeal. "Girls' night!"

"No." I yanked my hands away and waved them between us. "Absolutely . . . not. Did you forget this whole mess started with a girls' night? I don't know about you, but I've learned my lesson. At least for a while."

"Okay, then how about drinks after work tomorrow tonight?" She jumped in front of me, blocking my path. "We can unwind. Talk dirt on our men. It'll be fun."

"I don't think so. Besides, you and Ben made up, so you don't need to vent, and I don't have a man. Remember?"

"Sheesh, you're really stubborn sometimes." Kristi's pushed out her bottom lip in an exaggerated pout. "Fine. You win . . . this time." She backed out of the break room giggling. "We still on for lunch today?"

My stomach growled, reminding me I'd skipped breakfast again this morning. "Definitely."

"Perfect! That gives me a whole hour to change your mind."

MR. JAMISON's office door opened at 11:40. The three men emerged, laughing as Peter finished telling one of his favorite golf mishap stories, but I didn't dare turn around. Just kept my eyes glued on my computer screen. Their voices faded, moving toward the exit. *Finally.* I blew out a long, slow breath and waited for my body to relax.

I grabbed the stack of items I'd gathered for Peter, preparing to follow him into his office when he returned. He settled in at his desk and got back to work without even acknowledging me, which had become our new normal.

I'd stopped asking if I'd done something wrong or if everything was okay, but I still missed his warm and outgoing personality. The genuine smile he'd greeted me with for so many years.

I placed his mail in the bin, arranged the files he'd requested on the credenza behind his desk, and cleared the items left on the conference table after his meeting—including *three* used mugs. *Guess Nico wanted coffee after all.*

My skin tingled, the memory of that amazing kiss replaying in my mind . . . but that thought would have to wait. It wasn't the reason I'd come in here. I stood in front of Peter's desk, hugging the VanBergen account folder.

"Thank you, Danni." A few seconds passed. His head drifted up, and he peered over the top of his reading glasses. "Was there something else?"

Talking to Peter used to be easy, enjoyable even. "I was wondering if you've heard from Alexia."

He set down his pen and slipped off his readers. "If you consider a text message every morning telling me she's fine but won't be coming into the office, then yes, I've heard from her."

Wow. Alexia had told me they'd argued a few weeks ago, but she'd said it was no big deal. Apparently not. "I don't mean to pry—"

"Then don't. Please." He stood and came around to the front of his desk, leaning there with his arms and ankles crossed, and drew in a deep breath. "I'm sorry for—well, having her move here hasn't worked as well as I'd hoped it would. It's . . . complicated."

"I know about the baby."

Peter's head snapped up, his eyes wide.

"She told me her fiancé left her. Left both of them." My gaze wandered around the silent room. "Anyway, I promised to help her through her pregnancy. Figure out this whole baby stuff together, which is why I've been trying to get in touch with her. I told her about birthing classes we could attend, and they start tomorrow night. But she hasn't returned any of my messages for . . . at least two weeks now."

"Danni, you've been through enough." Peter rubbed his forehead.

"It's okay. I could use a distraction." Especially since trying to figure out my relationship with Nico had grown into a full-time obsession lately. "Besides, Alexia always says we're kinda like sisters. What better way to get to know each other?" I forced a laugh, hoping to convince both of us this would be fun.

Peter blew out a long, tense breath. "I'll have a talk with her." He returned to his seat and picked up his glasses, hesitating as though he had more to say. "I hear you spent a nice weekend at Elevations."

An involuntary smile stretched my cheeks. "I did." At least the first half was nice . . . amazing.

He nodded. "You deserve to be happy, Danni. Nico's a good man." Peter put on his glasses and returned his attention to the documents he'd been reviewing. "I think your dad would've liked him."

"Oh. I, um . . . thank you." *How did our conversation end up here?* I closed Peter's door on my way out, and turned, my step faltering. Nico stood by my desk, head down and fingers tapping on his phone.

"I'm pretty sure I told you I couldn't go to lunch today." I rushed past him and sat down, ignoring him and the fluttering in my chest.

Nico chuckled. "I meant to give you this earlier." He rested a hand on my back and leaned over my shoulder to place something in front of me. "Guess I got a little distracted," he whispered against my ear.

"What is this?" I sat frozen, staring at the tiny, pale blue box.

"I spent a few days in New York after—anyway, I was roaming around Midtown, saw this, and thought of you." He moved beside me, settling into the same spot he'd occupied earlier, and brushed my arm. "Open it."

My gaze drifted to Nico. "I don't—"

"Please." He grinned and shook his head.

I untied the white ribbon with trembling hands and lifted the lid, revealing the most beautiful ring I'd ever seen— sparkling diamonds surrounding a deep blue, oval sapphire . . .

the exact shade of the gown I'd worn to the gala. "Nico, this is . . . I-I can't accept this."

"You can. And I want you to." Nico took my hand, rubbing his thumb across Will's ring. "It's just a piece of jewelry, Danni. Whether you choose to wear it or not is up to you." He squeezed my hand before releasing it. "I'll see you tomorrow."

Nico walked away without looking back, leaving me with a thousand questions and a lot more to think about. He'd made his point—loud and clear—with a bold and way-too-expensive statement, but nothing had changed.

IT'S OFFICIAL
NICO

Danni had been avoiding me for more than a week now—one week, twenty-two hours, and . . . eighteen minutes, to be exact—and with each hour that passed, another chunk of my dwindling hope faded away. Hope that she'd call. Hope that she'd choose me. Hope that we could have a future together. A family.

Okay, so I may have been getting ahead of myself with that last thought, but the pending news on my paternity test had my nerves on edge and my imagination in overdrive these past few days. I snapped up my stress ball, squeezed it, and bounced it against the wall a few times. It didn't help. Not today.

My phone vibrated on my desk, and an email alert flashed on the screen. *BLS BioGen.* "Finally." I stared at the notice for a few seconds, my trembling finger hovering above the Open button, while I gathered the courage to read it.

Mr. Giardano,

This is to notify you that your DNA test results are available. To view them, sign into the secure account you were assigned when the samples were collected.

My grip on my phone tightened. I pushed to my feet and

stumbled across my office, unable to tear my eyes away from the message. I closed my office door, paced in front of it a few times, then locked the door and returned to my desk. "Just do it."

I scrubbed a hand over my face and pulled up the website I'd been checking all morning, waiting for the results. It seemed to load in slow motion, but then it was there. Right in front of me. Confirmation of what my heart already knew.

I shoved a hand through my hair and blew out a sharp breath, still staring at the screen—99.99999 percent. *That's pretty damn convincing.* A whirlwind of emotions sprang to life, battling inside me—fear, panic, anger, excitement . . . fear. Yeah, I already mentioned that, but it existed on two very different levels and deserved to be repeated.

I snapped up my phone, hands shaking more than they were two minutes ago, and struggled to type out a message.

Me: *Results are in. She's mine.*

Me: *I want to meet her.*

Me: *Today.*

I strummed my fingers on my desk, watching the dark screen. Waiting for a response. "What's taking her so damn long?"

A faint knock sounded on my office door, but I couldn't pull myself away to answer.

"Mr. Giardano?" My assistant's voice came through the intercom on my desktop phone. "Sir? Is everything all right in there?"

Tricia knew me too well. Knew I never locked my door. And she always seemed to have some sort of sixth sense about my moods and emotions. Sometimes I swore she channeled my mom's spirit.

I pressed the button on my phone. "All good. Sorry, I was just wrapped up in a project and got distracted."

Tricia paused before responding. "If you say so. I just

wanted to remind you about your meeting at The Next Level. You usually leave at ten, and it's quarter past."

Shit. I forgot I'd had to move Monday's meeting to this morning. "Thank you. I *did* lose track of time."

I closed my laptop then tossed it into my messenger bag, watching my phone the whole time. The screen finally lit up with a rapid succession of messages from my ex. The first was a nauseating smiley emoji with hearts.

Summer: *Tonight at 6:30.*

Summer: *We can't wait to see you!*

The last message contained an address.

I grabbed my jacket, pulling it on while I walked, and stopped at Tricia's desk on my way out. "Ben and Gabs still meeting with the auditors?"

Tricia checked her watch. "They should be back soon. You want me to give them a message?"

"No worries. I'll catch up with them later. Do I have anything urgent on my calendar this afternoon? I need to take care of something in town and may just finish up at my home office today."

Tricia studied her monitor. "Nothing that can't be pushed off until Monday." She lifted her head slowly and tipped it to the side, eyes narrowed and a crease forming between her brows. "You sure everything's okay?"

I nodded and gave in to the smile I'd been trying to contain. "All good. I promise." I tapped her desk. "Have a good weekend."

SET-UP AT FARLEY'S

DANNI

The elevator door slid open, and Kristi shuffled in. She sagged against the wall with a weary sigh. "So, so, so very glad this week is over. That boss of yours is driving me absolute bonkers."

I bit back a smile. Even worn down and exhausted, she managed to maintain her dramatic flair. "Isn't Mr. Jamison your boss too?"

Kristi rolled her eyes. "Well, I guess, technically, since he owns the company. I'm just used to—and quite happy with—hiding out in my little office all day without anyone pesterin' the crap out of me."

We exited the elevator into the parking garage.

"But enough about work." Kristi looped her arm around mine. "I want to know what's happening with you and Nico. You still playin' hard to get? 'Cause I notice you're *still* not wearing that gorgeous ring he gave you last week."

"More like he's playing hard to figure out. And I'm keeping my distance—and sanity—until I do."

"You two haven't talked about it yet? I mean, you're the queen of 'you need to communicate' . . . and I'm not talkin' about the way Ben and I spend countless hours communicating." She gave an exaggerated wink.

"Nico told me to take time and think. That's exactly what I'm doing." Thinking how crazy it was that I'd ever believed we both wanted the same things from our *relationship*, for lack of a better word."

Kristi tapped her jaw, giving a curious hum. "Ya know, I'm really surprised he's just sittin' back and patiently waiting."

"Oh, he's not. He showed up last Friday for our *date*, even though I hadn't accepted it, and hung out in my driveway waiting for me to come home." Good thing I'd decided to hide in my room and read all night . . . in the dark. "Then he sent me a huge bouquet of flowers on Saturday with a note that said he missed me, and I've gotten several random text messages from him every day since."

"But you haven't responded? Wow, poor guy must be goin' out of his mind." Kristi shook her head. "I don't know if I should be impressed by your willpower or smack you upside your head for bein' a stubborn fool."

I flashed Kristi a glance and laughed. "Totally changing the subject—we still going to Farley's?"

Kristi gave my arm a playful shove. "Of course we are. It'll be fun. Promise." We stopped by my car, and she gave me a quick hug. "I need to make one little stop on my way, but I'll see you there in a few."

AFTER THOROUGHLY EMBARRASSING myself the last time I'd been at Farley's Pub, the thought of facing Rob had my stomach in knots. I stepped inside the cozy rustic pub and drew in a mouthwatering breath of Farley's gourmet burgers, braved a glance behind the bar, then exhaled with a sigh of relief—the owner was nowhere in sight. This time.

"Danni! You're finally here." Kristi rushed toward me, singing her greeting, then threw her arms around me. "I was beginning to think you stood us up."

"Us?" My body tensed, every muscle going rigid, while one name flashed in my mind like a bright neon sign—Nico.

Kristi took my hand and dragged me past the bar. "Okay, now promise you won't be mad at me."

"And why would I be mad?" My gaze darted around the pub, searching for him.

"Well . . ." Kristi stopped and faced me. She flashed a *don't-kill-me* smile. "I know we said it would just be the two of us, and it's not that I think you're boring company or anything like that, but—"

My eyes fell closed. "Please tell me you didn't invite Nico without asking me first." As much as I missed him and really wanted to see him again, I still needed more time to find the courage. Decide if I could risk another painful rejection.

"Ooo . . . that would've been a really great idea, but nope. He's not here . . . at least I don't think he is. However . . ." She motioned toward the far corner—toward the same table I'd shared with Nico the day he'd followed me in here—only this time it was occupied by Kendra. "The more the merrier, right?"

"Kristi, why?" I groaned, rubbing the tense knot at the bridge of my nose. Suddenly hiding in my dark bedroom again didn't seem like such a bad option for tonight.

She tilted her head and stared at me, confusion in her eyes. "You two made up—least that's what Kendra said. And since tonight is supposed to be fun, you know '*girls' night*' and all that stuff, I figured—"

"We *semi* made up."

"Perfect! Now you can make up the rest of the way, and I can stop feeling like I need to pick sides." Kristi folded her hands beneath her chin. "Danni, please? We haven't had a Friday happy hour in . . . for-ev-er."

I closed my eyes and took a slow breath. "Fine. I know you meant well, so let's just make the best of this."

Kristi threw her arms around me. "That's the spirit . . . or at least *almost* the spirit." She giggled then grabbed my hand again and yanked, towing me through the maze of tables, most still unoccupied.

Kendra twisted in her seat with one arm casually propped on the chair back, watching us race toward her. "Gotta say, Tinkerbell, I'm impressed. I would've bet she'd try to bolt the minute she saw me."

"The thought crossed my mind."

Kristi laughed and elbowed my side. "But then she remembered how much fun we all have together, and she practically ran over here."

I raised one brow at Kristi, biting back a grin. "That's an interesting spin on what really happened."

She beamed at me and pulled out the chair next to Kendra's. "Now sit. We have a lot to cover, and since you were late, we only have twenty minutes left."

"Twenty minutes? I thought we were grabbing dinner here." Then again, I thought we'd be alone too.

"Nope." Kristi stood taller. She rubbed her hands together. "Surprise! You and Kendra can grab dinner. I have . . . plans."

Kendra shrugged, apparently as confused as I was. "You probably should have mentioned that little detail before you offered to pick me up." She turned to me. "My car's in the shop."

"Well, I assumed Danni would take you home." Kristi rolled her eyes. "Okay, now that we've settled the obvious—"

"Not so fast." Kendra held up a hand. "I want to know more about these mysterious plans." She drew air quotes around the last word.

Kristi tapped her chin and hummed. "Okay. Here's the deal—I'll add it to the end of the agenda . . . *but* we need to thoroughly cover the more important topics first. That means if you two want in on my secret, you need to cooperate." She motioned, again, toward the chair and gave me an impatient look.

I sank into my seat and glared at Kendra from the corner of my eye. "Was this your idea?"

"Hey, I'm innocent for a change." She raised her hands. "I was dragged here, completely unaware that we were being set up, same as you." She bumped my arm and grinned, a playful spark in her eyes. "I just wasn't as grumpy when I figured it out."

I grunted, resisting the comforting sense of familiarity springing to life after only a minute of Kendra's banter. "You're not the one constantly being pressed to ignore your feelings just because everyone else thinks you should."

"What the hell does that even mean?"

"It means I'm still having a hard time dealing with the fact that you kept Will's affair from me, and now I'm being forced to sit here and act like nothing happened between us. Like everything is just fine. But it isn't."

Kendra leaned toward my ear. "Sweetie, when are you gonna accept that telling you about Will wouldn't have made a difference?"

"It would have made a huge difference." I clenched my jaw. Why couldn't anyone get this?

She shook her head. "Nope. I know you well enough to call bullshit. You still would have taken the same damn path and tried to fix that pathetic excuse of a marriage." She narrowed her eyes, daring me to deny it.

I took a moment, let her words sink in. Considered the possibility. "You're probably right," I said on a sigh. "*But* . . . it would have been an informed decision. *My* choice. And that's a lot better than being lied to and feeling like a fool."

"Okay. I'll meet you halfway and concede that I should have told you." Kendra shrugged and settled back in her seat. "I made a mistake, and I've apologized for it."

"Really? I must have missed that. You've explained your choice, tried justifying if from several different angles, and admitted you were a shitty friend, but you've never honestly apologized."

Kendra hesitated, strumming her fingers on the table. A crease formed in her forehead, deepening with each passing second. "Damn." Her eyes snapped to mine. "You're right." She pushed to her feet and threw her arms around me, squeezing so tight I could barely breathe.

"I'm so sorry—for all of it. Keeping important details from you. Hurting you . . . even though I never meant to. And I'm especially sorry for being a shitty friend."

I bit my lip and blinked away the tears clouding my eyes. "Yeah, the shitty friend part really sucked."

Kendra laughed and winked. "But you love me, right?"

"Yeah. I do." I pulled her into another giant hug. "And I've missed you."

Kristi leaned back in her chair wearing a satisfied grin, her hands pressed over her heart. "Now this feels much better, and —ooh, perfect timing." She pointed toward a waitress approaching, carrying a tray with three large glasses. "I ordered chocolate martinis so we could celebrate . . . and because who doesn't love chocolate?"

We raised our glasses and toasted to good friends.

"So." Kristi drew out the word. She folded her arms on the table and focused her full attention on me. "Now that we have that settled, you gonna tell us why you've been avoiding Nico?"

I'd hoped to get through the evening without talking about

him, but it appeared that would *not* be an option. I rolled my eyes. "I guess pleading the Fifth isn't gonna work?"

Both ladies shook their heads.

"Great." I grumbled and flipped over my phone to check the time—see how much torture I still needed to endure—and squinted at the screen. I'd missed two calls from Alexia in the past ten minutes. Wow, maybe Peter finally had that chat with her . . . but she'd kept me waiting for three weeks. She could wait three hours—or until tomorrow—for me to call back.

"Tick-tock." Kristi waved a finger in front of me.

"Fine." I gave my phone a shove and sagged in my chair, letting out a heavy sigh. "I'm not avoiding Nico. Not technically. He's the one who told me to take time and think about what I want, but just like you guys, he can't give me the space to do that."

Kendra leaned onto the table, tilting her head to meet my gaze. "No offense, sweetie, but sometimes you need a push in the right direction."

Kristi grabbed each of our hands. "Like if I hadn't forced you to hang out with Kendra today, you two wouldn't be besties again . . . well, at least not yet."

"Maybe. But Nico never believes me when I tell him I want to be with him, so I don't get why he keeps pushing."

Kendra took my other hand, completing our friendship circle. "Because he loves you. Anyone who's seen you together can easily figure that out."

I let that thought soak in then groaned in frustration. "I'm sure those people miss the part where he hits the brakes every time things start to heat up, refusing to move forward with our relationship."

"You mean he won't sleep with you," Kristi clarified.

"Sleep, yes. Have sex? Totally different story. He seems to think I'm not over Will yet—"

"Gee, I wonder why?" Kendra poked my ring, her expression asking the question she didn't say out loud.

I pulled my hand away, staring at it as I had every day since Nico had asked me the same question. "I don't think—"

"Hey, Danni? Still can't believe you trust this chick, but you might want to see this." Kristi slid my phone in front of me and pointed at the text message on the screen.

Alexia: *Danielle, please answer your phone! Emergency!*

CONFRONTATION
NICO

I parked in front of the address Summer had texted me and tapped the screen on my phone, double-checking I'd gone to the right place. The "cottage" looked more like some old hunting cabin that had been roughly renovated and turned in to a rental property—not Summer's usual over-the-top, upscale taste in homes.

The door opened before I even reached the porch. Summer stood there, a welcoming fake smile plastered on her over-made-up face. She was wearing the kind of little black dress you'd expect to see in a club, and her blonde hair twisted in some sort of elaborate bun.

Maybe she doesn't plan on sticking around? The ridiculous thought vanished as quickly as it appeared. What mother in her right mind would leave her one-year-old daughter with a man the child didn't know? Then again, we were talking about Summer here, so I probably shouldn't put anything past her.

"You found me!" she called as I approached.

"Yep, pretty easy when you have an address and GPS."

A heavy cloud of the musky perfume she loved surrounded her, making me want to gag and cough. I'd always hated that shit, but she'd insisted it was sexy and mysterious. Summer leaned forward, apparently expecting a kiss. I side-stepped to avoid her and shoved my hands in my pockets.

Her eyes narrowed briefly before her cordial mask slipped back into place. "You look amazing, Nico . . . as always." She paused for a moment, pressed her lips together with a sigh, then moved aside to create an unobstructed path for me to enter. "Come in. Please."

The dimly lit, rustic room was sparsely decorated with a few pieces of mismatched furniture that probably came with the rental. A bright pink plastic box filled with a few toys sat off to one side, but no sign of my daughter. "Where's Sophia?"

"She's napping," Summer said, taking my jacket as I slipped it off.

"At seven o'clock?" I'm no parenting expert, but that seemed like an odd time to put your toddler down to nap.

Summer rested her hand on my shoulder then brushed the length of my arm. She didn't seem to notice—or chose to ignore—that I cringed at the contact, my body instinctively repulsed by her. "Dinner's ready. We can eat and have some quiet time to catch up until she wakes."

I dragged a hand through my hair. "The only 'catching up' we have to do is you telling me where the hell you've been— with my daughter—for the past year, and why you thought it wasn't necessary to even drop me a birth announcement to let me know she existed. You knew damn well I wanted a family. That I'd want to be a part of her life." *Even if I want nothing to do with you.*

She didn't answer. Just sashayed into the little kitchen where the old metal table was set with fine china, wine glasses, and two candles burning in the center. Soft, romantic music drifted from somewhere—maybe her phone on the counter? I couldn't be sure.

"I made your favorite—beef bourguignon." Summer lifted the lid on a casserole and stirred its contents.

Not *my* favorite. Maybe the guy she was screwing back then loved it, but I've always hated beef bourguignon. Whatever.

And I doubted that she actually 'made' it anyway—more like unpacked it from the delivery containers, same as when we were married. If I cared, and felt like searching, I was sure I'd find them stashed somewhere. I shook my head, amazed that I'd ever tolerated her little charades. "I already ate."

I pulled out a chair, moved it far away from the other one that had been strategically placed practically against it, and plopped down. "So back to our conversation. Where *have* you been? And why are you here now, finally telling me what you should have told me eighteen months ago?"

Summer handed me a bottle of wine and an opener, but I set both on the table and pinned her with an impatient stare. She drew in a slow breath and pulled back her shoulders. "Please don't make this difficult. I've made some mistakes, but I'm trying to fix that."

"Yeah, well, we've both made a lot of mistakes."

A sultry smile eased across Summer's face. "There, now that wasn't so hard to admit, was it?" She moved behind me and rested her hands on my shoulders, gently kneading them.

I shook free and jumped to my feet. "Maybe we should just start with the ground rules."

Summer folded her arms across her chest, pushing her silicone tits up higher, and arched a curious brow. "Rules?"

"For starters, no touching. We're done." I motioned between the two of us, reinforcing my statement. "I've moved on, and the sooner you accept that, the better it will be for everyone. I'm only here to see my daughter—now that I finally know I have a daughter, that is—and I plan to be a permanent part of her life, with legal shared custody." Summer grinned. "I'm all for joint custody."

"Second. This—" I waved a hand around the room. "We need to establish a neutral place for my dates with Sophia until we're all comfortable with me taking her alone."

Summer's grin widened, bordering on a conniving sneer. "About that." She drew out the words and inched closer, hesitating before brushing her fingers along my chest.

I caught her wrist and tugged her hand away. "Don't."

She rolled her eyes, appearing undeterred by my rejection. "I have an idea that will allow you to spend plenty of quality time with your daughter so you can get to know each other."

I recognized that look in her eyes—knew I shouldn't engage—but curiosity got the best of me. "I'm listening . . ."

"If Sophia and I were to move in with you, you'd become a regular part of her life. A *real* daddy." She glanced up, batting her eyes. "That would be perfect for both of you. All of us, really."

"Not. Happening. Sophia is more than welcome in my home. You? Not a chance."

Summer flinched as though my words had slapped her. It was a subtle move, and she regained her composure quickly, but I'd still seen it. Finally, something I said seemed to register in that thick skull of hers.

"Sophia isn't some pawn you can use in whatever twisted scheme you have planned to push your way back into my life. She's our daughter."

Summer rolled her eyes again. "Believe me, I know what she is. I'm the one who's been stuck with her every single day for the past year, not to mention what I went through being pregnant. God, you know I never wanted to do that to my body." She skimmed her hands the length of her torso, which looked as anemic as it had when she'd been trying to make her way as a runway model. "Do you have any idea what that's done for my lifestyle? Not to mention—"

"No! Summer. I have absolutely no clue, because you

deprived me of the opportunity to be a father. You stole the first year of our daughter's life from me. I wish I could have spent every day with her—not *stuck*, but watching her grow. Loving her!" Christ, what kind of mother thinks of her child as a burden? An inconvenience?

"You can gladly go back to your 'lifestyle.'" Which probably still involved screwing anyone she thought was a good investment in her time and effort—someone who could give her anything she wanted. "You want to be rid of the responsibility of raising and caring for our daughter? I'll gladly take over. You can walk away." *And hopefully spend the rest of your life dealing with the guilt of abandoning her.*

Summer reached for my arm, but I stepped away. "Nico, that's not what I meant. It's just been—"

A faint cry came from the back part of the cabin. The sound wrapped around my heart and squeezed, wringing out all the anger and frustration Summer had caused. "Sounds like someone's ready to meet her daddy."

Summer seemed unconcerned and waved a dismissive hand. "She'll be okay for a few minutes yet."

I arched a brow. "If you want to eat, I can get her up." It may be a bit unsettling for Sophia, since she'd only ever seen me one time before, and that was when another stranger swabbed the inside of her cheek. Not the best first impression to make.

Summer blew out a short breath, a less-than-subtle attempt to let me know she wasn't happy with the way this evening was going—as in, not at all to her plan. "No. Fine. I'll get her."

"Perfect." I couldn't control the full-on grin that followed, but the sense of excitement rolling through me quickly faded to jitters and self-doubt. *What if she doesn't like me? What if I suck at being a dad?*

Faint babbles drifted down the hall, followed by short monotone responses from Summer. She didn't sound happy to see our daughter—there were none of the sweet, maternal, nurturing responses you'd expect to hear from a mother reacting to her child's attempt to communicate.

A few minutes later, Summer returned to the living room, Sophia in her arms. Even though I'd seen her briefly the day we were tested, this was different. I was about to officially meet my daughter for the first time. My heart melted, and I swallowed the lump in my throat. "Hi there, sweetheart. Did you have a good nap?"

I wanted to scoop her up and hug her forever, or at least long enough to make up for all the hugs I'd missed, but I kept my distance. Gave her a chance to get used to me.

Sophia rubbed her eyes and buried her face in Summer's neck.

"She's still waking up," Summer explained.

I'd be willing to bet her bout of shyness had more to do with waking up in front of a stranger. Although, who knew how many "strangers" Summer had introduced her to over the past year. The thought sickened me, so I pushed it aside for now.

"Do you have a blanket to spread on the floor for her to play on?"

"You can grab the one on that ugly old chair." Summer pointed to the worn leather recliner by the fireplace.

While she got Sophia settled on the blanket, I went to gather some toys. "What are her favorites?"

"How should I know?" Summer gave me an odd look. "I don't think she has one. Just grab anything."

Was she serious? How could a mother not know what made her own child happy? I dug through the toy box and found a doll that looked well loved, a pink-and-white sparkly ball, some bright-colored plastic blocks, and one of those things with buttons you can push to hear animal sounds.

"This should be a good start." I spread the toys out around

Sophia and sat facing her. "Okay, sweetheart. What should we play with first?"

She stared at me for a minute, her warm chocolate eyes the exact shade as mine, but she didn't move.

"How about the baby?" I picked up the doll and gave it a hug, then held it out for my daughter.

Sophia smiled and pulled the doll into her arms, same as I'd done. Keeping one arm wrapped around her baby, she pointed. "Ball."

My heart exploded with pride. I flashed a glance at Summer, who stood cross-armed and leaning against the wall separating the living room from the kitchen. "She said ball! Did you know she could say that?"

Summer rolled her eyes. "She says a few words. Nothing too exciting."

Was she kidding me? I directed my attention back to my daughter—the only reason I was here. "That's right. Ball. Do you want to play with it?" I gave the ball a gentle push, rolling it toward Sophia. She laughed—actually laughed—and pushed it back to me.

After rolling the ball back-and-forth a few more times we moved on to the blocks. I'd stack them in a tower, Sophia would knock them down, clap and laugh, then hand them to me to stack again.

I couldn't remember the last time I'd had so much fun . . . aside from the time I spent with Danni. God, I missed her. Wished she were here to share this amazing moment with me.

Sophia crawled to me and tugged on my shirt, using it to pull to stand—something else I didn't even know she could do, but I didn't bother trying to share the excitement with Summer this time. "Look at you, baby girl. You're so big." I wrapped one arm behind her so she wouldn't fall.

Sophia grinned, one tiny dimple in her left cheek. She reached up and patted my face, rubbing her hand along my jaw. Her nose wrinkled at the rough texture of my short beard, and she babbled something only she could understand, then laughed again.

"Guess I'm not the only one who prefers you clean-shaven," Summer droned from the far corner of the room.

Sophia leaned closer and pressed her cheek against mine. She giggled again, then gave me a kiss. In that single moment, my life was perfect . . . well, *almost* perfect.

EXPLAIN YOURSELF
DANNI

I pulled up in front of the address Alexia had sent me, my stomach in knots. I hadn't been able to understand most of what she'd said on the phone, so my mind had been running wild with all kinds of possible "emergencies" during the drive here.

"Well that doesn't look good," Kendra grumbled. She tipped her head toward the house with its front door wide open and gave me a cautious look. "You sure you wanna go in there?"

My grip on the steering wheel tightened. I blew out a quick breath, peeled my fingers free, and opened my door. "I don't think we have a choice."

Kendra grabbed my arm. "You forget I was married to a cop for seventeen years?"

"No. But I also remember you love to binge-watch creepy crime shows and have a twisted mind." I lifted one shoulder. "Your authority's a bit tainted."

Her stare intensified. She dropped her voice to an ominous whisper. "There's no telling what you're walking into. It's not safe to go in alone."

"Alexia needs our help." I tugged my arm free. "And I'm not alone . . . I have you."

Kendra rolled her eyes.

"We'll be fine." *I hope.* "But if it makes you feel better, you can wait here and call Nate."

I hopped out of the car and ran up the front path before I changed my mind. A car door slammed behind me, followed by the slap of shoes on the concrete as Kendra rushed to catch up.

"Alexia?" I stepped inside, gravitating toward the hysterical sobs coming from the next room, and found her curled up in a wooden rocker, her hands wrapped around her abdomen.

Alexia let out a loud wail as we approached, rambling incoherent streams of nonsense. She sucked in stuttered breaths between words, talking about cramps and bleeding.

"The doctor said I have to go to the hospital, but I'm too scared to go alone. You've been through this. You're the only one who knows what I'm feeling." Tears streamed down her face. She cried out and doubled over. "Please, help me. Please! I don't want to lose my baby!"

Kendra looked at me with wide eyes. She leaned over, stroking Alexia's back. "What about the baby's father? Does he—"

"He's gone!" Alexia lifted her head to glare at me, pure hatred burning in her red eyes. "I already told you he left me here, all alone, and he's never coming back."

An icy chill ran down my spine. I shook my head and signaled for Kendra to let it go. Now was not the time to get into a debate about dead-beat dads, especially with a borderline psychotic pregnant woman. "Shh . . . let's just get you to the hospital. We can worry about everything else after you and your baby are taken care of."

My mind raced with memories of the time I'd been in Alexia's place, the fear and dread as real now as it had been back then. Losing my unborn child had been almost as painful as losing the love of my life . . . or at least I'd thought he was.

No one said a word on the short drive to Memorial Hospital, but the tension in the car was palpable . . . especially when we passed the one spot I'd hoped to avoid for the rest of my life —the site of Will's accident. The bitter image of Will twisted and morphed, changing into Nico and bringing to light my *greatest* fear—I could lose him too. Over stupid insecurities . . . his *and* mine.

"Danni?" Kendra placed her hand on my rigid arm. "Hey, slow down."

I glanced at the speedometer. In my moment of panic, I'd stomped on the accelerator, pushing the car to eighty miles per hour.

THE DOCTOR HAD CALLED the front desk to alert them Alexia would be coming. The staff whisked her straight to OB triage, leaving Kendra and me to pace the waiting room.

Twenty minutes passed, and still no word. This place, the sounds, the sterile smell all dragged me back to the night I sat here pleading for Will to live.

"I need to get some air."

"Danielle DeLaney?" A nurse called out before I reached the exit. "Ms. Jamison is asking to see you."

When I entered Alexia's room, she greeted me with an outstretched hand, despite all the wires and needles attached to her. The brief episode of pure evil she'd projected back at the house had vanished, replaced by her usual smile and overly-sweet demeanor.

"They found the baby's heartbeat. He still has a chance." She caressed her little bump of a belly, a dreamy look in her puffy eyes.

"That's great news." At least someone might get a happy ending. After the past few months, that small ray of hope was worth hanging onto.

Alexia patted the mattress next to her, motioning for me to sit.

"I never asked, how far along are you?" I tucked one leg underneath me and tried to look comfortable.

"Around twenty-five weeks. Too early for this little guy to come out. That's why they want to keep me here a while—to make sure he stays put." She took my hand. "I'm sorry for—"

A soft tap on the door interrupted us. "Excuse me, Ms. Jamison, I need to verify your health insurance." A young clerk came into the room, pushing her portable workstation. "The information we have on file is coming back as expired. Do you have new coverage?"

Alexia squirmed in the bed, looking around the room. "I should have a card in my bag, but I don't know where it got to."

"I have it." Kendra stood in the doorway, holding up Alexia's purse. "Sorry, the nurse let me come back. I was waiting in the hall." She crossed the room and dropped it on my lap.

Alexia pulled out her keys, her cell phone, and a pair of sunglasses before uncovering her wallet. Her phone screen lit up when she piled the items on the bed.

My eyes locked on the fading image, my heart pounding a ferocious beat. I picked up her phone with trembling fingers and tapped for the photo to return. I swallowed hard, staring at Alexia in the tiny emerald dress she'd worn to Logan's New Year's Eve party, wrapped in the arms of *my* husband. My fist tightened around her phone. "Why do you have this?"

Alexia didn't answer. Her lips twitched in an evil sneer.

"Explain why you're kissing my husband." My clenched jaw made it difficult to get out the words. Fear and fury collided, simmering in my veins.

"You seem to forget he was leaving you," Alexia sneered, taunting me. Gloating.

"For you?" I jumped to my feet, still clutching the evidence. "You're the whore who ruined my marriage?"

"Your marriage was a pathetic sham long before I showed up. At least that's what Will told me the first night we made love." Alexia responded in an icy voice while gently caressing her baby bump, the blips on her monitors coming at a faster pace.

"You know what? I'm just gonna stop back later." The clerk called out, cowering behind her computer and scurrying toward the hallway.

Kendra closed the door behind her. She eased toward me. "Danni—"

"Stay out of this." I held my hand up to Kendra but couldn't tear my eyes away from the scene in front of me. Heat scorched my face. Intense pressure built in my chest, threatening to explode. "Who is your baby's father?"

Tears welled in Alexia's eyes, but she didn't answer.

"Who's the goddamn father?" I hurled her phone across the room. It hit the wall, shattered, and fell to the floor.

She still didn't answer. She didn't need to. The tears streaming down her face told the story.

An alarm went off on Alexia's monitor. Two nurses rushed into the room, shouting questions and orders that no one paid attention to.

"How does it feel?" Alexia balled her hands into fists and slammed them into the mattress. "How does it feel to have someone you love taken away from you?" She narrowed her eyes, glaring at me with a deranged vengeance.

"What are you talking about? You lost him too."

One nurse called for security while the other instructed me to leave and tried to calm Alexia. Kendra attempted to pull me away, but I shook her off, determined to stand up for myself for once in my life.

Alexia leaned past the nurse who was trying to restrain her. "My father never had time for me after *you* weaseled your way into his life. You think I didn't know? Every moment he should have been spending with me, every memory we should have been creating, *you* stole. You needed to pay, and your cheating husband was easy and more-than-willing prey. The perfect revenge."

She grimaced, clenching her stomach, but continued her outburst in the same sickening, syrupy-sweet voice she'd used on several occasions in the past. "Oh, you poor thing. You don't think Will was faithful to you all those years before me, do you?"

Alexia let out an evil laugh and returned to a bitter tone. "You pathetic, delusional fool. I was the last in a long, *long* line of affairs. I never expected we'd fall in love, but that just made for a much sweeter revenge. And the surprise of our precious baby, well that—"

"Enough!"

"He'd still be here if it weren't for you. *He'd* be the one holding my hand. Taking care of our little boy. But you had to ruin everything. You manipulated him into ruining our perfect night—the night he proposed to me. He died going back to you!"

Another nurse ran into the room, followed by two security guards who grabbed my arms, telling me I had to leave. When I didn't move, they forced me toward the door.

"He died coming back to serve me with divorce papers," I screamed over my shoulder, tears streaming down my face, as the guards dragged me from the room.

When we reached the exit a police cruiser pulled up to the curb. Kendra's ex-husband climbed out of the driver's seat and approached us, his lips pressed together in a poor attempt to hide a smirk. He gave a subtle shake of his head and motioned toward the car. "Get in the back. Both of you."

The security guards exchanged a puzzled look and shrugged. "We didn't call the police," the tall one said.

"No, but they did." Nate hooked his thumb toward Kendra and me. "Friends of mine."

My head snapped toward Kendra. "You called Nate?" I said, my voice shooting up an octave.

"Texted him."

"Same difference." Were we really going to play this game? I crossed my arms and gave Kendra a stern look. "Why?"

She shrugged. The corner of her mouth twitched upward. "You told me to . . . back at the house?"

I rolled my eyes. "I was being sarcastic. Jeeze, I thought you knew me."

Kendra waved a dismissive hand. "Things were getting pretty ugly in there. I just wanted to have your back in case you completely snapped and crossed any legal lines . . . not that I would have blamed you, by the way."

Nate and the two guards laughed, reminding me of my current . . . situation, for lack of a better term. The latest kick to my fragile heart.

"I'll give them a ride to their car—make sure they leave, so you can go back to your nice peaceful evening." Nate shook both men's hands, thanking them when they offered him a light-hearted "good luck."

He climbed back into the driver's seat, shoulders still shaking with amusement from his conversation, and glanced at Kendra and me in the rear-view mirror. "Where'd ya park?"

RETELLING the whole story to Nate before he agreed to set us free only made me more furious, even if he had cringed at all the right places and offered several sympathetic nods. I paced the hospital parking lot, snarling with each step, as his taillights faded in the distance.

"Let it go, Danni."

I swung around, turning all my anger on Kendra. "Weren't you paying attention in there? How the hell am I supposed to let this go?"

Kendra reclined against my car, ankles crossed, and pulled a lip balm from her purse. "Yeah, you're right. Staying bitter and angry for the rest of your life is a much better plan. What was I thinking?"

Of course she was right, but I deserved a moment to rant. Have a tantrum. I'd earned it. I folded my arms with a huff.

"Look, at least they didn't threaten to press charges or tell Nate to throw your ass in jail. That's a good start."

"How can you joke about this?" My voice screeched with indignation.

"Who said I was joking?" She waved a dismissive hand and stepped into my path. "Will's gone. Karma's a bitch. And you're pushing away an amazing man—a man you *love*—to hang on to the pain and humiliation of your past?" Kendra raised her brows, pinning me with a look that dared me to argue. "The way I see it, you have two choices. You can continue to let Alexia screw with your head. And your happiness. Or you can let it go and finally move on."

I stared at the ground, trying to let her words sink in. "I know you're right. I'm—" I sucked in a shaky breath and raised my face to look at her, ignoring the growing sting of tears. "I'm just not sure how to move past all of this."

"Take some time. Have a meltdown. Go spit on his grave for all I care." Kendra grabbed my hands, giving them a gentle squeeze. "But don't think Nico's gonna to wait forever for you to get your shit together."

I blew out a heavy sigh, releasing some of my tension from the day's events. "Don't you ever get tired of being so bossy?"

A corner of Kendra's mouth lifted in a grin. "It's not bossy when it's common sense." She bumped her shoulder against mine, reviving the comforting sense of friendship we'd shared most of our lives. "So?"

"It's time to move on." My faint words felt like a small victory.

Kendra threw her arms around me, squeezing tight. "Good choice." She stepped back, held open the passenger-side door of my car, and motioned for me to get in. "Come on. Let's get you home."

I didn't move. "But this is my—"

"You really think I'm gonna let you drive right now?" Kendra shook her head and laughed then pulled me in for another tight hug. "Get in the car, sweetie."

I groaned, giving in to her better judgment. "I'm glad you were with me tonight." I pulled away to look at her. "It's really good to have my best friend back."

"Me too." She walked around and climbed into the driver's seat. "You know, it's about damn time you stood up for yourself —and I'm really glad I was here to see it—but don't stop now. Figure out what you need to do to let go of that bastard and get over this whole mess with his little bitch.

"Then go after Nico with the same intensity you showed in there . . . just try not to break any of Nico's equipment." Kendra gave a suggestive wink and grinned.

ALMOST PERFECT
NICO

Sophia and I had played for more than an hour before she'd gotten tired and curled up on my lap, rubbing her eyes. When she'd started to doze off, Summer got her dressed for bed then handed her back to me, and I got to kiss my sweet little girl good night for the very first time.

Forty minutes later, I'm still floating on cloud nine. I always assumed I'd love my children, but I hadn't been prepared for how hard and instantly I'd fall. It was the most amazing feeling in the world.

My life was so close to perfect—so close to what I'd always imagined for myself—but there was still one piece missing. One person. I turned my phone over in my hand again, debating whether or not I should call her, and gazed out my car window at Danni's dark house.

It had been eight days since I'd tagged along to Logan's meeting so I'd have an excuse to see Danni. Eight days since I'd kissed her and tried to convince her to choose me. Choose *us*. And eight days that she'd ignored every effort I'd made to keep in touch with her.

"Guess all that worrying about whether Danni liked kids,

and whether she would still want me when she learned about Sophia, had been for nothing." I tossed my phone in the passenger's seat and drove away. As long as I had Sophia in my life, "almost perfect" would be pretty damn awesome.

Tomorrow I'd call a family meeting to share my good news—and a *lot* of pictures—with them.

THE GREAT PURGE
DANNI

Kendra closed the garage door and strolled into my kitchen. "I don't know about you, but I could use a drink. And a snack." She dropped her bag on the table and opened the fridge.

"I don't need a babysitter." And the idea of putting food in my churning stomach wasn't too appealing either.

I drifted through the kitchen, straightening things that weren't out of place and tugging at the uncomfortable band around my finger.

Bottles rattled as Kendra continued her search. "Sweetie, you cried most of the way home."

"Did not." More like the *whole* ride home. I collapsed in one of the chairs at the breakfast bar, keeping that minor detail to myself.

Kendra turned and stared at me from beneath arched brows, her silent interrogation undeterred by the steady tap of my nails on the granite counter. She crossed the room and slapped her hand over mine to silence it, never breaking that damn stare.

I rolled my eyes. "Fine, but I still don't need you to stick around trying to cheer me up."

"Look, I'd be more worried if you were keeping all this crap locked up inside you, but I can't leave you alone like this." She released my hand and pushed away from the counter. "Besides, I feel guilty."

"You can't blame yourself for Alexia's sick, twisted mind. And . . . well, I probably should've admitted it before, but I'm pretty sure I overreacted, didn't handle things very well, when I discovered you'd kept quiet about catching Will on a date. I know you'd never do anything to intentionally hurt me."

"If I would have told you what I'd seen instead of trying to handle it myself, maybe things wouldn't have gotten so far out of control."

"I doubt it. I have a feeling the *damage* was already done by then. I just can't believe this was all some bizarre revenge plot for something I didn't even do."

"Yeah, that chick is seriously messed up." She tapped her temple. "Good thing that's all out in the open now."

Kendra searched through a few kitchen cabinets then went back to rooting around in the fridge and pulled out a bottle of wine. "So, what goes good with moscato?"

"More moscato." I dropped my head to my folded arms and let out a heavy sigh. "Skip the glass."

"Well, all right then." Kendra chuckled. "You want me to put that in a paper bag, or you gonna just guzzle it out in the open?" She climbed onto the chair across from me and set one wine glass on the counter. After filling it for herself, she pushed the bottle to me. "So you think your boss knew?"

The same question had been rolling through my mind since we'd left the hospital. I shrugged and took a long swig from the bottle. "It would explain his change in behavior the past few weeks, though."

I swallowed a few more gulps of wine. "The question is

what do I do now? About my job, I mean. I can't imagine ever going back there."

Kendra gave a thoughtful hum as she rolled her wrist, watching the wine swirl inside her glass. "Maybe things will settle down now that everything's out in the open." She peeked up at me with a wicked grin. "I'm more interested in what you're going to do about Nico."

I covered my eyes, preparing to hide from her reaction, but peeked out between my fingers. "I love him."

Kendra plunked down her glass. She slapped both hands over her heart. "Well it's about damn time you finally admit it. I've only been telling you that for months." She let out a laugh. "Seriously though, maybe you should start by telling *him* how you feel. And then showing him."

The same advice Jen had given me weeks ago.

All the ways I'd tried to seduce Nico flashed through my mind. A long series of humiliating failures. I shook my head and gave a frustrated hum. "It's gonna take more than that."

I let my gaze wander around the room at Will's laptop, his favorite ball cap, the book he'd been reading, the mug for his morning coffee that always sat on the counter. "Nico was right." Everywhere I looked, the house was a goddamned shrine to Will. I shook my head, stunned by the reality. "I never noticed it before, but . . . it all makes sense now."

Kendra took another sip of wine and watched me, a crease forming between her brows. "Care to let me in on that conversation you're having in your head?"

"It's just something that Nico said to me. I can see now why he—but I don't love Will. Not anymore."

Kendra pulled out her phone and tapped away then downed the contents of her glass. "I think you know what to do from here." She hopped from her seat, a satisfied look on her face, and grabbed her bag. "My ride will be here in a few minutes. I'm going to head home, see if Logan's up for a little cybersex."

I lifted my hand to stop her. "Please. No details."

Kendra smacked away my hand. "Relax. It's not like I'm inviting you to join us. Although . . ." She laughed and gave me a hug. "You sure you're okay?"

"No. But I'm sure I *will* be." And for the first time, those words didn't feel like a lie.

ALONE AT LAST. I roamed from room to silent room, all filled with glaring reminders of Will that made my stomach churn. My body tensed, muscles shaking from the anger building inside me again. "How could I have been so stupid?"

With a feral roar, I swept my arms across the sofa table, knocking every picture to the floor. The frames shattered, matching the tainted memories they held.

"You bastard. You goddamned fucking bastard!" I screamed into the air as though he were still around. Still able to hear me. *Probably laughing at what a fool I've been.*

How much of my life had been a lie? How many other times had he humiliated me that I didn't know about?

My chest heaved with each labored breath. The air stung as it passed through my throat, raw from my maniacal rant. I sank to the floor, trembling, and waited for the deluge of tears to wash away the pain of my former life.

A short burst of laughter erupted from me, followed by another. Then another. They continued, blending into a long, cathartic fit of laughter with tears streaming down my face.

Freedom. I'd finally purged the emotional baggage of my former life. "Time to get rid of the physical evidence."

I rushed to the closet, grabbed a box of trash bags, and began collecting everything that had been Will's. A few items would be packed in a box for the attic, but the majority would be shipped off to charities . . . and some would be therapeutically smashed into tiny pieces and tossed in the trash.

The decisions weren't difficult—no time wasted on sentimental journeys down memory lane. Something was either a keepsake or gone. I'd wasted fifteen years of my life on that man. Fifteen. There was no way I'd let him steal another precious minute.

As if to prove that point, while digging through a box in Will's closet, I found a receipt from the Radisson Hotel in New York City dated January 17th—the weekend he'd claimed to be in Chicago on business. The weekend I'd been racked with guilt for sharing one single amazing kiss with Nico.

I pinched the paper between two fingers, held it an arm's length away like the filthy piece of trash it was, and carried it down the hall to Will's office. After running the receipt through the shredder, I gathered the scraps from the bin and shoved them through a second time.

Note to self—any other boxes of unknown items will be going straight to the trash. No more unwanted surprises.

SO MUCH MORE
DANNI

I'd worked tirelessly into the wee hours of the morning, reclaiming my life and planning for my future . . . hopefully a future with Nico. After all that work and very little sleep, I awoke this morning feeling more rested, more energetic, and more hopeful than I had in months.

All of that faded the moment I'd turned onto Nico's long driveway. I'd been parked at the top of the circle, staring at his massive home, for the past ten minutes, a ball of nervous energy bouncing around in my chest. I blew out a heavy breath and checked my reflection in the mirror, adding a bit more gloss . . . one tiny step closer to making my big move. *Okay. It's now or never.*

I climbed the steps to his front porch, my left hand tucked behind my back. The door opened before I knocked, and Nico filled the space, staring at me with tired eyes. He leaned into the frame but didn't say a word.

I let my gaze wander over every magnificent inch of him—bare feet, faded jeans, a faded blue T-shirt that hugged his toned torso, and just a hint of the tribal tattoo around his left bicep peeking from under his sleeve. His hair was damp from a recent shower, tousled in his usual messy style. I closed my eyes and breathed in the heavenly scent that surrounded him.

Nico cleared his throat, gaining my attention. His dark eyes watched me with a guarded expression. He didn't say a word. Didn't reach out to touch me.

Did he want me to leave? Want me to stay? Had I taken too long to come to my senses? Make my choice? Butterflies swirled in my stomach, fear of another rejection intensifying.

You need to go after Nico with the same intensity you showed in there. Kendra's words of encouragement rose above the noise in my head.

My fist clenched around the stem of the single white rose I'd bought on impulse at a roadside stand. Intended as a romantic gesture, the idea seemed silly now. I swallowed hard and took a deep breath, focusing on the gorgeous man in front of me.

"Hello, beautiful." I extended my trembling arm, waiting for him to respond. Trying to figure out what to say next if he didn't.

Nico hesitated, staring at my hand, then swept his eyes over me with a heated gaze that touched every inch of my body. "You stole my line."

The deep tones of his soothing voice washed over me. I shrugged, biting back a grin. "Well, you stole my heart, so I, um . . . I guess we're even." I glanced past him into his quiet house, suddenly worried he might not be alone. "I-I'm sorry." I stepped back, shaking my head. "I shouldn't have—"

"Why are you here, Danni?" Nico shoved a hand through his hair. He pushed away from the doorframe and took the flower, his fingers brushing across mine.

"I—" I drew in a deep breath as he skimmed the soft petals along the side of my face . . . down my neck. "I m-missed you. Needed to, um, needed to see you."

Nico gave a thoughtful hum. He continued tracing my

collarbone with the rose. "If I remember correctly"—he leaned forward and whispered—"which I do . . ." He pulled back. "You wanted me to stay away. So I'll ask you again, why are you here?"

"I've, um . . ." Concentrating while Nico continued to tease me with the featherlight touches became impossible. I let my eyes fall closed, getting lost in the arousing sensation. My head tipped to the side as a faint sigh slipped past my lips.

Nico chuckled and lowered his hand, apparently pleased with my body's response to him. I hadn't expected this would be easy, but he seemed to be taking great joy in making me work hard for this. For him.

"I've spent some time—a *lot* of time—thinking. About Will. About us. What I want." I risked a glance at his face. "Just like you asked."

Nico nodded. "And what did you decide?"

I twisted my fingers in my dress. "Can I, um . . . can I come in? Please?"

He scrubbed a hand across his face then stepped aside, allowing a narrow opening for me to slip through. Our bodies brushed against each other as I squeezed past, the brief contact waking my senses. It had been nine long days since he'd held me in his arms, kissed me with a hungry passion. My heart skipped, beating faster.

Nico reached out and took my left hand, lifting it between us. The light through his front door illuminated the deep blue sapphire and reflected off the diamonds surrounding it, shooting brilliant rainbows in every direction.

He brushed his thumb across my ring. "It looks beautiful on you." His voice was thick with emotion. His eyes drifted to mine. "You're sure this is what you want?"

"Yes." I nodded and gazed up into Nico's warm eyes filled with hope. Everything I felt for him—everything I wanted to tell him—flowed straight from my heart. "I want to be with you. Not just for one night or one weekend. Not because of who you are or what you have. And not so that I can run around bragging that I'd been with you."

I dragged my fingers along his stubbled cheek, the rough exterior a total contrast from the tender man beneath. "I want *you*, Nico. The sweet, caring, passionate, and incredibly sexy man who makes me feel more alive than I'd ever imagined I could. I—I love you."

Nico's chest rose and fell with heavy breaths. He stepped closer, our bodies nearly touching. "Say it again." His words came out as a gravelly command, his voice thick with sexual tension.

"I love you," I whispered.

He wove his fingers through my hair, pulling my face toward his, and kissed me with a possessive hunger, claiming me. His lips moved down my neck, following the same trail he'd made with the rose petals earlier.

Nico pulled back to look at me, fire burning in his eyes. "You can't imagine how many nights I've dreamed you'd say those words. Imagined how it would feel to see the truth in your eyes."

His hands glided down the sides of my torso, caressing every inch of me. They continued past my waist, to my hips, the pressure there gently guiding me against his door. He groaned against my mouth as he kissed me, the vibration sending a tremor through my body.

Oh, God. Yes. This was what I wanted. What I'd needed for so long. I worked my hands under the snug fabric of Nico's shirt, exploring the ridges and valleys of his abdominal muscles.

He dipped lower, reaching past the hem of my dress to the exposed skin of my thighs, pushed his hands under the light cotton fabric, and shoved it up to my waist in one swift move.

Nico broke our kiss and braced his palms against the wall,

then dropped his forehead to my shoulder. His heavy breaths of indecision washed across my chest while his hips rolled against mine.

I clung to his back, afraid to let go. Tears burned in my eyes. Rejection—my greatest fear—would soon follow.

"Nico, please. Don't push me away this time." My whispered words came out as a desperate plea.

He brushed his lips across my neck and let out a low hum. "Not a chance. I've waited too long for this moment. Dreamed of touching you since the night we met." He placed a kiss below my jaw. "Loving you." Another kiss. "Making you mine."

Nico repositioned my clothes. He took my hands, lacing our fingers together, and kissed me—sweet and gentle this time.

"I promised you'd remember the first time I made love to you." He placed his fingers under my chin, tipping my face toward his. "I'm not going to degrade it with a quick, hard fuck against the wall." He chuckled and pressed his lips to my ear, nipping at the lobe. "We'll have plenty of time for that later. But this time should be special. Come with me."

Nico led me across the grand foyer to a wide staircase, pausing at the bottom. He turned to face me and caressed the side of my face, his dark eyes searching mine. "If this is another dream, I don't want to wake up." His eyes fell closed, and he brushed his lips against mine.

I STOPPED in the doorway of Nico's bedroom, heart racing as I scanned the familiar space. Memories of the day he'd brought me here after my drunken fiasco at Farley's came rushing back. The way he'd taken care of me without selfish expectations. The way he'd looked and smelled, emerging from the bathroom, fresh from his morning shower. The way he sat on the edge of his bed, wallet in hand, struggling to open it—unable to reveal his painful past.

And that bed . . . I drifted closer, wrapping my hand around one of the tall posts. The few clips I'd been able to remember from that night played in my mind.

Nico moved behind me and slipped his arms across my midsection, holding me close. "Thinking about some new dance moves?" He chuckled, his warm breath caressing my neck. "As much as I loved your sexy striptease, I have other plans for right now."

He turned me to face him. His lips glided along my neck—featherlight kisses mixed with the prickles from his stubbled cheek, the combination sending shivers through me.

My head fell to the side on a faint sigh, opening myself to him—my body's instinctive response to his touch. "Mmm . . . and what might that be?"

"I'll be right back." Nico pulled his phone from his pocket as he crossed the room, tapping on the screen. He placed it on his dresser and turned on a small speaker next to it, filling the room with a mellow tune that sounded vaguely familiar. "For starters"—he returned to me and extended one hand—"dance with me."

I reached out, letting Nico take the lead for whatever he had planned. He twirled me under his arm and pulled me to his chest, the same as he'd done at Elevations.

"This song, is it the one we danced to at the gala?"

"It is." Nico stroked my back, tender movements that sent out gentle ripples of desire. "'Here and Now.' I heard it a few months ago, at a reception. It made me think of you."

We swayed to the music, our bodies molded together as if they were meant to be one. Nico's lips grazed my temple. He gave a contented hum. "This is nice. I've missed holding you in my arms." He slid his hand to my hip and pulled me closer.

"I've missed it too."

But "nice" was a definite understatement. Every cell in my body hummed with excitement. Anticipation. Every movement of his hands, his lips, our bodies sent a new rush of desire through me, making me want him more. So much more than I had ever wanted any man.

As if hearing my thoughts, Nico eased down the zipper on my dress. His fingers traced over the opening, slipping further under the fabric's edge on each pass. He rested his hands on my shoulders, thumbs brushing the sides of my neck, and tipped my head to meet his gaze.

An intense passion filled his eyes, a need that mirrored my own. "I love you, Danni."

He lowered his mouth to mine, kissing me tenderly with raw emotion. Pouring himself into my soul. He eased my dress off my shoulders, guiding it down the length of my body. Nico dropped to his knees in front of me, caressing my legs and gazing up at me with fire in his eyes.

His hands drifted up my thigh, skimming along the edge of my panties. He leaned in and pressed his lips to the spot below my right hip then tugged the lace down to expose my tattoo. "So sexy . . . just like I remembered."

Featherlight touches traced each pink heart, gliding lower as he followed the trail at a leisurely pace. My lips parted, a reflexive sigh slipping out. My body ached with anticipation, eager for him to reach the end of the trail. "Nico. If you don't make love to me soon, I'm going to explode."

A faint chuckle was his only response, followed by warm kisses where his fingers had just danced across my skin.

My sighs turned to gasps. "Nico."

"Shh . . . patience," Nico teased then placed another kiss. "We only get *one* first time. I want it to be perfect." He stood and framed my face, staring into my soul. "I want to explore every inch of your beautiful body while I make slow, sweet love to you. All. Day. Long."

Nico reached behind me and unhooked my bra, guided it down my arms, and let it fall to the floor. He brushed his hands up my stomach, grazing his thumbs along the underside of my breasts with soft strokes.

"Come with me." He slid his hands to mine and guided me toward his bed.

Twirling me into his arms, he wrapped me in his warm embrace and resumed our dance, swaying his hips to the song that had been playing on repeat. He covered my mouth with a long, sensual kiss—a sinfully delicious kiss filled with promises of what's to come—then scooped me up and placed me on the mattress.

Nico shook his head, watching me with a heated stare that touched every inch of my body. "You're so damn beautiful." He bent down and kissed me again, lush and deep. "And you're finally mine."

He stepped back and reached behind his head with one hand, pulled off his shirt and tossed it to the floor, then reached for the button on his jeans.

"Wait." I sat up and pushed his hands aside. "You got to undress me. Now it's my turn." I flashed a glance at his face and the sexy grin stretched across it.

"That sounds fair." Nico laced his fingers behind his head. "Go ahead." He winked. "I'm all yours."

All mine. I'd dreamed of this moment so many times.

The sight of this gorgeous man standing in front of me, offering himself to me, took my breath away. I slid to the edge of the bed and pressed my palms against his chiseled abs, letting my fingers explore every ridge as I took my time working my way up his torso. Across his chest. And along his rock-solid arms. I traced the tribal band around his bicep then let my nails glide down the length of his back and around his waist.

I tugged his zipper, lowering it in slow motion, then slid my hands beneath the waistband of his jeans and guided them over his hips. "Mmm . . . now that's impressive." I traced my fingers along the length of his massive erection, barely contained by his black boxer briefs.

Nico groaned. His head fell back. "You're torturing me, you know."

I bit back a grin. "Shh . . . patience. You're the one who wanted to take things slow. Remember? Enjoy the moment."

Nico grabbed my shoulders and pushed me to my back, tackling me on his bed with my hands pinned above my head. "That's when I was the one doing the exploring."

"You mean *teasing*." I squirmed beneath him.

Nico winked. "It's not teasing, because I fully intend to follow through."

Nico grabbed my waist and eased me to the center of his bed. He straddled my hips and knelt above me, his gaze locked on mine. "I could look at you forever. Touch you. Kiss you."

He lowered his lips to mine, kissing me and exploring my body with his mouth. His tongue. Gentle touches that stoked a fire inside me. As promised, he took his time, drawing out the pleasure with such skill and patience. Easing off just before I fell over the edge time and time again. Wave after wave of erotic pleasure washed over me, each one more intense than the last.

I cupped his face, brushing my thumb across his lips. "For a man who claims to lose all self-control around me, you're doing a pretty good job of restraining yourself. Too good." I tugged at his shoulders, trying to bring him closer. "I need you inside me."

Nico nuzzled my neck, his fingers stroking between my legs. "Sorry, you taste so sweet. I can't get enough."

I let out a thoughtful hum, gliding my hands along his smooth chest. "So you're saying this is my fault again, hmm?"

Nico pulled back to look at me. He grinned and gave a slight nod. "That's what I'm going with."

"Well then, maybe it's my turn to see what you taste like." I traced a line down the center of his chest and followed the trail of hair from his navel to the waist of his boxers.

Nico caught my wrist and pulled it to his lips. He shook his head. "Not this time." He stretched across me to his night-stand, retrieving a condom from the drawer. "But I definitely like your other idea." His dark eyes locked on mine as he tore open the packet.

I tugged the condom from the packet and slowly rolled it down the length of his erection then raised my eyes to meet his. My heart pounded with anticipation, the same rhythm pulsing in my core.

Nico brushed his hand along the side of my face and twisted a finger in my loose curls. "That was fucking hot."

He lowered our bodies to the mattress and centered himself between my legs, his hips rocking against mine in a slow rhythm, easing himself deeper inside with each gentle push. His eyes locked on mine, reaching into my soul.

A sweet sigh slipped past my lips as he filled me. Physically. Spiritually. Emotionally.

Nico covered my mouth with his. He grabbed my hands, lacing our fingers together, and held them above my head. With one long, smooth movement, he pushed fully into me. Then stopped, his hips pinning me to the mattress. His moan vibrated through me, pure ecstasy, as he continued kissing me with a hungry passion.

The sensation of him filling me but not moving was driving me wild. My muscles clenched around him, aching for more. I opened one eye to peek at him. "Why did you stop?"

"Enjoying the moment. And the view." He grinned, staring

deep into my eyes. "You're so beautiful." He leaned down to brush his lips against my ear. "And you feel fucking amazing."

"You feel pretty amazing too." I squirmed beneath him, writhing with need. "But I bet you'd feel even better if you got moving."

Nico swiveled his hips, pulling back slightly, then pushed in with one solid thrust. My back arched, forcing out a cry of sheer delight. He repeated the same movement in an unhurried rhythm, over and over. His lips caressed my mouth . . . my neck . . . my breasts, each touch a new and wonderful sensation. Every slow, steady stroke pushed me higher as Nico skillfully massaged a sensitive spot inside me that I never knew existed.

My body tingled. The room turned black with sparkling white lights, and the pressure building inside me finally exploded, pushing me over the edge to the most powerful orgasm I'd ever experienced. I wrapped my legs around Nico, holding him to me as I cried out his name.

Nico's pace increased, his thrusts more aggressive, driving toward his own release. His grip on my hands tightened. His body tensed, and he let out a long, guttural groan.

He collapsed with his forehead on my shoulder, his breathing labored. "Wow. That was . . . just wow." Nico lifted his head. He brushed the hair from my face and tucked it behind my ear. "Amazing."

I bit back a grin and arched a brow. "Patting yourself on the back, champ?"

He nuzzled my neck, nipping at me with playful kisses. "Not a chance. *You're* what made it amazing. The way you feel. The way you make *me* feel. The way your body responds to me." He gave a slow contented hum and swiveled his hips. "It's like you were made just for me."

Nico held me a few minutes longer then sighed and gave me a soft kiss. "I'll be right back." He moved to the bathroom to dispose of his used condom then crawled back into bed, pulling me tight against his chest and wrapping me in his strong arms.

I snuggled into his warm embrace and let out a peaceful sigh, fully satisfied—physically and emotionally. That was so much more than mind-blowing sex—for the first time in my life, I'd made love.

SHOWER FANTASY FULFILED
DANNI

Waking up naked in Nico's bed, draped across his glorious body, had been one of the best moments of my life. The absolute best, of course, had come just before our nap.

I'd had plenty of vivid fantasies about him over the past five months, but none had come anywhere close to the reality of actually making love with Nico.

Making love. I let out a contented sigh, completely satisfied and relaxed. *What an amazing feeling.*

I swung my legs over the side of the bed and floated toward the double doors on the other side of his room. Nico had only gone downstairs to order dinner five minutes ago—ten, tops— but I missed him. *I'm sure he won't mind if I borrow something comfy and join him downstairs.*

Nico's massive closet had a large island in the center, built-in shelves, and a cushioned bench. Everything was neat and organized with one section holding all his business suits, the hallmark of his professional image as a powerful executive. I wandered to the other section—the casual side—and slipped on a soft button-down shirt that reminded me of the one he'd worn to our picnic by the lake.

When I turned to leave, my gaze settled on Nico's wallet on top of the island. Memories of the night he'd flipped it open to show me the picture of his ex-wife played in my mind. I drifted closer and brushed my fingers across the surface, tempted to peek inside.

How would you feel if he dug around in your bag? I winced at that thought but glanced over my shoulder anyway and flicked my finger at his wallet. The top flopped open. My hand flew to my chest.

Summer's picture was gone. In its place was a picture of Nico and me, taken at the gala. The expression on his face as he looked at me instead of the camera melted my heart. His—

Nico cleared his throat from the doorway.

My spine stiffened. "I was just coming down to find you." I slapped the wallet closed and spun to face him, relieved to find him smiling.

"So, dinner should be here in about an hour." He pushed away from the doorframe, where he'd been lounging, and strolled toward me. "Which gives us—"

I lunged forward, meeting him halfway, threw my arms around him, and kissed him with unrestrained passion.

Nico chuckled when I pulled away. "Wow, what was that about?"

"I, um." Maybe he didn't notice me snooping. "Guess I just really missed you." I twisted my lips. Starting a new relationship with a lie didn't feel right. "Sorry, I just wanted—but I shouldn't have, and—"

Nico pressed a finger to my lips. "I was going to show you." He kissed my cheek then pulled back to meet my gaze. "You were right. It wasn't fair for me to get upset about you wearing Will's ring while I carried Summer's picture with me. But more than that, I didn't want to look in my wallet and see her. I wanted to see you."

He set his phone next to his wallet and tapped the dark screen. It lit up, displaying the same image of the two of us. "Always you."

I clasped my hands behind his neck. "Always *us*."

"I like the sound of that." Nico skimmed his hands along my sides, a twinkle in his eyes. "You look awfully adorable in my shirt." He undid a few buttons and slid it from my shoulders. "But I like you better without it." He dropped a quick kiss on my lips then turned and walked away.

"Hey, where you going?"

"Shower." Nico chuckled and looked over his shoulder. "Care to join me?" He pulled the string on the front of his silk lounge pants and let them fall to the floor, then strutted into the bathroom.

Looking like that? No need to ask twice. I picked up his shirt and returned it to the hanger then rushed around his bed, slowing as I reached the doorway, and sashayed into the room. A light steam had already begun fogging the glass surrounding his walk-in shower. Nico stood in the center, hands in his sudsy hair, as several streams of water hit him from multiple angles. His muscles flexed and rippled with each movement.

"You planning to gawk all day, or are you coming in to play?"

"Hmm . . . definitely coming in." I stepped into the spacious shower and approached him, pressing my hand to his abs. "I was just taking a moment to enjoy this magnificent view." I let my fingers skim his waist while I strolled around him, taking in every angle of his perfect body. "You know . . . I had a fantasy about you making love to me in the shower a few months ago."

"Is that right?" Nico grabbed my wrist and pulled me to his

chest. "I think you need to tell me about it." He brushed his rough cheek against mine. "I bet I can make it come true."

"That's what I was counting on." I turned his hands palm up then filled each with a generous amount of shower gel. "You were behind me, washing me and caressing my whole body."

Nico grinned. "I can do that." He moved to stand several inches behind me then scrubbed his hands across my back and down my arms. "Like this?" Laughter laced his voice.

"Tease." I stepped back until our bodies pressed together, nestling against his erection.

Nico wrapped his arms across my hips, holding me to him. "Tell me what you want me to do, Danni." His low, gravelly demand vibrated against my ear.

My legs went weak. My grip on his arm tightened. I swallowed hard against the lump in my throat and tried to ignore the jumble of nerves bouncing around in my chest. I'd assumed Nico would take the lead.

"Danni? How can I make your fantasy come true if you don't tell me what to do?" He nipped at my ear, his rough stubble grazing the side of my neck. "And I want every dirty detail."

I sucked in a sharp breath, paralyzed by a sudden lack of confidence. I didn't know if I could actually *tell* him—share such deep, personal thoughts.

Nico waited patiently, continuing to hold me. Kiss me. He made me feel safe. Loved. Made me want to trust. To try.

"First . . . first you massaged my arms. My shoulders. My neck." I closed my eyes and let my head fall back, surrendering to him. To this exhilarating moment. "Then you skimmed your hands the length of my torso, down my thighs, and retraced the path."

Nico followed my directions, adding kisses along the way, and humming with pleasure against my skin.

"Mm-hmm . . . like that." I sighed and melted against him, getting lost in the arousing sensations—each touch more sensual than I'd imagined it could be.

"Next you caressed my breasts with featherlight strokes then caught my nipples between your thumbs and forefingers." My breath hitched, a gentle gasp slipping out, and a bolt of electricity shot straight to my core. I arched my back, grinding against Nico.

"Fuck, Danni." His husky voiced dripped with sexual tension. "Tell me what happens next."

I bit my lip, remembering the night I'd had that fantasy. How surprised I'd been that Nico could have given me such an intense orgasm without even being in the room. Heat filled my cheeks. "You slipped your hands between my legs, stroking me and giving me the most amazing orgasm I'd ever had. Well, until today, that is." I turned my head to peek at Nico and gave him a tender kiss.

He wrapped his arms around me, twisting my body until we faced each other. "Same for me." He pressed his lips to mine, his tongue sweeping into my mouth for a hungry kiss filled with need. Without breaking our kiss, Nico let his hand glide the length of my stomach and down the front of my thigh.

I caught his wrist, stopping him before he could retrace his path—before he reached the point where I might not be able to stop him—and took a few staggered breaths. "But I think I'd like to rewrite that ending." I angled my face to watch his.

Nico slid his hands to my hips, guiding me backward. A knowing look filled his dark eyes. "You have something in mind for this new ending?"

My back bumped against the cool tile. I bit my lip and nodded, meeting his gaze. "I believe you promised me a quick, hard fuck against a wall."

"It's like you read my mind." Nico growled, covering my

mouth in a passionate kiss. He dipped down and caught the backs of my thighs, lifting me to him, and guided my legs around his waist. "Hold on tight, beautiful."

He thrust up into me with one swift movement that forced a primal scream from my lungs. My nails dug into his shoulders, and I hooked my ankles together behind him.

"You okay?" Nico paused, a panicked look on his face.

"Hmm . . . so much better than okay."

Nico tightened his grip and continued pounding into me hard and fast, groaning with pleasure on each thrust. His mouth found mine, kissing me with the same hungry aggression. He slid his lips to my neck, sucking and nipping. "Christ, Danni, you feel so amazing. I just wanna stay here forever, buried so deep inside you."

I bit my lip as he swelled inside me, putting exquisite pressure on every sensitive spot. "Oh, my God. Yes. I—" I gasped, struggling to remember how to form a sentence. "So good. Just . . . don't . . . don't stop."

I nestled my head against his shoulder, finally understanding and fully appreciating his love of a good hard fuck against the wall.

MORNING APOLOGIES
DANNI

Gentle fingers brushed the side of my face, pulling me from sleep into the perfect dream come true.

"Good morning, beautiful." Nico's lips pressed against my forehead . . . then the tip of my nose . . . before settling against my lips in a slow, gentle kiss.

I hummed against his mouth as he woke every cell in my body, stirring them to an instant state of arousal. "Good morning, sexy."

Nico skimmed his fingertips across my chest and stomach, drawing random designs with featherlight touches. "Did you have a good night?"

"The most amazing night ever." I closed my eyes, getting lost in the memory. We'd snuggled together on the couch after dinner, under the pretense of watching a movie. In reality, we'd made out from the opening scene until the closing credits then came to bed and made love again. I let out a contented hum. "I don't think I've ever felt this happy."

Nico kissed me. "That's exactly what I've been thinking since I woke up." A crease formed between his brows. "Well, mostly."

He paused for a few seconds. His facial expression grew tense, and his mood shifted slightly—more serious. "About our shower yesterday . . ." His mind seemed to wander as he traced circles around my navel. "I, um."

I closed my eyes and let out a slow hum. As if the sensations rolling through my body from Nico's sensual wake-up weren't enough, memories of our hot and steamy shower sex pushed me to the next level of desire. "If you're asking me to take another shower, the answer is definitely yes. Assuming I can even walk that is." I let out a small laugh.

"Well, I'm certainly not going to turn down the offer, but what I was trying to say is that I'm sorry." He drew in a deep breath and shoved a hand through his hair, appearing to struggle with what to say next.

"What could you possibly have to be sorry about?" I wasn't an expert, but I'd give each of his performances yesterday a perfect ten.

He gave a cautious grin and pulled in a deep breath. "I'm not an irresponsible person—well, not normally." He rubbed the back of his neck. "For some reason I seem to lose all sense of self-control around you, but there's no excuse for me forgetting to use a condom. It's just that . . . well, if you—"

"Nico . . ." I let out a heavy sigh. "I'm not worried about getting pregnant."

A smile stretched across his face. "Well then, neither am I. I've always want—"

I pressed a finger to his lips. "Please let me finish. I've always wanted children too. Will and I tried for years." I shook my head. "I managed to get pregnant one time but lost my baby a few months in. After that, well—I guess it just wasn't meant to be."

I let my eyes fall shut, afraid to see any hopes for our future slip from his eyes. Family meant everything to Nico, and I suspected he dreamed of having a house full of kids someday. I couldn't give him that dream.

Nico pulled me into his arms. He pressed his lips to my temple. "There are other ways of creating a family. We'll work it out . . . when the time's right." He laced our fingers together.

"Just so you know. That was a first for me . . . other than Summer, of course." Nico scrunched his brows and gave a slight shake. "Sorry. What I'm trying to say is, I'm clean. I get tested every few months, but if you want me—"

I pressed my lips to his. "I don't want to talk about this right now." I eased out of bed and motioned for him to follow me.

Steam had begun to fill the bathroom when Nico wandered in, foil packet in hand and wearing nothing but a sexy grin.

I bit my lip and sashayed over to him, letting my eyes take in every magnificent inch. "Hmm . . . something's wrong with this picture."

He tilted his head, appearing confused.

I snapped the condom packet from between his fingers and tossed it toward the trash can. "I was tested a few weeks ago. I'm clean too." Without another word, I brushed my hands and stepped into the shower.

Nico froze, a stunned expression on his face. He scratched his jaw. "So, does that mean no more condoms?"

The hopeful tone in his voice made me laugh. "Unless you really *want* to use them." I pressed my back against the wall and extended his bottle of shower gel. "Are you planning to get your gorgeous self in here or must I come over and drag you in?"

I didn't need to ask twice.

FAMILY
NICO

Danni shifted in the passenger's seat and tucked one bare foot beneath her. A small whimper slipped past her sweet lips, still swollen from our latest round of up-against-the-shower-wall steamy sex.

"Sorry." I returned my hand to her knee, tracing lazy circles on her soft skin.

"Unless you're apologizing for insisting we get dressed and venture out, there's nothing to be sorry about. I'm just a little out of practice."

"I'm sure we can fix that." I slid my hand higher, easing up the hem of her dress, and brushed my fingers along her inner thigh.

Danni slapped her hand over mine right before I reached her panties, but she didn't push me away. "Mind on the road, mister." She laughed and shifted again, her hips rocking up enough for me to inch my fingers toward my target.

"Christ, Danni, how am I supposed to think about driving when you're so wet?" My mind raced, running through options for pulling off the road. Finding a secluded spot where I could get my mouth on her. Kiss those sore spots and make her feel better.

She purred as I stroked her through the thin fabric. "Maybe it would be easier if you didn't have your fingers where they are."

"You really want me to take them away?"

"Mmm . . . not really. I've waited so long for you to touch me like this. I don't ever want you to stop." Danni sighed and shifted beyond my reach. "But not here—while you're driving. It's not safe." She laced her fingers through mine and gave a gentle squeeze.

She didn't need to explain further, and I was glad she didn't bring up her ex's name. But the implication was there—he'd died from injuries he'd suffered in a car accident. Different circumstances, but fear had a way of blocking out the details.

"You're right. I'm sorry." I raised our joined hands and kissed her wrist.

Danni twisted in her seat, turning to look out all the windows. "Where are we going anyway?"

"About that . . ." I'd told her we were going for a ride, which we were . . . but I'd left out the minor detail that our *ride* had a specific destination. "Gabriela made me promise I'd be at family lunch today." I kept my tone flat then waited, flashing glances at Danni from the corner of my eye.

It only took a few seconds for the words to register. Her eyes grew wide. "You're making me do a walk of shame to meet your family?" Danni's voice shot up a full octave. She released my hand, tugged and smoothed her dress, then flipped down the visor to inspect her appearance. "Oh, my God, Nico. I look a wreck. What are they gonna think?"

"Sweetheart? You've already met my family." I glanced to the side again, trying not to laugh at her adorable, albeit panicked, expression. "And like I told you back at the house, that dress is *basically* clean—you only wore it half an hour, tops, to drive there yesterday."

Danni glared and smacked my shoulder, a hint of a smile on her lips.

"You look beautiful, so stop stressing."

She also had that just-fucked—multiple times—glow, which Gabriela would no doubt latch onto the minute she laid eyes on us. Not that I cared. Hell, I wanted the whole world to know Danni was finally mine.

I turned onto Gabriela's driveway, pulled off to the side, and twisted to face Danni.

"Are we there?" She squinted through the windshield.

"Almost. I wanted a minute alone first . . . to apologize. I shouldn't have tricked you into coming here with me."

Danni brushed her soft fingers across my cheek. "Nico, it's fine. I mean, I was a little shocked at first, but this is your family, and I understand how important they are to you."

"It's not fine. I wasn't honest, and *that's* important to you. To both of us." I tucked a curl behind Danni's ear. "I guess I was afraid you'd want to go home instead, and I couldn't bear the thought of being apart from you so soon." I stretched across the center console to kiss her. "Plus I plan to make love to you a few more times before we need to return to work tomorrow."

"Practice makes perfect?" Danni arched a brow.

"I don't know . . ." I pulled back onto Gabriela's driveway and took Danni's hand. "I think we're already perfect together. I just can't get enough of you."

Bella raced to greet me the second I stepped out of the car. "Uncle Nico!"

"Hey, munchkin." I scooped her up and kissed her cheek, carrying her around to the passenger's side. "I brought my friend, Danni. Do you remember her from the ball?" I opened the door and took my girl's hand, pulling her to me.

"I 'member you. You're Princess Danielle." Bella squirmed to get down. She curtsied then threw her arms around Danni's hips. "Did you come to play with me?"

Danni looked at me and lifted one shoulder.

"Only if you want."

A bright smile lit up Danni's face. She wrapped her free arm around Bella's shoulders. "I'd love to play. Is it okay if I talk to the grown-ups for a few minutes first?" Danni leaned down. "You know, so they don't get jealous?"

Bella nodded. "Come with me." She grabbed our hands, towing us toward the back deck. "Mommy . . . Uncle Nico's here, and he brought Danni with him."

"Really?" Gabriela poked her head over the side of the deck and shrieked. "Danni! This is such a nice surprise." She rushed toward us and pulled Danni into an overzealous hug, grinning at me over her shoulder—that fucking I-know-what-you-were-doing grin . . . just as I'd expected. She released Danni and moved on to me, squeezing tighter than usual, and whispered, "I'm so happy for you."

I pulled back and winked. "I'm happy too." I glanced around the empty yard and deck. "Where is everyone?"

"Well, Ben's running late—as usual—and Papa got called into the restaurant . . . but don't worry, I'll give him the update on your love life." She laughed and tapped my cheek. "Nonno and Troy are in the kitchen, getting the ribs ready for the grill. And the boys are down in the field. They asked me to send you down so they could kick your butt in soccer again, but I'll tell them—"

"No. It's okay. Don't change your plans because of me." Danni squeezed my hand. "Go play. I'll be fine here."

"Sure. Danni can keep me company." Gabriela beamed and draped her arm across Danni's shoulders, pulling her away from me. "It'll be nice to have a girl chat for a change instead of listening to you guys talk sports."

"You sure you're okay with this?" I kissed Danni's cheek and mock whispered, "You do realize she's going to interrogate you, right?"

Gabs laughed. "Actually, I was planning to share all your embarrassing stories."

"So . . . you and Danni, huh?" Ben set two tall glasses of iced tea and his phone on the table, then plopped down across from me. "It's about time."

We'd already discussed Danni and me at lunch . . . in much greater detail than necessary, if you asked me, but that was typical for my family. "You have a point to make?"

Ben chuckled, showing absolutely no remorse for his part in the lengthy interrogation. "Nope. Just sayin' that I'm really happy for you . . . and even happier for myself, since I won't have to put up with your moping around anymore."

"I'm in a good mood today, so I'll give you a pass on being a dick." I swirled the ice in my glass then took a long drink.

Ben laughed and checked his watch. "That's only because you spent the better part of the past twenty-four hours getting laid."

He had a point there. I let out a low hum, letting my mind wander through all the times I'd made love to Danni. "You notice Danni's ring finger?"

"I did. Looks like the one I caught you staring at in Tiffany's window. The one she wouldn't wear but suddenly put on yesterday?" Ben stared into the yard, strumming his fingers on the table. "I get the feeling there's more to that change-of-heart story than what you told us earlier."

"Yeah. A really fucked up part. I didn't want to bring it up with Danni around." I gave Ben a quick run-down of what she'd told me had happened with Alexia on Friday.

"Wow, that's just . . . I don't even know what to say about that." Ben shook his head, disbelief on his face. "Damn."

"I hate like hell that Danni got hurt again by that bastard's actions, but at least it finally broke whatever hold he had on her." I dragged a hand over my face and glanced toward the small table under a giant willow tree, where Princess Danielle and Princess Isabella were having tea with Queen Gabriela. Three of the most important ladies in my life, smiling and enjoying each other.

Danni took a sip from her cup then leaned down and kissed my niece on her cheek. That perfect scene hit me square in the chest—melted my heart—and I imagined Danni sitting there with my daughter.

"Does she know?"

"Not yet. I need to tell her tonight." Should have done it yesterday before I took her to bed, but hearing Danni say she loved me just blew me away. Made me forget about anything else but making her mine.

Ben's phone buzzed. Hi flicked away the message on the screen and gave his phone a shove.

"So when do you get the results?" He kept his voice low, even though we were the only two on the deck.

I'd been prepared to tell him and Gabs before I left the office on Friday, but so much had changed since then. Now . . .

Ben's eye grew wide. "You already got them!" He dropped his arms to the table and leaned forward, staring me down. The corner of his mouth twitched up. "Damn. This is good, right? I can be happy without you tryin' to kick my ass?"

I gave a slight nod, struggling to hold back my own grin while bursting with excitement on the inside.

"So why the hell are you keeping this to your—oh. Danni."

I nodded. "Not looking forward to that conversation." Every time I thought about it—practiced what I'd say—my mind came up with a new version of how it could go terribly wrong, always ending with Danni walking away.

"I don't think you have anything to worry about." Ben tipped his head toward the royal tea party. "It's obvious she adores Bella. I'm sure she'll love a little girl who's a part of you even more."

"Or hate that she's a part of Summer."

Ben swiped away another text message as soon as it appeared on his phone. He stared at the table for a moment, then let out a heavy breath and rubbed his neck before returning his attention to me. "I think you're overreacting, but we'll never know for sure if you don't tell her."

I sure hoped he was right, but the closer I got to having that conversation with Danni, the more nervous I got. I strummed my fingers on the table. "You know, you still didn't answer my question from earlier."

Ben narrowed his eyes. "What question was that?"

My brother had the worst poker face. He clearly knew what I was talking about. "The one you've been dodging since you got here—why were you so late? And when are you finally gonna break down and bring Kristi to these family gatherings?"

Ben groaned and flipped over his phone, ignoring the three new text messages that had just popped up. He leaned back in his seat, arms crossed, and stared at me. "That's two questions."

"Okay. Then I guess I'll need two answers." I sat back, imitating him, and waited.

"Fine." He held up one finger. "First of all, I was late because I was busy getting dumped, so . . ." He added a second finger. "Never. Any other questions?"

"Oh, shit. I'm sorry. I didn't—"

Ben held up his hand. "No worries. I was ready for it to be

over, so it's all good." He didn't look away. Didn't give any indication that he was lying about being okay.

"All right, but I do have another question—several, actually. Like, what happened?" I grinned and tipped my head toward his phone. "And what is with all the incoming messages?"

"She won't fuckin' leave me alone." Ben sighed and dragged a hand over his face. "Kristi's been seeing someone else for a few weeks—just casually, she said—but she wants to 'take it up a notch.' We'd agreed to an open relationship, so whatever. But it seems neither one of *them* felt comfortable with the whole 'sleeping with multiple partners' scene." He moved his glass while he talked, absentmindedly making patterns with the condensation circles it left on the table.

"And you were?"

Ben lifted one shoulder. "It's not like I'm looking for a committed relationship."

He snapped up his vibrating phone and lifted it to his ear. "You do realize when you dump someone, you're supposed to disappear, right? That means you can't text non-stop, then call because you don't like that I'm ignoring you."

He rolled his eyes, listening to the rambling voice on the other end of his call. "I already told you. I'm. Fine." Ben sighed. "Look, I gotta go. I'm in the middle of something." He gave a short, humorless laugh. "You don't get to ask that anymore either. Goodbye, Kristi."

He lowered his phone, shaking his head. "Christ, she's exhausting. How the hell did I survive five months with her?"

I laughed and took a quick look around to make sure we were still alone, then leaned closer and lowered my voice. "Well, you told me—on several occasions, actually—and I quote, 'the sex is fucking amazing.'"

Ben grinned, his head bobbing. "Oh, yeah . . . that's the reason."

I looked past my brother and focused on the beautiful woman approaching me. The past twenty-four hours with Danni had been amazing—and not just because of the sex—but I couldn't stop wondering how long this could last. Wondering if she'd still want me after—

"Everything okay?" Danni set a glass of wine on the table and snuggled in next to me, snaking her arms around my waist. "You look upset about something."

"I'm fine." I pressed a kiss to her forehead. "I was just missing you."

"Aww . . . you two are just so cute." Gabriela joined us, taking a seat next to Ben.

"Yeah, they're adorable . . . if you're into that mushy love crap." Ben laughed and looked toward the kitchen. "Where's Troy? You leave him tied up somewhere?"

Gabriela let out an exaggerated groan, closed her eyes, and shook her head. "And this is why I've always wanted a sister." She laughed and took a sip of wine, wearing a grin that stretched wider than the rim of her giant glass. Her eyes sparkled, dancing from Danni to me then back again.

Danni leaned closer and mock whispered, "Why is she looking at us like that?"

Ben and I burst out laughing.

"Sometimes it's best to just ignore her," I whispering back.

"Hey." Gabriela tossed a balled-up napkin at me, her smile never fading. "I heard that." She angled herself away from Ben and me. "So, Danni, I want to thank you for indulging my daughter. I'm sure you didn't come here planning to sit at the kids' table all afternoon."

"She's adorable, and I had a lot of fun playing with her, so no thanks necessary." Danni relaxed against me, a contented smile on her face.

Ben tapped his foot against mine, gaining my attention. He

gave a subtle nod in Danni's direction, his expression saying "told you."

I brushed my fingertips along Danni's arm. "You ready to head home?"

She nodded, her eyes finding mine. The sparkle in those baby blues told me exactly how she hoped we'd be spending the rest of our day.

Me too, beautiful. Me. Too.

I accepted Nico's hand, forcing a tentative smile as he helped me out of his car. "I had a really nice time today . . ." He'd been quiet most of the ride back to his house—tense, even—and I couldn't decide if he was upset, tired, or maybe just wanted to be left alone. "I should probably head home."

His grip on my hand tightened. "Stay. Please . . . at least for a few minutes, and then you can leave if you still want to."

I nodded, even more confused by his mood than I'd been a minute ago. "Everything okay?"

"Yeah," Nico said in a flat tone, guiding me inside with his hand at the small of my back. When we reached the kitchen, he turned to face me and took my hands. He pulled in a deep breath and blew it out slowly. "There's something that I need to tell you—one last secret. I should have told you sooner, but . . . this isn't a conversation I wanted to have in bed."

"Okay?" I dragged out the word. This didn't sound like it would be good news.

Nico stared at our joined hands, his thumb tracing the beautiful diamond and sapphire ring he'd given me. "You remember I told you about Summer?" He lifted his gaze to meet mine.

"Your ex?" I glanced away. "Yes."

He smoothed his fingers across my forehead, then placed a tender kiss there. "It's nothing bad, I promise. But you need to let me tell you everything before jumping to any conclusions."

"That's not really making me feel any better, just so you know. But I'll try."

"Good." Nico caught my waist, lifted me onto the kitchen island, then moved to stand between my legs.

He took my hands again and laced our fingers together. "About two months ago, Summer started calling Elevations—every day—asking to speak to me. My assistant would tell me, but she knew not to put Summer through or give her any of my contact information, which I'd changed after I left her.

"I thought everything was under control until the night you and I had our first date—" Nico winced at the same time I did, which made us both laugh. "I guess you already figured out that the woman you talked to in the ladies' room at Metro Sky was Summer."

I nodded, remembering how insignificant she'd made me feel. "She mentioned she was there to surprise her ex."

"I'm sorry. Ben saw her arrive at the club, and he'd texted to warm me while we were at dinner, but you wouldn't let me change our plans." Nico winked. "I didn't see her when we got there, and figured we were safe." He leaned in and kissed me, warm and tender. "Had I seen her, I *never* would have let her anywhere near you. Let her hurt you."

My eyes fell closed. That night I'd just assumed Nico regretted asking me out. It never occurred to me he might've been trying to protect me.

"Anyway, after that, Ben and Logan convinced me I couldn't keep avoiding Summer. I needed to talk to her to find out what she wanted." He swiped his thumb across my cheek at took a deep breath.

"Danni, I have a daughter." His eyes glazed over, and his voice grew husky. "A beautiful little girl, and she's . . . she's just amazing."

I blinked a few times, letting his words replay in my mind. Letting them sink in.

"Danni?" Nico brushed the side of my face. His eyes searched mine, silently asking for my thoughts. My forgiveness.

"I—I don't understand."

Nico took his time and explained everything, starting with the day he stopped by my house before meeting with Summer, and ending with every detail of his first visit with his daughter.

"Nico, I'm . . . I'm feeling so many things right now, I don't know where to start."

"Start by telling me you still love me, and you're not mad at me." He pressed his lips to mine, kissing me with a hungry passion. "Tell me you're not going to leave me."

"Of course I still love you. And I don't know why you would think I'd leave."

His posture relaxed. "I love you too." He leaned in to kiss me again.

"But . . ." I pressed my hand against his chest to hold him back this time. "I don't understand why you kept this from me."

"I kept it from everyone—well, everyone except Ben and Logan, but that's only because they dragged it out of me after the gala." He hooked his fingers under my chin and gently lifted my face toward his. "In all fairness, you were avoiding me most of the time while this was unfolding, so I wouldn't have been able to tell you anyway."

Nico brushed his thumb along my bottom lip, his gaze still locked on mine. "But I still tried. I stopped by your house Friday night. Wanted to tell you everything, especially how many times I'd wished you were there with me. But you weren't home."

He dragged a hand through his hair, a faint smile playing on his lips. "Staring at your dark house, I'd convinced myself you'd gone on a date and didn't want anything to do with me." He wrapped his arms around me. "While I'm really glad I was wrong, I hate what you were going through in that moment."

"Thank you." I rested my head on his shoulder, soaking in the warmth and strength of his embrace. That had been one of the worst nights of my life. In hindsight, it had also one of the best, because it forced me to see the truth—gave me closure on my past with Will. It led me to Nico and the loving future we could have together . . . maybe even to the family I'd always dreamed of having.

Someday . . . I hope.

"You know, I still don't understand why you waited so long to tell me about your daughter."

Nico lifted one shoulder. He slid me toward the edge of the island, holding me against his chest. "I was afraid," he whispered.

"I fell in love with you the second I met you." Mischief sparkled in his eyes. "Maybe it was the way you babbled incoherently and blushed whenever our eyes met."

I laughed and gave him a playful shove. "Well, we can't all be as smooth as you with your corny pickup lines."

A crease formed between his eyes. After a few seconds, he grinned and nodded. "Say what you want, but they must've worked, 'cause I got the girl." He winked and dropped a quick kiss on my lips. "Seriously though, after that night . . . the more I got to know you, the harder it became to imagine my life without you in it.

"I didn't know how you felt about kids—how you'd react—so I decided it was safer to wait until I had all the facts. It was foolish, I know, but I couldn't bear the thought of losing you again. And I worried you wouldn't want me when you learned about Sophia."

"Your daughter?"

He smiled, beaming with all the pride of a new parent.

"It's a beautiful name." I pulled his face toward mine, our lips almost touching. "And I hope I get to meet her soon." Before he could respond, I closed the distance between us, kissing him with all the love in my heart. *Showing* him my reaction to this new twist in our relationship instead of just telling him.

Nico slid his hands to my ankles and wrapped my legs around his waist. "Hold on tight, beautiful," he said, his lips never leaving mine. He slipped one hand under me and pressed the other against my back, then lifted me into his arms.

"Nico!" I shrieked with laughter, clinging to him as he carried me across the kitchen. "What are you doing? Where are you taking me?"

"Upstairs." He pulled back and gave me a suggestive grin, then winked. "I'm taking you to bed, so I can make love to you all night long."

For so many years, I'd convinced myself there was love in a place where it didn't exist. Shared my heart with a man who didn't want it. Didn't want me.

Now? I snuggled deeper into Nico's embrace, feeling like the luckiest girl alive, because I'd found so much more than love. More than sparks and amazing sex. I'd found my one true love.

The end . . . *almost.*

BONUS SCENE

Want more of Danni and Nico?
Scan for a special bonus scene to see what they're up to one
month later!

❦

Ben's story is next!

You won't want to miss his fun, sexy, second chance, enemies to
lovers story! Sign up for CJ Andrews' newsletter at
AuthorCJAndrews.com to get all the updates.

BEFORE YOU GO...

If you enjoyed *Our Love Was Meant To Be*, please take a moment to leave a brief review where you purchased this book.

Believe it or not, a book lives or dies based on its reviews. A sentence or two from you can make a difference! Besides, I'd love to hear your thoughts.

And don't forget to recommend *Our Love Was Meant To Be* to your friends. I always appreciate when a friend saves me from having to search for a new book to read and love. Yours will too!

Thanks again for reading! ~CJ

About the Author

Emerging author CJ Andrews writes contemporary romance stories filled with emotion and realistic characters that pull you in and make you feel like you're a part of their lives.

A lifetime fan of romance and rom-com, CJ creates captivating stories that are an entertaining blend of lighthearted humor and real-life drama. She takes her characters on an emotional journey, filled with a whirlwind of unpredictable twists and turns that will melt your heart one moment and break it in another…when you least expect it to happen.

But don't worry, in the world of Romance Books, all stories have a happy ending—or at least the promise of one.

CJ lives in Southeastern Pennsylvania, nestled between the historic city of Philadelphia and the scenic Pocono Mountains, which she uses as inspiration for the fictional towns in her novels.

She is happily married to her high-school sweetheart and is the proud mom of two adult sons. When she isn't glued to her computer or e-reader (which isn't often) you can find her enjoying time with her family, experimenting with new recipes in the kitchen, or dreaming of her next escape to a tropical beach.

CJ loves hearing from her fans. Connect with her on Facebook or at AuthorCJAndrews.com.

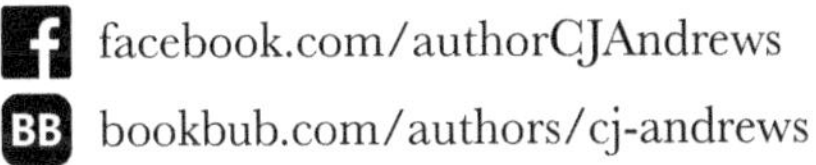